Also by Raymond Barfield

Poetry
Life in the Blind Spot
Dreams and Griefs of an Underworld Aeronaut
Bruno Glooms on the Bridge of Sighs

Novels
The Book of Colors
The Seventh Sentence

Philosophy
The Ancient Quarrel between Philosophy and Poetry
Wager: Beauty, Suffering, and Being in the World
The Poetic A Priori: Philosophical Imagination in a Meaningful Universe
The Practice of Medicine as Being in Time

Dreams of a Spirit Seer

Raymond Barfield

Fomite
Burlington VT

ISBN-13: 978-1-959984-47-4
Library of Congress Control Number: 2024932968

Fomite
58 Peru Street
Burlington, VT 05401
www.fomitepress.com
03-25-2024

For Samuel Wells

Day One

The Work of Martin Lampe, Asker of Questions

THE UNWASHED BODY on the straw mattress was stiff with cold. The air was cold, and the floor. The small fireplace was cold. The wooden box next to the fireplace held only a few fragments of coal.

A grunt came from the mound on the bed, trapped and tangled in the shroud of a tattered blanket.

As predictably as prisoners singing their foolish songs from behind dungeon bars to prove their souls' conversion, a mind began to chatter somewhere inside the mess of the body before it realized it was awake for yet another day instead of being dead.

The ideas it chattered about were alluring like the worst form of temptress, the black lace veil fluttering in the breath of God, so that only the faint outline could be discerned by the loon who gazed upon it from the outside, craving to jerk away the veil and, at long last, to get at the thing itself, the very thing-in-itself.

He felt drool on his cheek. Everyone else in Königsberg might waste their energy trying to appear groomed to strangers on the streets or in the marketplace where they bought their black bread and figs to stuff into their faces, trying to keep the furnace of the heart full of fire for yet another day. But not Martin Lampe. All of his energy was sucked up by his brain as it dragged some limp thought into the light from the muck of his dreams, like a cat dragging in half a squirrel and expecting to be praised.

Dreams seduced his mind, luring it into exuberant monologue all night. And then at sunrise, the dream would run off like a favorite whore scrambling after the next man, squandering devotion for a squirt in the dark as she turned from true passion, exchanging it for some peasant's phosphorescent eruption less consequential in mass and water content than any smashed slug under the boot, grunting her pathetic grunt as she squeezed and went pbbbbbbt, changing everything in his life, and leaving him alone to spin his tales on a straw-filled mattress.

He worked his hand free of the sweat-and-spill-clotted blanket and let it hang over the edge of the mattress, fingertips touching the floor, since four decades of service to the Great One apparently wasn't enough to grant a man even the dignity of a proper bed.

He just wanted to sleep without being harassed by ideas or dreams. But dreamless sleep was no different than death, and that thought throttled him with terror. Thus did Martin Lampe's mind spring awake against his will, leap to military attention, click its heels, and await further commands.

Meanwhile, only one of his eyes would open. The other eye was stuck closed by some dried excrescence that had squeezed its way out of his old lice-ridden head.

Before Lampe could lift his hand to pry his eyelids apart, he felt a tongue lick his fingers. "Ding," he gurgled from the depths of his phlegm-covered throat.

He wiggled his fingers. At the moment, it was the only affection he could manage to give the ancient beagle. The dog licked Lampe's fingers until a flea, or some such thing, demanded the attention of its back paw. Ding scratched and yelped.

Lampe pealed the tight-wrapped blanket down to his waist and forced himself up on his elbow. "Ding, for Christ's sake. You scratched open your tumor again."

The mass wrapping the upper part of Ding's right front leg had a small grin-like crevice revealing the red pulp beneath the fur. It had been growing slowly for months, but it didn't seem to hurt much, except when she tore it open with her claws.

Lampe's long, grey hair was tangled around his neck and matted to his forehead. He stroked the top of Ding's snout. "Your water bowl is empty."

As the dogs in the streets below filled the air with howls, God, or something, bellowed up from the gears and bells of the clock in the nearby square, and in the language of time it said, "Noon has arrived again, and you, Martin Lampe, are not so far from death that you can waste another day." When the clock finished its twelfth strike, the dogs also suddenly fell silent.

Something hit his window. Ding startled, knocking over the tin bowl Lampe used at night when he needed to dribble piss out of his leaky body.

"Demons from hell, those stupid birds." He looked down at the urine on his floor. Ding retreated with a limp to her corner.

She curled up on the old shirt Lampe had put down for her, eyeing Lampe to see what he would do next.

He rolled to his side, his mind still slopping in slow motion over the banks that contained the river of his dreams. His walls were grey with soot from the occasional times he had energy and money enough to buy wood or coal. Beneath this faint grey cover, the ideas he had scribbled on the walls hummed to his mind like emaciated drifters with eyes dulled by despair, staring at him through smudged windowpanes. Two years of scribbling on the walls hadn't silenced the ideas that haunted him in exile. But it was the only way he could rid his mind of the debris and prepare for the arrival of the idea that would open whole worlds, transforming the stuff of the universe into something that felt like music. These other ideas were mere preambles and distractions, minor derivatives from the Philosopher, and they had to be swept out of the mind and onto the walls to make room for the master idea.

Or maybe it was all just nonsense.

Over the rooftops he saw the eye-azure sky, clear except for one small cloud, like a cataract, dulling and blurring the sun.

Someone—probably one of those churlish little ruffians who were always mocking him when he went about his daily errands—hurled a stone from the street and cracked a windowpane in his cheap attic room. A lightning strike of rage flashed through his old flesh, but it quickly devolved into a vague agitation that deepened as the tangle of the tattered blanket knotted around his legs, an elderly man stuck in a woolen birth canal.

"Wait a minute, damn you!" He struggled free and limped to the window. There below was the injured titmouse, the dancing

Dunce, Johannes Kaufman, the villain who had taken over his life's work two years before.

Lampe grabbed the handles on the window frame and pulled. Frozen shut. He tried the window next to it. It opened just enough to let the cold air hit his groin through the thin nightgown he wore. The wind grabbed and garbled whatever Kaufman was yelling.

Lampe bent down to the crack to listen. His voice was hoarse and weak. "What do you want?"

Kaufman stopped jumping. He was a wiry little man, thirty years old with hardly a hair on his head.

Lampe said again, "What do you want, you fool?" His nightgown was as frayed as a whore's bedsheets and damp with the wet afterbirth of dream-induced night sweats. His voice cleared of phlegm a bit and grew stronger. "I don't have any wood or coal to warm wine for you, and even if I did, I'd sooner throw the jug down on your bald head." Lampe put his ear to the opening to listen for the Dunce's response.

"Then I've frozen my feet for nothing!" he said, and he turned to walk away.

"Wait!" Lampe cried. He was a fool for craving to know what he ought to care nothing about. The Dunce was his only source of information about the master, though he never said anything that Lampe didn't already know after forty years of service.

Kaufman continued walking away.

"I'm sorry!" Lampe yelled. He tried again to open the frozen window. It released and slammed up. Cold air hit his chest and made him gasp like a slapped newborn. He leaned out. "Come inside! I'll pour the wine and we can talk."

"No time," the little shit-meister yelled.

Lampe did not, could not, would not stop his foolish tongue. "Since when have you had no time? Wasianski does half the work I used to do, and the professor's too old to need the other half." He paused to see if he had offended the Dunce beyond repair for the day.

Kaufman put his feet together and squared his shoulders with the stiffness of a formal solemnity. He lifted his chin in the manner of those servants of the royal court who appear crisp, clean, and confident before the king's advisors, but who are usually perverted to their very depths. Then he announced in a clear voice, "Immanuel Kant is dead."

Two women passing by swung wide of Kaufman and looked up at the crazy old man half hanging out of a third-story window, his gray hair and nightgown blowing in the breeze.

Lampe gripped the windowsill to keep his hands from trembling, and he raised his face to the single cloud that was solemn as a slow-drifting ghost, thin, wispy, horribly temporary. Then he looked down and said, "Who sent you? Wasianski?"

Behind him, Ding scratched her inflamed tumor and yelped.

"Wasianski?" the Dunce said with a tone of contempt. "Please. I came on my own because I thought you'd want to know."

The wind carried the single cloud along, its edges fraying. A few blackbirds landed on a chimney across the street. Everything else was still.

"Were you there?" Lampe whimpered. He cleared his throat and tried again. "Were you there, at the actual moment?"

The Dunce shielded his eyes from the glare of sunlight. "I was beside him all night."

Lampe's mind whispered, *Forgive him, for he knows not what he does.* "Who was with you?"

Kaufman, an oblivious Centurion, continued to hammer the nails. "Vigilantus was there, and the professor's sister."

Ah, Vigilantus, the virile virgin voyeur. And it was certainly no surprise that Kant's money-sponge of a sister showed up.

"Who else?" Lampe could barely whisper.

"Sorry, what did you say?" Kaufman's upper lip was raised as he waited for an answer, exposing his hypertrophied gums.

Lampe despised him. "I asked who else was there!"

The Dunce's ears were set low with no proper hair to cover them, and his dull eyes squinted as he looked up and said, "Well, obviously Wasianski was there."

Lampe's will weakened at the mention of Wasianski—Ehregott Andreas Christoph Wasianski, the man most responsible for denying him the gift of witnessing the departure of the master's soul.

"Come up and tell me more!" Lampe cried out, all pain and welcome.

"Later."

"I have a jug of wine! It's my emergency jug!"

"Some other day. Wasianski says there will be hundreds, maybe thousands of people in Königsberg and beyond who will want to view him."

"View him?" Lampe's hands floated from his throbbing head to the windowsill.

"Pay their respects," Kaufman said. "Immanuel Kant is the most famous philosopher in the world."

Impertinent lackey. The Dunce understood nothing of Kant, and even less about the reasons for his fame. Lampe was the one who helped the little man to greatness. Helped? He devoted forty years of his life to getting the philosopher to his desk so his great mind could roam.

"One glass of wine!" Lampe yelled, traitor to his soul.

"Not today. I had to sneak out just to bring you the news. There's so much to do."

"But I can't be alone right now!"

"Find Eco," the Dunce suggested.

"He's rotting in the basement. Don't go! I must hear more!"

"Goodbye, Lampe."

"You'll come back?"

"It depends on Wasianski. There's work to do." The Dunce trudged away, swinging his arms from his droopy shoulders.

Lampe closed the window. He lowered himself to the straw mattress on the floor and watched in stunned emptiness as the single cloud drifted beyond the borders of his windows and out of sight. He lay back and closed his eyes.

When he woke, his spine crackled as he stood and went to his window. In the distance, across the rooftops, was the great castle, and next to the castle moat was Kant's house. He could see the tips of the chimneys. A small trail of smoke rose from the familiar hearth where, no doubt, the remaining friends of the philosopher had gathered in the gaping absence of Martin Lampe, the man who made Kant's greatness possible.

"He's gone," he said out loud, his voice over-ripe with new sorrow. "He left with no word of reconciliation, no goodbye, nothing."

Ding stared from her corner.

Lampe reached for his half-empty jug and sloshed the

wine around. It was hardly enough for an afternoon so bathed in grief. He opened the jug and drank deeply, then looked around at the thousands of scribbles on his walls from the past two years, his nonsensical groping for an elusive truth that had infected his brain during his four decades with the master. He drank again, but he got nothing more from the wine than mild relief from the headache he had found in the jug the night before.

"Why, Ding? Why did he leave without saying goodbye to his one true servant?"

Ding limped over to the mattress and lay beside it. Lampe stroked her fur, careful not to touch the tumor. He looked at her empty water bowl.

Where was Eco? He was usually awake, checking on Ding, making sure the dog didn't stink up the house because of Lampe's negligence. But he was a good man who endured Lampe with little complaint. Maybe he was at the market buying black bread and salted pork before Lampe could gripe about the logical point that room and board included actual food.

"The shame of it, Ding—to be forgotten." His sticky eyes moistened at the thought, but he felt little more than mild contractions somewhere deep in his belly, and instead of crying, he puffed out a few bundles of air.

Martin Lampe, recipient of high ideas during his forty-year tutorial with the world's greatest philosopher, was the best-educated man in Königsberg. He was prepared to take account of the general situation in the universe. Now was not the time to falter. Now was the time to turn to the work at hand, absorbing the terrifying fact of Immanuel Kant, dead.

He wiped the crust from his eyes, stroked his tangled beard, stood up, and began to pace in his small room, avoiding the urine that Ding had spilled on the floor. He picked up the book, given to him by the master, the dread and horrific *Critique of Pure Reason*, over which the entire world stumbled. It had broken some of the best minds, but not Martin Lampe's. No. His mind had become tempered steel in the furnace of Kant's ideas.

He took the book under his arm and held it tight as he paced. Like everything else in the room, its edges were darkened with soot, the pages worn from his reading and rereading. Thirty times, forty times, cover to accursed cover. He read with slack-jawed awe. He read with rage. He read with despair at the way the little Königsberg professor had undone the very heart of the universe. For anyone so unfortunate as to have understood the ideas, life was transformed into a paltry piece of fiction, a play in a theater with no real world outside into which a mind might pass when the play was over. Kant had utterly sequestered the mind from the thing-in-itself.

He opened his book, and for the thousandth time, he read the inscription on the title page written in the master's ratty scrawl. "For M. Lampe. Do not wreck yourself on the rocks of these ideas." Kant didn't even sign his name.

Lampe resumed pacing to relieve his agitation. "Why, Ding? Why couldn't he say a kind word without following it with some insult?"

He stepped in the puddle of urine, but he continued pacing, glancing out his window at the distant tips of the chimneys. "Look at that smoke, Ding. What conversations and recollections must be occurring around the bone bag of Kant's little corpse while you and I freeze alone in the chamber of ideas!"

It was unfair, unjust. Who had pulled the professor out of bed every morning? Who had arranged his breakfast just so? Who had endured his irritability when ideas didn't come as he wanted, or when ink spilled on those ridiculous slips of paper where he recorded moments of revelation for future testing in the laboratory of his uncanny mind?

Who? Lampe! Martin Lampe! He alone had poured the wine when all of Kant's friends had gathered to praise the little man after *The Critique of Pure Reason* was finally published.

Of course, no one understood the book, least of all Kant's Königsberg acquaintances. It would take the entire world of intellect to understand it. Kant knew this. When Lampe found the courage to ask for a copy, the master didn't even look up from his writing desk. "I have yet to find a philosopher on this continent who understands my ideas. Why do you think you'll understand them?"

Lampe answered, "I was at your side when you wrote the first word, and I was at your side when you wrote the last."

Kant bent forward in his brown coat with yellow buttons. His lopsided wig, covered with a hair bag, shifted with the momentum. The old man stared down at the floor long enough to make Lampe uncomfortable and embarrassed. Suddenly he waved his hand in front of his face with a little back-and-forth gesture as though he was clearing away the clutter of irrelevant thought or shooing away a fly. "Lampe, you surprise me."

He went to the bookshelf and brought a copy of the book back to his desk. He scribbled the unsigned insult, then he started flipping through pages, mumbling, "If I'm true to my maxims, I suppose … I suppose … I suppose … Ah, here it is." Then he read, "*The highest philosophy cannot advance further than is possible under the guidance which nature has bestowed upon the most ordinary understanding.*" He closed the great repository of dread and handed it to Lampe. "*The most ordinary understanding.* I suppose that includes you." Without another word, he turned back to his desk.

That night Lampe began to read. He scarcely understood a single sentence. As he read aloud in a subdued voice, he felt as if he had wandered into a cave so dark he could not see his hand in front of his face. But he could feel that the cave was massive, full of living beings at home in the darkness, and filled with dangers for those who did not tread carefully.

As he crept forward sentence by sentence, his own great principle—*the principle of the poetic a priori*—began to emerge from the inner workings of his mind, aging in the barrel of his skull, gaining complexity like the finest wines. He had to let it age since the master demanded all his time and energy.

———

Lampe's two years of exile had left him with nothing but time. His principle had begun to claw its way to the outer world in the form of scribbles on his walls. He was unsure how to connect all the moving pieces of his idea, but he knew he was very close to the secret that would synthesize Kant's life work in a way that even the master couldn't imagine.

"The idea is in the room, Ding. But I'm an old man, and I too will soon be dead. If I can't warm our room, I'll never unclench my hand enough to write."

Lampe's only furniture was the straw-stuffed mattress, two

worn-out chairs, and a simple desk with a single drawer where he kept his paper and ink. His hands shook as he stared at the drawer. "Is it time, Ding? Should I just be out with it? Just say it, the way the master did? Should I pull out the paper and ink, and make a clear statement of the principle before soot covers my ideas, or death snatches me away and leaves the world with no one who has understood?"

He gently tapped his chest and swallowed his desire to cry. "Ah, Ding. *The principle of the poetic a priori.* If I could get it on paper and complete the master's work, then I could die in peace. Imagine. They would find my body beside a stack of pages. Then all of Königsberg would finally recognize the genius of the system's highest organizing force, and they would be torn with wonder and grief that they ever called Martin Lampe a fool."

Lampe heard his door open, and he turned around.

"Want some biscuits, Martin?" Eco, his only friend, had stuck his huge, doughy head into the room. He sniffed, and said, "Martin! It smells awful in here. You spilled your pee on the floor again. And look, you walked all through it from one end of the room to the other!"

The great principle receded as Lampe contemplated biscuits and urine. "I live as I live," Lampe snapped. "You aren't my wife."

"But I'm your friend."

Lampe rolled his eyes and stared out the window.

Eco whistled to Ding. She made clunking sounds as she followed him down the wooden steps one at a time. He moved lightly, softly, despite his enormous bulk, as though he was filled with dry straw. He helped Ding out the door, leaving Lampe to sulk over his own unnecessary harshness and general superfluity.

Lampe went to the stairs and yelled, "I'm sorry for being irritable! But what's a man to do when his master is dead?" He stopped and listened. Nothing. Fine. He would just add guilt to everything else he had to carry in the continually chattering tribunal of his brain.

He walked back to his window to watch his little dog enjoy the simple pleasure of urinating. When she limped across the street, Lampe saw she had a biscuit in her mouth.

Good old gentle Eco. Who would guess he was Königsberg's most skillful hangman?

Lampe felt the cold in his brittle bones. He had to get warm. He was a man with important work to do. He had been deprived of the consolations of a mundane life, populated by normal things like fruit in the markets, the faces of dazzling girls, the smell of flowers, the songs of birds. Instead of living days filled with such delights common to all humanity beneath God's blue sky, he had been recruited by providence to silence the devil's whisper written into The Horrid Book.

"No more delay," he said to himself, feeling the eyes of invisible spirits, fallen and unfallen, turn toward him.

He sat in his chair and pulled out his ink, his quill, and his terrifying stack of empty, white paper. He had taken the paper from Kant's desk over many years. He took a sheet or two at a time so their absence wouldn't be noticed. It was a small tax for all the bother he endured from the exacting and exasperating professor. It was a well-deserved bonus, whatever the stingy old man might have said to make him feel guilty.

The master's books were important. Lampe knew this because Kant was famous despite being a terrible writer. But he was writing the truth of all humanity, too big for language. The final book he was working on was supposed to be the greatest of all, and therefore, it was the worst written. It remained unfinished, but Lampe believed it contained the secret to undoing the damage of the *Critique of Pure Reason*, which had hidden the Thing-In-Itself from humanity. The Dunce, plagued with an ignorance that wasn't his fault, said that Kant had worked on the book, but everything he wrote during the last two years of his life had been gibberish. At least that's what Wasianski told Kaufman.

Nothing about that was surprising since most of the important ideas had been suggested by Lampe before his exile. But the great book required both men. Left to Kant, it would turn into a mish-mash of armchair physics, organic bodies propagated by germs and eggs, and grocery lists for the day's meals. Lampe had pried him off small ideas. Instead of leaving the old man trapped alone with some horrid, inaccessible Thing-In-Itself bumping against the world's foundation, he had pushed Kant toward the mysterious consciousness shimmering fully forth like the wing-cases of insects with undersides tarnished blue. Lampe's imaginative prods and the ghost of Kant's once-magnificent mind were both needed to bring the great book to fruition and reveal the heart of wisdom.

Kant had begun to see and accept this. But then he invited Wasianski into the inner circle. After that, all was lost. Kant grew benighted and stubborn, until finally Wasianski pronounced the fatal words that led to Lampe's exile, destroying all possibility of repentance and forgiveness. Separated from the Master, Lampe was left alone in a freezing attic, with ten thousand ideas fueling the lantern of his chaotic brain, but with no way to forge a path through the dark forest that would lead to *The Idea*.

His head throbbed. If he could only get the idea on the page, his terror would lighten. He knew that writing even a single sentence would help. But every time he lifted his quill, he plunged toward dread without explanation, anxiety without object. Lampe had forged notes of apology on behalf of his master, he had made lists of chores, and he had scribbled many one-sentence thoughts on slips of paper he secretly stuffed into Kant's pockets. But in forty years, he had never written a single page of philosophy.

He sat shivering, feeling around the bog of his chaotic inner life for the words that would illuminate *the principle of the poetic a priori*. Then he put the quill in the drawer and closed it. He had borrowed it from Kant's desk many years before but had never found a way to return it. The quill had become the emblem of his grief and his guilt.

He knew Kant had intuited the principle when he wrote The Horrid Book that made him famous. After all, he had placed imagination—imagination!—at the heart of philosophy. And yet all the old man did was nod towards it and call it "a hidden art in the depth of the human soul." All of sense and thought, organizing the universe as we know it, was supposed to be brought together by the imagination, but Kant said he didn't feel like exploring it because it would be a "dry and boring analysis."

Dry? Boring? By the time Lampe realized that all of Kant's work would unravel without a richer account of the power of the imagination, it was too late. He had been labeled an idiot.

After Lampe was exiled, he fantasized about giving birth to a fully formed idea that would triumph over the master's myopic prejudice and restore him to his proper place at Kant's side. But the idea would not come forth. Sometimes his great principle called to him from just beyond the words scribbled on his walls, or else whispered like wind on the other side of the window, untamed, a force with no sign of its origin. At other times it billowed in unformed haze, powerful, but still unspoken, and carried the web-mesh of his mind up towards the clouds like the animals floating in Montgolfier's hot air balloon. But it would never simply state itself, once and for all. Lampe was suddenly distraught at the possibility that he would die before he put his ideas about the *poetic a priori* on paper, and the scribbles on the walls would fade, or worse, be whitewashed in preparation for the next tenant.

Only hours before, the master had departed from his bones, and no doubt Kant's ghost was wandering somewhere in the city since he almost never stepped beyond the boundaries of Königsberg. He no longer had a hand to write with, nor a voice with which to talk about the ideas he might snatch from whatever air his mind breathed after death. But what if Swedenborg had been right about action at a distance, the kind of action a lingering ghost could bring about? Could Lampe offer the master his bony hand and his meaty brain as a way for the spectral philosopher to continue incarnating ideas in words on the page? Maybe. Possibly.

What if he could preserve the walls as they were? What if the walls became an eternal monument to himself, Martin Lampe, a shrine to his lifework, the mystical fragments of philosophy that grew from the forty-year tutelage for which he traded his life as he meticulously cared for Kant's tiny world—carrying his umbrella, cleaning his chamber pot, searching for his stockings, straightening his wig, finding the way home when the old man was tipsy, or waking up the philosopher at five in the morning, which was the only proper hour to begin the life of thought—all so that the great works might be deposited on humanity's doorstep.

If the citizens of Königsberg had ever grasped the horror of Kant's inner world, they would have been shocked at what Lampe endured and overcame. But his history had prepared him for travail. He had overcome a dubious beginning after being planted in his mother's flesh by a bookish philologist from Naples before she followed a dark captain to the Baltic Sea, where the man deposited her, hangover and all, at the Königsberg harbor in the Vistula Lagoon among braying animals, crates of fruit, and bags of spices.

His mother had been a whore, but he admired her. She had used multiple languages to curse the finicky Italian scholar who had so quickly tired of her, leaving only Lampe-in-the-womb as evidence of their relationship. Sitting on her knee, Lampe had learned to herd words into lively phrases, though a lack of coordination between his brain and his tongue kept his more intricate thoughts tucked in the dark crevices of his magnificent mind, leading to his reputation as a dullard among Kant's friends and colleagues. Only Eco the Hangman would patiently wait to hear the words crowding up behind Lampe's tongue as they all clambered to get out at the same time. Good old Eco, treasure trove of doomed men's regrets, confessions, and final requests.

As a servant, he had learned to hide in the wings of life's theater. Dinner appears, order in the house appears, and the local genius appears on time for his lectures on logic and metaphysics. But the excellent servant remains hidden.

There are those who discount the servant. Not Lampe. He knew that servants are venerable beings who do not appear, but who are the secret to everything that does. The servant incarnates one of the deepest patterns of reality, like those hidden truths the mind must catch in flight from the corner of the eye, or those mysteries that shimmer forth in the disturbance of leaves among a few waving trees in the light of dusk.

—⁓—

Lampe's tattered military jacket hung on a nail by his desk. He put it on over his nightgown to add a layer between his old body and the cold air in his drafty room, then he went to the bedroom door to watch Ding struggle up the dark stairwell. Because of her tumor, she yelped when picked up, so he let her climb at her own pace. She looked towards him as she labored, occasionally glancing back at Eco who watched her from the base of the stairs. The chattering ghosts in Lampe's brain scattered at the approach of Ding, who was real, and completely herself.

Lampe whispered, "Ding, Ding, you purity of presence. You always wake me from my recurrent sleep."

At each step, Ding paused for a moment. When she arrived at the top of the stairs, she walked past Lampe and curled up on her blanket by his desk. He closed the door and locked it. Lampe and Ding slept for several hours.

When Lampe awoke, he felt a strange resolve. "Ding, I must begin the great tale that will complete the master's work. I must do this to honor his death."

Ding watched as Lampe got out of bed, went to his desk, and once again pulled out his paper, ink, and quill, laying each in its proper place.

He picked up the quill, dipped it in ink, and looked out toward the smoke rising from the chimney of Kant's house in the distance. Wasianski and the crew were probably there, droning on and on about the professor as though they really knew the man. Eventually, they would write their stories in biographies and epic poems to fortify their own careers and reputations. But none of the men at the hearth had been pummeled repeatedly with the master's endless critiques of mundane life, nor had they endured his fits of pouting and complaining if there was something wrong with the fish, say, or the soup.

Lampe alone knew the real Kant, whose calm outward appearance was like the outward calm of the surgeon in wartime cutting off infected limbs, doing things that would unnerve the common man. For decades Lampe had listened to Kant endlessly describe how he faced mountains of danger, pits, and monstrous beasts grown up from centuries of wayward speculation and foolhardy forays into untouchable realms of form and verity. And he had watched Kant's university students lose their minds and souls as they tried to do philosophical battle armed with their wooden swords and flimsy shields, inevitably becoming good-for-nothings with no ability to think. But after tasting the world of eternal ideas, they could never again be satisfied with simple, useful work. Those tragic creatures were the ghosts of Königsberg, and thanks to Professor Kant, they were everywhere.

As he lingered over miserable memories, a single drop of ink gathered ominously at the end of his quill, hovering above the abyss of horrid whiteness on the page. And then, with no other change in the universe, it fell to the page in a sudden flash of black. A hint of blue and green appeared at the creeping edge of the ink.

He put down his quill and stared at the splotch, the great work of Martin Lampe, the sum and substance of his own wisdom, his insight, his contribution to the world. He said, "Ding, what if this is as far as I can go?"

Eco called from outside Lampe's room, "Martin?"

Lampe didn't answer.

Eco twisted his key in the lock, stuck his enormous cloud-like head into the room, and said, "We need to clean up this mess, Martin. This is not a proper way to live."

Lampe looked up from the black splotch on his sheet of paper, his gaze drifting out the window toward the sky. He grumbled, "Don't you have someone to hang?"

"Be nice, Martin."

Lampe turned around slowly, unsteady on his chair. He was twisted up in his nightgown, and the creaking and cracking of his back vibrated its way up to his inner ear. He felt his chin quiver, which he hated, betraying feelings he preferred to keep to himself. He looked up at Eco and said, "He's dead."

Eco held out a jug of wine he had purchased, bless his soul, and he said, "I heard at the market." He stepped into the room. Resting his soft, pale bulk on Lampe's bed, he opened the jug of wine, took a sip, and handed it over to Lampe.

Lampe drank three large swallows. He paused, and noticing how miserable his hollow soul was, he drank three more.

Eco held up a fleshy, cautionary hand, and Lampe handed over the jug.

—⁓—

Darkness crept into the city as the two men sat in silence. They drank together without a word until the last of the sunlight was gone and only a quarter of the large jug of wine remained.

Eco lit a lantern. Lampe's eyes were half-closed.

"We'll clean up tomorrow," Eco said. He struggled to rise from the mattress on the floor. "I have one hanging in the morning, but it's early. I can come back and help you by afternoon. I'm sorry about your old friend."

Lampe was unexpectedly moved when Eco, with his tender sensibilities and feelings, described the master as his old friend. He looked at the white globe of Eco's soft head. The moon outside his window glowed benignly, the night version of the single cloud that had begun the strange day. The sky was full of dark blues, grays, blacks. In the lantern light, the scribbles on his walls looked like scratches from some beast's claws.

"I'm afraid, Eco."

"What are you afraid of?"

Lampe thought for a moment. "Do you think they'll invite me to view his little corpse?"

Eco intertwined his thick fingers and looked down at his absurdly large feet. "I can go to his house and ask them tomorrow after I finish work."

Lampe closed his eyes and sighed, "No. I'm in exile. I can only go if they invite me on their own."

Eco was intimately familiar with the looming shade of Lampe's melancholy, and there was nothing to do except to give him over to whatever demons would torment him through the night and wait for the sun to dispel the shadows once again. He looked at Lampe from inside his flour-pale bulk, white as innocence, lost for words. Lampe saw Eco's pain, but he had no relief to offer. Pain was the order of the day.

Eco said, "Goodnight, Martin." He left Lampe alone with the moon and the rhythmic breathing of Ding from the dark corner of the room.

Lampe called out, "If they don't invite me, I'll die of sorrow!"

The lantern light faded in the stairwell as Eco continued down to his room in silence. Nothing could answer Lampe's final fear.

Day Two

The True Estimation of Living Forces

THE MOON WAS GONE when Lampe's brain jerked him awake. He stood and put his face close to the cuckoo clock that hung over his head. "No!" He could just make out the black hands against the white background. Four o'clock. "No, no, no!" He had long lost the habit of waking in time to prod Kant out of bed, and he didn't want it back.

He lay down again, pulled the blanket to his chin, closed his eyes, and waited. His brain was completely awake and there was nothing he could do about it.

"Go away!" he yelled at Kant's scrawny ghost that was almost certainly somewhere in the room. It didn't help. The choir of imbeciles in his brain took over the day shift, relieving the dream choirs that rarely gave him peace. Resistance was useless.

Before Lampe was exiled and his lifework destroyed, he would light the kindling in Kant's fireplace every morning at five. Then he would go to the bedroom where Kant's tiny body was wrapped in the thick eider-down blanket pulled up to his ears. The master barely wrinkled the blanket because of the co-

cooning procedure that was Lampe's duty every night at exactly ten, pulling and tucking first one corner, then another so that Manuelchen was bound and snug.

"Up!" Lampe would bark as he lit the candle beside the bed, illuminating Kant's still-closed eyes and floppy nightcap. He pulled the cap from the brow-heavy head. "There's work to do. The world is waiting for you to scribble something about how things are, or how they ought to be. The king himself waits! Königsberg sleeps, benighted for the lack of the philosopher's industry!" Alas, nothing but snores in the face of his eloquence, morning after morning for forty years. But if Kant ever missed those morning hours, not only was his day ruined, but Lampe's was considerably diminished as well. So he persisted.

Lampe had learned the necessity of morning boldness. He pulled away the covers, exposing the philosopher's small, absurd buttocks, an arse no good for sitting, nor for much else it was designed to do, raising the perennial question about where God was when Kant's intestines were created.

"Up, up, up!" Lampe said.

"I'm up!" Kant birthed himself from the bed with a strange, slow-motion aggressiveness. "Give a man some peace. It takes time for a mind to come alive."

Time? No, it took Lampe. And tea. And a pipe. And a breakfast table arranged just so. But once the philosophizing had begun and the master's attention had returned to a review of his notes in his battered copy of *Meier's Logic*, preparing to sate the knowledge-hungry students who would soon gather in the lecture room downstairs, was there any word of thanks to Lampe? And when some great idea, which might have slipped into oblivion if Kant had slept through the hours of revelation, was instead captured on one of his hundreds of slips of paper, was Lampe thanked? Even once?

But none of this was really important, was it? The great question residing in the neighborhood of all secrets about Kant's miraculous achievements was ignored by the whole city. If Lampe was the one who woke the great Immanuel Kant, who, or what, woke Martin Lampe? Was it the gods who lifted him from his river of dreams? No. Old Lampe woke Old Lampe—or at least his marvelous brain did. Lampe was the first mover, the prime mover who set in motion the productive monstrosity of the Philosopher. Morning after morning, Lampe was the ghost unseen in the intricacies of Kant's great Architectonic.

Ding was under the blanket, curled at the foot of the bed. She nuzzled her way up until her face emerged, and she licked Lampe's ear.

"Ding, this is absurd." His mind was gaining its old precision, and his senses were darting about, each in their own way, gathering data. He was suddenly aware of the pungent smell of urine. He paused and collected himself. "Ding, I have a plan. We can go wake up Wasianski. The master has been dead for a day. The shock should be gone. We must do what men must do. We must close out business and care for remains and remainders. We will settle this now, like men, like soldiers. I will offer to work with him. To collaborate. Of course, Wasianski sleeps until the stars are blotted out completely from the sky. But that gives us time to eat a little black bread and some strands of flesh off that nasty pork bone Eco keeps. Then we will confront Wasianski. Is that good, Ding? Be patient."

Ding perked up at the mention of eating and bones. She was the most complete beast Lampe had ever known.

If he could enter the house and see the body that had reluctantly carried the philosopher's mind for so many years, maybe the resentment that had taken up so much space in his own mind—endlessly bellowing, endlessly spinning retorts, endlessly constructing arguments about the fundamental injustice of his exile—would finally go quiet. Maybe breathing in the smell of the house and feeling the master's cold flesh and wrinkled skin would allow him to slam the door shut on his shame with a firm and final clap of wood against wood. And with the harsh sound of a driven nail, he could say, "It is finished."

Then, in the newly won peace and silence of his mind, he could turn to his own great work, bringing together what a perverse genius had sundered, reuniting things as they are and things as they appear.

He felt much better now that he had made a resolution.

But he couldn't go until the Dunce visited, to ensure that he had any last-minute information. And the Dunce would visit, of course. Even if Wasianski had him working double-time, which is to say working half of what had been expected of Lampe, he wouldn't resist the chance to rub it in, mentioning, just in passing, the details he knew Lampe craved, details that should have been delivered to Lampe's own eyes instead of being filtered through the so-called "mind" of a moron who had never read a word of philosophy.

Ding produced a sympathetic groan as Lampe got out of bed and lit the candle on his desk. He pulled out his paper and quill again but didn't risk opening the ink. The idea would come. It had to come.

But how, exactly, do ideas come? He had seen Kant sitting on his stool, writing sentences up the side of a page and onto random slips of paper, as though he were poking the heads of demons back into hell as they tried to force their way up through white paper in the guise of angels. His intensity was almost unbearable to watch as he dipped the bone from the bird's wing into his ink pot, scratching and crossing out words until the hands of the clock reached quarter-to-one, when he would call out to the cook in a voice much deeper and louder than anyone would expect from his small body, "It's three quarters!"

At that cry, the ornery, reclusive cook would set out the liquor Kant would drink after the first course, and then return to her soup, racing to finish it, while the philosopher struggled to get the thought on paper before the hour arrived.

Lampe played his part in the game, of course. But he still kept some piece of himself to the side, watching and wondering why the master rushed, since there was no one in the house but an old-lady cook, a melancholy soldier who had seen too many deaths on the battlefield, and a frail philosopher writing about that mysterious "something = x" deep in the soul.

What was the source of the urgency? Kant's haunting, horrific, ecstatic will, of course. His will would bend nations, the world, and God himself, if that's what it took to get the system right. Europe might fear Napoleon, but Napoleon was nothing compared to the world-destroying Manuelchen. What was God up to?

Lampe looked down at the accidental drop of black ink

on the white paper. The idea was somewhere in that black splotch, but his room was like a silent stranger's brain with thoughts inscribed on the inner cave. If only they would coalesce into a speech, so the whole thing could be said at once and with clarity.

Lampe had skimmed the cream from the professor's writing and lecturing, and he had stored away a little philosophy for himself. But his work demanded long hours of waiting. And he had waited. He had waited forty years. Now it was time to show the world something new, to redeem the master's work from its worst sins by completing it through benevolent heresy.

"Hoards!" the Dunce said as he walked in. He had knocked at the door, but he hadn't waited for an answer.

What could Lampe do except force himself out of bed and coax the Dunce to elaborate, purchasing information with the wine Eco had delivered the night before?

"Tell me more," Lampe said.

"It smells like piss in this room," Kaufman said, despite his usual aversion to direct statements of fact, or anything substantial enough to suggest the presence of a real mind.

"Forgive me. I'm an old man, and my dog is not well."

If the Dunce had not picked his nose and scraped the dried wax from his ears, Lampe might have conjured some modest modulation of his disdain for the idiot. Not that Lampe, smelling worse than a goat, was any better. But exile does things to a man.

Lampe continued, "Hoards, you say? Hoards of strangers are coming to see the professor?"

"As soon as Wasianski opens the door they start in, looking around, mumbling among themselves. But when they come to his little corpse, they fall silent."

"Why? What does he look like?"

"Like a small, dead man," the impudent Dunce said, doubling his offense by reaching for the wine jug at Lampe's feet and pouring a second glass without asking permission.

Lampe pulled his chair closer to the Dunce and leaned in so that the odor of age and abandon, and the flaking, caked-up accumulation of excrescence that penetrated even the smell of dried urine drifted in Kaufman's direction. He bent forward so that he was looking up at the fool from under his bushy eyebrows. Beneath the dull light of the wary Dunce's gaze, he adjusted his head slightly to the right, forging a visual evocation of the master, whose head often bent to that side because of a deformity in the shoulder.

"I was with him for forty years." The rasp of his voice steamed up from his lungs in the Königsberg cold. He grinned, not to grin, but to show the Dunce his swollen gums and missing teeth, and to make him smell the breath of a mule.

He felt Kaufman's satisfying repulsion, so close to the effect he had calculated to achieve—the judgment that he was mad. Then he sat up straight, raised his index finger into the air, and said, "Here's the thing. I have several ideas of my own and some work that needs to be finished. But unlike yourself, I'm an old man. You're at the age for love, right?"

Kaufman looked down with a weak smile and his face blushed, as though a drop of blood had fallen into a bowl of milk.

Lampe leaned in again, this time with a chuckle and a wink, wagging his finger. "All I have is memory. The work of old age is to get memory straight, and old men's brains are as brittle as their bones. Memories escape like sand from the clutched hand of an excited child." Lampe curled his fingers into a fist. "In fact, I suggest that you think of me as a child. Just think of me as a child."

"He used to say that!"

"Did he?" Lampe hated this inevitable phase of conversations with the Dunce in which Kaufman told stories he had heard about Kant, forgetting that Lampe had lived the stories for forty years.

"All the time! As he got older, he said to everyone who visited, 'I'm old and frail. Consider me as a child, consider me as a child.'"

"Well, old men are old men," Lampe grumbled. "But listen to me. I've wandered off again. You were about to tell me what he looks like."

"Like a skeleton wrapped in wet paper," the Dunce said, picking the dirt from under his nails.

Lampe reached for the walking cane leaning against the wall. The cane was as heavy as a hammer. "I'm sure there's more to say."

"What do you want to know? His skin looks like the ash in your fireplace, with a little of your yellowish color mixed in."

"Which room is he in?"

"The backroom, with no fire, so he stays cold and doesn't start to stink. Wasianski only allows fires in the front room and the kitchen."

"What else? Tell me more about the end, the last days and hours."

"What is there to tell?"

"Everything!" Lampe yelled. Then held his fingers to his lips and said more quietly, "Everything. Was he afraid? Did he eat? Did he drink? Tell me, did he keep working on the last book, all the way to the end?" Lampe looked up at the ceiling to keep his tears in check. "Did he mention me?"

Kaufman took too much time to answer, time an old man does not have, so Lampe asked, "Do you go to him at night? When the room is empty?"

"Why would I do that? The room's freezing. Besides, of all the people in Königsberg, he's least likely to change."

"Do you ever touch him?"

Kaufman was mid-sip. He glanced over his glass. "Are you losing your mind?"

"No. I'm finding it."

Kaufman shrugged. "I helped to move him, of course. I just picked him up. He hardly weighed more than his clothes. No wonder he always slumped in his chair. No muscle at all."

Lampe closed his eyes, imagining the little professor in the familiar parlor, sitting with a benign smile on his smug little face, enjoying the presence of friends until some manner or maxim was trodden upon. "Did he write?"

Kaufman put his glass on the floor and looked around as though he was searching for something to eat. "I don't know if you could call it writing." He had the condescending smirk of a man who must bear irrelevant questions of those who miss the deep point of a conversation. "He sat at his desk and scribbled. But I looked at the pages. They made no sense at all. He stuck the names of dinner guests and shopping lists between the ideas. Nothing made any sense."

"Of course not." How could it make sense to someone like the Dunce?

"There was one funny thing, though." He began telling his anecdote, but Lampe was weighing the advantages and disadvantages of cajoling Kaufman into bringing the final manuscript to him, knowing that Kant's ghost would be in the very pages.

Lampe said, "I'm sorry. My mind wandered. Please start again."

Kaufman waved his hand and said, "It doesn't matter. I need to get back."

Lampe reached out and touched Kaufman's knee. "No, please, tell the funny story."

The Dunce looked down at his knee with renewed condescension and Lampe removed his hand.

"Well, as I already said, the old man would sit slumped in his chair with his eyes closed, covered up with his blanket, like he couldn't hear anything around him. But Wasianski had this little trick. He would lean over and whisper into the professor's ear, and the old man would sit up and start right into a lecture on whatever topic Wasianski had whispered. Usually, it was something about planetary motion or the Moors of Barbary. I heard those so many times I could nearly give the lectures myself. But the guests would give a little round of applause as Kant sunk back into a slump, and Wasianski would take a little bow. Then he would …"

"Horrible!" Lampe said, hitting both hands to his knees and shaking his head. A small cascade of dandruff fell from his tussled grey hair.

"I thought it was funny. Why do you say it's horrible?"

"Toying with the master? Displaying him like some magic doll?"

"You're one to talk," the insolent Dunce answered.

Wagging his finger like a metronome counting the beats of his denial, Lampe said, "I never, never, never, never mocked him."

"That's not what I heard. You bickered with him all the time."

Lampe sat back. "Our differences were philosophical."

"Hah!" Kaufman said, reaching for the wine as though this new line of conversation would take a while and couldn't be missed.

Lampe grabbed the jug. "What have you heard about this?"

"It's not worth discussing. The man is dead."

"But *I'm* not!" A lambent fire lit up in Lampe's eyes. "I'll raise a swarm of wasps around your ears with my words, even though fools and knaves half stung to death still can't hear the truth!"

"You're upset."

"Upset?" Lampe's voice thinned into a breath. "Kaufman, I missed the end, and everything is still unfinished!"

Kaufman stared at the jug. "He could certainly keep a secret."

"What do you mean by that?"

"He wouldn't say why he fired you after all those years."

Lampe stood. "Wasianski was the one who sent me away."

"Wasianski wouldn't have done it unless the professor wanted you gone. The only thing the old man said was that you had shamed him in some way."

"Shame?" Lampe said. "He knew nothing about shame."

"Then tell me why he fired you?"

"He didn't fire me. He chose the one punishment that would hurt me more than any other. He sent me into exile."

"Same outcome."

"No." Lampe glared at the Dunce's placid, uncomprehending face. "A person is fired from a job. He is exiled from a life."

Kaufman stood up, unsteady from the wine. "Wasianski will be looking for me." He closed one eye and focused on walking toward the door without swaying.

"Kaufman!" Lampe tried to hold the blurred gaze of the Dunce with the force of his eyes.

"What?"

"That last manuscript he was working on."

"The one with meal plans and guest lists?"

Lampe bowed his head. "Yes."

"Wasianski thinks he should hide it to protect the professor's reputation. The old man had lost his mind."

"Can you bring it to me? I want to read it."

"Impossible," Kaufman slurred, wagging the thumb of one stub-fingered hand. "It's locked in the desk, and I don't know where the key is."

"What if I told you how to get into the desk?"

"Impossible," he said again with the same gesture.

"Maybe we can talk more tomorrow." Lampe's clarity was increasing. The Dunce would never understand what was at stake.

"I can't come tomorrow."

"Why not? Your visits make me so happy."

"I have to tend the vigil."

"Later in the afternoon, then. Or evening. Or early morning. Please, I need news about who is visiting, who is keeping vigil."

"That's easy," the Dunce said, unaware of the dagger he carelessly wielded. "Everyone is visiting. Everyone is keeping vigil."

Lampe nodded as Kaufman turned and stumbled his way down the stairs. There was nothing else he could do. He was the only man in Königsberg who couldn't pay last respects to Immanuel Kant, philosopher. He was also the only man in Königsberg who actually loved the old son of a bitch.

Only an invitation could cancel his exile. He imagined Wasianski sending a small, handwritten note. He would put on his livery of white with red trimmings and go to the house, just as he did each day when he was Kant's servant. He would step into the front hall and shake off the cold. He wouldn't go immediately into the freezing room where Kant's little body lay on the table. Instead, he would stand in the warmth of the old parlor, maintaining a pace fitting for the sublimity of a vigil. Then he would see them. He would see Jachmann, Porschke, Wasianski. He would see dear Baczko. And he would say, "No, no, don't stand. And look! Vigilantus! So good to see you."

He would say, "Yes, certainly I'll have a sherry. Just a small one. I want to keep my head about me."

And then, "A story? Of course, certainly, a story. But which one? There are so many, and the sherry is raising my thoughts to the heavens. Yes, I will have a bit more. Just a bit. There. Or a bit more than that, perhaps. Yes, there. Thank you.

"Well, where to begin? On the way over I passed by the gallows where that unfortunate fellow hangs. Yes, yes, I agree. I hope they take him down soon. Distasteful. But I do see their point. Why make an example of someone and then hide the event?

"Anyway, when I passed the gallows, I was reminded of a story you've probably never heard. That's one of the many advantages of being a servant. You hear all the ramblings when too much wine has loosened the mind and tongue.

"Speaking of which, yes, one more glass, and then no more. Excellent.

"Now, the story. When little Immanuel was living in the Satterstrasse where his father worked with leather, he was forced every day to live among dangers, surrounded by swamps and irrigation channels, and full of the living forces blowing in off the seas. It invigorated the sickly young philosopher, even as the atmosphere of drying hides made it harder for his inadequate lungs to breathe. His father did well enough as a strap maker, cutting belts and thongs from the hides of dead cattle. But he had friends poorer than himself. One of them lived in the basement below the butcher's shop, enduring the mundane reminder of death as blood soaked through the ceiling. Death was everywhere, my friends, everywhere. And Manuelchen, with his thin shoulders folded in, breathing heavily as he tried to keep up with other children, always felt a suffocating sense that even to run in childish games was to outrun his own breath so that air became like water.

"But he was no coward, gentlemen. Far from it. And this is where the story finally begins. The king had learned of a merchant who was selling raw wool without permission, undercutting the king's economy at a time when he was building his great army. And so, as some things never change, he not only allowed a man—a family man, mind you—to hang all day just in case anyone thought of doing business independently of the king's own plans, but he went further. He had the body thrown outside the city gates where it was to stay until the birds turned it into a skeleton. When the master told me this story, my first thought was how horrid it must have been for the family to look down at every bird dropping and wonder whether some part of the poor man was in it. But I didn't say this to the master. As you know, he didn't like interruptions, digressions, or excessive note-taking while he spoke.

"Imagine! Manuelchen trying to run with the other boys, left behind again and again. And he stood there, knowing his poor mother would never allow him to go past the gates. But the dead man on the other side fascinated him. The gate was a fixed chasm. Inside the gate, life was preserved, and the city was ordered according to the king's law. Outside the gate was the swampland, the fog of the unknown. And out there, the dead man rotted, forcing people to avert their eyes.

"Think of it, friends. The little boy crouched by the road, playing a game with pebbles, somber and taking account of this king and his laws.

"Then, when no one was near, Manuelchen picked up a stick and plunged past the gate into the world of flies and swamp creatures who breathe the watery muck. And for the first time, the master said that it—It!—was right there for all the world to see. This man had been a father and a husband, but what lay outside the gate was nothing other than death. The flesh was already bloating. The parts exposed to the sun were pale and white, and the parts seeping into the earth were purple and black. One arm was folded across the neck, and the other was palm down on the dirt.

"Gentlemen, there was a force emanating from the body, keeping Manuelchen from approaching. But he stepped forward anyway. Both of the man's eyes were open. The power of the sun and wind had clouded them.

"The voice of some anonymous busybody called from the gate, 'You, there. You ought not to be out there.' But our hero didn't turn around because he was inquiring into the truth of reality. He was delicate, yes, but he was unafraid of even the darkest facts about the world. He bent forward and reached out with his stick. He nudged the body's index finger, grey and purple, so that the finger lifted—then slipped. The stick caught the long fingernail and pulled it off the nail bed. He always emphasized this part.

"The voice of the woman at the gate was muffled by his great concentration. The nail was lifted at an angle, and immediately an insect crawled up onto the rich nail bed to feed. When he got to this point in the story, the master would always thrust his finger into the air with a jab and say, 'There it was!' And then he would jab toward the fire, pausing as a faint grin appeared, revealing his fearlessness. He had swallowed the thoroughness of death, and he knew something true about the world.

"Just weeks before, that very hand had reached out for illicit money in exchange for the hide of a sheep. Days before, that very hand had satisfied the living man by scratching an itch on the neck or back, and it had lifted food to the now fixed and gaping mouth where flies moved in and out. And why were things as they were? Because the king condemned him to rot outside the gate. The king condemned him, and thus was he condemned!"

No doubt Wasianski would be taking notes as Lampe told how something—precisely some *thing*—called out to the boy's heart. No doubt he would recognize that there, outside the city gates, beside the meat of the dead man's corpse, the idea of the very thing-in-itself was born, haunting dreams and philosophy. From the rotting flesh in that dark theater came the revolution that would change the way the world thinks.

—◦∾◦—

Ding suddenly yelped, breaking Lampe's reverie. There was a blood stain on the quilt. Ding's tumor was bleeding again. Feeling the stiffness of his own joints and his helplessness in the presence of suffering, Lampe leaned over and gently held a cloth to the scratched tumor until the bleeding stopped.

A sense of final doom was pursuing him without mercy. A simple invitation to join the others in vigil would redeem him from the paralyzing horror of his solitary shame. One line scribbled on a piece of paper by Wasianski would undo his exile.

He needed a plan. As a military man, he knew that good plans are based on resources that actually exist. His only link to Wasianski was the Dunce. So that was where he had to begin.

Day Three

The Sword

"Why are you wearing that silly coat?" the Dunce asked.

"Because I'm cold."

Kaufman was unusually talkative, but for the first time he had brought a jug of wine, so Lampe waited patiently to hear news from the vigil.

The Dunce said, "That's a military jacket."

"I know."

"You were a soldier?"

"I was."

"When did you fight?"

Lampe waved his hand. "It doesn't matter."

"It does," the Dunce said.

Lampe sighed. "The march on Saxony."

"Was the king there?"

"Yes."

"Did he fight?"

"Like no one I've ever seen." Of all memories, this was one of those he least wanted to discuss. But it gave him an idea. "He had no fear of death, which meant the rest of us had to fight like we also had no fear of death. But the experience tempered the iron of my courage and made me an excellent guard." Lampe leaned in toward the Dunce, who was casually attentive. "With so many people coming through the house and eyeing the famous man's things, maybe Wasianski should hire a night watchman."

"The locks are excellent," the Dunce said from inside the dry well of his glib incomprehension of Lampe's painful and intense desire to be invited in from exile. After he had performed his dramatic pause, he asked, "Why didn't the king fear death?"

Lampe allowed the diversion for the moment. "Do you know anything about Frederick the Great?"

"F the G? Every child knows that he built our canals, drained our swamps, and created new crops of potatoes and turnips. My mother loves the turnips."

"He was also a poet and a philosopher."

"Not much help on the battlefield," the Dunce said, as though knowing how to grow potatoes and turnips helped in a fight.

Lampe glared at the Dunce. "On the battlefield, nothing helps more than philosophy."

"How does nothing help in a battle?"

Lampe rolled his eyes to heaven for relief. "When Frederick was young, he tried to escape his father. He and a friend ran off to England. But his father had them tracked down, arrested, and brought back to Prussia. He beheaded the friend in front of Frederick, then he beat his son bloody." Lampe drank deeply. "The king didn't think about death in battle because there was no room inside him for anything except rage and hatred for his father."

Predictably missing the poignant sadness Lampe described, the Dunce said, "Too bad you lost the battle."

Lampe ignored him and continued. "I remember General William of Fermor riding into Königsberg with his soldiers and taking over the castle so that everyone could feel his victory in their bones. The Russians were everywhere, and I was reduced to begging an occasional swig of vodka from them. But I enjoyed them, especially when they were drunk. They were always morose, even after winning everything. If you asked why, they always answered, 'We'll still die someday.'" Lampe took a long drink of wine. "That was an excellent answer."

"Sounds miserable."

Lampe shrugged. "Without the Russians, I never would have worked for Kant."

"What do you mean?"

"He never told you about how we met?"

The Dunce looked around at the scribbles on the walls as though he had just noticed them. "No one was allowed to mention you in the house."

"I heard that," Lampe said, dejected.

"He even wrote down a reminder in his little notebook that he must not mention your name."

"At least it took some effort to forget me."

"For a few weeks. After that it was easy."

Lampe tried to glare, but the Dunce was paying no attention, fidgeting as he always did before announcing he had to leave. "I first heard of Kant from the Russians who attended his lectures on geography."

"Where did he learn geography?" the Dunce asked.

"Wasianski said in his eighty years, he never went far from Königsberg."

"That's true. But he knew more about geography than anyone." Lampe paused, turning a weighty gaze toward the Dunce's eyes while he figured out how to best make use of him. "The Russians had accumulated more than enough philosophy from their own endless wells of melancholy. But they loved his lectures on geography. The way they talked about Kant, I imagined him as a large man who could hold the attention of victorious soldiers with his daunting presence."

"I should tell Wasianski about that," the Dunce said. "He's always looking for tidbits to put in his biography."

Lampe saw an opportunity emerging. Perhaps he could supply the Dunce with information to share with Wasianski in exchange for a chance to see the master's final manuscript.

The day he first met Kant, Lampe had just been released from the castle dungeon. He had spent a month there for insulting a nobleman's wife. When she turned out to be the whore Lampe said she was, did anyone apologize to Lampe? Certainly not.

The day he was released, he was wandering along the piers looking for a bottle of decent vodka, a loaf of bread, and a couple of silbergroeschen to persuade a woman to join him for the evening. The piers were covered with items from all over the world. You could find anything. Grain, flax, ash, tar, spices, leather, wax. The thought of all the people who had to mine the metals, grow the fruits, build the ships, decipher navigation routes, and complete the thousand steps needed to get a product into town at a reasonable price exhausted his brain. The traders from Poland, England, Denmark, and Sweden all seemed cheerfully unaware of life's brevity as they haggled over five thalers this way or that for a box of smoked beef. It left Lampe feeling like little more than a thinking barnacle on a ship's hull.

"I like that," Kaufman said. "A thinking barnacle."

"The vodka helped."

"Always does."

Before being thrown into the dungeon, Lampe spent his days meandering through the city, lingering in the market, chewing on hard bread, and watching girls pass by. He was in his late twenties, and he thought about nothing other than whatever birdsong, bee's buzz, or shapely backside caught his post-war, sensuous, death-wilted mind.

But one bright day, a little man passed by him with a step that was too spritely and hands that moved in the air like tethered birds as he talked to the friend walking with him. He had neat little cuffs, a fine little coat, and a ridiculous little sword on his belt.

Lampe immediately despised him. "Why the toy sword?" he blurted. "You're no soldier."

The stranger turned and said, "Neither are you."

Lampe had walked on a few more steps before he realized that he had been insulted. Strictly speaking, the little man's statement was true. The Russian occupation had ended his military career. He stepped back and stared at the slender, dainty man. With the serrated edge of a vodka-induced slur, he said, "Don't carry a sword unless you're ready to use it."

Kant tipped his head to the right, grabbing Lampe's otherwise wandering focus with the barbs of his pure blue eyes. He studied Lampe like an entomological specimen. There was no hint of a grin or frown to alter the thin-lipped line of his mouth, nor was there any fear when he said, "Don't carry a tongue in your head unless you know how to use it properly. It's meant for eloquence, but you wag it at strangers with reckless stupidity."

"We'll be late for the play," Kant's friend said, pulling at his elbow.

Kant kept his eyes fixed on Lampe's downturned face.

His friend persisted, "Kant, let's go and leave this unfortunate man to his drunken wanderings."

"Kant?" Lampe said. "Immanuel Kant?"

Kant waved his right hand once to the left and once to the right, and then shoved it into his pocket. "A man wants a pleasant stroll with his friend without encountering tiresome vulgarity. But you've disturbed my walk for no reason other than your need to make a loose and inappropriate comment to a stranger."

"I was only …"

"What if I were the sort who merely walked on?" Kant interrupted, allowing his pale hand to emerge again and fly briefly around his head before returning to the nest of his pocket. "Then I might regret my lack of boldness. This would shame me and ruin my evening meal. One loose insult, and you would deprive a stranger of half a day's joy, a stranger who has never done you any harm. And then that half-day would be gone forever."

"Yes sir," Lampe said, cowed, grabbing the fingers of one hand with the other as though holding a hat in contrition.

Kant inspected the newly humbled young man. "You used to be a soldier?"

"Yes sir."

"What work do you do now?"

"I have no work just now, sir."

"Manny!" Kant's friend called out again. "This is one of my favorite plays. Please hurry."

Kant lifted his hand. "I suggest that you find some useful occupation and spend as little time as possible wandering around. Free time will never benefit you. This should become your maxim." He turned and walked toward his friend. Then he turned back and said, "Young man."

"Yes sir?"

"What is your name?"

"Martin," he answered. And then he completed the utterance and changed the course of his own life: "Martin Lampe."

Kant took a step forward, "Lampe?" He took one more step forward. "Your name is Lampe?" A slight grin formed on his thin lips and his cheeks grew pink.

"Yes sir." Lampe was sure the man was mocking him.

Kant pulled out his little sword in an elegant gesture and pointed to his feet. "Do you see these shoes?"

"Yes sir."

"Could you keep them clean like the shoes of a soldier summoned to the general's office?"

"Easily."

"Can you keep a home clean? Run errands?"

"I suppose."

"Do you need work?"

"Yes sir."

"Do you want work?"

"Yes sir."

"Lampe," Kant said with manifest seriousness. "I will consider this."

The friend called out, "Manny, the show, the show!"

Kant said, "Come to the university tomorrow and ask for Magister Kant. I will let you know my decision. Do you agree?"

"I do," Lampe answered, as though he were agreeing to a marriage.

Kant turned and walked off, bellowing into the air and the sky and all that is beyond the sky, "Lampe! Imagine that! His name is Lampe!"

———

Lampe looked up at the Dunce to see if he was still paying attention. "That was the beginning of my education."

"Your education."

"Yes. My education. I never received a degree. But for forty years I listened to his lectures. I saw the great books drip off the bony end of his quill. I served wine to foreign guests who brought news and new ideas, and who hoped for some trinket of wisdom from the great philosopher to carry home."

"Is that what all this is?" Kaufman waved his hands towards the scribbles on the walls.

Lampe looked around. "Well, yes. It wouldn't be possible without my education."

"What wouldn't be possible?"

"The work."

"What work?"

"This!" Lampe pointed to his walls.

"What is this?"

The moment had arrived. Lampe stood and began to pace with his hands behind his back. "Excellent question. Yes, what is this?" He spoke with gravity, trying to impress upon the Dunce the great privilege at hand. "You and Eco are the only people who have seen these markings on my cave."

Kaufman looked at the wall nearest him and squinted at the scribbles there. He was a terrible reader, and he was embarrassed by his ignorance. Lampe understood because he too had once been ignorant. He knew the pain of humiliation.

Lampe said, "This is only half the work. This is my half of the highest point of view."

"It's hard to see the words with all the soot on the walls."

"We always see reality through a fog, my friend." He raised his hand toward the heavens to match the pitch of his rising voice and rhetoric, then he placed his hand on the Dunce's shoulder in a fatherly way. "Here's a question for you. Would you like to help finish the work?"

Kaufman said, "You lost me."

Lampe looked down at him. "You can help me complete the work of the greatest philosopher ever to have been born of a woman."

The Dunce stared.

"I'm not being clear." Lampe resumed his pacing.

Kaufman glanced at the cuckoo clock. "Wasianski will wonder where I am if I don't get back to the house soon."

"Yes, you're indispensable. But please listen." The Dunce wilted in his chair as the pitch of Lampe's voice rose. He only needed to grasp the merest glimmer of what Lampe was saying. "Do you see these walls? This is the other half of Kant's final book, his greatest work. His friends thought he was losing his powers. Lunacy, they said. The imbecility of a second childhood. But that wasn't true! He was about to break through his earlier system and its constraints. His ink pot was a tea kettle boiling over. The ideas seemed like lunacy only because they were incomplete. The so-called scholars who have seen the manuscript and dismissed it make me want to howl. Kant knew I was the only person who understood his final ideas, and he hated me for it."

Without thinking, Lampe got down on one knee. Every muscle and joint ached. His back crackled as he put his hands on the Dunce's knees and said, "I was exiled, and I despaired of ever being invited back to the house. But if I could have the manuscript, even for a day or two, or perhaps three, I would see how to turn all this random scribbling into a book that would crown Kant's glorious life, and my own."

At first the Dunce's face was blank. His lips puckered and unpuckered, giving the impression of a rabbit considering which dandelion to nibble. But the grossly expressive request slobbered by Lampe made Kaufman uncomfortable. "I don't know anything about why you were fired. And I don't know anything about this book. But I do know that if I don't get back, I'll be fired too."

Lampe almost tipped over when Kaufman stood. Feeling the strain in his shoulders and knees, he returned to his kneeling position. Pushing on Kaufman's vacated chair, he stood up and quietly said, "Of course."

The Dunce backed toward the door and left.

After a few breaths to calm himself, Lampe reviewed his

disastrous strategy. There is no negotiating with an idiot, and Kaufman was an idiot. An actual idiot, not just someone who seems like an idiot.

—⁂—

Lampe often seemed stupid to Kant's guests because sleep deprivation and daytime drinking led to occasional verbal blunders. This offended him at first. But he was working for a genius, and he soon realized that if people thought he was stupid, he could stand around like a lamppost and listen in silence as they spoke without restraint. Because he was always running in and out of rooms, he only caught partial phrases. But over decades he pieced the phrases together to grasp the whole philosophy.

Kant didn't make Lampe's education easy. He refused to discuss philosophy at the dinner table or over wine. At the mention of any metaphysical concept, he would change the topic to politics or billiards. But if the conversation turned to something like the possibility of inhabitants on Saturn, Kant would leap at the idea. "Reason can't get us to an answer, but I have concluded that there must be intelligent life on other planets! Furthermore," he would say as he leaned toward whatever local scholar or visiting stranger was at the table, "is there any reason to suppose that our souls cannot somehow continue to live on one of those planets?"

Inevitably the guest, completely missing the point, would ask, "Why would living on another planet make any difference?"

Kant's eyes would flash. "Imagine how light life would be on another planet! How unencumbered with the weights and constrictions common to Earth! Might not the immortal soul inhabit those distant orbs of the universe and behold the excellence of that plan which so arouses curiosity even here? Globes in the planetary region might be forming even now, new mansions in other skies we might one day enjoy. With thoughts like these, the sight of the starry sky on a clear night gives profound pleasure to noble souls. Amid the universal silence of nature and the repose of the senses, the hidden faculty of the immortal spirit speaks a language which has no name, expressing ideas that are felt rather than thought." Kant would repeat such statements to different guests until he was pleased with the formulation, and then these would often end up in his books. And as often, his readers would be as baffled as his dinner guests.

But not Lampe. He heard the master where others seemed deaf. These were the first embryonic murmurings of the great *principle of the poetic a priori*, which he understood even before Kant, whose soul timidly retreated to the confines of his narrow chest and his uncooperative bowels.

Kant's bowels were a formidable philosophical adversary. The master often indulged in a physical reverie, dreaming of being whipped on the silver tether of life from earth to another planet, reaching not toward eternal verities, nor Platonic forms, but rather toward the pathetic hope that just for once he might breathe easily, and perhaps, finally, take a decent shit.

"Well, there's no going to other planets," Kant's literal guest would usually remark.

"Why not?" Kant would ask irritably, like a toddler asking why he can't have a cookie. "Why can't we reach them with our minds?"

"Our minds?"

"Certainly." Kant's tone would regain its mature equanimity

as he began his explanation. "It happens here on earth all the time, with no regard for distance."

"How so?"

"Suppose you're in India or Arabia or some country in Africa. If you've been righteous and carried out the rules of morality, you are as embedded in the community of good souls as if you were sitting here at this table. Physical presence doesn't matter." With a dove-like gesture of his hand, he would indicate the approach of his central point. "On earth, our crystalline minds are wrapped up in a dark covering of flesh and blood. But if all sense were to drop away, you would suddenly apprehend that you are already in heaven."

"What if I'm not righteous?" the benighted guest would ask.

"Then your eyes would be opened to the hell you occupy already, the community of the depraved."

The guest would persist. "So you believe in this business of spirits?"

"I understand what is necessary."

"What about tales of visions, or communicating with the dead? You say you believe in a heaven, and a hell? This is rather different than …"

"Lampe!" Kant would interrupt.

"Yes sir," Lampe would dutifully respond.

"You were a soldier."

"Yes sir," Lampe would say as he clicked his heels together neatly and lifted Kant's empty plate from the table.

"When you stood your post, did you worry about the affairs of the general, or did you simply stand your post?"

"Stood my post, sir, stood my post."

"Exactly. In the same way, we are to remain morally good in this post. The future world will take care of itself. Morality is all that matters. But enough of that! Lampe, get my hat and walking stick. It's time for a stroll." The master didn't like to talk about philosophy at the table because it drew blood from the stomach to the brain, causing his bowels to be upset. He would turn to his guest. "Do you care to join?"

The shift from God to digestion aids could be disorienting, but guests learned to accommodate the quirk. "Thank you. Yes, I suppose I could do with a walk."

"But no more philosophy," Kant would demand. "Now tell me, what have you heard lately from Berlin?"

As Lampe listened, he heard something new. He had never encountered it among his mother's lovers, his fellow soldiers, nor in the chatter of his own brain when he was alone. Here was a mind that lived in an invisible world of ideas. Kant observed earthy people who lived fully in the world of bodies and conflicts of will, but he never participated. Instead, he tried to convert people to reason, offering maxims to guide action. Some of his friends returned the favor, most especially Johann Georg Hamann.

Hamann was sent to London on business when he was a young man. Once he was free of the provincial eyes of busybodies in Königsberg, he tasted the open pleasures found only in cities such as Paris, Berlin, and London. There, a sticky web of charming, ravenous men led him to new understandings of abandon. He didn't resist. They shared each other, along with the booze his money bought.

But before long, instead of being in the middle of a parlor

full of sensuous men, he found himself in London, alone in a cheap attic room with no money for bread and no excuse to give to the businessman who had sent him there. His room had a window, a bed, and a spider in one corner. The only other furnishing was a bible someone had left behind. Hollow, unclean, and afraid, he opened the book and read it straight through. He began the book as one man, and he finished it as another.

When he returned to Königsberg, his friends quickly discovered that everything except his appearance had changed. They diagnosed him with the disease of religious fanaticism, and Kant set out to reconvert him to enlightened thought.

Lampe listened closely, astonished at how close Hamann was to discovering *the principle of the poetic a priori*. Hamann's forehead was high, and his eyebrows were almost always raised, as though he was perpetually surprised, or about to make a controversial point, or both. He had a slightly receding chin offset by strong cheekbones and a perfect nose, giving the impression of haughtiness supported by wealth, except that he was neither haughty nor rich. He barely had money for anything beyond the occasional visit to the theater. But his brain made up for this.

Hamann said, "Lampe, you mentioned your mother was from Italy?"

"My mother, sir?"

"Yes, your mother. Didn't you say she was from Italy?"

"I don't remember saying. She was familiar with Italian ports. And English ports. Various ports, I'd say."

"Why ports?" There was no judgment in his voice.

"She was an entertainer."

"I see. Your ears are red, Lampe. It would be a terrible thing to be embarrassed by your mother. Your mother is your mother."

"I'm not embarrassed."

"Say what you want."

A loud fart came from the next room where Kant was on the chamber pot, struggling with his destiny.

Hamann said, "We show up as bodies lured and tempted by drives that are rammed into the very core of our lives. Can tweaking some postulate of reason stay the volcanic flood of fiery feeling and desire? Kant can't even control his own bowels. How can reason control the human heart? There is such a pudder and racket in the schools of the learned about essences and quintessences. Even the great theatres breed confusion with words of little meaning. You need say nothing more, Lampe. I understand"

"She was a whore."

"As I said, I understand. But don't be too presumptuous when you think about your mother. She likely had her own reasons you could never guess."

"I'm glad you've found your way back to the light of reason," Kant said as he walked into the room, apparently more comfortable than before.

"Back?"

"Yes, back."

"I'm not back."

"You're here."

"I'm in Königsberg, but I am not back to the absurdities of faith in reason."

Hamann lit his pipe. Kant only held his pipe to his lips because, aside from special occasions, he allowed himself no more than one bowl of tobacco each morning, though the bowl grew bigger over the years.

Kant said, "The disturbance of your vision will take some time to heal."

"My vision has nothing to do with it. I've been overcome, and I welcome defeat. The enemy is already inside the camp, and it's stronger than you ever imagined. The weapons you and your professors are forging in philosophy's shop of reason are fired at too low a temperature. They'll crack in battle."

"The only enemy is reason misunderstood, misused, and stretched into areas where there is nothing firm, nothing certain."

"Manny, the most important things in life are misunderstood, misused, and uncertain. If you limit reason to areas where you think it reasonably functions, you're proving the strength of your sword by keeping it out of battle. You're slicing at the wind in play. Your philosophy is too thin a gruel for conversation about the soul. Souls need saving, and that is a bloody dangerous business. Your philosophy can't save a soul."

"I don't want to save your soul. I want to save your mind."

"What I really need is help with my finances."

"We'll get to that. I've already found you a job, in fact. This is the first step toward a full return to reason."

"What's the job?"

"In a moment. Restoring you to reason is far more important."

"Why? Reason left me defenseless when I was in bed with two men at once. I don't even know what you mean by reason anymore."

Kant blushed, but his tolerance for perversion was astonishing, especially since the master was a virgin.

"That's precisely why you need saving," Kant said. "Your confusion has a different order of magnitude than most. But I agree that misunderstanding reason is the central problem of our day. It's at the root of so much folly, including most of yours, old friend."

Hamann said, "Your philosophical problems and conundrums are artificial. Almost every problem in your philosophy is a product of your strange use of language."

"If reason isn't the solution, what is?"

Hamann again lit his pipe and held his glass out for Lampe to pour more wine. Then he winked at Lampe and said, "The loneliness of moral chaos is excruciating. The solution, Manny, is faith like a child."

Kant sighed and held his own glass out to Lampe, who was distracted by Hamann. "Lampe, more wine."

"Sorry." Lampe poured the wine and stepped back to his usual position by the door.

"When you talk like that, you put yourself outside reason. *Not*," Kant raised his hand to underscore the word, "in the sense of disagreeing with this or that idea. I mean reason as the only safeguard against folly and darkness."

"Folly and darkness? The only time reason seems to make progress is when it isn't up against real darkness. To face real darkness, we need something outside reason."

"How would you ever evaluate something outside reason? How would you know it's good?" Kant was sitting upright now.

Hamann said, "I know by knowing."

"But reason is the condition for knowledge. You're verging on a tautology."

"And you're verging on a kind of timidity that will make you miss whole worlds."

"None that are properly human," Kant said.

"What do you mean?"

"I'll never miss a human-sized world. If I miss the worlds of the gods, so be it. I'm not a god and neither are you."

"How do you know we aren't gods?" Hamann asked.

Kant shook his head. "Because you're too poor to be a god."

"Finally, something we agree on! I barely have enough money for pipe tobacco."

"The job, then." Kant left the prospect of converting Hamann for another time. "It's yours if you want it, but I doubt you'll like it."

"I'll do anything that's honest."

Kant again held out his glass for more wine, promptly poured by Lampe.

Hamann asked, "So, what's the job?"

"You'll work in the tax office of the king."

"Ah, the king. Marvelous."

Kant looked at Hamann, holding his gaze. "I know you despise the king, the court, and royal taxes."

"I also despise being hungry," Hamann said. "Besides, it'll be temporary. Everything is."

"Are you writing now?"

"Always."

"What are you working on?"

Hamann looked down at his hands. "A trifle."

"How far into it are you?"

"I just started."

"When?"

"Five minutes ago."

"I look forward to reading anything you write," Kant said, though he didn't like any of Hamann's books.

"I also look forward to reading it." Hamann stood up. "I'll leave you and Lampe to your evening tasks. I'll never be moved by your catechism of reason, but I'm grateful for your help with this job."

Kant gave him a slight nod of the head.

When Lampe returned from showing Hamann to the door, Kant said, "He's a strange one Lampe. I don't know what will come of him."

Lampe shrugged and began to clear the table. "At least he's honest."

"You can be honestly mistaken." Kant picked up the book next to him, signaling that the final judgment had been spoken for the night.

Lampe disagreed. He had heard the rumors and the gossip, but it didn't matter. Hamann was guided by something he called *the principle of the union of opposites*. It was a marvelous, bloated precursor to Lampe's own lean *principle of the poetic a priori*. Even Hamann's titles hooked Lampe's imagination and gave his brain something new to chatter about. *Fragments. Clouds. Flying Letter. Golgotha and Scheblimini*. Hamann would rather cure others of their philosophical maladies than add another intellectual corpse to the wasteland of endless systems. The incremental creeping of *Meier's Logic* left him cold. His search began in a cauldron ignited by orgies, a fire at first destructive and then purifying, leaving him empty in an attic populated with angels and spiders, unable to ignore the still, small voice at the heart of the universe.

He showed Lampe the way to the master principle. But he also inadvertently led Kant down the road to perdition by translating a small fragment of David Hume's philosophy and publishing it in the Königsberg paper. The little piece unwittingly planted the seed of madness by inspiring the idea that led to *The Critique of Pure Reason*, the idea that isolated all of humanity from things-in-themselves. Fortunately, almost no one understood the master's ideas, and those who did seemed more enthralled by his genius than horrified by his philosophy.

"Eco! Eco, are you down there?" Lampe called down into the darkness that Eco seemed to crave. "I haven't seen you for two days. You'd best not be rotting. Not today."

No answer.

"Eco!" he called out again. *Rotting* was the name Lampe gave to the stretches of solitude Eco sometimes fell into, lying in the dark, a blanket over his window, one candle lighting the spooky collection of toy guillotines he'd built. When the huge, pale man fell into these dark times, with no one to execute, he could stay in his room for a couple of weeks, which meant Lampe had to find his own food, buy his own wine, and care for Ding's bodily needs. It was terribly inconvenient.

Maybe Eco was just out gathering supplies. Or perhaps he went to the church to sit. He had no friends besides Lampe, so he certainly wasn't out on a social visit.

Lampe left his door open to listen for Eco's return. He dreaded this third night filled with thoughts about the emptiness in Kant's house beneath the moon.

He coaxed Ding over to this mattress. She still hadn't eaten the crust of bread from the day before. Why did that morsel of panting dog flesh comfort him and calm his panic? He didn't know.

If he couldn't figure out the meaning of such a small creature, was there any question he could answer? Not on his own. But if he could see the final manuscript of Kant's late poetic struggles to free himself from the thorns of the demonic architectonic that had trapped his mind for so long, it would be as good as a visit from Kant's ghost. Together they could finish the work of the great philosopher and his faithful servant: *The poetic a priori, by Immanuel Kant and Martin Lampe.*

Otherwise, all the scribbles on his walls added up to a bunch of nonsense no one would care about. He would never move past the absurd splotch of ink that mocked him.

And what then? He would rot in silent solitude. The reality of *the poetic a priori* would hover in the realm of the forms until some other mind stumbled across it and stole his treasure.

It wasn't fair. His treasure had been stolen too many times before. This idea was his, and no one was taking it from him.

He gently snuggled with Ding. He felt her tumor. Maybe it was larger, maybe not. At least it wasn't bleeding. Exhaustion carried him beneath the surface of conscious torment, while terror kept his mind buoyant and awake against his will. It was a clash that made for troubling dreams.

In that middle territory between waking and sleep, only one

face appeared more often than the master's—his mother's. But it was almost always contorted in passion, or in rage, beneath, or on top of, the men who diluted Lampe's joy from the time his mind first woke to sex as a child.

Sleep was more welcome than ever.

Day Four

The Only Possible Argument in Support of a Demonstration of the Existence of God

"They let me take the poor man down. The gallows are finally empty." Eco's voice was thick with phlegm. He sat like a large blob of bread dough on Lampe's mattress.

Lampe had been awake from before dawn, sitting at his desk, staring at the ink splotch on the first page of his terrifying stack of otherwise empty white paper, and feeling the discrete ideas scattered in the cold mass of his mind like the plucked petals of a flower caught in clear ice, their perfect forms made still, beautiful, lifeless. The intellectual force that was needed to conquer the problem of *the poetic a priori* now tumbled limply into the fourth day of grief. Lampe said, "Eco?"

"Yes, Martin?"

"Do you enjoy the gasps and groans of the people dying on the end of your rope?"

"I wish you wouldn't say it that way." Eco's massive hands were rubbing together like two bereaved old women hugging in church.

"Does it bother you?"

"What bothers me is when we leave a man to rot at the end of a rope, just hanging there for days after he's dead. He's paid for his crime. Why can't we do things with more respect and dignity? I get very sad when everyone in the city goes about their business like there wasn't a dead man hanging in the center of it all. But it's my job."

Lampe picked at a scab he hadn't noticed before on his arm. "Maybe it's good for a criminal to rot in the public square. His stench reminds us of evil. Maybe we need to see birds picking flesh off his carcass to force us in the right direction, because the average citizen can't be trusted to choose rightly."

"You don't believe that."

"I'm tempted. Nothing is fair. I can't even cast my shadow on the front steps of my master's house after forty years of service."

Eco said, "You could go ask if anything has changed. You could ask if you might be forgiven."

"Ha!" Lampe stood up and wiped the oil from his forehead. He looked at it glisten on his fingers. "I'd starve to death. All I have is the pathetic little pension the master left me on the condition that I never return, and Wasianski would cut me off the moment I appeared on the doorstep. When a wrong has been done and a sentence pronounced, grace is no longer an option. It is finished. It is done."

"That's very sad," Eco said. "There should be more mercy in the world."

"Mercy? From Kant? Let me tell you a story. Once, in the middle of a delicious meal, when everyone was having fun, the old man looked across the table at a guest who was going on about the harshness of the law or something, and he said that if you were on a ship transporting a prisoner condemned to death, and the ship began to sink, and everyone jumped so that only you and the prisoner remained, and the prisoner was chained and doomed to certain death by drowning, even then, Eco, my only friend, even then, you would be obligated to execute him before leaving the ship."

"That's horrible."

"You wouldn't execute the prisoner?" Lampe asked.

"Certainly not. They pose no danger to anyone, and they would die anyway."

"You're a hangman, Eco!" Lampe shook his head and rubbed the gray stubble on his face. "I know it's horrible. But it's also beautiful. The master's maxims were pure, and his devotion to them was so strong. I can't ask for release or permission. It must come from the other side."

"That's hard."

"And there is so little time."

———

Lampe obtained his incomparable education standing by the doorway between the dining room and the entrance hall, his back straight against one wall, his gaze fixed on the opposite one. He would stand still until he had to do something like straightening the professor's wig, crooked from overzealous argument. The first time Lampe straightened the wig, Kant was annoyed. But eventually his hand was no different than Kant's own hand absentmindedly straightening the wig. This was the fullness of that ontological category, *being a servant.*

Once Lampe tasted the strange form of thought and exploration called philosophy, he could never go back to gutting fish or sorting fruit to make his way. He might well have been undone from the inside were it not for Hamann's persistent resistance of Kant's demonic wooing, with his little ebullitions of sub-acrid humor, and his droll and witty peevishness at the rubs and vexations of life.

Lampe didn't understand why Kant was so devoted to converting Hamann back to reason. He always had at least one young man as a philosophical project, but Hamann, with his fleshly past and inclination toward joyful skepticism and prayer, became one of Kant's obsessions.

"Faith is fine for a child," Kant allowed. "But you're not a child."

Hamann cleaned his nails, listening to Kant's same old failed argument, before giving his usual response: "Let's go play a few games of billiards."

Kant waved away the distraction, his hand flying around his head and quickly returning to the nest of his pocket. "The child has no reason for this faith you insist on. Therefore, it will, at some point, become unstable in its belief."

"Is that what happened to you?" Hamann asked.

"I'm not unstable in belief, because I don't rely on belief. But yes, like any thinking child, I eventually discovered the faults of faith. Religion cannot grasp why a God might exist."

Hamann said, "A child doesn't need to see *why* God exists. A child merely sees *that* God exists. It's the same with me."

Kant reddened as he always did when someone claimed to see something his rules did not permit—God, ghosts, the thing-in-itself. He leaned forward, reaching out toward Hamann as though grabbing at him from the edge of the philosophical abyss. "There is no organ for such sight."

"Certainly there is." Hamann continued to stare at his nails. "Otherwise, I couldn't see what I see. But I do, as long as I am not distracted by false questions and convoluted philosophical diversions like yours."

Kant sat back. "There is one idea that might clear up your confusion."

"I'm not confused, Manny. I see more clearly now than I ever have."

"I mean the idea of moral sense. We are pushed, commanded even, to pursue the highest good. Call it seeing if you want, but the logical consequence ought to be perfect happiness."

"Find me a perfectly happy man. If he agrees, you win."

"But you're making my case for me."

"How so?"

Kant said, "There's nothing within the moral law that guarantees perfect happiness, even if we're perfectly obedient to the moral law."

"Then why do you insist on connecting the moral law and happiness? How does that replace my sense of God?"

"Because there *ought* to be a connection. I merely postulate a means for the connection. And since such a means cannot be in nature, it must be outside nature."

"And that would be God," Hamann said.

"Exactly," Kant said, calm and satisfied that he had broken through Hamann's fog. "I postulate God, the guarantor of perfect happiness in another world to reward the moral work we do here."

"Do you believe in this God?"

Kant immediately waved his hand in the air as if he were shooing away flies. "Belief has nothing to do with it. I begin with what is the case. I start with the moral law, and what ought to follow. And this leads me to see that I must postulate God."

"I hope you never need God for anything other than the completion of a philosophical treatise."

"At least my God accomplishes that much."

Kant was sitting in what he called his observatory position, with his hands crossed over his belly and his eyes at half-mast. He finally grinned. Perhaps the closing jest had finally arrived. Then a strange turn occurred in the conversation, one Lampe grew to expect, and Kant looked down at the belly protruding off his otherwise thin frame. He asked, "How are your bowels? Did my suggestion that you take honey to lubricate them help?" The several hypochondriacs in Kant's group of friends relied on his observations about the physical, even more than the metaphysical.

"I'm finding my way well enough, I suppose."

"You don't appear to be bloated. Your breathing seems to be quite regular with none of that shortness of breath I suffer from."

"You should have been a physician, Manny."

"No, my mistress is metaphysics. But look at this." Kant off his coat while Hamann observed. "I have such a narrow and flat chest. I've never been able to breathe." He turned to the side allowing Hamann to fully appreciate the flatness of his chest. "There's no room in my body. That's why I suffer so horribly when I have insufficient exoneration."

"Oh good God," Lampe muttered to himself.

Kant lashed Lampe with his eyes. "What was that you said?"

"I was just saying to myself how hard it must be having everything crammed in so tight."

Kant's blue eyes stared, head tilted, mouth fixed in a straight line, as still as if he were posing for a portrait. "You have no idea."

Hamann said, "In my case, it's not my intestines that distract. It's love."

Kant turned his eyes from Lampe who noticed a wink from Hamann. "You may think it's love, but don't be too quick to dismiss your bowels. If you stop paying attention, trouble will brew down there. It's quiet at first. But suddenly you find yourself stopped up, miserable for a week, hardly able to think. There's a reason for this too."

"I thought we were finished talking about reason."

"Never."

"So, what's the reason for this great suffering?"

Kant leaned forward into his lecturing posture. "Our organs are like the organs of the four-footed beasts. When we stand up," Kant again stood up to demonstrate his point, "our organs hang, pendulous. The heart hangs from the vessels, stretching them."

"Stop!" Hamann's imagination was vivid. One mention of the heart straining the vessels, and he imagined his own ready to tear. "We can talk about anything else, even reason. Better yet, let's just go for a walk."

Kant refined his point. "The intestines, weighted by feces, are uniformly supported by the abdominal musculature in animals. But in us they sag, elongate, and threaten to rupture."

Lampe said, "That's why I prefer to lie down and sleep as much as possible."

Kant ignored Lampe and said, "It all begins when we are in the womb and our mothers stand upright." He thrust a finger high into the air and then thrust it forcefully toward the ground.

Hamann said, "I don't get it."

Kant answered in triumph, "As fetuses we are vertical, but head down!"

In the lingering silence, Lampe felt the sagging of his heart and guts for the first time, after thirty years of being quite happy about his organs.

Kant sat again and crossed his spidery thin legs. Lampe stepped towards him and straightened his wig, which had suffered from the excessive enthusiasm of his pronouncement.

With his eyes now bright and his smile placid, Kant offered Hamann his conclusions. "This is the price we pay for our greater rationality. The downward flow of blood when we are in the womb nourishes our brain and allows it to grow into a superior state. That's why you should embrace your natural state as a man, committed to the rational faculty, rather than allowing yourself to be led by the leash of blind faith in things beyond what you can find in reason."

"Our rationality grows by virtue of the extra blood flowing from our shit-filled guts? The status of reason is worse off than I thought." Before Kant could respond, Hamann stood and said, "Manny, thank you for the meal, the conversation, and the image of my heart and guts that shall never again leave me in peace."

Kant merely nodded.

—•••—

In the evenings the little philosopher rarely spoke to Lampe. He used the time to finish writing a piece, or to read, or to prepare for the next day's lectures. He seemed to enjoy the silent presence of Lampe, like the presence of a cat or some other disengaged, low-maintenance, domesticated beast.

Lampe obliged him by sitting and polishing the spoons, but he did so willingly because he didn't want to be alone with own his thoughts and nightmares about war.

Many of Kant's friends viewed servants as partially defective, as people who could not sustain their own lives, and who needed to latch on to the more stable and durable lives of others. Battle had broken enough of Lampe that he wouldn't dispute the charge. People thought he was simple because of his tolerance for menial tasks such as standing by the wall or polishing spoons for hours. But he needed rest from the violence of war. Polishing one spoon, and then another, and then another, was a meditative act that kept his mind focused on something besides death and the stench of fields full of torn corpses. Reading pornographic stories also helped.

But few people realized that some parts of the job made every nerve in his body raw.

"Lampe, more wine."

"Lampe, more fish."

"Lampe, time for a walk."

"Lampe, don't interrupt."

Guests frequently chuckled at Kant's dull, foolish servant. But because he'd had a front row seat so close to the master's astonishing mind, his silence grew. After absurd conversations about his uncooperative intestines and the incomprehensible effects they had on speculation about metaphysical subtleties, when the guests finally put on their coats and departed, Lampe remained alone with the master, meditatively polishing spoons in the vicinity of that high forehead veiling the ethereal verities as they migrated in and out of Kant's mind. The master's forehead became the object of Lampe's contemplation while the master extracted terrifying ideas from the ink jar. A little sip from his vodka flask helped him to endure, tempering his gift for bearing witness, dampening the fire before it became intolerable.

Sometimes the little professor would sit in silence for hours with no fidgeting, breathing his shallow breaths. He would stare at the poplars swaying in the wind like metronomes set on slow. He would placidly watch the birds that came and went on the windowsill. And then, like a possessed man who had only minutes remaining in his life to write out his will or profession of love, he would take up the quill, dip it into the ink jar, and start scratching philosophy across the page, up the edges, onto scraps. Where did it all come from? Who or what was he listening to as he wrote and wrote and wrote?

Most men would say, "Here is a swamp. Here is a frog. Here is a mug of beer." Those were the things in the world.

But the master put sanity at risk by daring to produce the very proof, or failure of proof, for nothing less than the existence of God, making the mystery of the universe appear on paper with ink in the same room where, a few hours before, he had complained to his guests about his bowel movements.

After episodes in which Kant's bowels clashed with his attempts to prove the existence of God, Lampe usually had nightmares, if he could sleep at all. But Kant, that horrifying little man, would simply yawn, ask for warm tea with sugar, and then sleep as peacefully as a well-fed dog after a long walk.

Lampe's mind sprung back from these memories, and he rushed to his desk. But the piece of paper with the ink splotch felt like a reproach. Only silence met him as he held the quill that had once belonged to the master.

Who was he to write ideas? Who was he to grab at these strange entities inhabiting the world of the invisible, forcing them to appear as sentences on a page like God forcing souls into frail, lustful bodies, vulnerable to judgment? Could philosophical contemplation spring from pure emptiness, dereliction, and the spirited darkness of night?

Ding lapped water from her bowl. Then she curled up, careful of her tumor, and she began chewing the piece of smoked hide Eco had left for her.

Lampe put down the quill and retreated to his mattress.

Kant had infected him with the desire to question the universe, and once it was too late for him to be cured of philosophy, the intellectual bully had hinted that the questions he wanted to ask were unanswerable. His only consolation was to follow in the steps of the youthful Rousseau, who confessed to reading erotic literature with one hand. It was enough to lead one to terminal despair.

A prayer suddenly swept through his mind: "Thank God for Ding."

He relaxed into his straw mattress. He smelled disgusting. The odor would have embarrassed him if a woman were present, but since he was alone, he found it strangely pleasant, even though it smelled like a preamble to death.

All his ideas were fading. He was an old man on a divinely constructed gallows. God's hand was pressing gently on his lower back. Eternity's hangman was visible at last.

Day Five

Illnesses of the Head

"I NEED A LITTLE BREAK now and then," Kaufman said. He had discovered that his daily errands were more pleasant if he dropped by to visit Lampe for a nip of wine. "Wasianski's showing off for the wealthy people who are curious about the old professor, but it's tiresome and he's bossy."

Lampe said, "Kant has already been dead five days. You'll be able to rest soon."

"I doubt that." The Dunce eyed wine jug. "The lines keep getting longer. I don't think Wasianski expected the entire city to come pay honor. And he makes everything worse when he brings an official to the front of the line and serves him refreshments. He's becoming impossible."

"Tell me more." Lampe pushed the wine jug towards the Dunce.

"Wasianski wants to be famous." The Dunce reached for the wine and took a couple of swallows. "He plans to write a book. But the professor wouldn't be happy with some of the notes he's scribbling."

"What sort of notes?" A dim glimmer of hope was breaking through the darkness in Lampe's soul.

"Notes about this, notes about that."

"Can you be more specific?" Lampe relaxed his clenched hands and spoke carefully, trying not to offend the dullard.

"Notes about his life. When he was born, where he went to school, daily habits. Blah, blah, blah."

"Habits?" Lampe said. "Of course, I know nothing about his habits."

"He's put together a pretty good little list." The Dunce again missed the hint that Lampe could share vast stores of information that resided in the reservoir of his brain.

Lampe asked, "Which of his notes would offend?"

"His private notes."

"About what?"

Kaufman took another drink from Lampe's wine jug. "About his sleepwalking. Or the strange comments he started making before dinner."

"Does Wasianski mock him?" Lampe asked.

"He says it's just for completeness."

"It's wrong to make fun of an honorable man."

"Wasianski knows an opportunity when he sees it. He's had visitors from the king's court, barons, military officers."

"He would have grown old and anonymously dropped off the face of the earth if Kant hadn't died at the right time."

"If anyone knows that, it's you." The Dunce grinned like a toddler with a sharp knife. "Wasianski stays busy making sure the commoners don't take any relics. But after everyone has gone for the day, when I'm tired to the core, do I get a rest?"

"Let me guess," Lampe said flatly, devoting all his energy to preventing a mighty eye-roll.

"Nope. None." Kaufman lifted the jug.

"Let's use real glasses and toast your good work." Lampe felt a new opportunity lurking, so he took his two glasses, and he handed the cleaner one to Kaufman.

Once the wine was poured and they had tapped glasses, Kaufman continued his complaint. "While I'm mopping away footprints, dusting, and preparing food for the next day, Wasianski just sits at Kant's writing desk, scribbling his book about the old man. Then he begrudges me my private time in the mornings."

"I'm honored that you use your precious free time to visit a decaying old man like myself."

"I don't know how long I can stand it. And I tell you, I've had offers myself."

Lampe sat up straighter and topped off the glasses of wine. "What kind of offers?"

"I've made a few connections on my own." A look of second-hand haughtiness rippled under the surface of the Dunce's bland face. "One or two wealthy visitors told me they'd welcome Kant's servant into their home. I have my own stories to share, you know."

Lampe suppressed a groan. After only two years of working for the master, was the Dunce known as Kant's servant? But there was no time to argue. "I agree," he said, and he held out his glass.

"With what?" The Dunce tapped Lampe's glass a second time.

Lampe said, "You deserve better than this. Who is Wasianski to determine your life? He didn't hire you. Kant did. He didn't pay you. Kant did. You worked for Kant. Even now it is Kant's money that supplies your income. This treatment is unacceptable. It's outrageous. Do you want to know what I think?"

The Dunce took a gulp of his wine and eyed Lampe as though he were selling magic potions on the street.

Lampe nearly folded in half as he leaned forward with his legs crossed and his hands clasping each other, squeezing rhythmically, pumping like a heart. He took a deep breath and said, "Kaufman, as soon as Kant is buried, you'll quickly be forgotten." He held up his hands in solidarity when he saw the putty of the Dunce's pale, pink expression of limp shock. "I know it's not fair. But that's how people are. When the novelty wears off, these wonderful opportunities will fade away. If you want a permanent position and the security you deserve, you must act now, while people are still enchanted with Kant, and with you, his, you know ..."

"... trusted servant," the Dunce said with sudden, grave illumination as his face slowly transformed into a vague look of interested concern. "What do you suggest?"

"Don't wait. Go today. Go now. Accept the best offer. By tonight you could be working for more pay at a permanent job. If you wait until the professor is buried, it will be too late."

Kaufman draped his arm over the back of his chair, like a shrewd negotiator who will not be taken in. "I'll have a job for a while. The lines still stretch around the corner all day."

"But think ahead. Even the melancholy fact that the master will soon begin to stink will surely bring the crowds to an end."

"The room he's in is freezing. Wasianski says he could stay there for weeks."

Lampe allowed a small grin to appear on his face. He felt another strategy bubbling up from the deeper parts of his own brain. At last, the words arrived. "You're young. I dare say you have a girl somewhere."

The Dunce grinned and looked down at his feet. "No, no. No girl. Not yet."

"Oh, now, I don't believe that," Lampe lied. Kant's maxim, *Always tell the truth*, was fine unless some truly wonderful outcome was only possible with a tincture of deception.

The Dunce awkwardly confessed, "There might be a girl or two with some interest. Actually, one of them is so lovely ..."

"And think about this," Lampe interrupted before the Dunce could descend into sentimental drivel about some perfectly plain and dull girl whom he had seen once at church or in the market, saying a single, stumbling, *Hello*, before finding his own pathetic voice choked up with a confluence of desire and self-doubt. "You've been in the closest circle of one of the world's most famous men. Impressive! All that remains before you woo her and have her fall into your arms is a steady income. Women love security."

"I don't know. Things are so busy right now. There's time for all the rest of that."

"There is no time!" Lampe demanded. Then he asked in a steadier voice, "Do you know why the professor never married?"

"I've heard some theories," the Dunce answered with an insolent wink.

"Whatever theories you've heard are wrong." Lampe was well aware of the gossip, and he had no interest in discussing it. "He didn't marry because he refused to make a decision until everything was perfect. But things are never perfect. He was forever dissatisfied with his finances, or job security, or home. And then it was too late. Simple as that. Do you want to grow old and die alone?"

"No."

"Do you think a chance like this will ever come along again?"

The Dunce shrugged.

Lampe wagged his finger close to Kaufman's nose. "Don't waste it! Go today!"

The Dunce breathed in and, with a voice strengthened by enthusiasm, he said, "Yes! I must get out of that house of death and away from Wasianski's constant nagging."

Lampe immediately poured another glass of wine to fortify the resolve growing in the spineless young man. "You're wise beyond your years."

The Dunce sat back and let his gaze wander without comprehension across the thousands of scribbles on the walls of the strange Martin Lampe. "I do wonder, though."

"Wonder what?" Lampe tipped his head forward, unsure how much longer he could bear this conversation. Hours were passing irrevocably and adding up to days, pushing him closer to the silence of his own grave. Lampe felt a need like lust to see the old man, to see the last work of the master, and to move past the humiliating ink splotch that was his only achievement.

After the Dunce paused for effect, imitating the look of a man capable of real thought, he said, "I probably shouldn't leave Wasianski to manage the crowd alone."

"You're so generous," Lampe said, noting the presumptuous nod of the Dunce's small head. "But you shouldn't let this concern disrupt your own life."

"I don't know, Martin."

The answer was so exquisitely clear, but the Dunce couldn't see it. Lampe shut his eyes and plainly stated the self-evident solution that held the potential to transform and redeem his life. "Perhaps I can help."

The words blew past the undiscerning Dunce like a wind transiently rustling leaves, portending nothing. "I'll just carry on. That's easiest." He began to pat his pockets as though he was about to leave. His glass was nearly empty. Lampe quickly moved to refill it, but the Dunce held up his hand. "I've had enough for now." As he moved to stand, he felt just how much wine he had drunk, and he had to sit again.

Lampe made immediate use of this and patted Kaufman's knee. "Listen. There were some old misunderstandings that you need not worry about. But our dear philosopher is dead. This is a time for letting go of all that, you know. Forgive and forget. New beginnings and so forth. By this I mean new beginnings for you." He patted Kaufman's knee again, unsuccessfully trying to appear benevolently paternal. "Here's the important thing young man. I'd be willing to step in and help Wasianski while you pursue your important new goals of financial security and a family."

A small snot bubble appeared when the Dunce suddenly snorted a laugh through his nose. "You'd hate being bossed around by Wasianski. His high-pitched, look-down-your-nose voice would be a needle prick in your ears. I couldn't ask you to do that."

"No, listen." Lampe had to focus mightily to restrain his tone of desperation as he reached out and took hold of Kaufman's arm. "It would also help me. I'm an old man myself. This would give me a chance to revisit old times, you know, and all that sort of thing."

"I can't afford to miss any of my pay while I consider jobs. I'd best just stay."

"You can keep your pay! I don't need it. I'll give it to you. Then you can have your pay, and you can also have the time you need to seize these rare opportunities."

"You would do that for me?"

Lampe's heart pounded as victory approached. "You're a young man. I couldn't sleep at night if you missed this singular opportunity."

"Unfortunately, Wasianski isn't very enthusiastic about you, sorry to say. Your name is off limits there."

Lampe swallowed a barbed lump of pain. "I'm not beyond apologizing. I would know what to say."

The Dunce seemed genuinely thoughtful at the prospect. "What should I do?"

"Go to Wasianski and tell him that you need time to explore opportunities. You're right that he won't be happy. That's when you let him know about our conversation."

Kaufman scratched a pimple on his chin. "I'll need to ask those folks if the jobs are still being offered."

"Fine! Do that immediately and then go to Wasianski. But remember, you must make the right decision for yourself, your future wife, and your future family. All Wasianski has to do is to send a simple note, one sentence asking me to come. And I will come right away."

"You'll have to work on your grooming."

Lampe looked down. His fingernails were long and cracked, with some unspeakable collection of gray matter beneath them. His nightgown and old soldier's jacket were filthy. He smelled bad and his long hair was tangled. "I'll take care of that today. When I get that single sentence, I'll go to Wasianski. Can you do this?"

"Yes," the Dunce said with a hint of encouraging excitement in his voice. He struggled to stand again. "I think you're right."

Lampe's heart nearly burst with longing and anticipation. He stood up and said, "Go on son, don't miss the chance. Run if you have to. Remember the fine wife you will win when you are well employed in the house of a rich man." And don't forget that Wasianski only needs to scribble one sentence on a slip of paper and send it my way."

"Thank you Lampe." The Dunce walked to the door. Before he left, he turned around and said, "You're a good man."

"This is what friendship is for." Lampe smiled his first sincere smile in ages.

———

At last. Five days he had waited, while a small forest burned in the fireplace of the master's home and the world marched by Kant's dry little corpse. Now Lampe might also be allowed to cross the threshold, to wander about the old house, to visit the bedroom that Kant kept dark for fear of bugs, and then to step into the cold room where the little, gray corpse lay.

The torment of exile affects a man's composure, but now a plan was in place. It was a good plan. An excellent plan. From long experience, Lampe tried to keep some skepticism in reserve since the plan depended on the Dunce doing a few simple tasks, and this introduced a measure of uncertainty.

But still, it might happen. In fact, it would probably happen. The Dunce would move on to his simple new job, find a wife, and bring imbecile duplicates of himself into the world, God be praised.

Wasianski was another story. Would he be able to see the sublime rationality grounding the prospect of reconciliation? Could he grasp that only Lampe was able to help him write his biography of Kant? Surely Wasianski knew that. It was self-evident.

Maybe he should show Wasianski the quill he stole from the unmagical Kant. If he did, he would have to say it was a gift. He didn't want to jinx things with a lie, but if he told the truth and confessed that he stole the quill Kant used to complete *The Critique of Pure Reason*, he might be thrown out as quickly as he had gained entrance. And yet, if he told the truth, he might be seen as truly repentant and be welcomed back into the only place where his mind thrived.

Everything was too uncertain. Better to stay silent about the quill and avoid complicating things. He would do nothing until he heard from Wasianski.

He went into the hallway and yelled down the stairs, "Eco, are you here?" Soon he heard the heavy footsteps of Eco, the lumbering ghost, and who appeared at the base of the stairs. "Eco, I'm feeling better, and I want to eat. Get some money from the box and go buy two jugs of wine, a loaf of black bread, sausage, and some figs. After that, we can play cards."

"Okay, Martin. I'm glad you're feeling better. I was worried about you."

While Eco was getting food and wine, Lampe straightened his bed sheets, folded his nightgown, and dressed. With his scissors, he clipped his beard close to his face and he combed his hair. He pulled his small throw rug over the dried urine on the floor and gave Ding a piece of smoked hide to chew, hoping to distract her tongue from her tumor.

When Eco finally returned, the slowest man in Königsberg, they set up their little feast in Lampe's room.

"You do seem happier today," Eco said in a tone that made him sound like he was offering condolences.

Lampe gnawed on a piece of sausage and a slice of hard bread. He had not been this hungry in years. He popped a fig in his mouth and washed it down with wine.

Eco finally asked, "Why are you so cheerful? Did you get your invitation?"

Lampe grinned a greasy grin. "Not yet. But it's only a matter of time."

"Very good, Martin." Eco wiped his plump white fingers on his pants and then reached for the card deck. He took up a card and looked at his hand. He had a perfect face for cards—round, pale, and padded with fat. But there was a sadness that covered his face like the pox.

Lampe took up one card and put down another. "I am on the cusp of a Copernican revolution."

Eco cautiously put down a card and reevaluated his hand.

Lampe quickly put down a card.

Eco slowly placed his cards on the table. "I win."

Lampe looked at the cards. "Fine, then. You win."

With the soft but relentless attention a mother gives to the evolving personality of her child, Eco said, "You play too fast, Martin."

"You play too slow," Lampe answered. "It distracts me."

"I should go nap. Then I need to get things ready for tomorrow."

"Another execution? Already? That should put you in a good mood."

Eco stood and walked slowly to the door. "Be nice, Martin. We should show respect for the man's family in their grief."

———

From inside the vocational constraints of a servant, Lampe learned to pay quiet attention, shepherding the vast expanses of mind residing in the tiny body of the philosopher with his clockwork discipline. The average mind would break under the weight of the ideas that emerged. Kant's writing desk was a brutal ship on a raging sea, where the foundations of the mind were tested and the weaker parts thrown overboard.

Lampe knew the destructive effects of philosophy on the unprepared mind. The most extreme example he had witnessed involved a student named Johann Friedrich von Funk. Kant had said a few too many times, "I'm fond of that student, Funk. He has a sensitivity about him, a fragility that bodes well for his receptiveness to true thought." And he gave Funk special attention, gifting him with benevolent pressure to continually improve in his philosophical endeavors.

Unexpectedly, Funk died of exhaustion a few days before Kant's fortieth birthday. When his friends found him, they were shaken and terrified. Amidst all the emotion and confusion, an argument broke out among them regarding who would bury poor Funk.

Lampe was sad about the death of the young man, but he didn't realize the impact Funk's death had until after the burial when he noticed a new silence in the master. For weeks, if Lampe said anything, Kant only looked at him with a sad grin. No amount of cajoling or encouragement could lift the professor from his gloom.

One day Lampe saw a letter on Kant's desk addressed to Funk's mother. It was in Kant's handwriting, but it sounded nothing like him:

"Every human being makes a plan for his destiny in the world. There are skills he wants to learn, there are honor and peace, which he hopes to get from them, and lasting happiness in conjugal life, and a long list of projects that make up the pictures of the magic lantern which he paints for himself, and which he allows to play continuously in his imagination. Death, which ends this play of shadows, shows itself only in the great distance, and is obscured and estranged by the light that envelops the more pleasant places. While we are dreaming, our true destiny leads us on an entirely different way. The part we really get seldom looks like the one we expected, and we find our hope dashed with every step we take until death, which always seemed far away, suddenly ends the entire game."

Kant never talked like this before or after the letter. But death had infiltrated his life in a new way. Death was indecipherable, and acceptance of it required repeat treatments. Kant said nothing more about Funk, the loss, the death, the terror. But he was driven deeper into his philosophy, where he could float in the atmosphere of timeless, deathless, death-like thought. He continued to refine his skills at billiards, and he ate out regularly, making jests with his friends, going to the theater after dinner, and appearing generally healthy. But he also began to read medical books as much as he read philosophy, and he talked about his ailments more than ever. His hypochondriacal tendencies began appearing in his books.

It was obvious to Lampe that much of what the philosopher wrote was silly. He was working on a ridiculous book called *Observations on the Feeling of the Beautiful and the Sublime.* His notes began badly, in Lampe's opinion, attacking anyone who claimed to have a revelation, who sensed the presence of heaven, who claimed to understand prophecies, or who filled their mind with thoughts about the size of the seas. Such thoughts led to delusion, fanaticism, and dementia. There was a surprising amount about sex in the book as well, all of which was naïve to the point of absurdity. If only Kant had asked for insight from Lampe, son of a whore, his books would have been best-sellers.

One evening, smelling strongly of the cheap whiskey that bolstered his confidence, he looked over Kant's shoulder as he wrote and asked, "Shouldn't you have a romp with a real woman before writing about sex?"

The master stopped writing, but he didn't look up from his paper. After a few moments, he said in a whisper, "Say that again."

Lampe didn't say it again. He had come too close to losing his front-row seat at the writing desk, where discoveries emerged from The Mind.

But he still wondered how Kant could possibly think he knew the things he claimed to know. To a casual observer, the discovery process would look like nothing. For hours he scratched the bone of his quill against paper, trying to define concepts such as visionary, crank, trifling, fop, dandy, chatter, silly, insipid, and grotesque. He dissected the melancholic, the sanguine, the phlegmatic. But he seemed to have an especially keen eye for women and their secret magic, their inborn feeling for the beautiful, cleanliness, and delicacy in respect of all that provokes disgust. He insisted that they were intolerant of commands and incapable of principles, but at least they were neat. He was dogmatic about his conclusion that a sexual inclination ultimately lay under all their charms, and with the boldness of one stating self-evident truth, he pronounced that if a woman has a head full of Greek or mechanics, she may as well have a beard.

This was no work for a true philosopher. It was embarrassing, and Lampe had to intervene. Kant needed a new kind of discipline if it was ever to escape from drivel about dandies and fops. Lampe was trained as a soldier to observe *Kadavergehorsam*— cadaver obedience. He was prepared to die, if that is what it took to bring the master's philosophical genius into the world.

But nothing hinted at what was coming. The book on the horizon would change reality itself. It would turn the universe inside out, and it would bequeath to Lampe the life-long task of recovering the thing-in-itself from utter isolation.

The truly great idea—whether it arrives from God or from the Devil—demands that the whole universe conspire. The birth of a real idea requires labor that contorts the mind as the womb is contorted, and made bloody and wet, in the birthing of an animal. The ideas in *The Critique of Pure Reason*, the great book of horror, would only find their way into the world with a midwife who was ferocious, because the ideas were huge, and they were breach in the womb. But who could bear to be midwife to such a monstrosity?

Kant's life appeared routine and pleasant, with a predictable schedule of writing, lecturing, eating, and sleeping. But in the early mornings, he gathered the trappings necessary for the birth of the idea of the horrid book. He laid the foundation and assembled the scaffolding so that the structure might be built, the great architectonic that would become the temple within which the thing-in-itself would remain, hidden behind the thick curtain, imprisoned in the most secret place, until Lampe could figure out which key unlocked the prison door and release it back into the world of the awakened mind.

Honing the master's discipline was made easier by the death of the unfortunate Funk, which suffused Kant's once-jovial life and smothered any residual concerns about fops and dandies. But writing philosophy didn't pay the bills, so Kant made some extra money by joining the king's effort to educate the troops. He was not yet famous as a philosopher, but he was sufficiently known for his knowledge of mathematics, mineralogy, and geography to be of use to the soldiers. Numbers, rocks, and maps cleared his mind of brush, and allowed it to lie fallow while the great ideas germinated in the dark place. He had little regard for soldiers, Lampe not excepted, because a soldier simply follows orders, and that is not a noble aspiration for the human soul. His opinion didn't change when Lampe pointed out the soldier's visceral mastery of loyalty, courage, devotion to comrades, and sacrifice. Nonetheless, Kant enjoyed the company of any social elite, including that of higher military officers, and they usually enjoyed his company as well.

When General Meyer sent a carriage each day to pick up the little professor, Lampe, who venerated generals, was transiently intimidated. How did this little professor, by mere force of mind, gain such a place in that world, while Lampe, who had risked his life in war, could only wave goodbye as he stood on the steps with his spoon-polishing rag? Just when Lampe was close to smacking Kant if he said another word about the consistency of his stools, one of Frederick the Great's generals would invite the master to lunch, leaving Lampe mute with admiration.

But how quickly things can change. One day Lampe was waiting for the professor to return home from one of these lunches. When the carriage pulled up, Kant stepped down, walked past Lampe, and went to his room without a word.

Lampe asked the driver, "What happened?"

The driver leaned over and said, "Wine."

"Wine? He drank too much wine?"

The man shook his head. "Spilled too much."

Lampe attempted a gasp of horror to cover his delighted fascination. General Meyer had a reputation for being obsessed with elegance, and Kant was obsessed with appearing elegant. "Terrible!" he said as he imagined the event, wishing he had been there to see it.

"Terrible indeed. Your man there spilled red wine on the general's most exquisite table setting."

"The general must have been furious!"

"Nope."

"He wasn't furious?" Lampe asked.

"That's what I just said."

"Well, I'm sure the professor was mortified. He'll be embarrassed to show himself in public again."

"Not if the general has any say. When your man spilled the wine, the general took an entire glass himself and spilled it right across the tablecloth. They had been talking about the Dardanelles, so the general started drawing illustrations in the red wine on the tablecloth."

"What did the professor do?"

"He listened to the general's explanation of the Dardanelles. Then he stood up with a newly filled wine glass. He held it high and bowed. Quite the gentleman he is."

"Yes," Lampe said. "So is your general."

The carriage pulled away. Lampe stood alone, hesitant to go inside. Kant would be a miserable companion that night. Social appearances may have been saved, but Lampe's increasingly nuanced sense of the master's moods told him that Kant would seethe in solitude. He would isolate himself for a while, with Lampe as the only animated object he would tolerate, simply because he considered Lampe to be more like talking furniture than like a man.

Kant was sitting in his chair by the window staring at the church steeple. He said nothing for nearly an hour. Then he suddenly stood, walked back and forth across the room several times with his hands in his pockets, and looked up at Lampe, who was pretending to dust the furniture. "Do you hear all that noise? The loading and unloading of carriages? The loud ship workers wandering the streets? I can't work here anymore. I must move!"

Lampe shrugged. "I'll help you pack."

Kant ignored him and resumed staring out the window. Something was changing and Lampe wasn't sure what it was. But he remained present, watching in the quiet before the thunderstorm.

Kant was feeling for a power that he mumbled about more frequently, a secret art in the depths of the human soul. As the nature of the universe and our place in it gained new and horrific clarity in the master's mind, Lampe forced himself to watch instead of running off to the solace of women, wine, and oblivion.

—༺༻—

Such memories made Lampe feel close to death. He was comforted only by a dying dog and the city hangman. In his solitary vigil, he wondered at his own secret art and why art took so long. The scribbles on his walls, each a discreet idea, floated like asteroids searching for a moon, moons searching for a planet, planets searching for a sun, all drifting without a center. Would he ever get to the secret that pulled everything together?

When Kaufman brought the one-line invitation from Wasianski, and he could finally kneel by the master's side and hold the last manuscript in his hands, then he would know.

The room was dimly lit by the moon. Ding was snoring in the corner. Lampe lay down on his mattress, drew his knees to his chest, and fell asleep.

Day Six

Molyneux's Problem

LAMPE HADN'T FELT SUCH EXCITEMENT in years. He watched and waited as Kaufman meandered toward the front door of the house, slammed the door behind him, walked up the stairs, and finally arrived at Lampe's small room.

"Johannes! Have a seat."

The Dunce was apparently growing a beard, and he was wearing small reading glasses of the sort writers and intellectuals sometimes wore. Lampe kept his thoughts to himself as he pulled out the jug of wine and a loaf of black bread wrapped in newspaper. "A bit of breakfast?"

"Perhaps a morsel," the Dunce said.

Lampe broke off a piece of bread. Then he poured a glass of wine for each of them. Kaufman bit into his bread and chewed it with exaggerated chomps, as if the bread were stale.

"So," Lampe finally said. "What news do you have for me today?"

The Dunce plucked a piece of straw from the bread and flicked it to the floor. His eyes looked huge behind his ridiculous glasses. "A whole world is opening up for me. I've met professors, barons, merchants, and poets."

"Yes, yes, just as we talked about. A world of opportunity for a bright young man."

"I've started to wonder something."

"Yes?"

"What is it about Kant that makes people want to see him?"

What words could Lampe use to show the Dunce the universe that occupied the philosopher's mind? What words would not be instantly lost as they entered the echo chamber of Kaufman's head? "Well, he knew a lot about math and rocks. And he knew a lot about morals and whatnot."

Kaufmann said, "Maybe I should learn more about philosophy."

"I've seen many young men distracted from a productive and fruitful life by getting involved in philosophy too soon."

"I'm nearly thirty."

"Thirty! My boy, the master didn't begin his real work until he was in his fifties. The book that made him famous didn't come out until he was in his sixties. That last book he was working on he started in his seventies. So, let's talk about opportunity, not philosophy. You seem a little down today."

"I work beside a rotting corpse all day. I guess I've started thinking about death."

"Johannes, leave that to us old men. You're young!"

Kaufman rubbed the patchy stubble of the beard he was growing.

Lampe was becoming impatient. "Something else is wrong."

"Do you remember the girl I mentioned?"

"Yes, yes, of course."

"I told her my plans, but she seemed offended that I dared to speak to her, like I had touched her with my, with my ..."

"Your poetic muse?" Lampe interjected before the Dunce embarrassed himself. "Tell me, where did you meet her?"

"In the market."

"And?"

"And, we had a silent understanding."

"How silent?" Lampe asked.

Kaufman's eyes grew moist, and he gulped down his glass of wine.

The jug was growing light, but Lampe refilled his glass and said, "Now, now." Keeping droll boredom out of his voice was like keeping moisture out of a basement. "If one girl doesn't work out, another will. Trust me. But you might lose the next one too if you aren't well situated to dazzle her."

"Wouldn't a girl be dazzled by my job in the house of a famous philosopher?"

"You'd think so, but it never helped me. I suppose most people don't understand philosophy the way you and I do."

The Dunce nodded and appeared to be reflecting on the surprising revelation that he understood philosophy. Then he asked, "What's the magic in that manuscript you mentioned? It seems like a confused mess."

Lampe put down his glass of wine. "You're reading it?"

"I glanced at it."

"Glanced at it?" Lampe's chest constricted, and he dug his fingers into his thighs to hide the trembling of his hands.

"It's just bundles of notes wrapped up in old newspapers

and so forth. One stack is wrapped in the diploma of a medical doctor. Dr. Hubschmann."

"Hubschmann," Lampe said, trying to lighten the tone of his voice as he recovered his breath. "Well, at least his diploma was finally put to good use. He wasn't much of a doctor."

The Dunce took off his absurd little round spectacles and cleaned them with his shirt. "The book makes no sense."

How could he possibly explain the book to the Dunce? But he had to try. "Kant planned to call it *The Highest Standpoint of Transcendental Philosophy in the System of Ideas: God, the World, and Man in the World.*"

"That sounds dreary."

"Dreary? It would have crowned and completed his philosophy. It was supposed to be the story of everything, and I was going to help him finish it."

"Why would he need your help on a philosophy book?" The Dunce had sharpened his daggers.

"My contributions were insignificant, of course," Lampe said, feeling his breath return on a wave of indignation. "But he was missing the secret that would bring order to the book. That's why it looks like a mess."

"And you know this secret?"

Lampe, growing agitated, pointed to ideas written on the walls. "It's all around you! Can't you see?"

Kaufman leaned back in his chair and glanced toward the door.

Lampe knew better than to throw his pearls before swine, so he hid his despair and changed the subject. "Enough! Let's talk about you!"

The Dunce eyed Lampe over the rims of his round glasses.

When he was sure that Lampe had calmed down, he said, "I've started having the same nightmare the old man had."

"Which nightmare?" Lampe hoped the Dunce wouldn't start trying to plumb the depths of some meaningless dream.

"Last night I dreamt that I couldn't breathe."

"Oh, that dream," Lampe said. "Yes, Kant used to wake up from the dream and will his breathing to continue. He thought the nightmare would kill him otherwise."

"Would it have killed him?"

Lampe calculated for a moment before answering. "Probably not. He dreamt of all sorts of frightening things. Once the scaffolding of his mind began to loosen, all the things he had ignored or dismissed as nonsense began to show up."

The Dunce's expression dulled, a cold wick on a blob of candlewax.

Lampe was wasting time. "My dear young man, I'm sorry you're having bad dreams. I only hope the house isn't haunted." If ghosts would help him get to the master and to the book, he would use ghosts.

A glimmer of concern flickered across the paste of the Dunce's face.

Lampe couldn't wait any longer for Kaufman to tell him the news he needed to hear. "Tell me about the people who want to hire you. What did they say?"

"What?" The blankness on the Dunce's face was disconcerting.

"Yesterday. Our conversation. The people who want to hire you. Kaufman! Don't you remember? Wasianski and the slip of paper with my invitation?" Lampe stopped before he lost his battle with rage.

"I haven't actually talked with them yet."

Blood rose up into Lampe's neck, his head, his eyes, pounding as his heart punched against his chest like an animal trying to escape its cage and attack. "Why not?"

"I was too sad about Maria."

"Maria?"

"The girl I mentioned."

"There will be other girls, Kaufman!" Lampe nearly choked on his own words. His eyes drifted to one corner of the room where a spider was spinning a web that obscured several precious sentences he had scribbled on the wall.

The Dunce looked over the top of his small scholar's glasses with an unearned look of condescension. "You sound angry."

"I'm not angry," Lampe lied. "I'm trying to help you. Forget Maria and talk to the people who are offering real opportunity. It's barely past noon. There's plenty of time today."

Still looking over his glasses at Lampe, as though this gave him some leverage, some authority, the Dunce said, "I've been thinking."

"Have you?" Lampe's mind retreated from the trickling drivel the Dunce identified as thought.

"With so many people still coming to view his little corpse, better offers might come along. Maybe I should just wait until it's buried, and then follow up the best offers."

"It?" Lampe said with a sudden jolt of electrical energy.

"The corpse."

"It?" Lampe said again.

"Sorry. Until he's buried?"

Lampe stood up and began pacing as an alternative to

strangling the balding rodent who was drinking his wine and wasting his time. "I know these people. I watched them for forty years. When the master is in the stone vault, they'll return to their business and forget about you. You'll have no job, and no girl. Your floppy little peepee will remain unsheathed forever."

As Lampe's voice grew more insistent, the Dunce leaned farther back in his chair.

"Don't you see my point?" Lampe demanded. He knew he had lost composure, and with each lash of anger he was moving farther from his goal.

The Dunce pushed his glasses up the bridge of his nose. "I'll think about it."

"Don't think too long." Lampe flailed his hands around for emphasis, and he hit his nearly empty glass, sending it to the floor where it broke right beside Ding. Ding yelped as she jumped from her blanket.

"You're terribly irritable today."

Ding yelped again as Lampe lifted her away from the broken glass, trying not to squeeze her tumor.

"Your dog looks awful. That tumor's getting worse."

"It's not!" Lampe yelled. Then he pulled in his voice like a kite caught in turbulent wind. "Johannes, I'm an old man. All night I'm up dribbling in this stupid pot. I never have a roaring piss. I'm tired."

"So why would you want to come help Wasianski?"

"I have my reasons." Lampe was suddenly weary of trying to persuade the Dunce. "Are you going to talk to them about the offers or not?"

Eco's heavy footsteps on the stairs distracted Kaufman for a moment. Then he said, "They didn't make an offer, exactly. It was more of an offhand suggestion."

Eco knocked on the door. Then he tried to open it, but the door stuck.

Lampe pinned Kaufman to the chair with his eyes. "I thought," he said slowly, deliberately, like he was culling Kaufman's insides with the blade of his tone, "you said you had an *offer*."

The door slammed opened as Eco pressed his weight against it. "Are you okay? I heard something break."

The Dunce said, "Tell him Eco. You saw the crowds at Kant's house. It's a lot of work keeping up with a vigil for a world-famous man."

Lampe turned to Eco. "You visited his house?"

Eco, the ghost-white hangman, paled as much as such a man can pale. He folded his massive hands into a clot of white dough and bowed his massive head. "I was out buying flowers for my room, and I noticed that I was near the house."

"Why didn't you tell me?"

"I didn't want to upset you."

"I'm always upset!" Lampe held his clenched fists to his closed eyes. "I could have told you details to notice."

"What kind of details."

"Anything. Changes in furniture, new rugs, how much dust there is on the bookshelves."

The Dunce said, "There's no dust on the bookshelves."

"Ashes in the fireplace, scraps of paper with his ideas on his desk."

"No ashes have built up in the fireplace," the Dunce said.

Eco explained, "I just strolled up to the house and waited in line."

"Was the line long?"

"Oh yes. Full of strangers. I didn't recognize anyone. Everyone was so nice."

Lampe whimpered, "The whole world satisfies its curiosity gawking at his rotting little body, while Lampe the Faithful festers alone in exile!"

"He's not actually rotting," the Dunce said. "I told you he was in the corner room with no heat. He's practically frozen solid."

Lampe rested his head in hands. At least the master was frozen. At least the lines were long. There was still time. "Are you going to do as we agreed?"

"What did we agree about?" the Dunce asked.

"Just give my message to Wasianski!"

The Dunce paused and wiped his glasses with his shirt. Both lenses were smudged when he put them on again. "Will you tell me why Kant fired you?"

Lampe shook his head and glanced over at the pathetic ink splotch on his paper. "I think I'm getting sick."

The Dunce stood. "Then I'll leave you alone."

He walked out before Lampe could catch his breath. He was halfway down the stairs when Lampe jumped up and called after him. "Johannes, please come back tomorrow."

The Dunce didn't look back, but he raised his hand and waved it in the air. Did that mean he would return or was he waving goodbye forever?

Lampe knew he had fatally offended the man. He sat down again and said to Eco, "I'm not ready to die."

"You're not dying," Eco said in his most consoling tone.

"We're all dying," Lampe said irritably. "We've been dying from the moment we were conceived."

"Okay, Martin." Eco looked dejected. "I didn't know it would bother you so much."

Lampe added, "You could have grabbed part of the manuscript for me."

"Manuscript?" Eco asked.

"I need the notes from his final manuscript. That's my only hope."

"I couldn't steal, Martin. You know that."

"You hang people by the neck every week, but you can't take a manuscript I wrote?"

Eco's face went sad like a shot deer falling in the forest. "I only hang people who have left the human bond of trust." After thinking for a moment, Eco asked, "You wrote the manuscript?"

"Parts," Lampe said, frustrated at how difficult it was to explain his role in the master's work, even when he was talking to his only friend. "As Kant grew older, he frequently got stuck on this or that piece of fruitless nonsense. So, when he would leave the room, I'd scribble a few sentences in the margins. I was good at imitating his handwriting. Once he noticed the sentences, he thought they were his own, and he would head off in the right direction. We needed each other. But I can't finish the work unless I see what he wrote after I was exiled."

"I still couldn't steal."

Lampe waved Eco away. He needed to think. He needed to be alone.

Königsberg had forty thousand people, three hundred roads, one thousand stables, twenty- three churches, seven schools, two bookshops, six hospitals, four plague houses, ten pharmacies, three poor houses, one orphanage, and four prisons. The city was a living thing for Lampe. Kant's rooms on the Pregel were especially wonderful, because the sounds of the river vessels were so clear. Boats carried goods back and forth from the English ships moored in the lagoon. Carriages brought goods from Poland. The bustle of the market consoled Lampe and saved him from solitude. It was a bustle of production, not devastation. When he woke up terrified by dreams about war, the night sounds of city revelers comforted him.

But Kant hated noise. He complained that the boats and carriages distracted him while he was writing. He woke at five in the morning so his mind could unfold from its cocoon of sleep in quiet rather than with the jabs and prods of the city.

One day, Kant unexpectedly announced, "If I'm ever going to get my work done, I must get out of these noisy rooms soon. But I can't move unless I have more money." He looked at Lampe and pressed his lips together. He folded his hands over his small belly, which was always a bad sign. After a calculated pause, he said, "I could cut the household budget."

Lampe stood still, sweeping the same spot. He felt like a beagle looking up at the master, wagging its tail, certain it has done something wrong, but with no idea what it could be.

Kant stared at Lampe with disconcerting tranquility. Lampe increased the pace of sweeping until he couldn't stand it. He threw down the broom and said, "Think about how much time

I save you! Think about everything you don't have to worry about because of me!"

Something about Lampe's loss of control further calmed the master. He spoke with a tone of conclusiveness usually reserved for the assertion of a firm maxim, or else for the end of a crushing philosophical argument aimed at an enemy. "These rooms are loud and stifling. I need more silence."

"But there's so much life here."

"Nonsense. I must move. I'll find a way." The philosopher's face beamed with its inexplicably small beaming ability. He refused to discuss his plan further, leaving Lampe to grasp that his livelihood, and indeed his life, depended on the master.

This forced Lampe into his only anxious recourse. He had to become the Ideal of a Servant. At least for a while. Where Kant's rooms were mostly dust-free, they became utterly dust-free. His clothes were neatly arranged. His silver teaspoons were polished and free of tarnish.

After a week of this, Kant asked, "Lampe, what has gotten into you?" But he knew precisely what Lampe was experiencing. He closed his eyes halfway and pressed his lips into a condescending grin. Then he said, "I'll need your help moving my things."

Lampe made his face glum. "Where do we move them?"

"I've decided to take rooms in Kanter's house."

"Why Kanter's house?"

"It's the center of literary society. I belong there, not stuck in desolation listening to the grunts and howls of river workers."

"Charming." Lampe swept his way to the corner of the room with his back to Kant. The professor was expansive and witty with his students and friends, but with Lampe he was like a boy pulling the wings off a fly.

After a few minutes of silence, Kant finally said, "The library."

Lampe continued to sweep and didn't respond to the uninterpretable sentence fragment.

Kant clarified, "I will make extra money by working at the library. The government has appointed me the sub-librarian."

Lampe swept.

"It sounds dreary," Kant said, "but a thaler is a thaler. I'll owe nothing to any man, and I'll never tremble when there is a knock at my door. That's my newest maxim."

When Lampe still said nothing, Kant continued. "The library is in disarray. Drudgery lies ahead. Even when no one is there I'll have to be present, frozen to the bone. But this is the only way to get on with my work." He paused before saying, "And it will allow me to pay your salary."

Lampe swept in rhythm a few moments more. Then he went to the kitchen and returned with one of Kant's favorite cookies.

Kant picked up the cookie with one hand, while the other waved in a circle above his head before diving back into his pocket. "I'll work there Wednesdays and Saturdays from one to four o'clock. But that doesn't mean you can go out for drinks while I work."

Lampe allowed the master to have his ridiculous little jab. The work would be miserable and boring, and it would freeze the master's bones. But Lampe would make sure that Kant arrived home to warmed, spiced wine. He would keep the rooms spotless. He would encourage the frail philosopher. But he felt how expendable he was.

Kanter's house may have been the center of literary and cultural life in Königsberg, but Lampe hated it. He and Eco had recently become friends, and he whined to Eco when they met in the pub. "The house is freezing. The only reliable source of heat comes from the lust of the men and women who meet there. They pretend to be pious, but they don't fool me." Lampe looked for a response in Eco's puffy face, but he found none. "There's one young woman, Maria Charlotte, who makes particularly good use of her breasts. It doesn't bode well for her elderly husband, I'll tell you that."

Eco focused on his black bread and morning beer, and he said nothing.

"You don't know what I am talking about, do you? The professor doesn't see it either. He thinks her husband, Jacobi, is a great man, and he insists that Maria is a reasonable woman. Conception only comes in one form for him. But it takes more than a vow to feel confident about a wife with a body like that."

Eco shook his head slightly, refusing to be drawn in by his strange and talkative new friend.

Lampe was bewildered that Kant could be so completely blind to the way Goeshen the Munzmeister gazed at Maria Charlotte while Jacobi chattered on about whatever idea was on his mind.

Eventually, Lampe realized that the master was oblivious because he was increasingly possessed by the dark shadow of the thing-in-itself, and his exile of the thing-in-itself was grounded in his physical horror of blindness. Kant thought about, talked about, and read about every agony accessible to the heart, lungs, and bowels because he was terrified that his own health was tenuous. But nothing frightened him so much as blindness, and though he didn't trust anyone on the faculty of medicine with his own body, new developments in eye surgery drew him to their lectures.

One morning Kanter was giving a breakfast for friends and visitors. He used these breakfasts as a send-off for foreign guests who were returning home so that their last memories included the intellectual vigor available in Königsberg, refuting the notion that they were in some backwater town that was behind the times.

Kant was seated across from an eye surgeon. Before he could interrogate the doctor, a professor at the table named Woland introduced himself to Kant and said, "I know your work well."

Kant offered a humble nod of gratitude.

There was something odd about the stranger. His German was fluent, but his accent was hard to identify. He had several platinum crowns on the left side of his mouth, and several gold crowns on the right. His hair was dark, but not exactly brown or black. His suit was gray. He had a walking cane with a knob in the shape of a poodle's head. The most unusual thing about him was that his right eye was blue and his left eye was green.

Kant asked, "What do you do?"

The stranger thought for a moment as his eyes rotated up toward the ceiling before his gaze returned to Kant. "I'm in theology."

Kant grunted, "Ah, how interesting," indicating his complete loss of interest.

But before Kant could turn his attention to the far more interesting surgeon, Professor Woland said, "I read your proof for the existence of God."

"Ah," Kant said again.

Before he could add the word "interesting," Woland forced him into silence. "You think that order in matter leads us to the concept of God as a necessary thing? That's a bizarre way to talk about the almighty, don't you think? Do you even believe in this God?"

Kant grinned. "It's more complex than that. Out of deference to our host, perhaps we should eat breakfast rather than arguing philosophy."

The stranger said bluntly, "Your proof for the existence of God is clever, but if you continue to argue that way, people will think you're mad." Then he smiled, showing his gold and platinum caps.

Kanter turned to the eye surgeon to interrupt this unwanted confrontation. "You mentioned a child you're treating, an eight-year-old, blind from birth."

"I am," the doctor said.

Kanter asked, "Why was he blind from birth?"

Kant said, "That sounds like a question for our theologian."

Professor Woland aimed his strangely tenacious grin at Kant and said nothing.

"Actually," the doctor said, "congenital inflammation blocked the flow of fluid and clouded the eyes."

Without looking away from Kant, Woland said, "So, the child has been blind from birth, and you can make him see?"

"I plan to try."

Woland's face suddenly broke into an affable look, and he turned toward the doctor. "How?"

Kant glanced around, trying to catch the eye of anyone who

noticed the theologian's arrogant manner. But all the guests were enthralled by the doctor.

"We used to slip a needle through the sclera, here, where the pupil is blocked." The doctor took up a teaspoon and demonstrated with the handle, closing his hand like an eyeball. "Unfortunately, you end up with injury of the ciliary body."

The theology professor said, "The benefit is always transient with that operation."

"Exactly!" the doctor said. "The surgical area scars down or fills with exudate. Do you know someone who's had the operation?"

"I've done the operation," Professor Woland said, stunning the doctor and everyone else at the table. "I studied medicine before devoting myself entirely to theology. The patient glimpses the world, and then it all goes back to near darkness, with only a vague sense of light coming and going."

Kant said, "That's hideous."

"What's hideous?" Woland asked. "To see? Not to see? Or to see, and then not to see?"

Kant said, "The exudate! Only seeing light refracted through a scar!" He looked at the doctor. "Is this what you'll do for the boy?"

"No." The doctor leaned back in his chair with the cheerful demeanor of a physician who can control the very thing that frightens all other humans. "My friend Dr. Sharp developed a technique in which we transfix the cornea and iris by one incision across the anterior chamber. If his parents can find the necessary funds, this will change his life."

A businessman named Joseph Green was at the table. He had been silent. But at the mention of money, he said, "What if I paid?"

Kant glanced at Green and said, "I'm willing to help with funds as well."

Green nodded to Kant, then looked down at the bulky English watch on his wrist.

The doctor said, "That's quite generous of you both. But you don't know the boy."

Green said, "Knowing him would add nothing to the act."

Professor Woland glanced at Kant and said, "But he would settle the Molyneux problem. That's what you're really interested in, right?"

Kant stared daggers in the direction of the strange theology professor. This was exactly what he was thinking, but he didn't consider it proper to say so. Woland seemed to read his mind.

Kanter asked, "What's the Molyneux problem?"

Woland said, "Seventy years ago Molyneux wrote to John Locke and suggested that we could understand how much of our perception is learned and how much is innate by correcting the vision of people born blind, and then assessing what they perceive, if anything."

Green said, "I'll contribute half the money."

"I'll give the other half," Kant said. "But I want to watch the operation and to be present when the boy first sees."

"To answer a philosophical problem?" the doctor asked. He now had a hint of wariness in his voice.

"Not only that. I hope he'll be able to see, just to see."

"Wrong," Lampe mumbled.

Kant turned to Lampe who was standing just behind him. "What's wrong with it?"

"He's just a boy," Lampe answered.

"Who is blind," Kant said.

"And you want to solve a philosophical problem by cutting on his eyes."

"And if he sees?" Kant asked.

"Then he sees," Lampe answered.

"So where's the problem? What do you want me to do? Weep first? What good is a philosopher or physician who can't detach themselves from such things?"

Green looked at his watch again. "Nine o'clock. I must be going."

"Yes," Kanter said. "Thank you all for coming. Time to start the day."

The obliging guests backed away from the table. Woland leaned toward Lampe and said, "Your man wants to pry his way behind the appearances, and the appearance of appearance. He thinks he'll get closer to the thing-in-itself by observing the globe of the eye, the muscles, the gelatinous humour. But he'll fail."

Lampe had never heard the haunting phrase *thing-in-itself*. No one else at the table seemed to have heard the stranger except Kant, and he was silent the rest of the day.

———

Soon after that gathering at Kanter's house, Joseph Green began visiting regularly. Before long, he was at the center of Kant's private life. Green was a businessman who wanted to be a scholar. He ordered life his according to the precise increments with which time was meted out, registered on his enormous English watch. He was intolerant of tardiness and intolerant of earliness. "Why not simply be on time?" he would say.

Green was a foot taller than Kant, and he moved like a man surrounded by fragile objects that might easily break. He spoke in the same way, measuring words and phrases as though misplaced ideas could harm the minds of others. His business partner, Motherby, took over Kant's finances. No greater gift could have been given to Kant. Green carved out a circle of safety around the little professor. Inside this circle, Kant beamed. He began to trust Green with his system of ideas, which Green approached in the same way he approached business ventures. He was open but cautious and full of questions. He taught Kant to use the language of business when the language of philosophy wandered too close to poetry. Green acknowledged that he couldn't recognize poetry unless it was written on the page. This baffled Kant, but it didn't matter.

They enjoyed each other's company. Green was always amused when Kant ate more than anyone at dinner. If a guest asked Kant about the secret to his health, he would answer in his deep voice, which was disarming because it rose up from inside such a small frame. "The true metaphysics of life is good eating and good drinking." If a guest took that as permission to discuss philosophy, Lampe would quickly bring more food—a ragout of cod, turnips, barley pudding, dried fruit, or whatever the next course might be. Kant would dig into the food before anyone commented on this or that metaphysical point. He would say, "Philosophy interferes with the digestion by drawing blood to the brain at a time when it is needed in the belly.

My maxim is never to take up speculative topics while dining."

Green beamed at the gusto of his small friend for the bounty of the table. Even Lampe felt safe near Green, not because of anything he did, but because of his steady, bemused, and attentive presence. But throughout the meal he would look at his watch as though he was timing his bites, forcing the final bite to correspond exactly to the arrival of the hour's end.

"Green, what business are you in?" a guest would ask.

"Trade." He never gave a tad more answer than was needed.

"Ah. And what do you trade?"

"Timber, fruit, and spices."

"Ah. And where do you trade?"

"Prussia, England, and the Indies."

"Ah."

Nothing more could be wrung from the wealthy man. He became a source of wonder and speculation in Königsberg.

Unlike Kant's sometimes threadbare, though consciously elegant, clothing, Green's clothing never had a frayed hem. He seemed to be spared the spattering of mud from carriages. Even when the snow melted in spring his shoes were clean and dry.

When conversation clipped along at the pace Kant enjoyed, especially after a few glasses of wine, Green's reserve deepened. He observed the unwavering passage of time, and he seemed to derive serenity from this.

If they had agreed on a time for a walk, Green would stand up, no matter where the conversation was, lay his hand on Kant's shoulder, and say, "Manny, you'll be late for your walk." Then he would gently push Kant out of the room, leaving Lampe to direct the confused guests toward the door before grabbing the umbrella, in case of rain or excessive sunshine, and running up behind the two men.

Kant had filled up with a rich darkness and melancholy months before when Funk died. He had become obsessed with death, and he had kept a morose silence. He even stopped wearing wigs. He had spoken incessantly about the shortness of life and about how difficult it was to find love, driving Lampe to the most effective critique he could think of: "You're turning into a poet!"

But Green drew Kant out of the darkness by the light of his own certainty regarding the value of time as an ordering force, time as a lens that makes sense of the world, forcing it to march forward predictably and reliably, second by second, minute by minute, hour by hour. Precision was liberation.

"You are well," Green would pronounce whenever melancholy took hold of Kant. Darkness often settled on him. Before he met Green, would go to plays to escape his memory of Funk and his thoughts of death. Green offered an alternative solace, and often Kant was strangely pacified as Green repeated the words, "You are well."

But sometimes he resisted, and in a voice that was low and polite, he would say, "I am not."

"Nonsense. Manny, you allow these dark moods to descend. It's unnecessary and distasteful. When I say you are well, I mean it."

If Kant still resisted, Green would pull out a small pocket-sized ledger, and he would calculate the sum of money Kant could expect to have with regular investment. Kant's attention would waver at first, but Green won the full focus of the master's mind as he went through the ledger line by line, with no vagaries, and with only well-founded hope for the future of Kant's financial security.

The light in Kant's eyes and the smile he would try to conceal enlivened Lampe's heart as well because it was good news for his own employment. As Green talked and calculated, Lampe stood by, ready to serve. They would spend an entire hour talking about currency, investment, and returns, and by the end of the hour, Kant would stand up and pace with a buoyancy Lampe had witnessed only when a stretch of writing was going particularly well.

Green would say, "Manny, the language of commerce has an essential clarity about it. It's clean. I can tell you with coins how much I value each object in the world."

Kant listened intently. For Lampe, this view of the world was bland and dreary, but for the sake of job security, he was willing to tolerate it.

"Financial transactions involve words, gestures, and firmness of resolve. But in the end, the coin is exchanged for the loaf of bread. One man has a real coin. The other has a real loaf of bread. It's beautiful. What is the currency of your work, Manny? What is the product, and what is the coin exchanged for the product?"

Kant closed his eyes as he waited in thought. Then he opened his eyes and out flew the bird of his right hand fluttering briefly in the air. "You ask an interesting question, Joseph. In philosophy, silly talk of spirits, forms, and so forth abounds. But metaphysics isn't some Atlas holding up the world. She's a magus, throwing a cloak of invisibility around superstition. I'll think about your question."

Just then Green looked at his watch. "Seven o'clock, Manny. Time for me to leave." Immediately he stood up, put on his coat, and took up his walking stick. "Always remember that your old age will be comfortable, with no anxiety. I can promise you security because I make decisions based on the irrefutable coin and the clear rules of commerce. If you can achieve that in your philosophy, you will be the greatest philosopher the world has ever met."

Green bowed and walked away without waiting for a response that might delay his precise moment of departure.

When the door closed, Lampe turned around and said, "That was rude."

But Kant couldn't stop smiling, and he left Lampe's comment unanswered.

—⁓—

The next day Hamann and Kant met at the pub for dinner. At the end of the meal, when they were tipsy, Kant told Hamann about Green's question. "What is the currency of philosophy? What is the hard currency that has reliable value we can use in the world of thought?"

Hamann examined his fingernails and said, "I'm certain you won't like my answer."

Kant struggled against the exuberance of the grin that was forcing its way onto his face. "The answer is clear! Maxims!"

"Maxims?"

"Yes. A man's worth is no greater than the firmness of his maxims."

"But Manny, look around the pub. It's filled with merchants, sailors, and lonely women. Do you see the way that woman

118

cleaning the glasses stares at the pub owner? Does she hate him? Love him? Both? How much of the real world can you fit into a maxim?"

"Any part of the world that can be grasped by reason will fit into a maxim. Whatever doesn't bleed into the realm of nonsense can fit into a maxim if it is formulated clearly and held with firmness. Maxims would even help you with your stomach problems."

"How can maxims help my stomach?"

Kant answered, "Can you listen without rolling your eyes?"

"Certainly. Anything to help my stomach."

"Maxims establish boundaries for the mind. Otherwise, the mind wanders into swamplands like a child unaware of danger. Then it's vulnerable to suggestions from the body. Think of your own abdominal sensations. The sensation isn't quite pain. But it's new, and it has no clear cause. You worry this might be cancer. Am I right?"

Hamann resumed looking at his fingernails.

"That thought upsets your equilibrium. This worsens the sensation, which further disturbs your mind. With minds like yours and mine, only the corrective of firm maxims can reduce our vulnerability to an early and otherwise avoidable death."

"The firmness of a maxim doesn't make it right."

"Foot soldiers!" Lampe blurted out while calmly shining the already gleaming silver spoons.

Kant looked towards him with one eyebrow raised. "What's that you say, Lampe?"

"Foot soldiers follow their leader into anything, including death. They never doubt the leader." He placed the spoon in the drawer and closed it. "But what if the leader is a fool?"

"Exactly!" Hamann said before Kant could dismiss Lampe. "Why would a fixed maxim be superior to the mind of a man who can judge and revise and change directions based on a real situation? A man is alive, a maxim is inert."

Kant said, "You don't see the consequences of your argument. Your approach would leave us afloat in a dark sea beneath a dark sky."

"Manny, we're already afloat! Go outside and look at the night sky. It's darkness without end!"

Kant said, "The night sky is part of what convinces me that our lives are best ordered by maxims, just as the stars are ordered by natural laws."

Lampe signaled the server for more alcohol to nudge Kant's mind toward the clouds where Hamann was at home. The Magus, Hamann, was a genius who could help save Kant from himself, and save the world from the master's devastating mind.

———

The single morsel of poetry that existed inside Kant had tried to find its way out in *Dreams of a Spirit Seer*. He had written it quickly and with an astounding focus, as though he was trying to get it out of the way in preparation for something else. When the flurry of thought was complete, he had placed the stack of paper on his desk and announced, "Lampe, I'm going for a long lunch and a few games of billiards at Gerlacks. When you finish your work, you may leave. I won't be back until late in the evening."

After he was gone, Lampe continued dusting, peering at the stack of paper containing the new mystery that had percolated up from deep within the dark soil called Immanuel Kant.

When he was sure that Kant was not returning for some forgotten thing, he sat down at the desk and looked at the manuscript.

Dreams of a Spirit Seer. The scrawl that flowed off Kant's quill was now as familiar as his own handwriting. The master began in the realm of shades with its visions, miracles, tales told at the breast, and those false apparitions that arise from the swift winds of hypochondria. He had been intrigued by the spiritual ideas of Swedenborg, even though Swedenborg had ignored the letter Kant sent him. And in his new manuscript, he seemed to affirm his belief in the possibility of immaterial natures, including his own soul.

Lampe felt a thrill like sex, or music, or divine hope.

But as he read on, his heart darkened. Kant wrote that any philosophy appealing to immaterial principles is lazy. *Of course, master. Kill the mysterious infant you conceived in the early pages and let the devil unburden you of it, you cretinous little monster.*

Lampe knew intuitively that there was more to the world than the accidents of flesh and physics. But his cowardly master had retreated into doubt at every threshold, and Kant's doubt always became Lampe's doubt. While Kant drank and played billiards after getting his doubt onto paper, Lampe was left in desolate solitude to struggle with the universe. His own great *principle of the poetic a priori* was trying to be born, but now it was choking on its own umbilical cord.

Lampe continued reading *Dreams of a Spirit Seer.* After Kant finished mocking experiences of ghosts, spirits, and conversations with the dead, he concluded his book by saying that the butterfly wings of metaphysics that lift us to converse with spirit forms are folded using the styptic power of self-knowledge on the low ground of experience and common sense. And he proclaimed that he was happy to stay with what is useful.

Lampe returned the manuscript to the desk exactly as Kant had left it. But he carried with him the image of the folded butterfly, and he despised his master for that thought. He stopped speaking to Kant beyond cursory answers to mundane questions. He just served the food, dusted, and shined the spoons. Kant finally asked what was wrong, but only after a full week of silence.

"Nothing," Lampe answered.

Kant shrugged and returned to his book.

Lampe recovered by the simplest philosophical move imaginable. He didn't fight Kant's folding of the wings of metaphysics. He didn't argue against Kant's low ground of experience. He didn't resist Kant's cowardly denial that there might be more to this universe than meets the eye. He didn't work out implications, nor enumerate axioms, nor worry over contradictions, nor plan a treatise to defend his idea. He simply began to know and to know fully.

In the end, it cost him twenty years of work to see that only *the principle of the poetic a priori* allowed this knowledge, not of physical mechanisms beneath appearance, but of the true reality that spoke through appearance. His own principle was more fundamental than any that Kant had ever discovered. That thought frightened and thrilled him, except in the frequent moments when doubt consumed his joy and he felt like a charlatan, spinning nonsense out of the nothing.

The instrument of *the poetic a priori* was a lantern in an infinite cave lighting now one part, now another, deriving the felt whole. And the deepest discovery it revealed was that the thing-in-itself, far from being hidden, continuously shines forth through appearance.

———

Each night Lampe felt his life shorten. His own great work was splattered across his walls. But part of it was also hidden somewhere in the last work from the master's hand. During the day he was enlivened by the possibility that the Dunce would bring him a piece of the manuscript or an invitation from Wasianski to join the vigil. But at night these possibilities withdrew, and a raw haunting descended upon him.

Ding's snore would have comforted him, but the tumor was a constant reminder of Ding's transience. In his motherless solitude, he listened to the wind coming from the lagoon, the wind that drove ships of commerce toward their goals, the wind that fanned the fires and blew the pendulums of the men caught in crime who hung in the public square.

He felt something, a presence that might have been the master, but might as easily have been the Devil hidden in darkness along the rooftops.

What was he actually afraid of? That no one knew he existed? That his life of service to Kant was forgotten before it was even over?

He was no better off than Ding.

It was late, and he was old and tired. If he did not die in the night, he would awaken shortly past four o'clock, forced by memory. But there would be no master to awaken and no tasks to do, other than to wait for the call from exile as the days repeated themselves.

Day Seven

The Antinomies

IN THE FURNACE OF KANT'S MIND where indomitable ideas began to be forged, quips about human behaviors and comments about spirits were burned to cinders along with anything that could not be abstracted from blood and sex. The philosopher no longer fit in the literary society he had once craved at Kanter's house.

The men and women in Kanter's inner circle easily moved from literature to politics to fantasies about airships flying up to the moon. From noble and well-connected friends, they gathered gossip about Voltaire and his odd relationship to Frederick the Great. But Lampe's ear was trained to listen for what was meant rather than what was said. He predicted the circle's downfall from the moment Johann Julius Goeschen joined the group. He had come to Königsberg as the master of the mint after the Russian occupation, and he was the sort who quickly and indiscriminately made friends. He was soon known across the city as the Munzmeister.

"Goeschen wants to master more than the mint," Lampe said

to Eco one evening when he was giving a long answer to Eco's courteous inquiry into his day at work. The large and pasty executioner was distant and quiet, but Lampe enjoyed the reserved presence of this cloud of a man.

Eco offered only the placid gaze of condolence to Eternal Purity for the foibles of humanity.

Lampe went on. "The Munzmeister has already sniffed out the young Maria Charlotte Jacobi. He deflects suspicion by flirting right in front of her husband. Her very much older husband. The entire evening was about sex. They gossiped for hours about Voltaire and his many women. Apparently, he even had a fling with Frederick's cook. But Maria's husband was oblivious."

Eco seemed more burdened than elevated by such talk, so Lampe allowed the theater of memory to play silently in his mind.

When Maria asserted that writers and artists should be allowed a bit more freedom than everyone else enjoys, Kant said, "Really?" The impertinent young woman was obviously borrowing gravitas from her elder husband.

"She makes a fair point," Goeschen said. "But not only because they are writers. They need experience to make their books and plays realistic. Have you seen *Zäire*?"

"That dreary play?" Jacobi said.

Maria said, "Any play is interesting when it's set in a harem in Jerusalem."

"I agree," Goeschen said, "Why do you say it's dreary, Jacobi?"

"A palace full of wives and concubines?" Jacobi answered. "You've obviously never been married, Munzmeister. The play just goes on and on with a Turkish Sultan about to marry Zara, who then pleads for the Christian slave and another man who, surprise of surprises, turns out to be her father, as the slave turns out to be her brother. They want her to be baptized so she delays the nuptials for one day, making the Sultan suspicious that she is unfaithful, so he kills her, only to discover his mistake, and then he kills himself."

"Well now you've ruined it," the Baroness said. She was the unofficial leader of the literary group.

"I merely saved you from predictable tedium so you can use your time in a way better suited to your considerable mind."

"I've read the script of the play," Maria said. Then she turned to Goeschen and added, "I think it's fascinating that they had a seraglio in Jerusalem."

"Why?" he answered. "They had men in Jerusalem. Besides, I've heard that it's part of their religion."

"Their religious habits don't matter," she said. "You're a Christian."

"For now," he answered.

She looked straight into his eyes, not even pretending to be embarrassed. "Some of Voltaire's lines are wonderful."

"What's your favorite," Goeschen asked.

"*One cannot desire what one does not know,*" she answered

Goeschen said, "He was right in saying that."

"You think desire precedes knowledge?"

"Sometimes desire is knowledge."

Maria thought for a moment, then said, "Sometimes, knowledge of desire leads to desire."

"And that can lead to another kind of knowing."

"Do you desire that to be true?" she asked.

"I know it to be so."

"In knowing, then, do you cease to desire?"

Goeschen said, "To desire more fully, I must know more fully."

She answered, "Sir, if you want to know more fully, then clearly you must desire, and you must desire more clearly."

While Goeschen pursued his catechism with Maria, Herr Jacobi refilled his scotch and argued politics with Kant.

Then one of the visitors, who was doing business in Königsberg, said, "Should we be talking about this in mixed company?"

Frau Jacobi turned to him and said, "It's a literary society. Why shouldn't we talk about Voltaire?"

"I didn't mean Voltaire," the man said, flushing.

"Who, then?" Maria asked.

One of the other men said, "Tissot was mentioned in passing."

Suddenly everyone stopped talking and turned to give their attention.

"I'm not familiar with Tissot," Maria said.

Kant said in his deepest voice, "There are many other worthy authors we can discuss without subjecting ourselves to the chicaneries of an ill-instructed reason like that of Samuel Tissot."

"Now I'm intrigued," Maria said. "Tell me more."

Kant blushed. Goeschen immediately took advantage of the moment. "He's a physician from Switzerland, very famous. I am surprised you haven't heard of him. His book has been translated into many languages."

"And what is the book?"

Goeschen said, "It's called *L'Onanisme*."

"*L'Onanisme?*" she asked. "From Onan, in the Bible?"

Herr Jacobi, who had drunk three scotches more than was good for him, solidified his fate by saying, "My dear, it's a book about the effects of masturbation on the body. Another dreary read, I assure you. Kant is right. There are much better topics for the evening."

Maria would not be stopped. "And what are the effects of masturbation on the body?"

Even the baroness, who was no stranger to difficult ideas, began to fidget in her chair.

Goeschen answered, "Tissot says it's worse than smallpox. And, apparently, it's more dangerous for women than for men."

"Really?" she asked with disarming calmness, never looking away from Goeschen's eyes. "Has this been demonstrated scientifically?"

"I can't imagine how it would be scientifically demonstrated," he answered.

"Yes, you can," she said.

The visitor who had initially objected said, "No, it hasn't been demonstrated. But it fits with the long judgment and experience of humanity."

The others nodded their heads in agreement. Lampe noticed that most of them had apparently read the book, though he had never seen the book on anyone's bookshelf, including Kant's.

The objector continued. "Dr. Tissot says that if we made use of the act only when there is need, it would be okay. The problem is the habit, conjuring up fantasies, making oneself want to do it. You always need more and there's never satisfaction. He says it causes every disease from tuberculosis to blindness."

"Nonsense," Maria said.

"How do you know?" Goeschen asked.

"Do I look sick?" she answered.

"Immanuel!" Jacobi immediately said more loudly than necessary, finally attempting to dampen his wife's loose talk. "You're a philosopher. What do you say to the issue?"

Kant looked down at the floor and said with solemnity, "It's worse than suicide."

Groans erupted in the room. Kant raised one hand and put the other in the pocket of his coat. When everyone was quiet, he said, "A man gives up his personality when he uses himself merely as a means for the gratification of an animal drive. He violates his own duty to himself."

"And a woman?" Maria said.

Jacobi quickly interjected again, "But worse than suicide?"

"Most definitely worse than suicide," Kant repeated, his voice low and steady. "When a man commits suicide, he treats himself as an object, and this is wrong. But it's a response to real despair." He looked around the room, leaning forward the way he did in the lecture hall, tipping his head to the side. "When a man does this other thing, he treats himself as an object, but he creates the need himself, and that is both wrong and absurd."

The objector said, "Rousseau has a few interesting thoughts on the topic."

Kant, who kept Rousseau's portrait above his writing desk, nodded vigorously.

The man continued, "He said it was a kind of mental rape in which one person uses another but avoids a real encounter with them in the world. It allows men to dispose of the entire female sex at once, and to make any attractive woman who tempts them serve their pleasure without obtaining her consent."

Goeschen said, "Are you suggesting that we should get permission from a woman to imagine her in this way?"

Lampe noticed a wink from Goeschen to Maria.

The baroness said, "I think what we need is permission to change the subject." No one resisted her.

Later that evening, when Lampe was finishing his work, he looked at Kant and said, "Interesting conversation today."

Kant kept reading without answering.

Lampe said, "Frau Jacobi is …"

"Married!" Kant said, raising a finger in the air. "She's the subject of a vow!"

"Of course. The mighty vow."

"The gates of marriage are firm."

Lampe said, "Not so firm that she can't flirt with you."

Kant glared. "You've been reading my letters again."

"No."

"You have."

"No."

Kant said, "Her notes are playful. They must be read in context. Jacobi is a good friend."

"And more than a few years older than Herr Goeschen."

"Enough, Lampe!" Kant stood up. "I'm going to bed. Don't mention this again."

—⁂—

Two months later Maria Charlotte was having an open affair with Goeschen.

"No shame," Kant whispered to his friend Hippel, who was

visiting for lunch. "She shows no shame whatsoever. She flaunts the affair!" His voice was full of indignation and shock bordering on disbelief, as though he was saying that Jacobi himself was pregnant.

Hippel said. "You're a pure soul."

"No. I merely know something about the moral world. And this…"

"It's sex," Hippel said. "It's just sex."

Kant was pink with indignation. "She asked for a divorce. She dared to say publicly that she wants to be rid of 'the worthless old man.' Imagine that. Shameless."

Lampe stood behind Hippel, cleaning the bronze on the clock.

"Enough out of you, Lampe," Kant said with a guttural growl.

Lampe stopped polishing the clock and looked up. "I didn't say anything."

"It's the way you didn't say anything," Kant replied.

Hippel said, "Manny, if you bring up the topic in every conversation, people will talk. Some already say you have an emotional attachment to the young woman."

"Nonsense," Kant answered. "I'm committed to maxims."

"You're angry," Lampe said. He placed Kant's bottle of port on the table.

"No, Lampe. I'm committed to the value of a vow."

"Twaddle diddle, tweedle diddle," Lampe mumbled, opening the spoon drawer to focus his mind with the act of shining. "These things happen all the time,"

"Lampe is right," Hippel said. "If you force every conversation toward Maria Charlotte and her …"

"Yes, yes, yes," Kant said. "You've said it before."

———

Lampe calmly predicted to Kant that sex would destroy the literary society. Frau Jacobi had opened the gate of possibility, and Frau Kanter soon followed with an affair of her own.

At first, Kant was angry with Lampe for presuming. But when it came true, he became disoriented and isolated himself for a time. For months Kant was obsessed with the affairs, and everyone, Lampe included, was embarrassed for him.

Kant redoubled his commitment to maxims, which baffled Lampe. There were plenty of maxims tossed around the literary society, but none of them restrained the tides of lust. The fire was raging, and the maxims were dry planks, hardly the material with which to build a protective wall. Under the tutelage of Green, Kant tried anyway, and his dependence on Green became complete.

Green brought the relief of meter, without variation, into Kant's life. The meter was not the rhythm of poetry, nor the movement of music. It was the unchanging click of the second hand and the unvarying sweep of the hour hand on Green's enormous English watch. The chaos of lust that erupted in Kanter's literary club was replaced by the calm, measured, calculating mind of Green. In his new training regimen, Kant no longer played billiards. He no longer played cards. He did not go to the theater. He almost never walked beyond the city gates of Königsberg, and he vetted all decisions with Green.

One afternoon he told Green, "I'm turning down another university position, Joseph."

"Another offer? Where is this one?"

"Berlin."

"A wonderful city," Green said.

"It would shorten my life," Kant said. "I'm healthy, but in a weak way."

"And the salary?" Green asked.

"Very good. But if I don't live to enjoy it . . ."

"Your finances are coming along nicely, Manny. Don't you worry."

Exchanges like this were generally followed by Green smiling his faint smile and closing his eyes for a brief nap. Kant would the same, and Lampe would stand by, bored to distraction. His only workable solution at these times was to have a little vodka in his pocket to lift his thoughts to heaven.

Then one of the nappers would awaken. Then the other would awaken.

Their placid exchange had none of the fire that roiled around Maria Charlotte. If the uninitiated watched the energy-depleted habits of the two men, they would wonder whether anything worthwhile could ever emerge. But Lampe knew that the answer was *yes*, without qualification.

His master was giving birth to something new in the world. From the outside, his training with Green looked like nearly nothing—two middle-aged men, eyes half closed, testing propositions from finance and philosophy as though they were the same things. But this was the preamble, the preparatory process of stuffing the butterfly back into the cocoon with a revolutionary styptic approach to philosophy, the radical cutting of the wings.

Lampe saw the power of Kant's evolving ideas, and he hated

them. He preferred the *conceptus fantasticus*, the genius of fine parts and fertile fancy cajoled by devils breaking out of their holes. But he endured the distilled spirit of conversation between Kant and Green. This was the price for his front-row seat at the spectacle of the master's great, clean mind pulling itself up from the muck of Königsberg's slop, mud lanes, animal droppings, and swampy meadows where children drowned, ascending through the fog made up of constipation, asthma, frozen books in the unheated library, crowing roosters, howls, laughter, and all the bawdy world that Lampe cherished.

Kant's strange and crystalline globe of pure thought rose, and Lampe reluctantly admired the unremitting horror of this new form of abstraction. He had to drink to tolerate it, but he was disciplined, imbibing only, and exactly, as much as he needed to put up with his master. No more. But also no less.

One evening after Green had departed, Kant said, "The delusions that have entered the world of thought are thoroughly rooted and nearly impossible to separate from sound thought. They're a cancerous growth mingled with healthy tissue. The sick limb must be removed in order to save the whole."

Lampe was not yet sure whether this was a threshold of discovery, or a precipice. But he experienced a new kind of dread he had not met even on the battlefield. It was intellectual dread, and the silence within which it arose made it worse than the trembling of the body when death looms in the smoke of war. The deeper his dread went, the more he craved to be with a woman.

Thus was he smitten by an ephemeral appearance in the shadows and vapors of the dim pub, a perfect shape, a form that conquered him with the completeness of an argument in mathematics that somehow makes the universe interpretable. She sat with her back straight and her high breasts cast in flawless silhouette, countering with their mere being the whole world of Kant's abstractions.

Lampe had never been very successful in romance, even though his mother was a whore who provided him with ample opportunity to master erotic patterns and exigencies. His occasional success was always the result of a direct approach, befitting a soldier. So he walked over to the table, bowed in the lantern's light, and sat down. "Lampe. Martin Lampe."

Her head was tipped forward so that the shadow from the large brim of her hat hid her face.

She didn't answer him.

"I'm chief assistant to Professor Immanuel Kant." He waited for a response. None came. "He's a very famous philosopher. Maybe you've heard of him."

Her hands retreated into her lap. As they disappeared, he glimpsed their ghostly whiteness, though it was hard to trust one's eyes in the dim light obscured by a cloud of pipe smoke and the inward fog of beer.

He tried again. "Do you come here often? I don't think I've seen you before."

She looked up. The lantern on the table lit her face, her hair the color of a sable mink, and the blue of her eyes that was so dark it nearly looked black. Overlying the beauty of her face were the webbed and lace-like scars of healed burns. Her clothes were the sort Lampe saw when he followed Kant to the parties of nobility, but they were worn at the edges. She looked past her scars, daring Lampe to let his eyes drift from hers and linger on her disfigurement. Her eyes held his in a throttle while he searched for something to fill her aggressive silence.

Finally, he said, "I can see you want to be alone."

She nodded, then lowered her eyes again. There were nods of mere agreement, nods of dismissal, and nods of gratefulness. He wasn't sure which sort of nod this was. When he stood up, she briefly glanced at him with the faintest of smiles, then looked down again.

As he stepped back into the bright sunshine, he decided it had been a nod of gratefulness. The scars on her face seemed faint in his memory, but the beauty behind those lacy scars had transformed him, as the fire had transformed her. He was in love, and he didn't know what to do. When he returned to work and closed the front door behind him, he emptied his flask of vodka in three gulps, rested his head on the dining room table, and smothered his storm of emotion with the transient silence of sleep.

He was jarred into reluctant consciousness when Kant slammed the door and said, "You have mustard sauce in your hair."

Lampe sat up and touched his mussed hair. His head had migrated to the dish of mustard sauce on the table. He was still too drunk to focus. He closed his left eye so that he only saw one image of Kant. The master was smiling. When Lampe smiled back, Kant's smile disappeared.

He allowed Lampe to sit in squalor a moment more and then said, "I've finally been given the professorship I wanted." He was suppressing a grin, which always made him look silly. He had waited fifteen years for the position of *Professore Ordinario der Logic und Metaphysic.*

Lampe began to wipe his hair with his sleeve, and he brought all his faculties to bear on the single goal of not saying something stupid, which in this case meant saying nothing at all.

Kant looked again at the mustard-clotted hair. "I'm planning to have some friends over for a little celebration. Would it be too much trouble for you to tidy up the place, and yourself?"

Lampe nodded. Kant turned to leave, but he stopped at the door. "Why are you drunk in the middle of the day?"

The only answer that occurred to Lampe was the truth. "I met a woman."

"You met a woman." Kant stepped toward Lampe. "And that caused you to curl up in my mustard sauce with whatever vodka-diluted fragment of reason you retain?"

"She's beautiful, but ..."

"I can only imagine."

"She's beautiful, like Frau Jacobi except ..."

"Lampe!" Kant held up his hand, unamused at the mention of Maria Charlotte.

Lampe continued, "... except that she has scars on her face and hands."

"Scars?" Kant said.

"Burns." He paused to gauge the level of annoyance on Kant's face. "She's otherwise flawless."

"No woman is flawless, I assure you."

"Her shame makes her beauty hard to turn away from."

"I'm sure that observation will win her heart. But enough! I must write my inaugural dissertation." The joyful grin burst back onto his face, and he left Lampe to wallow in the agony of love as the alcohol wore off.

—⁂—

Lampe never understood why it took so long for Kant to get the professorship he coveted. Didn't they realize that the greatest philosopher in the world lived in the backwaters of swampy Königsberg? Was Lampe the only one with eyes to see? The master had been passed over repeatedly while the theology faculty spun tales from a storybook, and the medical faculty did little more than administer opium, saltpeter, greasy unctions, purges, clysters, and succedanea.

The day of Kant's inaugural address was rainy and cold. "Come, Lampe! We'll be late on the one day I must not be late."

"We have plenty of time," Lampe snapped. There was no reason to rush, only to stand around with a bunch of damp old scholars and youthful inquirers who would stare at Lampe without speaking to him. Lampe had snuck a peak at the lecture titled *On the Form and Principles of the Sensible and Intelligible World*. The devil was already in it, severing the mind from the world, creating an a priori substitute invulnerable to the fire of desire, the pumping of blood, or the spurting of essential fluids.

The men gathered in the lecture hall were unprepared for the devastation they were about to witness, but almost none of them would even begin to grasp Kant's ideas. Lampe recognized some of the young men who smirked as he sloshed along beside Kant, crossing the university courtyard, protecting the philosopher's lopsided wig from the rain with his umbrella since the master refused to hold it himself.

Lampe looked around at the jowls of the elders, and the sharp jawlines and noses of the lean youth, many of whom would be crushed by the ideas if ever they truly strained their minds to understand. The soggy scholars dressed in black nodded and rubbed their chins as though they comprehended the direction of Kant's quick flits and flights. But only Lampe moved among the ideas with the confidence of one navigating familiar furniture at home when everything is dark. He stopped listening as his mind drifted from the lecture and Kant's crisp gesticulations to the window and the trees, the clouds, and on beyond until suddenly the room erupted with the sound of men knocking their hands against the desks, chairs, and walls to praise the newly promoted professor of logic and metaphysics.

Green offered exuberant congratulations that evening to a content and sleepy full professor. As usual, he departed at precisely seven o'clock, leaving Lampe to tuck in the philosopher and tend to the great mind's surroundings, keeping them tidy and in order.

When Lampe closed the bedroom door and prepared wood for the next day's fire, his mind was alone at last with the woman's image. How does a delicate scar, something so faint, so nearly nothing, alter a life so completely? And yet ideas are infinitely lighter, without even the substance of a scar. But they too can change everything.

Kant had his full professorship, but his real work, and Lampe's, had hardly begun. The writing desk was covered with scraps of paper on which Kant scribbled ideas as they came. He stuffed them into pockets and drawers, like Noah gathering materials before the flood, preparing to build the ship that would save the creatures of the earth.

Slowly, day by day, sorting through slips of paper, reading and rereading drafts of chapters as they inched along in scrawled and weedy growth, the scales dropped from Lampe's eyes, and he began to understand the airship of ideas the master was building. It was a perfect, impenetrable world of madness, forever separating the mind from what is real. Lampe felt a chill as the universe began to grow cold and dark through the power of Kant's mind, and he wondered how the professor could think such things, and still stroll in the world of ordinary scholars, countesses, and politicians.

Kant's well-swept, dustless, and spare spherical airship was an ark where space and time were tucked as pure intuitions, science was given its certainty, and the wild and untamed reaches of metaphysics were brought to a disciplined end, forced to recognize the limits and boundaries of accessible truth. The airship would be complete, self-contained, and safe, with a couch for sitting, a neat little row of books, and a fireplace. But there was also a single darkened window onto the reality forbidden to pure reason, with its unalterable structures, despite its lust to reach past appearance and touch the ungoverned things-in-themselves and the impractical God who could not be reduced to a prop for a moral treatise.

The most terrifying part of this evolving philosophy of horror was the idea that Lampe-in-himself was also outside the airship. He could never know his real self, but only the self that appeared to himself as himself. Why couldn't the master create a philosophy more like Montgolfier's balloon? Why couldn't it be more open so that Lampe could float along with Montgolfier's dog, chicken, and goat? The reason was simple. That would be too dangerous.

As Lampe huddled in his room with Ding, recollecting the slow dawning of Kant's horrific ideas on the horizon of his mind, he knew he could open Kant's closed airship to the wildness of mystery. The Dunce was his only hope. But he felt like a man in a desert watching water drip from his leaky canteen, except that the water was time.

Salvation would require a miracle, but he did not know how to pray.

Day Eight

Night Thoughts of a Skeptic

IN EXILE, LAMPE WAS HAUNTED by morbid doubts about whether Katarina, the scarred owner of his heart, had ever truly loved him. After they first met, he visited the pub daily. But he didn't see her for weeks. When she finally showed up again, he asked for permission to walk her home.

"If you must," she said.

Unscarred, she would have married a nobleman. Without the burns, her beauty would have been overwhelming. But fire had incarnated her in alien flesh against her will, just as Lampe's mother's flesh was made incarnate by sailors and the occasional lascivious scholar or merchant. It thickened her physical presence so that she was always aware of herself as a body, feeling her slightly crooked smile, the tug of skin when she blinked, the roughness of her hands when she rubbed them together. Her wings were scarred down. For two months, Lampe accompanied her when she walked from home to the shop where she was a seamstress. Her potency and desire were wrapped in scar tissue by fate, but Lampe craved to unbind her like the risen body of Lazarus.

One day she said, "Martin."

"Yes, Katerina."

"The fire destroyed almost everything I loved. These scars are my veil. I want to live as a nun. I've accepted it."

"Why are you saying that?"

"I only fascinate the part of you that pities."

Lampe stopped and turned to her. "No, you fascinate the part of me that desires."

"I don't believe you."

"Why?"

"I just want to be alone."

Lampe said, "You don't want to be with me because I'm only a servant."

He thought she would disagree. But she said, "There may be some truth to that, but not for the reasons you think. It's not because my parents were wealthy that I'm wary of you. It's because you talk about Professor Kant more than anything else. Can't you see that he's your life's passion?"

Lampe went down on one knee. "Katarina, marry me."

"No."

"Marry me, please."

"No."

"You're afraid."

"Martin. Death wrapped his fingers around my face and neck and left his mark. He raped my lungs and choked me. He took my parents and all that mattered to me. I'm not afraid of anything."

"Then marry me."

She opened the door to her home. "You've only seen the scars on my face and hands."

"Katarina, you're beautiful."

She grabbed his face and locked her gaze on his eyes. "Go home and imagine where else a woman might be burned. Then ask me your question again."

She closed the door leaving Lampe to carry out her demand. He imagined her experience. He imagined all the way down to the details of screams and agony. The scars on her face and hands were so delicate, for him hardly a blemish. What else had been disfigured? Would it matter? She was calm, cold, quiet, private, injured. In any other circumstance, Lampe would have been her hired servant. But he felt the growing fire of his desire for her.

The next day he arrived at the shop, knelt down, and said, "Marry me."

"Did you do what I asked?"

"Yes."

She looked at him past the delicate webs of scars at the outer corners of her eyes. "I'll marry you. But not in a church."

He was surprised by this. "Why? Don't you believe in God?"

"I do believe in God. He's the one who let this happen to me. Is this settled?"

"Yes. It's settled."

She put out her hand, but Lampe stood up and kissed her. He felt the scar at the corner of her mouth. When he stepped back and looked at her, he worried that even marriage would not bring her close to him. But there could be no better wife for Martin Lampe, apprentice philosopher, afraid neither of bitterness nor of truth. He quickly arranged the private ceremony before she changed her mind.

Lampe wanted to tell Kant about his marriage, but the news wouldn't be welcomed, and the master had become increasingly distracted by Hamann. Everyone else had given up on converting Hamann back to reason as the lusty, hypochondriacal monster of faith labored away at his strange writings.

Kant grew frustrated as Hamann wielded his *principle of the union of opposites* with more boldness. His noble principle addressed the brokenness of human experience and the fragmentation of human knowledge.

Hamann was becoming known as *The Magus of the North*. He gave Kant the starting point for his true work as a philosopher through a little piece called "Night Thoughts of a Skeptic." He published it in the Königsberg newspaper and then forgot about it. It was a translation of a treatise by Hamann's hero, David Hume, whose ideas he carried home from London, where he had whored around and found God. Most people skimmed it before moving on to local gossip.

Kant was irritable when he picked up the newspaper. He had just returned from lecturing on mineralogy to a group of students who insisted on seeing the cabinet of minerals over which he was the reluctant caregiver. He opened it, staring off to the corner of the room while the students said uninteresting and stupid things about the rocks.

But as Kant read the newspaper, a peculiar silence grew. Lampe polished spoons, periodically sipping from his flask of Russian Vodka, contemplating the enigma of the universe. Kant sat at his desk without moving for two hours. He didn't ask Lampe why he had time to polish the spoons yet again. He didn't try to catch Lampe in the middle of a sip from the flask so that he could accuse him of drinking too much.

He just sat there.

When Lampe could no longer ponder the heavens and the earth, the watery wastes, the lucent globe of the moon, the sun, and the stars existing through inward spirit, their total mass permeated by mind, he asked, "Are you pissed off about something?"

Kant turned and looked in Lampe's general direction with his eyebrows raised high on his broad forehead, as though he had heard a rat clawing in the walls. Then he turned back to reread the article as if Lampe had said nothing.

"I'm leaving early today!" Lampe waited for a complaint about what, exactly, he was paid for if there were so many things that were more important than his work.

None came.

As Lampe gathered his things to leave, Kant spoke into the air. "Where's Green? I must talk to Green."

"I'm sure he'll come at some precise time," Lampe said.

Kant wasn't listening.

———

Lampe woke Kant the next morning and was stunned when the little man got out of his bed without delay and without being cajoled. This was always a clue that the master was onto some fine project. Kant sat down before Lampe had even set the table, and he buttered his bread without complaining about the lack of a napkin.

Lampe asked, "What was that you read yesterday?"

"A review," Kant said.

"The one by Herr Hamann?"

Kant glanced at Lampe with genuine surprise. "You saw it?"

"*Night Thoughts*," Lampe said. "It was hardly more than a paragraph, but it seemed to bother you."

"You surprise me! Why do you think it bothered me?"

"Because I polished the entire set of spoons without a word from you."

"I wasn't bothered." Kant smiled his thin smile. "Or rather, I was bothered because something I had never seen became utterly clear to me. It will take a couple of months to work out, but the conclusions will be of the highest importance. The highest!"

Kant was never happier than when he found an idea that presented itself whole so that he could dissect it, discard unseemly parts, filter it for impurities, and place it under a philosophical microscope. He wrote and rewrote notes and scraps, feeling for the joints of the idea that he would bend, loosen, and sever. The process was opaque to Lampe, and his careful and secretive reading of every scrap and note he found did not illuminate it. But once Kant found such an idea, Lampe sensed that something new was clawing its way into the world.

"A couple of months," Kant said again.

It took ten years. For ten years Lampe watched Kant try to lift the skirt of appearance, only to find appearance. Appearance. Never the thing-in-itself that was beneath appearance.

"I don't understand," Eco said the first time Lampe told him about the idea.

"No one understands! You must let go of everything in the world. He has discovered the thing-in-itself, something we cannot sense, but can only think."

"And it exists?" Eco asked with his habitual and meticulous politeness. A look of childlike incomprehension shaded the uncooked pancake of his face as he waited to be enlightened, though sometimes Lampe wondered if Eco tried to make him feel smarter by pretending not to understand.

"It must exist," Lampe said. "But here's the horror. If he's right, there's a me-in-itself that I can only think about but never experience."

"Very strange, Martin. Would it make any difference if you got to it?"

"How could we know? We can't get to it!"

"Never?" Eco asked.

"Never!" Lampe affirmed. "It's utterly isolated from us."

"One less thing to worry about, I suppose." Eco's mind was a bowl of tepid milk.

—⁓—

Hamann's article so thoroughly lifted Kant's mood that Lampe decided it was time to tell him the truth about Katarina.

"Professor?" He stood in the doorway of Kant's writing room. "May I show you something?"

Kant held up his hand while he finished scribbling down a thought. The rooster next door crowed, and then crowed again. Instead of commenting on the hated chicken, he turned with both hands on his tiny knees and glared at Lampe. "What?"

"I want to show you a magic trick."

Kant let his head drop forward. "I have too much work, and that chicken next door will not be quiet." He turned back to his desk.

"It's a good one."

"The chicken?" Kant said without looking up.

"No, the trick. It's a good one."

Kant put down his quill again and stared out his window. "I don't have a single clean shirt for tomorrow."

"You should have told me earlier," Lampe grumbled.

"Your job is to know these things."

Lampe refused to be diverted. "I will take care of it. But this trick…"

Kant breathed in as deeply as his small chest would allow, and he sighed. "Show me."

Lampe performed his card trick. He was pleased with his performance.

For a few moments, Kant stared. His face turned pink as he tried to suppress a grin.

"Not bad, eh?" Lampe said as he reached for the cards.

At first, Kant said nothing, quickly trying to think his way through the trick, to find the secret in his mind. He finally shook his head. With his reluctant grin still drawn across his face, he said, "How'd you do that?"

Lampe looked out the window where the neighbor was chasing the rooster around, making more noise. "It's magic."

Kant's grin disappeared. "I'm serious Lampe. I must get back to work. Show me."

"No, it's magic." Lampe tried to resist the pleasure this small superiority in knowledge brought him, even though it worked against his primary purpose.

The rooster crowed again, a long and piercing crow.

"Show me, Lampe."

"Magicians are sworn to silence," Lampe said, examining his ungroomed fingernails.

"Then I hope you can make a living performing your trick."

Lampe tried to not drift from his goal of confessing marriage, but he was carried by a wave of desire to make Kant beg. "I'm sworn never to reveal the secret."

"By whom?"

"By the confederacy of magicians."

"Nonsense," Kant said, staring out the window toward the hated chicken, turning pinker. "Someone had to teach you. You can just as easily teach me."

Lampe returned to his purpose. "Let's have a little exchange."

"You're growing too bold, Lampe."

Lampe shrugged. "I'll show you the trick. All I ask in return is that you let me say something without you getting angry."

"Did you break something?"

"No."

"Lie?"

"No."

"Steal?"

"No."

Kant thought for a moment. "Show me."

"Do you promise?"

"Yes. Now show me."

Lampe took the cards. Moving slowly, he showed the trick to Kant.

The master pondered the simplicity of the thing, annoyed that he had not figured it out himself. "Interesting. So, what do you want to tell me?" The rooster crowed again, and a grimace flashed across Kant's face. "Come, come. What do you want to tell me?"

"I married last week."

Lampe understood the ways the great mind was affected by being ensconced in the inadequate body of the little professor, constricted by the narrowness of his chest, suffering his absurdly skinny buttocks that pressed against the tripod of his thinking chair. He understood the tension in the muscles of Kant's jaw, the wrinkling of his brow, and even the shape of his mouth with its slightly downturned corners. The unexpected news of the marriage might even have seemed humiliating to Kant who pored over his ledgers in solitude, but who was never satisfied that he had enough money to marry. Still, Lampe trusted Kant's devotion to maxims such as *Never break a promise.* He stood confidently, like he was standing before a tiger secured by the reliable bars of the cage, certain that the maxim would hold firm and protect him from anger.

After a few moments, Kant said, "I hate that chicken."

"What?" Lampe said, surprised by the sudden shift in topic.

"The chicken." Kant's voice was tense with agitation. "I hate the chicken."

"It's just a chicken," Lampe observed.

"Don't scoff!" The warning shot out from the slit in the canvass of reality that was the philosopher's small body.

"Why bring up the chicken now?" Lampe asked.

Kant's voice rose in pitch. "Why does it scream all day long? To find a mate? To bring more chickens into the world so they can screech and holler and mate together, and bring even more chickens into the world? It interrupts my work. The world will end up with less philosophy and more chickens. It's absurd, and I hate it."

"Just buy the chicken," Lampe suggested, trying to maintain an atmosphere of mature sensibility. "We can roast it."

Kant slapped his hand on his knee and turned back to his desk. He grabbed his quill and dipped it in ink. But instead of writing he just held it over the ideas on the paper. A drop of ink slowly grew at the tip, threatening to blot out some crucial word and, for the moment, worrying Lampe more than his marital and vocational turmoil.

"I tried to buy it," Kant mumbled. "Twice. I offered the man three times what the scrawny bird is worth, but he refused to believe that a philosopher can be bothered by a chicken."

Lampe didn't say anything. Kant's anger directed toward the chicken was best left to the chicken.

Kant sulked. He complained to his dinner guests about how little money he had for unexpected occurrences. He told them that he didn't see a way to avoid making a few cuts in his budget. And, with ever-increasing bitterness, he cursed the screaming chicken who wanted to procreate. But he never said a word in anger about Lampe's marriage. Not one word. His maxim was inviolable.

A few days later he told Green, "I'm taking quarters in the Oschenmarket."

"That's no surprise, Manny. The stress of all that has gone on must be terribly distracting."

"And that chicken," Kant added.

Lampe poured each of them a glass of wine in response to Kant's raised finger. "The new quarters will be more expensive. I'll have to tighten finances somehow."

"Perhaps," Green agreed.

"I'll give it some thought," Kant said.

Lampe cleared his throat and said, "A man gets married sometimes! A man just gets married!"

"Indeed," Kant said, as though responding to a dullard's observation that sometimes people die.

The memory of Kant's refusal to delight in the prospect of such a mundane source of happiness weighed heavily upon Lampe as he paced back and forth in front of Ding, but it didn't come close to the dread he felt as he stared at the package on his desk. The Dunce had brought it to him with clumsy stealth and quickly departed. Even the Dunce's presence would have been a comfort in a room where the master's final thoughts were buried in ink and paper.

"Be careful with this," the Dunce had said, adding unnecessary words to the atmosphere. "We're very busy. There are twelve of these packages, but this may be the only one I can bring. I carried it in this potato sack. But Wasianski still looked at me suspiciously when I left. So just be careful, careful, careful."

Lampe's hands trembled when he lifted the fascicle, the repository of final ideas from the world's greatest mind. It was wrapped in an old, oversized invitation to a commemorative address for Jacob Freidrich von Rohd, the Prussian secretary of state, labeled May 22, 1801. It was the final fascicle. The moron had accidentally done something right. He may have thought he was avoiding Wasianski's eyes by selecting the bottom fascicle, but Lampe knew that God had forced the Dunce's hand to deliver the final words Kant ever wrote.

The fascicle was illuminated by the moon's light. Lampe drank wine and procrastinated. He tried to remain calm, but the fascicle terrified him. This was the death-poem of the master. If the secret to *the poetic a priori's* completion was anywhere, it was in this manuscript. And if it wasn't there, *the principle of the poetic a priori* would fade away, and Lampe would have nothing left to do but die.

Something had called out to Lampe the first time he watched the genius tear into a world of things that can only be thought. It had called out from the chaos that surrounded the master. It had called out from the chickens, from the unfaithful women, from the stalwart Green with his cylindrical head and measured ways. Everything accumulated in Lampe's memory, his storehouse of thoughts and images, labeled and organized, but meaningless because he did not have the key, the guiding rule that would bring *the principle of the poetic a priori* to full fruition.

He had been the only person to witness the entire forty-year arc of world-bending thought, but he had missed the last two years when the poetic finally began to pick at the cracks in the master's wall of reason. Now the last part of the record of those years, months, days, and hours was on his desk, in his hands. Many people gossiped about the master's decline and senility. But reality was not senile. It was still trying to break through, and the spirit of the work had settled upon Lampe.

Or something had settled upon him. The fascicle glowing in the moonlight was not mere paper and ink. It was the mind of Kant, more powerful and terrifying that any spirit or demon. He didn't need a theory of ghosts to feel the presence of the master staring with disdain through the window, luxuriating in his ethereal, bodiless duration, mocking his most vilified, but longest-living, student.

Courage was needed. Courage of the highest order was needed if the thing-in-itself was ever to be saved from the threat of nothingness. But on the threshold of this demand, Lampe could not even open the manuscript.

When the idea of separating our world from the thing-in-itself wormed its diseased and wriggling way into Kant's mind, it was perhaps the Devil's greatest victory over God. It relegated God to a place inaccessible to reason, and it turned God into a postulate, while the deepest reality of creation was hidden from the human mind. The Devil's strategy almost succeeded.

Green had been the only person besides Lampe to witness the evolution of the idea. He listened to Kant, but he neither accepted nor rejected any idea quickly. He turned them like a pig on a spit. What Lampe immediately saw as true or false, Green probed and tormented until the philosophical machinery was so complex and unwieldy that it no longer fit into clear sentences.

One evening the two of them were sipping port, and Kant said, "I'm getting closer to it."

"To what?" Green asked.

Kant ran his finger around and around the rim of his small glass of port as though he was nervous about answering the question. The control of his life, his frail body, his time, and his mind had been won by Joseph Green. He worked, and he measured his work against the economic order of Green's mind. "I'm getting close to the idea that will allow me to finish *The Critique.*"

"Tell me more, Manny."

Kant looked like a schoolboy asking to hold hands with a girl at recess when he said, "There are appearances. And there are categories of the understanding. Each of these is irrefutable and complete on its own. But ..." Kant paused and took a dainty sip of his port.

"But to gain the dividends, you need a way to connect them," Green said, drawing a smile from the inner chamber of the professor.

Dividends? Lampe smoldered.

The ocean of a universe was at stake, and Kant was building the ark, a philosophical ark with a great hull to divide the waters. But Green dissolved everything into a means of exchange that could be stored in a safe. His mercantile caution denied Kant the fiery engine he needed, so the ship went nowhere. It just floated, waiting for the waters to dry.

"Dividends," Lampe mumbled, nearly bending the spoon he was shining. "Thank God he'll maximize return on his investment."

Kant ignored him, and he pulled a couple of slips of paper from his pocket. "To connect the appearances and the categories of the understanding we need schemata, Joseph. Schemata."

"And what are schemata, Manny?"

"Rules," Kant said. "The schemata are rules that allow everything coming through the senses to be related to what is most pure."

"And that is ...?"

"Time, Joseph. Time! I've discovered that time itself is determined by these rules."

Lampe rolled his eyes, but he immediately wished to withdraw his eye-rolling from the universe because his master had said something that, on second thought, was intriguing.

Green saw the eye-rolling and shook his head slightly as a reprimand before looking at his huge English watch. "Time?"

"Yes!" Kant said more boldly. "Time! Schemata determine time according to rules."

"The schemata determine time according to rules," Green said with the tone of a businessman being offered a chance to get in early on the sale of leaf mold for the cure of itchy skin rashes. "This sounds promising. I'll need to hear more. But not tonight. It's seven o'clock."

Lampe saw the slight shrug of Kant's shoulders and his suppressed expression of annoyance. It was justified. Even Green's strict adherence to his watch should soften to accommodate the first revelation of such a breakthrough.

Green said, "We'll talk further, Manny. Goodnight."

The schemata looked like handwaving to Lampe, no better than Descartes' pineal gland bringing the mind and body together. But it was a start, and he trusted that the mind of Kant could sail past the schemata and find a better idea.

Unfortunately, after many weeks of conversation, Green approved of the schemata, which meant that the universe would simply have to shift to accommodate Kant's idea. "It's like the Copernican revolution, Manny."

"Yes," Kant replied with a smile. "A Copernican revolution."

So instead of continuing to search for the truth, Kant spent month after month and year after year working out the details of his disastrous idea as eager anticipation grew among his colleagues. In time, he could see the world in no other way. He was making his mind as he made up his mind about the truth of the world. And he dragged his friends and students along with him.

Lampe couldn't save Kant from philosophical folly as he constructed the airship that carried his thoughts to rarefied heights until the air thinned and the mind grew giddy, becoming devilish by mistaking itself for a god.

Philosophy and madness finally merged one rainy day when Kant made Lampe carry the umbrella on a visit to a student who had lost one eye to the pox and the other to a surgical procedure for a cyst. On the way to the young man's house, Kant was sullen and irritable, reaching for the umbrella to correct its position every few feet, as though Lampe was incapable of holding an umbrella.

Did Lampe complain about getting soaked while Kant fretted over a few unpredictable raindrops blown by the wind? No. Lampe endured.

When they arrived at the student's house, his mother showed them into his room where the young man sat, empty eye sockets directed toward nothing in particular, and the student immediately exclaimed, "Professor Kant!" before his mother said a word. "You're so kind to visit. And the man with you smells damp, and he's dripping on the floor. Could this be the famous Martin Lampe? Is he holding the famous umbrella at the famous angle?" Lampe blushed when the student's smile erupted into an exuberant manifestation of unbridled joy.

"Indeed, indeed," Kant said.

After the boy's mother stepped out of the room, Kant answered questions about new events at the university, staring the entire time at the boy's eye sockets, leaning to the right and then to the left to get a full view of them. Lampe wondered if he would reach out and touch the sockets with his thin fingers. The boy's head followed the nasal breathing of the gawking philosopher. Suddenly, Kant shocked the boy by announcing in a firm tone, "You're *not* blind!"

His mother, who had been listening at the door, stuck her head into the room but didn't interrupt the great professor. Kant stood up and began pacing before the stunned student. "You're not blind, I say!" His voice rose to the formal confidence of a lecturer feeling his way toward an idea. He lightly tapped his walking stick on the floor as he paced.

The boy directed his eye-sockets toward the corner of the room and smiled an excessive smile, showing too much of his teeth and gums. "Professor, I assure you that I'm blind." His voice was calm, joyful even, heightening the distress of the professor.

"No!" Kant raised his finger in the air. "You have concepts."

Lampe said to the student, "He has his finger in the air," just to ensure that the young man could participate in the theater of the absurd.

"Ah," the student said. "Thank you. This must be the big point."

"What was that?" Kant looked at them. Then he continued in the same tone. "You have sufficient concepts from past intuitions."

"Concepts? Well, professor, I certainly smell, hear, and touch as never before. I've started to wonder if vision is like the sun. It blots out all the stars with its brightness. I wish I wasn't blind, but I'm also glad that I'm no longer limited by vision."

"You're not blind!" Kant repeated, lifting his walking stick and slamming the end against the floor, jolting Lampe, the mother, and the student. "I insist! You have sufficient concepts from intuition and concepts to overcome the lack of sight."

"Professor," his mother said as she stepped into the room with a worried look on her face. "Perhaps we could talk about something more pleasant."

Kant looked at her as though she had just turned down a cure for her son's blindness.

The visit continued awkwardly for a while longer, and then Lampe took up the umbrella and they left. When the front door closed, Lampe shook rainwater onto Kant's wig and hissed, "Embarrassing!"

Kant flicked away the water. "Yes, his mother should be ashamed. If only he could see my point."

"If only he could see at all," Lampe answered.

"You wouldn't understand. He was one of my brighter students. He should've had a chance."

Lampe glared, then handed him the umbrella and walked away.

Kant called after him, "What are you doing Lampe? You're becoming peculiar! Do you hear me? Too peculiar for my taste!"

Too peculiar. Lampe pulled up his blanket, covering himself and Ding, but he was still cold. He thought about the blind student who learned that vision can hide other experiences. He knew the boy was right because he too suffered from the invisible. In the deep part of night, the spirit of the dead professor delivered vague, disturbing doubts to Lampe's inner world. What should he do? What could he do? The invisible had drifted up from Kant's final manuscript, bringing night thoughts, fear, and dread.

The invisible tormented him. If he were courageous, he would just give up his pension, see the body, and be freed of the ghost. Then he could starve like a brave soldier, die in a frozen room, and be forgotten by everyone.

Day Nine

Concerning Volcanoes in the Moon

LAMPE'S BRAIN YELLED, "Four o'clock!" dragging him from fitful sleep, with half-dressed dreams still clinging to the edge of his mind until he stomped on their fingers, and they dropped away into oblivion. His mind blew on the flickering thoughts glowing in the embers of the prior day's melancholy, philosophy's fuel. A question appeared from the edge of philosophical darkness, crawling toward the growing light. Did exile demand that he not even linger, unobtrusively, in the general vicinity of the dead master's house?

As the question warmed itself, rocking gently and wringing its hands, he felt a gravitational force pulling on the thousand glowing pieces of thought scattered on his walls, causing them to move, not yet with the sweep of a galaxy's spiral, but with a kind of vibratory and musical delight, each in its small allotment of space made of ethereal anticipation.

From his mattress on the floor, in the milky light of the moon, he could see the fascicle on his desk. The presence of Kant's final manuscript pinned him between a cliff and an abyss. He had to choose whether to climb up the cliff with his fingernails locking into crevices and terror shrouding his ascent, or else to drop into the undifferentiated solvent of the void below and relax into death.

The bundle of paper held nothing but ink marks, all wrapped in some stupid invitation because of how cheap Kant was. And yet the fascicle was the organizing presence of the sun, orienting the planets and smaller bodies that circled it, giving everything a sense of place in the infinite universe. Ten thousand words were scribbled on the walls, each an individual shard scattered from the breaking up of Lampe's own attempt to forge a great thought. But they suddenly ordered themselves around the sun of Kant's final fascicle, his final words, like an army of soldiers standing at attention when the general arrived.

This was a beginning, and it was necessary.

But a philosopher such as Lampe ... Well, there it is—a philosopher such as Lampe ...

Such a philosopher needs something else. And though he did not yet grasp the reason why, he knew that the vagueness of this *something* resided in the vicinity of Kant's body. Lampe was forbidden to approach the body until Wasianski delivered an invitation to suspend the exile, but perhaps mere proximity to the house would be enough to stoke the fire of his imagination. And why not?

Fact: From the road in front of Kant's house, a person could enjoy the sight of the frozen gardens and the moat of the castle, breathing in the air of history, and the deep secrets of ancient powers and of war that wound amongst the castle's towers.

Fact: Lampe was capable of walking back and forth all day, in this place or that, if he chose to do so.

Fact: Lampe was as free as any other citizen of Königsberg to walk back and forth on the road in front of Kant's house.

No one could exile him from such experiences without exiling him from life. Lampe was like any other man. He had standing as a citizen. Indeed, only an imbecile would deny that he was an elder of Königsberg.

He was finally wide awake, scratching Ding's ear. Ding needed a long walk. It would do her good. The plan was forming.

So, what if, just hypothetically, Lampe happened to be standing near Kant's door when Wasianski stepped out for a moment of relief from the death vigil? He would be shocked by Lampe's presence, but in that moment, Lampe would demand a fair hearing and beg for relief from the disproportionate harshness of the exile that banished him from the only thing that kept his mind intact. Lampe was nothing apart from Kant. He was nothing apart from the work, the writing, the revolution, the man. Katerina had been right about this before their short, unhappy marriage began. He had chosen to dedicate his life to the philosopher.

As he imagined asking for a fair hearing, he could see himself approaching Wasianski. But before he could get the formulation of his imaginary repentance out of his mouth, he heard Deacon Wasianski pour words into his ear like hot oil. "Lampe! Can you not honor the professor's wish, even in this solemn and sacred season of grief? Have you no shred of respect? Leave! From now on you get nothing. Beg on the street if you want to eat. You think were banished before? Well, now you are banished indeed!"

And what shame he would feel if it occurred in front of the strangers lined up to see the famous corpse. Lampe would hang his head, covering it with a cloth, and he would slink past the anonymous gawkers who so easily gained the only thing he desired. No, better that he suffer the shame and sorrow he had been dealt. Why compound his risk while all the world stared at the master, who was hidden from his sight as surely as the thing-in-itself?

When *The Critique of Pure Reason* was finally published, it crept into philosophical minds far from Königsberg. In time, renowned thinkers from other countries journeyed to see the great professor. For Lampe, the most important consequence of this fame was that Kant finally had enough money to buy his own house.

He bought it from the widow of Johann Becker. Becker had painted the portrait of Kant that hung in Kanter's house, and his patience with the philosopher's strange and fussy vanity about the tilt of his head had impressed Lampe.

Kant bought the house for 5500 guilders after Green assured him that the investment was excellent and that any resale price was certain to be high. "My dear Manny, we're growing older. My own health is failing faster than yours. With a permanent home, you'll feel more secure. And security is gold to an old man."

"We're not old, are we?" Kant asked.

Green answered, "We're old enough to know in our bones what age means."

"And in our bowels," Kant added.

"You'll outlive all of us, Manny. But you must buy the house."

From the moment Lampe first entered the house that was suffused with musty charm, he knew it was perfect for his philosopher. The financial wisdom of the purchase was irrelevant.

It was bordered by the moat of the castle, whose gardens, narrow alleys, and owls were perfect to provoke and support a philosopher in his thoughts. Lampe was filled with domestic joy as he walked from room to room, sucking the marrow from a gnawed chicken bone he had in his pocket. Saucepans and frying pans hung in rows over a gigantic hearth, which had a jack that turned to roast every side of a succulent sirloin of beef. The oak rafters and beams were black with age. Around the dining room table were paneled seats with tall backs. In the parlor were polished tables on which pewter tankards had left rings. Soft light drifted through the leaded windows, and well-polished lamps hung from the raftered ceiling. Lampe imagined cheerful, cozy, clouds of tobacco smoke floating up from long clay pipes as rain tumbled down the chimney and made the wood fire sizzle in the hearth. The house was the true architectonic, the condition for the possibility of real philosophical thought, standing against the demonic residue of unwarranted speculation.

Unfortunately, once the philosopher moved in and sat down to his work, a sound worse than the screaming chicken rose up and assaulted his mind. Every morning and evening, the prisoners in the castle dungeon sang praises to God for their salvation.

"Lampe!" Kant said a few days after moving in. "Why didn't you warn me about this hideous musical farce? Weren't you once in the dungeon for something or other?"

Lampe said, "I like the singing. It helps me while I devote my mind to the high work of sweeping your floors, dusting your furniture, and straightening your wig."

"Your work might be compatible with the bellowing of the newly devout, but mine isn't."

Lampe looked over Kant's shoulder at the piece he was working on. "*Volcanoes in the Moon*," he said. "Well, that sounds important."

"It's gravely important, and I can finish it soon if those transient converts will stop trying to persuade God to forgive their sins in exchange for a few badly written songs."

Lampe recollected his time in prison bellowing hymns to drown out the crunching sounds of rats searching for breadcrumbs in the empty bowls of the men. "The dungeon stokes gratitude in the soul for things we take for granted."

"Singing doesn't influence God or change the moral law."

"Prisoners are still people, and most of them have great stories from their lives which they tell with skill."

Kant said, "I don't care if they're poets, political rebels, or dandies unfortunate enough to have offended a nobleman's wife. They can repent in silence. Go ask them to be quiet."

"I could close the window," Lampe suggested.

"And let me suffocate? I can barely breathe all winter, and now that it's spring. I should at least be allowed some fresh air. No, they must stop. Go tell them that Immanuel Kant demands silence. Tell them I'll never finish another book if they're not quiet."

"That'll do it." Lampe sighed the sigh of the worldly man who knows the truth that reaches past the cradle of innocence.

"I'm sure they're just trying to convince the guard that they've changed."

"If they were truly redeemed, they wouldn't beg to be released. They would demand that they serve the full sentence demanded by justice. Every false hymn is further proof that they have not repented. Tell them that. Logic and moral insight will silence them if my pain is not enough."

"I know the guard," Lampe said.

"Good."

"No," Lampe corrected. "I know the guard. He's a troll. If I say that a philosopher is bothered by his prisoners' songs, he'll either beat me or laugh at me. Probably both."

"You were a soldier. Show some authority."

"I don't have any authority and I won't go!" Lampe stomped out of the house.

Kant stepped outside and called after him. "Lampe! Go by Hippel's house and ask him to dinner. He'll help us!"

Help us? Lampe thought.

Theodor Gottlieb von Hippel had become the Mayor of Königsberg, and he had mastered the art of the dual life. Publicly, he was a trusted administrator with a reputation for effectiveness and pragmatism. But Lampe learned from Hippel's servants that in private he enjoyed being chased around the house naked while they whipped his buttocks with wet towels.

Hippel had studied with Kant, and now he was a friend. Kant ignored his sexual oddities. For a man with such tenacious virginity, Kant had a surprising, if selective, tolerance for perversion. Lampe, son of a whore, appreciated this.

The mayor was plump and soft, with a very attentive manner in conversation. He often jotted notes to himself. People took this as a sign of how determined he was to remember and honor their requests about the way Königsberg should be run, but he was actually recording strange behaviors, comments, and indiscretions to use in the anonymous novels and plays he wrote, among which was a play about Kant and Lampe. Kant didn't want that kind of publicity, but Lampe enjoyed it, despite being portrayed on the stage as a dullard.

One evening, when Hippel came for dinner, Kant insisted on taking dessert in the study. He told Lampe to open the window for some fresh air.

Hippel said, "It's chilly outside."

"Fresh air will cleanse the nostrils and improve the flavor of the dessert," Kant replied.

Hippel shrugged and reached for the port. "Are you going to Countess Keyserlingk's dinner party tomorrow?"

Kant leaned forward in his chair, cupping his hand behind his ear. "What was that?"

"Countess Keyserlingk," Hippel repeated. "Are you going to her dinner party?"

"There!" Kant said, thrusting a finger into the air. "Hippel, do you hear that?"

"Do I hear what?"

"The singing! Night and day they drone on, trying to prove their flimsy repentance."

Hippel looked toward the open window. "Their voices aren't too bad if you ask me."

"But listen to them!" Kant complained. "They're so loud!"

"I'm sure they have their reasons, and they're probably bored. What of it?"

"What of it?" Kant said. His face turned the darker shade of pink that usually bloomed when a student failed to see a self-evident truth. "I can't think and I can't write. You must make them stop."

"I'm the mayor, not the warden. Let's talk about something we can achieve. How are the plans for the inauguration of the king coming along?"

Because of his position at the university, Kant had been asked to head the ceremonies for the inauguration of Frederic William II. "The plans are fine."

Hippel said, "This is important, Immanuel. The king already thinks our city is suited for little more than training bears. If the ceremony isn't magnificent, all of Prussia will think the same thing. And then Germany and France. And then the whole world."

Kant stared at Hippel. "The ceremony will be fine unless this singing continues. I need quiet to do my work. If you can't silence them, they will silence me."

"Just reassure me that the ceremony is coming along."

Kant waved his hand above his head. "Everything will be fine. But only if the prisoners are silent."

Hippel said, "I can't stand by them and hit them over the head whenever they sing."

"No, but you can tell the jailor to hit them. It's unbearable to be subjected to this noise when I'm so close to grasping the very idea."

"The very idea of what?"

Kant waved his hand again, then he stuffed it in his pocket. "If you silence them, you'll see."

But even Mayor Hippel couldn't entirely stop the prisoners from singing, though he did reduce their cries for salvation enough to accommodate the thickening isolation of abstruse and abstract thought in Kant's perfect, icy world where Lampe smoldered like the last coal in the hearth. The morbid quiet that ensued was only occasionally interrupted by the singing of a prisoner who had not yet heard of Mayor Hippel's rules. When the lone singer would suddenly fall silent in the middle of a verse, Kant would grin over the top of whatever book he was reading while Lampe glared in judgment.

Unfortunately, the boys who played in the street created their own disruption when they began throwing stones over his fence. The more Kant objected, the more they threw stones. He spoke with the police, explaining the problem in detail. But they just shrugged and said, "What do you want us to do? They're always gone by the time you tell us."

"Wait here! They'll return. Then you can lock them up in their own closets and fine their parents."

"In their closets? They're just boys. We can't act unless someone in your house is hurt."

He hit the ground with his walking cane. "I'll only be able to punish them when I'm sick, wounded, or dead!"

Kant's philosophy expressed a desire to be disembodied and freed from roosters, lusty women, rough boys, prisoners, and sluggish bowels. But when he came up against the real world, it pushed back. It wasn't susceptible to argument.

Even monetary metaphors faded as Green's health declined

and he stopped visiting. Kant never felt comfortable around the sick, so he asked Lampe to deliver occasional notes.

His isolation grew. Hamann, the Magus of the North, was becoming famous because of his critique of Kant, so the master distanced himself in protest. Hippel was a busy mayor who spent his free time writing his novels and enjoying his naked chases with wet towels.

At first, Lampe resented the isolation. But he also hated being in his own home. The scars on Katerina's body seemed to extend to her soul, and she was so distant that Lampe felt more alone than ever when he was with her. Her world was ensconced in memories of sorrow, encased like an insect in amber, while Lampe's mind was dragged into the upper atmosphere of pure thought as he followed the master in his philosophical airship.

——————

The pressure of the impending inauguration of Frederic William II grew. To curb the master's irritability, Lampe suggested that Kant enlist an assistant—someone accustomed to Kant's habits and ways of thinking, someone with military discipline who could embrace Kant's instruction, sacrificing his own projects, and even his own marriage, if necessary.

Kant liked the idea of an assistant, so he recruited Christian Jakob Kraus.

Kraus! Nephew of pastor Buchholz, of all people—the confessor of the sex-craved god-lover, Hamann.

Kraus! Whose reservations about Kant's lectures nearly drove his fragile mind insane.

Kraus! Whose uncle had died, leaving him with no support,

so that he was especially vulnerable to Kant's offer of substitute support.

Kant had periodically coerced the unfortunate Kraus to work on smaller writing projects, gathering together messy essays cobbled from slips of paper, and producing a clean draft for Kant to revise. But now he began to invite Kraus to dinner, and he hinted at plans that Kraus couldn't have anticipated. Lampe offered no warnings or advice to the frail little scholar who was thirty years younger than Kant. The sooner he broke, the sooner Lampe would have a chance to prove to Kant that he had chosen the wrong man.

As the inauguration approached, Kant talked about it incessantly.

He talked instead of planning.

One evening at dinner, Kant said, for the thousandth time, "Jakob, I must lead and plan this inauguration because of my position at the university."

"I know," the sullen Kraus answered.

"You must do more to assist me if you care a whit about me."

Kraus' face was red with the fear and frustration of the weak, and he was already weary of Kant's endless demands. But he said, "It will be my pleasure."

"Excellent," Kant said. He had heard Kraus' response, but he ignored the true answer on the young man's face. "Now, tell me how your diet is going."

Kant had prescribed a diet as a remedy for Kraus' persistent stomach troubles. Kraus said, "Everything's fine," but he refused to share details about his bowel movements.

Once Kraus accepted the task of organizing the inauguration, he committed to it fully. He drew a detailed map of the area in which the ceremonies would take place. He wrote up a list of people who should give speeches, provide music, and participate in different stages of the ceremony.

Kant frequently told him that the reputation of Königsberg depended on the inauguration, and Kraus accepted the burden of the task with a tremulous sense of what was at stake. A couple of weeks after being charged with so much responsibility, his eyes dull from a lack of sleep, he offered the results of his work to Kant.

Kant half-listened to Kraus' presentation, picking at his remaining teeth and making a sucking sound as his tongue searched for the freed debris. After a long pause, he said, "The task was entrusted to me, and with good reason. I've already decided how the ceremony should be arranged."

Kraus turned red with anger before pushing it down into the basement of his vulnerable soul.

Kant noticed, and he suddenly turned charming and kind, like an old man watching a favorite nephew, content that his own life had been well-lived, thinking only of the flourishing of those who would outlive him. "Ah, my dear Jakob. If only you knew how your presence warms my old heart. With you, and you alone, I share everything." He reached over and stroked Kraus' head. "Lampe! Bring my friend some wine. The good wine, Lampe. The best wine."

Lampe walked out muttering, "Get it yourself. I'm busy." Then he brought the wine and poured it for the two men.

—⁂—

The a priori structure of the inauguration had formed in Kant's mind, crowding out all of Kraus' suggestions. Once it was in place, it could be no other way. But as the inauguration approached, Kraus increasingly worried that the professor's calm assurance was not merited by the quality of the planning.

Several nights before the event, Kant rehearsed the details to Kraus, who had stopped objecting or offering suggestions. As the two of them pressed forward in the wonderful world of Kant's mind, Lampe stood by trying to reconcile his horror with his grave amusement at Kraus' choice to trade so much of his short time on earth preparing to fail in such a spectacular and public way. But Kraus never wavered as Kant polished the surface of his ideas about how the inauguration would proceed, one part following another part in a perfectly ordered way, as inevitably as any effect follows a cause in our mind's reception of the world.

"The inauguration isn't your great *Critique*," Lampe whispered as Kant bent over to pick up the pipe he had dropped. "The real world won't conform to your mind."

Kant sat up with his pipe. "What was that? You said something, Lampe?"

"Nothing."

Kant opened the drawer where he kept his tobacco pouch, but it wasn't there. "Where's my tobacco?"

Lampe looked around the room without moving. "I don't see it."

"You're in one of those peculiar moods again, aren't you? Jakob, may I have some of yours? Tomorrow is the day I have an audience with the king."

"He's a fierce man," Lampe said. "I fought beside his uncle. Can I go with you and see what happens?"

"Certainly not." Kant tipped his head and sucked his few teeth as a reprimand. "It was hard enough to get a spot for dear old Kraus."

Kraus blushed.

Lampe looked at Kraus and said, "You'll get used to it."

"Get used to what?" Kant said. "Speak plainly, Lampe."

Lampe ignored him and left the room.

When Lampe arrived to wake Kant on the morning of the inauguration, he was already sitting in his study fully dressed, though his wig crooked as usual. But he looked exhausted from lack of sleep.

Lampe said, "Smoke your pipe. I'll make you a small breakfast. Then we can go. And straighten your wig, for God's sake. Everything will be fine. The king will be the king no matter how the inauguration goes."

Kant looked up at Lampe and then looked down at the floor. The man obviously didn't know what to do next. He was finally caught between a sense of obligation and depletion.

Lampe had seen this look when soldiers slowed down and said they couldn't go on. He knew what to say on the battlefield: another two miles and we're there; come or you'll be left alone; dinner lies ahead; if you make it, you'll save your honor, but if you stop, you'll feel shame in the presence of the soldiers who march onward.

But Kant looked old in a new way. He was bundled up, lost in a pile of cloaks to keep his bones warm. Lampe saw the truth, and he gave a gift to the master. "I won't let you go. I'll be blamed by everyone, but I'm forcing you to stay at home."

Kant looked up. "What?"

"You've done your duty, and the ceremony will happen as it happens. But you're exhausted, and your health is weak. I can't let you go."

Kant sat for a moment. Relief appeared on his face. "Are you sure it will proceed without me?"

"Quite sure." Lampe helped Kant out of his blanket, coat, vest, over-shirt, and shoes, and tucked him back into bed for more sleep, which had never happened before. He hid this treasure in his heart.

Kant was still asleep in the late afternoon when Kraus knocked on the door, furious that he had been left alone to watch the event fall apart. Processions didn't know whether to go to the right or the left. Hippel was in front rolling his eyes and whispering insults about Kant to his noble neighbors.

The king, at least, was unflustered since he didn't care about anything that happened in Königsberg, including his own inauguration. The event began, the event ended, and the king left for his palace.

But Kraus was irate. "Where is he, Lampe?"

"Herr Kraus!" Lampe said. "Good to see you."

"Where is he?" His face was an unfortunate shade of intense pink that diminished the effect of his rage.

"The professor fell ill, I'm sorry to say. He's in bed resting."

Kraus was trembling with fury. "He has done me wrong!"

"He's an old man," Lampe said. "Old men get sick."

"He forced me to appear before the king, and then he left me to hang. He ignored my plans. He lived the entire event in his own mind, and then left me alone to suffer the king's glare.

Even worse, I had to endure the glare of Hippel and the whole university senate! I've been publicly shamed. And I'm not the only one. He didn't give passes to several important dignitaries, and they were turned away at the door!"

"Well, sir, come to dinner tomorrow. He'll be feeling better by then. He'll want to hear all about it."

"Oh, I'll come back tomorrow. But it won't be pleasant. Tell him that. Tell him I'm not happy!"

Lampe said, "Of course, sir. Of course."

Lampe didn't tell him. He knew how fragile the master's digestion had become. Kraus simply didn't know how to work with the master to achieve something as simple as the inauguration of a king. Kant had chosen the wrong man to assist him, in Lampe's opinion.

The forgotten professors and dignitaries who had been left out of the inauguration wrote letters to Kant that agitated him. "I meet these men in lecture halls. Do they think I overlooked them intentionally? What a tiresome bother, Lampe, what a tiresome bother."

"It will all be forgotten soon enough," Lampe said. "Just like me."

Kraus came to dinner expecting an apology from Kant. Lampe left them to themselves. When he returned to check on them, Kraus was sitting next to Kant with a pink face full of abject silence. Kant had obviously castigated him for the discrepancy between the imagined ceremony and the actual one, and he had placed the burden of the poorly executed event on Kraus.

Lampe shrugged his shoulders and shook his head, as though to say that some partnerships are simply not destined to endure.

Later in the day, Lampe visited Hippel's servants. He brought them vodka and almonds, and in return, they gleefully recounted Hippel's rant from the night before.

The next morning while Kant was smoking his pipe, Lampe whispered, "Mayor Hippel isn't happy."

"What do you mean?"

"Never mind," Lampe said. "Just silly servants talking."

Kant tipped his head forward and lowered his voice. "What did they tell you?"

"Nothing! Mayor Hippel had drunk a few glasses of wine. Much can be forgiven a man when he over imbibes."

"Lampe!"

Lampe faked a wince. "Well, according to his servants, he said, 'Kant and Kraus may be great scholars, but never let them rule a land or a village. In fact, they are incapable of ruling a chicken coop!' The chicken coop got a laugh. But who can trust servants, right professor? They probably had too much wine themselves."

Kant didn't speak to Hippel for a month. Every evening he sat alone with Lampe, gnawing on his cold, unlit pipe, grumbling about the roles of Kraus, Hippel, and the king in the unraveling of his perfect plan.

But to Lampe's astonishment and dismay, Kant eventually persuaded Kraus to stay by his side like an abused dog, throwing him bones of praise and insisting that everything depended on him.

Administrative duties receded into the past, while the implications of the horrific *Critique of Pure Reason* continued to dawn upon the thinking world. Kant's attention turned next to wrestling morality and beauty into his system, scribbling ideas on slips of paper stuffed into his pockets and saved from the washerwoman by Lampe who arranged them in drawers and on the desktop, as he saw fit.

When the devil blinds a mind to things-in-themselves, it is actually the mind that is hidden from itself, and it can never stop searching for itself. But as it does, madness lurks, and the master had become untethered from any possible view but his own. In the preface to his new scripture, he had written, "In this inquiry, I have made completeness my aim, and I venture to assert that there is not a single metaphysical problem which has not been solved, or for the solution of which the key has not been supplied."

Kant might not have been able to govern a chicken coop, but he was becoming the very deity of his a priori world. It was a world of pure nothingness, a new madness on the face of the earth.

If Kant was right, reality was a solitary darkness, perhaps hidden even from the mind of God. Reality's core of light no longer shined through appearances like the sun shining through stained glass windows.

Hippel was the first to attempt a public presentation of Kant's ideas in the form of a three-volume novel called *Descriptions of Life in an Ascending Line, with Additions A, B, C.* He portrayed Kant in the role of an examiner named "His Spectability." At the beginning of the humiliating novel, His Spectability was happy because he had become a Grandfather the night before, with Grandmother Lampe by his side.

But Hippel had only picked up a few fragments of the master's ideas in his lectures on encyclopedia and anthropology, and he misunderstood even those morsels.

Kant dismissed Hippel's trivial portrayal. Anything that didn't conform to Kant's maxims had to be rejected. A voice of inerrancy accompanied the revelations in his new scripture, and Lampe worried that a new inquisition was not out of the question.

When Kant stopped fretting over the botched inauguration, he began to think more seriously about his strategy for achieving divination. But becoming a god is never easy.

One day, when Lampe was trying to repair the loose leg on Kant's three-legged thinking stool, the master blurted, "My work is a Copernican revolution. So why does everyone claim they can't understand it? I think they're being willful in their misunderstanding."

"It's a hard book to read," Lampe said, aware that Kant was complaining to him only because no one else was present to listen.

"But once you see the truth of it, nothing else makes sense."

"Sounds like you need a preacher to spread the word. And maybe a defender against the devil."

"Sometimes I wish I had your simple view of the world."

Simple?

Lampe stood at the philosophical spring where wonder, longing, and insight were born from the deepest parts of the mind. But Kant was standing guard over the imprisoned thing-in-itself. It had to be rescued and reunited with the thing-as-it-appears. The devil had given Kant the idea of cutting humanity off from the thing-in-itself, because this was the only way to cut humanity off from God, now that sin had failed as a strategy.

Lampe had been chosen to stand again this severance. He was chosen to fight a battle not of swords and cannons, but of mind and wit. As the mind of God was incrementally embraced, the world would be incrementally transformed. As the world was transformed, more of the mind of God could be seen. Only a person who had acquired the mind of God could play midwife to the thing-in-itself and allow it to be born again.

Of course, this required Lampe to use subtle methods to avoid being noticed. Otherwise, everything would end. God was obviously the one who had chosen him to be the professor's servant. Now that he had been tutored in philosophy for so many years, he could choose to spend his time like Hamann, writing public works against Kant. Or he could choose to pursue fame by writing, say, *The Critique of Poetic Reason*, or some such thing. But books disappear in time unless they are works inspired by God, or by the Devil. *The principle of the poetic a priori* descended from the mind of God and increasingly haunted Lampe. But the principle had to flow from the quill of the great Immanuel Kant himself in the form of a second revolution, healing the way humanity views the truth of the universe after the great sundering wrought by *The Critique of Pure Reason*. Lampe could only lead Kant to write the book if he waited patiently, listening for the moment that the music of thought opened into the apparent dissonance that would bring about a higher order. Then he could insert slips of paper into Kant's pockets with ideas written in the aging man's scrawl, which he had mastered.

Such boldness could only be risked when the professor was

especially susceptible to suggestion. But unfortunately, Kant had stopped drinking large quantities of wine, so Lampe had to wait for age to soften him. Meanwhile, other books would be written to fill the time, while the highest point of view brewed in that deeper cauldron of thought where the mind of Kant and the mind of Lampe were nearly one.

—∿∿—

Lampe stared at the fascicle on his desk. It was Kant's last attempt to give birth to the principle that Lampe had nudged him towards over years. He felt the weight of what remained to be accomplished. But what could he do in his wretched solitude? He could add pages to the fascicle and have the Dunce sneak it back, but there was so little time. Nine days had already passed by while he dawdled and tormented himself.

Not that it was Lampe's fault. His imagination needed to be reawakened, and the great gaping hole wrought by the master's death had to be filled. He only had one fascicle, but he needed the entire manuscript, and wine, and time. He needed to live in the house again. He needed to work at the master's writing desk. He needed to become Immanuel Kant.

But first, he needed to be forgiven. Tricky. Kant was dead and could no longer say, "Lampe, I forgive you. Return here to your true home."

What could be accomplished if he visited Kant's house without being invited?

Perhaps Deacon Wasianski would hear the sincerity of Lampe's regret and consider the way Lampe's marriage was broken—nay, sacrificed—in service to Kant and to the Ideas. He might say, "Old Lampe, poor man. Have you really suffered so much these past two years? I tell you, the master forgave you in his soul."

Then Lampe might answer, perhaps visibly holding back a sob, "But Kaufman told me that the master carried around a notebook where he wrote reminders to himself never to mention my name. My name! Blotted out! Forty years of devotion gone!"

"Yes, yes," Wasianski might then say, in a pastoral effort to console. "But listen, old man. I had private conversations with the professor. He told me—not in so many words, no—but he told me that he forgave you. Or here's what he told me. He told me that he still had a fondness for you."

"A fondness," Lampe might then say, holding the emotion in his mind, turning it over, contrasting it with alternative possibilities, but resisting anything that distracted from the possibility of redemption. "A fondness. Yes. That will suffice."

In the solitude of his room, the ninth night of dwelling in a world from which Kant had departed, Lampe knew that even if he died with nothing more than the assurance that his forty years of work was not be summed up in a single story of concluding shame, he would be satisfied.

Or not satisfied, exactly. There could be no satisfaction apart from the completion of Kant's great architectonic. Everything that came before merely plowed the ground and planted the philosophical seed that had to die in order to grow into the flourishing plant, the flower of wisdom slowly showing forth the meaning, and purpose, and end of the whole—*the principle of the poetic a priori.*

"I am an old man!" he cried suddenly toward Ding who was

184

licking her tumor. "I have no children. I have no shelf of books to prove the value of my life. I have no fortune. I have no house. I have no collection of students to fondly remember my harsh but deep teaching, or to tell stories of my wisdom after my death. Ding, I have nothing to show that Martin Lampe existed in the fair city of Königsberg!"

He lay down on his mattress, heavy with sorrow, and he pulled his blanket to his chin. The system wasn't the only thing that needed redemption. Lampe wanted to demonstrate the sum and meaning of his own life's work. Was there anything wrong with that? His vision of what would suffice was so modest. He only wanted to be escorted past the waiting gawkers lined up to look at the great philosopher whose corpse weighed less than a child. He wanted them to feel a slight tug of resentment at his privilege. All he needed was to hear, just once, the common people asking one another, "Who is that man?"

Who is that man?

He heard the answer in his inner chamber: that is Martin Lampe, the devoted servant of the famous Immanuel Kant. That is the man who tended to all practical tasks and made the great works possible. He may have played a few harmless little jokes on the philosopher. But he is also the man who introduced the regimented discipline into the master's mornings, a discipline the philosopher needed but could not achieve on his own.

Martin Lampe. Ah! What a repository of secret stories he must have about how the philosopher worked! How deep must be his knowledge about the master's struggle to uncover the truth of human existence in the universe! How great this man's learning must be after forty years in the presence of the world's greatest philosophical mind, where ideas like diamonds, like nuggets of gold and silver, were brought up from the darkness within and displayed in the glorious light of reason and imagination!

When the philosopher felt the strain of age, Martin Lampe cajoled and chortled and even played the fool if necessary to prod the master toward higher levels of thought. Stand aside and let this man pass by!

Martin Lampe? Martin Lampe? Let us now praise Martin Lampe! Let us bring his life to the stage of memory! How fortunate that Königsberg has the bottomless well of Lampe's memory to plumb, uncovering the true history of Immanuel Kant! Let us visit Lampe!

Indeed, let us sit at his feet and absorb his insight into the mind and work of Königsberg's difficult philosopher! Was he not in a novel by Hippel? Was he not portrayed on Königsberg's theatrical stage? Let us, then, write another novel and another play! Or two! Or three! Let him be dressed in fine new clothes and invited as our special guest into the lecture hall where new students are first meeting the daunting trial and wonder of philosophy! Fresh students who can never hear the voice of Kant can still be gifted with a glimpse of the philosopher through his singular pupil!

Yes, yes, and a thousand times, yes!

Martin Lampe's forty years of work could be transformed from the shame of exile to a fitting conclusion for a life. Even if he died before finishing the last great work that he and the master were writing, Martin Lampe might yet be freed to enjoy his last days, and to die with honor!

But it could only begin with an invitation. Otherwise, it was shame upon shame. It could only begin with a legitimate annulment of exile. Without this, his redemption would devolve into begging and end in disgrace, poverty, and a sorry death indeed.

So much memory should not be lodged in the brain of an old man soon to die. The weight of memory was too much. The untapped power of *the principle of the poetic a priori* panicked the withering flesh of his brain. His room was a dungeon. He wanted to howl a song to save the subtle aura of his soul, but he had no one at hand who might hear.

Oh, for a woman, even a virgin, suffused with the serous and globular parts of blood heated by an uncritical fever, just to keep an old man's body warm and his soul unafraid. Anything but the *aurea medoritas.* A happy medium can be no comfort to a dying man with much left to do. He needed a new form of excess.

Day Ten

The Ideal of a Woman

When four o'clock in the morning arrived on the tenth day, Lampe didn't notice. He had already been up for an hour writing the Dunce a letter to remind him about the invitation from Wasianski, on which everything depended.

So far, he had only written, "Dear Johannes …"

Lampe put the quill into his empty wine glass and stared at the words.

Should he begin by asking him to bring news? Maybe. Should he ask for another fascicle? Not yet. The coward might lose nerve and take back the one fascicle Lampe had, leaving him with nothing. Less than nothing. Just a desk, ink, paper, and a quill.

He tried underlining. "Dear Johannes …" It didn't help.

He tore up the page and pulled out a new piece of paper. The waste would have infuriated the master, but this task demanded perfection.

He again wrote, "Dear Johannes," but no new words came. He probably needed a break from the strain of composition.

He pulled the fascicle to the center of the desk. Kant's friends believed that his mind had begun to regress toward childishness. But to Lampe, the master's mind had at last relinquished its rigidity and become more malleable, as long as suggestions that came from outside were offered with deference and humility. This allowed Lampe to redirect the great ship of Kant's philosophy.

Sometimes Kant became distracted and began writing lists of lunch guests or long, ridiculous paragraphs on a priori matter. When Lampe witnessed such diversions, he would write a phrase or two on a scrap of paper in Kant's handwriting. "If God is, he is only one," for example, or something similar. He never asserted concepts, such as the idea that God actually exists. Kant would have to discover that on his own. He only wrote hypotheticals—*if* God exists—and then watched what followed.

And why was that? Because Lampe craved definitive proofs. No one in the universe had a better chance of finding the proof of proofs than Immanuel Kant. As fabulous as Lampe's own tutored mind was, he served the world best by coaxing the mind of the singular professor.

He had seen many of the notes for the final work, but he had never seen the last draft of any portion of the manuscript. Lampe's principle of the poetic a priori had emerged under the gaze and force of divine providence. But for many years it had been bound in a cocoon. Kant's final manuscript was ordained as a portal through which the principle might struggle forth, stretching its wet and sticky wings. For Lampe, the fascicle held the sweet notes of a philosophical gavotte.

He pulled the beeswax candle close, and he ran his fingertips along the top margin of the first sheet. Then he read the words written in the familiar script: *Transition to the limit of all knowledge—God and the World.*

His eyes suddenly sprouted tears, and he let out a cry of sorrow. He released all control and said into the air, "My master, oh my master! My master, my life! I am afraid in the marrow of my bones! Haunt me!"

Ding sang out a long howl, provoking the neighborhood dogs. The universe became barking dogs in the street, countless stars in a dark sky, and the feeling of a tingling force at the window, a flying beast perhaps, or a spirit, or a witch.

He rubbed his dripping nose on his sleeve and touched the first few lines of the text. What brilliant avoidance of reality the nearly illegible scrawl contained.

In the order of the system of synthetic knowledge through a priori concepts (that is, in transcendental philosophy) ...

Forty years of Kant's philosophy had shaped Lampe's mind so that this horrid language, so resistant to the warm heart of the bleating, bleeding world, enlivened his soul to the point of ecstasy.

The principle which provides the transition to the completion of the system is that of transcendental theology in two questions: 1) What is God? 2) Is there a God?

In the margin Kant had scribbled a note expressing his confidence that if there is a God, there can only be one. Where did such presumption originate? From the slip of paper on which Lampe had scribbled the idea, obviously. The world should be grateful. God should be grateful. Suddenly, Lampe felt a rush of indignation. After everything he had given to the master, Kant had chosen to inflict the extreme punishment of exile on him.

According to the Dunce, Kant would only give a one-sentence explanation: "Lampe has so offended me that I'm ashamed to say how."

"Shame?" Lampe could not hold back his weeping. "What did the master know of shame?"

Lampe looked at the crusted blood on Ding's tumor and took up his jug of wine. He drank deeply and drank again.

When Green became so ill that he was no longer able to visit, Kant began to seem lost after sunset. But he never visited his friend. He said he wanted to wait until the illness was gone.

Lampe found Green's dead body on a routine visit to deliver Kant's good wishes, assuaging the coward's conscience. When he returned home, he cried, "Herr Green is dead!"

Kant tipped back his head. He breathed in deeply through his nose until his small lungs were full. Then he breathed out with no words, no comments about the news. He didn't allow a single tear to escape his eyes. But soon after, Lampe felt a nebulous, unbounded emptiness open up in the house. Into that void, Kraus haplessly wandered ever further.

The transformation of the young scholar with whom Kant strolled and dined was like the spider's venomous transformation of the web-trapped butterfly. The young man's devotion needed to be consolidated. His wings were still beating too vigorously on their own. The change didn't come from within Kraus. It was the product of Kant's own mind, injected into Kraus.

One evening, Kant was sitting in front of the fire, leaning forward on his walking stick to reduce his heartburn. He had invited Kraus to dinner, but Kraus had a previous dinner engagement. Kant insisted that he come later and have cordials and dessert. The weary but devoted Kraus conceded to the plan.

While they waited for Kraus, Kant grew impatient, and he lashed out with a demand that Lampe polish the spoons again.

"I've already polished them."

"They must be spotless. No one likes spots on their spoons."

"They're spotless," Lampe said. "The silver will come off if I keep rubbing them."

"They're pure silver," Kant replied.

"Then I'll rub them to nothing," Lampe said. "Pure nothing."

"Is dessert ready?" Kant asked.

"It's been ready since the afternoon."

Kant paced, glancing repeatedly at the clock on the mantle. "Where is Kraus?"

"Caring for his own business, no doubt. You only asked him over at the last moment. I'm sure he doesn't keep his schedule clear in case you wish him to come over."

"Bah! This is an important day."

"Why?" Lampe asked.

"None of your concern. Polish the spoons."

The gulf created by Green's death had to be filled quickly. Because of Green, Kant had become possessed by time, day by day, hour by hour, pulling all the world into order by an act of will that occupied the space between a tick and a tock. But something more was agitating him as he waited for Kraus.

When Kraus finally arrived, Kant didn't castigate him for

being late. Instead, he welcomed the young man. "Come, Jakob, come."

"Thank you, Immanuel. It's good to see you."

"Come, come, sit in my chair!"

Kraus took off his coat and submitted to sitting in the professor's favorite chair.

"Thank you," Kraus said. "It's good to see you."

"You said that already." The old man was nearly prancing around Kraus as he barked, "Lampe! Dessert! Bring our favorite port! Hurry now!"

Lampe hurried as ordered, but only because he didn't want to miss anything. As far as he could see, two things bound the men together. The first was hypochondriacal attention to the body's habits. Kant had finally found someone who seemed genuinely interested in the challenges of his intestinal life. Lampe could write an entire treatise comparing the bowels of Kant and Kraus. The second thing was their complete conversion to Kant's critical system of philosophy. The master craved a trustworthy, young defender, a supple recipient of his penetrating will to whom he might safely bequeath his madness.

But it was folly to think that in a matter of months, some young scholar such as Kraus could grasp the details of the magisterial system Kant produced in his second birth, his palingenesis. Decades were needed just to understand the artifacts that appeared in the form of books. But the reality toward which the artifacts pointed, and the mind-fount from which they came, located in the constipated, wheezing crevice of a man named Immanuel Kant, required something more than time for anyone who wished to understand them. It required a miracle.

In his better moments, Lampe feared for Kraus' soul and well-being. Kant's hunger for a disciple who would carry on after his death was ravenous. Lampe had seen less robust minds break on the rocks of Kant's philosophy. But the unmourned death of Green and the growing clamor of conflicting news from around the world forced the old man to treat his books and ideas the way that others treated their children, protecting their progeny, anxiously awaiting the arrival of grandchildren who would guarantee the survival of the family.

The night Kraus came for dessert, the cook—a strange woman who rarely spoke, who preferred to be alone, and who never greeted Lampe—had left a beautiful bread pudding in the kitchen before going home. Lampe dipped up the pudding and poured the sticky cream sauce over it. When he took the plates into the parlor, he saw Kant's hand on Kraus' knee. Kraus was pink with discomfort, but Kant seemed oblivious, or at least unconcerned.

"Bread pudding!" Lampe announced, loudly.

"Thank God," Kraus said.

When Lampe handed a plate to Kant, he put it on the table without taking a bite and said to Kraus, "I have some news."

Kraus looked at Kant and drained his glass of port. Kant flicked his fingers toward the glass as though Lampe was not already about to fill it again.

"Now is the time!" Kant said.

A stranger might not have noticed that Kant was nervous, but to Lampe it was obvious. Kraus glanced at Lampe with a questioning look on his face. Lampe shrugged.

"Now is the time!" Kant said again.

"Yes?" Kraus finally said. He sat with his bread pudding balanced on his knees, his port glass in one hand, a spoon in the other.

"Yes!" Kant answered. The master walked over to his desk, pulled a small box out of the drawer, and stuffed it in his pocket. "Tonight, you get your wish!"

Kraus' strained grimace was a command for Lampe to continue refilling his glass with port, bolstering him for whatever was coming next.

"You've been my dearest and most trustworthy friend, Jakob."

Kraus looked as confused as Lampe.

"We have shared ideas," Kant continued, pressing his fingertips together, forging ahead as though constructing an argument. "We have conversed and mingled our minds. You alone truly understand my work."

Kraus saw Lampe roll his eyes, but Kant was focused on his own hands. His thumbs and index fingers formed a triangle into which he stared. "You respond to the criticisms of others as I would. It's as though my own thoughts flow from your quill."

"You're a good teacher," Kraus said with the dull tone of one who has been complimented in a way that feels like an insult since he was becoming known as a fine scholar on his own.

Kant waved away the comment. His hand landed bird-like in his pocket and then emerged with the small box. He held the box in front of Kraus for a moment before opening it to reveal a diamond ring. "This is a *pretium affectionis*, meant to show you how my heart is forged to yours. Take it!"

With no table nearby, Kraus had to negotiate the plate of

bread pudding on his lap, the spoon, the napkin, and the half-full glass of port. He put his spoon on his plate and it fell to the floor, flicking pudding.

"Here, just hold out your finger," Kant said. "No, the index finger! There, good." Kant slipped on the ring. "Yes! A pretium affectionis. With this, we have entered into a union in which we shall live only for each other."

Kant grinned, satisfied with the exchange. Now that the relationship was sealed with a ring, he stuffed a spoonful of bread pudding into his mouth, ready for the next topic of conversation.

Lampe's face could not unrage itself in the glare of Kant's betrayal, shamelessly favoring Kraus.

Kraus stared at the ring. His hand trembled slightly.

Kant said, "Lampe, get Jakob a new spoon and wipe up the pudding."

Lampe did not.

Kraus said, "I can't find the words to say what I'm feeling."

Kant responded, "The less said the better. I've set up a shared bank account for us. The money will cover our common expenses. I'm so happy!"

To Lampe's jaundiced and angry eye, Kant didn't look quite so old as he sat basking in glory, assured and bolstered by the gratefulness he assumed Kraus felt.

Kraus cleared his throat of pudding. "You honor me beyond what I deserve." Then he tried to add conviction to his tone. "Well, yes, then. I will accept this ring of friendship."

"Of course you will! Lampe, more port!" Kant turned his hungry and mortal eyes onto the flaccid paleness of young Kraus' face. "In this union, we live only for each other."

Kraus filled his mouth with bread pudding, stuffing in more than he could comfortably chew, staring at the fire as Kant, scarcely able to contain his grin, sipped his port and glanced over at the diamond ring on Kraus' hand.

Lampe could have warned Kraus that the master's phrase, *We live only for each other,* meant they would both live for Kant. But the time wasn't right. So he observed, patiently and quietly, as Kraus endured the busy work of writing metaphysical reviews and responses to confused criticism, and the phrases and ideas Kant threaded into the quilt of Kraus' thought, testing the similarity of their responses to the world's misunderstandings.

Occasionally Lampe felt sorry for Kraus as he miserably jotted down absurdities like Kant's new idea that the ultimate goal of the human race is to establish a perfect constitution. Kraus had to mute his own voice and replace it with Kant's. Complete conversion required a catechism. The catechism filled the day, as though Kraus were a schoolboy, rather than a respected member of the university faculty.

For a while, he carried out every detail of Kant's bidding. But in time, as tensions grew between the two men, Lampe had to act. He had to find a way to recover the quiet intimacy that flourished when he and the professor worked alone. The old cook didn't count, of course. She existed only to produce puddings, breads, and meats for them.

The opportunity to get rid of Kraus came when another of Kant's prior students, Johann Herder, began to criticize the system. Herder had become famous, and though Kant stung under the critique, he was too busy to allow the criticism to distract him. So he demanded that Kraus step up and do the work.

But when Kraus read through Herder's criticism, his response was, "What a wonderful mind he has! Have you read his arguments? They're beautiful."

"Nonsense," Kant said. "His thought is confused. He covers it up with poetry and metaphor. I can hardly believe he was ever my student. I'll write the response myself if you aren't up to the task."

Kant became increasingly short-tempered after this. If they were having dinner with guests and Kraus said, "The king shouldn't insist on pietism while he runs a brothel in his palace," Kant would interrupt with, "Do you know the king personally? Have you spent even a single night in the palace? No?"

Kraus would answer only with a red face and silence for the remainder of the meal. Then Kant would continue discussing politics, directing questions and comments toward everyone except the dejected Kraus.

Lampe wondered how long a man like Kraus could endure. Would he break and become Kant's servile double, or would he stiffen his spine and end the relationship?

One evening the cook made a marvelous piece of beef. Despite her sullen and distant melancholy, she could cook a muscle like no one else. Kraus had a nearly beatific look on his face as he took a bite and said, "This beef is so excellent that its flavors could only be diminished by a topping."

There were nods all around the table until Kant blurted out, "Nonsense, Kraus. There is no meat too excellent for a dollop of good English mustard sauce." And he spooned more mustard sauce than usual onto his piece of beef.

Kant might as well have insulted the memory of Kraus' dead mother. Kraus threw his napkin onto his plate, half-covered with uneaten food, stood up, and weakly yelled, "Next you will say that I can't distinguish wine from water, or potatoes from, from, well, from a clump of leaves." He seemed suddenly embarrassed by his lack of a potent comparison, and he stomped out of the room without another word.

Unfortunately, in his fluster, he stomped into an adjacent room with no exit while Kant grinned at the guests, calling out, "Leaves? Leaves? As a matter of fact, Kraus, I think your intellectual gifts are exactly suited for the task of distinguishing potatoes from a clump of leaves."

Kraus had to return to the dining room to get to the door, and he looked at the floor as he passed through the room without a word.

Kant called out, "Ha! Kraus, come back to the table. Or don't, if you're having a fit!" He turned to his guests and said, "He's a good young man, but he's moody sometimes." And he shook his head, embarrassed at his assistant's poor manners. It was a minor problem that he would correct later, as he might correct a child in private.

When Lampe handed Kraus his coat, he knew that the so-called union was over. Before Kraus stepped out of the house, he took off his diamond ring and handed it to Lampe. He offered no explanation. Lampe didn't require one. Kraus was clearly trying to save his own soul.

—⁓—

The next morning Lampe had to cajole more than usual to get the master out of his bed.

Once Kant was propped up in his chair, smoking his pipe, and warming himself beside the fire, Lampe took the diamond ring from his pocket and gently placed it on the table.

Kant said nothing until Lampe was about to open the curtains. "Leave them closed." He picked up the ring. "Where did you get this? Did Kraus leave it by mistake?"

Lampe said, "He handed it to me as he left."

Kant puffed on his pipe and picked wax out of his ear. He shifted in his seat, first one way, and then the other. "Did he say why he handed it to you?"

"Did he need to?" Lampe asked.

"What do you mean by that?"

Lampe turned back toward the professor and glared. "You humiliate him every time you're with him."

Kant folded in his shoulders and retreated into his chair. "You exaggerate."

Lampe said, "Kraus doesn't even have a flask of vodka to help him bear your grating criticism."

"I'm correcting him." Kant said in a louder voice, and his shoulders unfolded a bit. "Everything is at stake. I intend to bequeath my work and legacy to Kraus. A successor must be groomed. Do you hear me?" He leaned forward and pointed his pipe. "Do you hear me?"

Lampe grumbled, "The price is too high for him."

Kant settled back in his chair. "What would you know about that?"

"If you only knew…" Lampe started, but Kant raised his hand for silence. Lampe left the room without another word, but he looked back at the little professor who had picked up the diamond ring. The light from the fire was too dim to see his expression beneath the shadows that covered his face.

Kant stayed in his room until close to noon. When he finally came out, he was whistling and cheerful. "Lampe!" he said. "You must go to Kraus' house and invite him for dinner. Just him and me. Here's the ring to give to him. On your way, purchase a fine rose. You must tell him that I need his help. I'm an old man, and I'm frail. Tell him everything is his, my whole world. Tell him we must not allow small arguments to interrupt my ... No, our ... No! Tell him we must not allow small arguments to interrupt *his* great work!"

Lampe took the ring. "And when he says he *doesn't* want you to be his life's work?"

"Lampe, just go and do as I say. He won't refuse. How many people have such work bequeathed to them? None! Because there is no other work like this!"

Lampe took the diamond ring and bought the rose. On the way to Kraus' home, he noticed more dogs in the streets and a surprising number of cats climbing along the fences. The gutters by the streets seemed fouler with no rain to wash them clean. The air carried the smell of roasting meats, mingled with the smell of raw blood and newly harvested hides hanging but not yet dry. As he walked, he began to feel nauseated. Perhaps he was becoming ill.

An old woman stared at him from her potato cart as he approached. She had a small fire in a pot over which she warmed her hands. She said, "You look like the devil has your spleen."

Lampe looked up at her. "What did you say?"

She cut a piece of raw onion and lifted it to her lips. "You look like the devil has your spleen."

"What does that mean?"

The old woman grinned, and Lampe handed her the rose. She said, "I'll pray for you," and then she laughed.

Lampe continued to Kraus' house and knocked. When Kraus didn't answer the door, he knocked again.

Kraus answered mid-knock.

"Lampe," Kraus said with an easily discernable lack of luster. His face never had very malleable features, but now it was locked in a tolerably persuasive expression of frustration mingled with fear.

"Herr Kraus." Lampe bowed.

Kraus looked tired. "What do you want?"

"The professor sent me."

"Did he?" Kraus' hands were trembling just slightly.

"He wanted to know if you've finished that review of Herr Herder's book. He said it's overdue."

"The review?" Kraus said, his face turning first a ghostly pale color, and then dawning with the deepening pink of feeble disbelief.

"Yes sir," Lampe answered, clicking his heels together. "The review. Of the book. By Herr Herder."

"The review?" Kraus asked again, buttoning his jacket as though he was trying to keep the last fragment of his dignity from escaping.

"That's right, sir. He said something about giving you a second chance, but he seemed disappointed that the review isn't finished yet. It sounds rather important."

"Wait here." Kraus closed the door and went inside. Soon he returned with a small manuscript. "Here. This is what I have.

It's not my best work, but it's fair. If he wants revisions, he can tell me."

Lampe looked at the manuscript, surprised at the depth of Kraus' generosity toward a man who showed him so little respect. "I'm sure this will be fine, sir. Thank you."

They stood looking at the manuscript in Lampe's hands. Then Kraus said, "Was there anything else?"

"No sir. Is there anything I should pass on to the professor?"

Kraus again reddened. "Please pass on my regrets for my atrocious behavior last night."

"It was not atrocious, sir."

"Ah, but it was," Kraus said. "It was humiliating to everyone."

"If you ask me, sir, the professor was the one who was humiliating."

Kraus stiffened his back, which placed his height at roughly Lampe's own. "Is it appropriate for you to say such things about your employer?"

Lampe's heart untangled from any sense of residual worry over Kraus' fate. He bowed again. "You're right, sir. I misspoke."

Kraus nodded and closed the door.

On the way back to Kant's house, Lampe thought about the weight of a single moment in which anything could happen. He approached the old woman selling her potatoes. This time she said nothing. He walked up to the pot of fire, dropped the manuscript into the flame, and said, "A little more fuel to warm your hands."

"I'd wager that it warmed you even more than me." She grinned and Lampe noticed the color of her eyes, one blue, one green.

Before Lampe could take off his coat, Kant came into the hall and said, "Well?"

Lampe took the diamond ring from his pocket and held it out in the palm of his hand. Kant stared. He took the ring from Lampe's palm and chewed on his pipe as his eyes moistened and reddened. "What do we do now?"

Lampe rarely saw the professor at a loss for what to do. He offered a modest solution, the only solution. "I know what you need."

Kant walked back into the parlor to collect himself.

Lampe followed him and said, "Kraus has his own life."

"Apparently." Kant sat down and resumed chewing on his empty pipe.

"All young men have lives that distract them."

"What's your point?"

The moment had arrived for Lampe to offer himself as more than the servant, the bringer of port, and the shiner of spoons. He breathed in deeply and said, "You need someone who has observed the growth of your entire philosophy and who is utterly devoted to you."

Kant looked at the ring. "That's obvious."

"All the men around you have their own books to write. Their minds are clogged up with their own ideas."

Kant looked up, his eyes now dry. "You've paid more attention than I gave you credit for, Lampe."

"Yes sir." Lampe's voice choked with emotion, with possibility.

Kant thought for a moment. Then he straightened his frail spine and gripped his pipe between his teeth with a look well known to Lampe. It was the look of ideas dawning and breaking through. "Kraus had great promise, but he was weak. I need someone who is steady. Someone with humility who does not always need to put themselves forward."

"Yes!" Lampe said. "Someone who can resist the devil!"

"I need a man who can see the value of the work," Kant said, not responding to Lampe's comment about the devil. "I need an intellectual soldier who can defend the work, the truth."

"Yes!" Lampe was giddy with the inner knowledge that he alone fit the description. "You need a soldier who will go to battle for you with no thought besides defending the work!"

Here at last was something worthy of lifetime dedication. He would no longer need to drink to assuage his boredom. He would dress better. He would use his gift for languages bequeathed to him by his mother the whore, both to redeem her memory and to carry the gospel to everyone with ears to hear.

Kant stared at the floor, deep in his own thoughts. Finally, he looked up and said, "What's the name of that man? The one we met at that interminable wedding."

Was he ignoring Lampe?

Kant stood up and waved his hand in the air. "That man, that man. Oh, how my memory is becoming an unruly child."

"There were a lot of people at the wedding," Lampe responded as gloom descended upon him.

Frustrated with his memory lapse, Kant said, "You know the one. That deacon! He was at the university some years ago. Very interested in my work. Not terribly bright, but quite capable as a scribe. I'd wager that he's also quite capable of devotion and loyalty."

"I don't remember," Lampe lied.

"Wasianski!" Kant said, his face bursting into a beam of victory. "That's it. Andreas Wasianski. He was annoying at first, but I'm sure he's matured with time. Perhaps he'll be at the countess's dinner tonight." Kant stuffed his pipe into his pocket and rubbed his thin hands together. "What do you think?"

Lampe choked out a whisper. "Do you really want to know?"

Kant didn't answer. He pulled out his pipe again and granted himself a rare second bowl of tobacco, grinning his oblivious grin.

With this, at long last, Lampe began to truly despise Kant. He walked out of the room, went to the attic, and drank the last of the vodka in his flask to fuel the fire of his hatred for the stranger, Wasianski. He felt the wretchedness of an abandoned bride as he imagined Kant luring Wasianski into the inner circle they had shared for so many decades. But his furious grief consolidated into clarity, and he saw that refusing to go to the countess' house with Kant would only make it easier for Wasianski to wedge himself in.

That evening, Lampe stood by the front door, offering no help as Kant struggled with his overcoat. But the little professor was nearly giddy as he spoke about the countess. "Her ability to bring people together is miraculous. She's the ideal of a woman."

"She's rich," Lampe said. "There's nothing miraculous about giving people free food and wine."

Kant buttoned up his coat, oblivious to Lampe's smirk. "You're wrong Lampe. I've never met anyone like her."

The countess's intimate inaccessibility was intensified when she would take Kant's arm, nuzzling it as she introduced him to foreign visitors. He couldn't see that he was making love to the countess. Concept and conception mingled in his heart. They were hidden from his mind but felt vaguely in his viscera. This gave him a pleasurable disturbance in his ghostly sense of transient living forces. He was "the philosopher," and he was glad for the standing invitation to her palace.

———

"Immanuel!" the countess said. She walked over to him with a warm familiarity while Lampe straightened Kant's crooked wig in the ornate mirror hanging in the entryway.

"Cleo," he beamed. He had chosen this nickname to demonstrate his small sense of flirtatious daring. "I wish Javotte were here to see how lovely you look."

She held his arm and leaned toward him so that he blushed with pleasure, and she pointed to a group of men. "If Javotte were here, he would quickly control the conversation in that corner before if got out of hand. Hippel is driving the guests into a frenzy over the question of whether the Russians are friends or enemies."

"And what do you think, Cleo?"

"After Javotte's experiences as a diplomat in Germany, Austria, Poland, and Russia, I think he would say the Austrians are the enemies, not the Russians."

"I agree." Kant handed Lampe his cane. He tugged at the lapels of his coat and thrust his jaw forward in an exaggerated way that made the countess smile. "Tonight, I shall defend Russia in honor of Javotte. And you." He concluded with a bow.

"Immanuel," Hippel called out across the room. "Come, we are discussing the king's pietism," which meant they were actually gossiping about his sex scandals and the Rosicrucian advisors who stayed in his favor by looking the other way.

"I thought you were discussing the Russians," Kant said as he walked toward Hippel and the small crowd gathered around him. He didn't notice Wasianski snaking his way closer under the glare of Lampe's resentful gaze.

When Kant saw him, he said, "Wasianski! I was hoping you'd be here. Do you know Mayor Theodor von Hippel?" Then he hooked arms with Wasianski as though they were the best of friends.

With a borrowed bottle of wine under his coat, Lampe left the banquet hall to skulk around the mossy stones at the base of the palace while Wasianski wormed his way into the vacuum left by Green's departure and by the failing of Kraus' nerve. His place in the master's work was fading even as his thought was carried by ganza birds past the dark horizons of the earth. He leaned against the cold moss, watching the movement of clouds in the moonlight.

He stayed outside with his thoughts until Kant's voice broke through the darkness. "Lampe! Lampe! Where are you?"

He quickly finished the last of the wine and dropped the bottle to the ground. Then he stepped out from the bushes that concealed him.

Wasianski stood next to the countess, waving goodbye to his new comrade.

Kant waved back as he and Lampe climbed into the carriage that was waiting for them. Kant looked up and said, "How I love the starry sky." He was in a good mood, which was a terrible sign. "Deacon Wasianski is an excellent man. Not brilliant, but definitely reliable."

Lampe said nothing as loudly as he could.

The memory of that night was painful. Lampe rolled over in his bed and once again reviewed the history that positioned Wasianski as the leader of the vigil for the dead genius.

Lampe had come so close to achieving fulfillment of his true purpose. But he learned how much small things matter. Kant's old neighbor had refused to believe that a cockcrow could interrupt a great thinker's work, and his friends balked at the idea that constipation could prevent the revelation of the secrets of the universe. But Lampe knew, with agonizing clarity, that the entire work of a lifetime could be undone by something as insignificant as a single shit in a pot.

Day Eleven

On Enthusiasm and the Means Against It

LAMPE NO LONGER RESISTED when his mind forced him to wake up at four o'clock in the morning. His voice was husky with phlegm as he whispered, "Are you here? What do you want?"

Waiting for an answer in the silence frightened him. The quiet and the solitude were thick with Kant's spirit. Ding was at the foot of the bed under the covers, and she crawled up toward the head of the bed. Lampe reached down and scratched her back and head, careful not to bother her tumor.

He stood up from his mattress, sore in the cold of the morning, and he sat at his desk with his blanket wrapped around him. The only warmth was whatever seeped from the rooms below. He lit his candle and opened the fascicle, that graveyard where Kant had buried the bones of things-in-themselves. There was no other way the master could speak to him now.

What is a God? he read. *Is there a God?*

Again and again, the same questions.

He forced himself to read on. Soon he came to a passage that Kant had scratched out:

~~To bring about the highest object of moral practical reason in the world—God and the world form the objects of reason's willing. The totality of things: ens summum summa.~~

Why did he scratch out the passage? The answer was obvious to Lampe. The mind can't will God and the world into existence out of nothing. Reality expresses the divine imagination, and it can only be explored through a divinely touched imagination. If a shrunken version of reason is given priority over the imagination, everything shrivels into the twigs and matchsticks of logical form, rather than being voluptuously clothed in reality.

"What did you discover about God and the world?" Lampe said to the spirit of Kant, to the universe, and, incidentally, to Ding. "Show me!"

Kant's deep voice gained clarity and volume in Lampe's mind as he read on.

Self-love (in soul and body) is not generally true or permissible; but benevolence toward oneself, without pleasure, is.

"That right there, old man, is the problem!" Lampe said to the air.

In between philosophical jabs, the master had scribbled a list of dinner guests. *Herr Schultz or Pörschke and Chaplain. Herr von Hess and Prof. Kraus.*

Kraus? So, good old Kraus made it back to the table? Was Lampe the only man in the world with whom Kant couldn't reconcile?

Herr von Hess und Prof. Kraus.

Everyone gathered in his imagination to keep vigil, sharing wine, smoking pipes, sitting before the fire in the reverie that settles on people when a great death rends the veil.

He forced himself to read past the list of dinner guests.

The problem is thus: First, what is God? Second question: Is there a God?

The same questions. Again and again. What was tormenting the old man?

There exists a categorical imperative in the mind (mens, not anima) of every man in which a rigorous command of duty shows the transgressor his own reprehensibility (unworthiness of being happy).

Why was he so unhappy? Why did he see himself as reprehensible?

If abstraction is made from sensible appearance, not only is the transgressor's worthiness of being happy denied him, but he himself is condemned through an irrevocable verdict (dictamen rationis).

Lampe's hands began to tremble. Maybe Kant was not talking about his own reprehensibility. Perhaps he was talking about Lampe's. Lampe was the one condemned through an irrevocable verdict. Was this a letter from Kant to Lampe? A message? Obviously! What else could it be? The Dunce said that Kant wrote reminders to himself never to mention Lampe's name. Lampe must have occupied Kant's mind while he worked on the final part of the final and greatest book. But the message was not one of redemption. It was condemnation without hope. Dictamen rationis. His condemnation was a dictate of reason. In Kant's world, there was no defense against that.

He began reading out loud with a voice full of gravel.

Nature deals despotically with man. Men destroy one another like wolves. Plants and animals overgrow and stifle one another.

Nature does not observe the care and provision which they require. Wars destroy what long artifice has established and cared for.

He stood and paced. Ding watched him, wary but present.

"Men destroy one another like wolves? Old man! What are you saying?"

Among all the characteristics that are attributable to a thinking being, the first is to be conscious of oneself as a person. I am a person; consequently, a moral being who has rights.

"Ding!" Lampe cried. "The master is saying that I am a person with rights. But he has also said I am irrevocably condemned and unworthy of happiness. I hate him!"

No one else who read the manuscript would know that a message was buried in these repetitive concepts. Each repeated *dictamen rationis* was borrowed from Kant's past ideas and thrust into the fire to temper the iron. His words labored under the strain of *the poetic a priori,* rattling the cage, trying to break the bars of Kant's architectonic.

"Enough! I must get closer!"

The impulse to see Kant's body, right then, rose from he knew not where, but Lampe put his coat over his nightgown, pulled on his boots, and left the house. Only a few people were out in the cold dawn as he walked toward the bridge. When he reached the middle of the bridge, he ran his hand along the old, solid banisters. He leaned over the edge, looking down at the bridge's supporting columns thrust into the earth beneath the cold river that flowed from the dark heart of Russia to the darker leviathan-filled waters of the Baltic Sea.

He was invigorated. He had been isolated for two years with

nothing more than a quick scuttle to the nearby market to buy food, wine, and, as he could afford it, coal for his stove. The feeling of life arose in him even as the gray clouds thickened overhead. He walked past the gate where, in Kant's youth, the dead man's body had been tossed to be eaten by the birds. A visceral chill tensed his gut at the thought that some part of the dead official might even be inside him, everything intermingled in plants and animals, unbearably close.

He meandered toward the castle as though he was just taking a stroll for his health and happiness. But when he turned the corner and saw the small road leading to the house of pain where the dead body of the master was exposed to the eyes of everyone in Königsberg, the red whip of his heart lashed his chest wall, warning him of his folly.

Pebbles, whitewashed fences, and the plastered walls of houses and pubs formed a corridor leading to the forbidden place of vigil. These were not mere objects. They were the dwelling places of his imagination. A breeze carried the smells of early-rising pub masters cooking the pork and the burnt butter for the brown sauces that hungry men going to work would later pour over potatoes to give them strength. These smells would undo him if he didn't retreat, or else go forward to claim his rightful place at the dead man's side.

His path was clear, the only path for a devoted soldier. He had to demand the manuscript that should have been his inheritance. He had to declare that no exile, no rupture, no indiscretion, and no misunderstanding could possibly be so terrible that condemnation snuffed out the final illumination of the system. He had to go forward.

Or he could retreat.

"Walk forward Martin Lampe," he whispered to himself. He went to the corner of the pub and leaned against the wall while his breathing slowed. Then he peeked around the corner and beheld the doorway for the first time in two years. His body ached with tension as he shuffled closer. The house was a stone's throw away. He crouched and trembled. His legs grew stiff.

There was already a line of people at the front door. Suddenly, the door opened and Wasianski appeared, an angel of doom. He filled his pipe and lit it with slow leisure, as though the people waiting in the cold were not there. Then he gave instructions to the first few people in line, and he stepped back inside, allowing the visitors to enter.

"Who are these people?" Lampe wondered. He had only been secluded for two years, and yet besides one or two vaguely familiar merchants from the market, he recognized none of them.

A firm hand grabbed his shoulder. "What are you doing here old man?"

Lampe turned, "Kaufman! My heart nearly stopped."

"So you decided to approach Wasianski?"

Lampe suddenly felt small, exposed, with none of the confident disdain he had when the Dunce visited him. He shook his head. "No! Too risky. I already know the answer, and the result would be unbearable poverty. Please keep this to yourself."

"Have you finished reading that thing I brought to you? Wasianski hasn't noticed yet, but I hate to think what he'll say if he finds out that I let you borrow part of an original manuscript."

"Has he read it?" Lampe asked.

The Dunce said, "He thumbed through part of it. He's more interested in writing the biography than in deciphering the old man's senile drivel. But I need the package back soon because he plans to show it to a couple of people after the professor is buried."

"Give me one more day." Lampe swallowed hard and let the comment about drivel pass. Then he added, "Please."

The young Dunce's face registered a brief, haughty flash of deliberation over Lampe's fate. "I'll come get it tomorrow. But you might want to run on back to your room before Wasianski sees you."

"You're probably right." After a brief pause, Lampe asked, "Those job opportunities—have you made any progress?"

"There's more opportunity now than ever. I'm not worried." Kaufman patted Lampe on the back and walked away whistling a discordant tune.

—∿∿—

When Lampe was back in his room and sitting at his desk, he began to despise himself for his cowardice. The servant of a genius would be a prize for any biographer, unless that servant was Lampe, unjustly labeled a sot, accused of treachery, and charged with thievery and the keeping of sordid secrets. What good was his vast trove of memory when his mind was contained in the rotting old body of a coward hiding in an attic?

At least he had once been a soldier on battle. When had Kant ever shown real courage? Oh yes, the master may have occupied himself with the stars, the place of God, and the workings of kings, but it was always from the safety of his writing desk or the dining table. And his knowledge of the world outside Königsberg came from others who ventured past the city boundary, and whom Kant invited to dinner only to hear their updates.

"News!" he would bellow when the guests were all seated.

The guests rarely offered more than gossip. But one evening, a businessman who had just returned home said, "I heard that a French jail stocked with thirty thousand pounds of gunpowder was stormed. There is now open rebellion against the king of France."

Kant's eyes glistened and he was immediately enthralled. His understanding of the significance of the event was uncanny, and he had to calm himself before speaking. "Friends, the light of reason and liberty will stand against the darkness of despotism and deceit. The French are scrounging for food. They are in debt from funding the American Revolution. Millions of farmers are watching their children starve while the nobility and the religious elite stuff themselves. This is the moment we've been waiting for. This revolution marks the season when ideas and theories will finally bleed when cut."

His guests politely agreed. But to Lampe, they seemed more embarrassed than impressed with Kant's grand pronouncements. They apparently thought it was just another rebellion of dissatisfied commoners.

That evening, when the master was safely lodged in his chair, he said to Lampe, "Do you know what this revolution means?"

"That a lot of people will be dead soon?"

Kant ignored the comment. "It means I can finally say something I've never been able to say before."

"And what's that?" Lampe asked.

Kant looked up as though he could see through the ceiling to the heavens that were drawing back like the waters of the Red Sea. "Now let your servant depart in peace, for I have seen the glory of the world."

Lampe liked this phrase at first. But it grew tiresome as Kant repeated it every time the topic of the revolution was mentioned. Day after day Kant would sit at the dinner table, newly animated, his mouth greasy with the food he sumptuously consumed, and he would expound on the revolution as though he was God's chosen prophet.

He began to speak about the revolution as the incarnation of his own ideas. He had never once lifted a finger to bring it about. He had never risked his life, his home, or his fortune. He had never even risked the chance of missing a meal. But in his view, the entire world was conforming to his thoughts. His mind had imposed itself upon the realms of metaphysics, morality, and beauty, and now he was convinced that it had imposed itself upon the very workings of history. He was competing with Providence from his armchair. Lampe would have dismissed Kant as a loon, the way some of his guests did. But the master had also discovered the retardation of the rotation of the earth from the same armchair, and his discovery won the Berlin Academy Prize. So, Lampe always returned to attentive, silent, patient waiting.

Events in France became the only topic Kant allowed at the dinner table. He was interested in any facts his guests had to offer, but he wanted to hear nothing of their political theorizing. He had already settled theoretical matters definitively.

Not every guest understood the rules. One evening a professor visiting from Hamburg said, "Professor Kant, I'm surprised by your enthusiasm for the French Revolution. I thought you opposed revolution."

At the word *enthusiasm*, Kant's forehead wrinkled, and his thin lips retreated into his mouth like the antennae of a snail. He looked down at his soup and stirred in a dollop of cream. He said, "I do oppose it," and began slurping his soup while his guests glanced at each other, wondering if the rumors of his diminishing intellectual powers were perhaps true.

Lampe knew the master was in full control, but Wasianski, the self-serving idiot, stoked the ignorant glances of the guests with a look of mocking sadness and embarrassment at the elderly man's performance. Lampe was furious.

A thick and balding guest who had accompanied the Hamburg visitor said, "Well, then how is it …"

"Tell me!" Kant interrupted, directing his question toward the professor from Hamburg and ignoring the bald guest. "Who decides the justness of the law?" There was an edge in his voice that sharpened whenever guests strayed from facts to theory at his dinner table.

"The lawmakers, I suppose."

"And when the law is made, the citizens have no right to disobey!" Kant wiped the soup from his mouth and nodded to Lampe, who removed the empty bowl. "None! The citizen's rights are defined by the law, and the law cannot be whole and, at the same time, open to legal disobedience."

"But surely we can question the justness of the law."

Kant picked at his teeth. "Obviously. Question all you want. Pick up your pen and go to work. But!" he said, suddenly raising his hand and nearly hitting the platter of sea bass that Lampe was trying to place on the table. "You may *not* lift your sword to make your point!"

"Marvelous!" Wasianski said. He saw Lampe roll his eyes, and he glared at him with a scolding expression, to which Lampe bowed slightly. Wasianski had no power in that house. Not yet.

"But you support the French Revolution?" one of the guests asked.

Kant's eyes brightened as he plunged his knife into the sea bass. He breathed in as deeply as his small, inadequate lungs would allow. "It's one of the greatest moments in history! Of course I support it!"

Wasianski laughed and offered a small clap, forcing another eye roll from Lampe. Lampe met Wasianski's pursed-lip glare with another slight bow.

The other guests seemed stunned that the old professor was so fully mired in such a contradiction and apparently unaware of it. The rumors about his failing powers sadly must be true.

"Gentlemen!" He met their looks with a firm gaze from his blue eyes. "Louis abdicated when he made the estates general. Don't you see?"

They did not.

Kant continued with a look of astonishment at their obtuseness. "The French Revolution was not a rebellion. The king himself opened the way. There is no contradiction!"

"Of course!" Wasianski said. "Outstanding!" He didn't look at Lampe, who had indeed rolled his eyes a third time.

Lampe muttered, "Good God, help us," at the same time

Kant bellowed, "Let's stretch our legs and go to the study for dessert. Lampe! Dessert! Port!"

Kant walked out. Wasianski passed by Lampe on his way to the study, but he wouldn't look him in the eyes.

No one besides Wasianski seemed convinced by Kant's argument, but Kant gave no ground. He had decided how the world was, and therefore it could be no other way.

—⁓—

As Wasianski moved closer to the center of Kant's world, he became more deliberate in his praise. He carefully avoided effusions that might be interpreted as unwelcome enthusiasm. He noticed the smallest detail of Kant's behavior, and he often jotted his observations in his notebook. But he had little comprehension of Kant's ideas, and he was able to wedge himself into the role of paternal caregiver only as Kant's mind slowed. This took time.

Kant's synoptic gospels had been written in the form of three critiques. The fourth gospel was underway. Minor epistles had been written first by Kraus, and then by others. But he needed major epistles, the strong voice of a prophet if his immortality was to be assured.

Unfortunately, the year the French Revolution began, Kant had a revolution in his health. He could keep up appearances for the duration of a meal with guests, but he was growing weaker. Wasianski saw the decline, and he began visiting more often and at strange times, interrupting the rhythm Lampe and Kant had established. If Kant invited Wasianski to dinner at two o'clock, he would arrive at one. He often brought some little gift with him, such as a special kind of writing paper, or a copy of an essay the professor wanted.

Wasianski had not yet infiltrated the inner-most circle, but he was testing for the secret door, pushing at bricks to discover the hidden chamber. He finally found it.

One day when Wasianski arrived early, Lampe opened the door and immediately felt that something was different. Wasianski didn't even feign courtesy to Martin Lampe, keeper of the house. He handed his coat to Lampe and gave only a one-word greeting, "Lampe." He walked past him without waiting to be led and entered the sitting room where Kant was taking his temperature.

"Immanuel! So good to see you."

Lampe hung the coat in the closet and then stood at the door of the parlor to listen.

Wasianski said, "Yes, Immanuel, I'm quite willing to help. These details cause you so much worry."

"What a great relief!" Kant said. "Keeping track of money is becoming a burden."

"Don't fret a moment more," Wasianski said as his fawning ingratiation dripped onto the freshly swept floor. "Now, may I ask a favor? I hope this isn't too much, but I wonder if I might have your permission to write a biography of you so that all future generations will know about the great genius, Immanuel Kant? I've thought about this, and I'm prepared to make it my life work."

"Oh, good God above," Lampe cried out from the hall.

Wasianski stood up and closed the door, leaving himself and Kant alone.

That did it. The offer of security and immortality was irresistible. Wasianski devoted himself to the professor. He swept into the position of intimate helper and carried out responsibilities that Kant had performed perfectly well his entire life.

Lampe seethed. This would further weaken the old man, but he had been outmaneuvered. He should have been elevated from servant-in-charge-of-the-chamber-pot to biographer and literary executor. He could write a whole book on the hardships of being a servant to genius. But biography was not his calling. His divinely appointed task was to ensure that the fourth gospel was completed, and nothing would stop him.

One day, when Wasianski's cloying presence was disrupting the equanimity of the house, Kant received a letter from a woman named Maria von Herbert of Klagenfurt. He held the letter up to Wasianski's nose so he could sniff its faint perfume. And then Kant said, "Listen to this. She wrote, 'As a believer calls to his God, I call to you for help, for comfort, or for counsel to prepare me for death.' Apparently, she has lost the love of a man because she revealed a drawn-out lie to him. What do you suppose the lie was?"

Kant's face molded itself into a look of concern fitting to a conversation about the moral life of a reprobate. The woman had expressed her devotion to Kant, and there was a demanding edginess to her letter that agitated him, or perhaps, given the redness in Kant's cheeks, excited him.

Wasianski also forced a look of serious attentiveness, bringing his professional insight as a deacon to bear on a problem of interest to Kant, which made it a problem of interest to Wasianski. "Read those last lines to me again, Immanuel."

Kant read the lines again.

Wasianski made his diagnosis. "I'm inclined to say that she's enthusiastic."

Kant, an enemy of enthusiasm in any form, nodded in agreement and read on. "She says, 'I have read the metaphysic of morals and the categorical imperative and it doesn't help a bit. My reason abandons me just when I need it. Answer me, I implore you, or you will not be acting in accordance with your own imperative.' You're the deacon, Andreas. How do you think I should respond?"

Wasianski's expression turned smug. "I would be inclined—working, of course, from your principles—to offer a moral sedative."

"A moral sedative." Kant licked his thin lips as he contemplated the turmoil of the young woman. "I like that phrase. She seems more concerned that she lost a man than that she told a lie."

"I think you've touched on the very heart of the matter," Wasianski said.

Lampe was putting away the clean dishes, and he muttered, "Rubbish. The girl is in despair."

"What was that?" Kant said. "I can't hear you while you're clinking the dishes."

Wasianski, the insufferable prig, answered for Lampe. "He thinks the woman is in despair. It's a simplistic assessment, if I may say so. But if she is in despair, she desperately needs the remedy of a physician of the soul such as yourself."

"Yes, Lampe," the elderly, virgin professor said with authority. "She needs instruction and penalty. She calls on us as physicians. We must not allow her to sink further into folly and enthusiasm. I have no time to write back to her at the moment. But later, later. Lampe, put this letter on my desk."

Lampe took the letter to the study. As he read the words

Maria von Herbert had written, his heart softened towards her. How unfortunate that she looked to the categorical imperative for guidance. She begged Kant for help. "My heart splinters into a thousand pieces. Either damn me or comfort me." Lampe wondered what she would think if she met the professor in person.

Later that night when Wasianski was gone and Lampe had drunk an extra glass or two of vodka to compensate for the stresses of the day, he asked Kant, "What did you think of the letter?"

"It was peculiar." Kant wrapped a blanket around himself and sat down in front of the fire.

"Will you write back to her?" Lampe asked.

"I suppose. But first, I will ask the countess Keyserlingk her thoughts on the matter."

Lampe said, "At least that's better than asking Wasianski."

"You're terribly rude to him, Lampe. Especially when you've been drinking. You should stop. I've been very careful to maintain my delicate health, but my teeth are falling out, my skin tears with the slightest trauma, and my intestines seem to be growing ever more uncooperative. If you don't moderate yourself, your old age will be even worse than mine."

"I feel good enough."

Kant pulled the blanket tighter. "Well, I won't be here forever. Every day brings news of yet another friend's death. I have so much work left to do. Don't be rude to deacon Wasianski. I need his help."

"But he's so, so . . ."

"He's so helpful, Lampe."

Lampe put up the last dessert plate and said, "In any case, you should write back to that woman. But be kind. Now, come to bed. I'll tuck in your sheets."

Kant had closed his eyes, but he opened them again and nodded. Lampe led the weary old man to bed and tucked him in so that the covers were taut. He was so thin under the thick blanket that his body barely seemed present, as though he was just a head on a pillow. Instead of saying thank you, he closed his eyes and said, "You stink of alcohol, Lampe. You must stop drinking."

Lampe said, "How else can I bear this life?" But Kant was already asleep.

—⁓—

Several days later Lampe was delivering letters and purchasing tobacco for Kant. He returned in the late afternoon to find Wasianski emerging from the study with a finger to his lips. "Lampe, the professor has asked for some time alone."

Lampe said, "He can be perfectly alone with me in the room."

"No, Lampe, I'm quite serious."

"So am I."

Wasianski said, "Lampe, the countess fell ill and kept it to herself. But she died this morning. It was dreadful and unexpected, and it has shaken him terribly."

Lampe suddenly felt nauseated. He said, "You don't understand. He needs me now more than ever." The unexpected death of the countess made him sad, but his true worry was the effect her death would have on the master. He pushed past Wasianski with the jar of tobacco under his arm and went into the study.

Kant was pale, slumped into his chair, holding the note

from the countess's household informing him of her death. He looked up and stared at Lampe as though he were a stranger.

"I have your tobacco," Lampe said.

In a weak voice Kant said, "You've heard?"

Wasianski came in behind Lampe. "My apologies Immanuel. I told him you might need some time to yourself."

Kant waved his hand in the air. Lampe glared briefly at Wasianski and said, "I'll fill your pipe. You need a second bowl today."

Kant didn't respond. When Lampe handed him the pipe, he took it and allowed Lampe to light it for him. After he smoked in silence for a few minutes, he said, "I'm sad to the point of fear. I'm sad with sadness like pain."

Kant never shed tears for friends who died, but this was more like losing a wife. His mood swung from melancholic brooding to sudden irritability. He would demand that Lampe dust tables and chairs that were already clean. He would complain about his spoons when he was eating soup. "I need a clean spoon, if it's not too much trouble!"

Trouble indeed. Did no one care that Lampe was also grieving in his own way? He understood what the countess had given the master despite his embarrassingly virginal contortions. And now, she was dead. Nobility didn't change the cold reality that she would soon smell like any dead squirrel on the side of the road. She was only weeks from being a skeleton with a few rotten pieces of flesh hanging from her bones, and she was mere months from being forgotten by all except her closest friends.

Lampe suffered in silence and solitude while Kant was soothed by Wasianski's excessive doting as he used his pastoral training to ease Kant's grief at her death. Now that she was dead, she was elevated to the status of pure idea. Kant invited the pure form of this ideal into his neat but tightly crowded little world, and he permanently ensconced her on the altar of philosophical moonshine as *The Ideal of a Woman*.

Though Kant obsessed over the dead countess, he had no regard for Maria von Herbert, who was a living woman in real pain. He waited until spring to write back to her. Lampe thought the delay was abominable.

Meanwhile, Wasianski strategized like a businessman taking over the assets of a town, slowly gaining power. "Your fame is growing all over the world, Immanuel. Look at these requests to have dinner with you." He held up letters that may or may not have been such requests. He sorted through the mail, supposedly relieving the great man of mundane tasks. Lampe had to sneak around for glimpses at Kant's letters, manuscripts, and ledgers, while Wasianski was granted unlimited access. Kant was cheating on him like an unfaithful husband.

Lampe lay in his bed feeling the pain in his legs from his journey to Kant's house. He longed for spring, though he was unsure if he would live to see it. In all the universe, Ding alone gave him a sense of immediate, whole, and marvelous goodness. How he would miss her when she died.

Almost everything about the world was the same as twelve days before when Kant still breathed. But almost everything about Lampe's world was different.

What, exactly, did he need?

He needed to be the one watching over the professor and

leading people to the little corpse as he told stories about the great man. Providence should have given him that small measure of dignity. Then he wouldn't have fretted over whether or not to let the black ink flow off the bone of his ostrich feather, painting mysterious sentences onto paper. He wouldn't have cared if the manuscript ended up as fish wrap, and *the principle of the poetic a priori* was lost forever.

He could have had peace. But it was not to be.

Day Twelve

On the Old Saw

DAY TWELVE, FOUR O'CLOCK IN THE MORNING, and though his body ached, Lampe lit his candle, wrapped himself in his blanket over the top of his coat, and continued reading the final fascicle of the master's last and greatest book.

Winter nights stretched too far into the morning, but the candle flickering shadows across the page was comforting to him. The glow of his pipe tobacco and the warmth of the wine that eased his aches allowed him to feel the cold without despairing. The fascicle was his only concern at the moment.

He looked again at page one.

God and the world.

These concepts are altogether contained analytically in the idea of the highest being, which we ourselves have created. But the problem of transcendental philosophy still remains unresolved: Is there a God?

Had the idea of God ever once consoled, or comforted, or cheered the withered old philosopher?

Lampe wrapped his blanket tighter, sipped his wine, breathed in the pipe smoke, and stared at the glow of his reflection in the window. The wind rattled a loose shutter as death paired his nails and shook his head, refusing to say, *a priori*, what happens when we die. Death remained *a posteriori*. Concepts analytically contained in the idea of the highest being did not suffice in the presence of death. If there was to be any hope, a philosopher needed a god who was actually *God*. But the inn of Kant's philosophy was full, and it had no room for such a God.

God is not the world soul.

Spinoza's concept of God and man, according to which the philosopher intuits all things in God, is enthusiastic (conceptus fanaticus).

"Ah, master, you little shit," Lampe whispered to himself. "*Conceptus fanaticus,* eh? You came so close to the truth, but you should have looked again."

Page two.

God and the world.

There are gods as little as there are worlds; rather, one God and one world.

Page three.

It can be said without qualification: 'There are not gods; there are not worlds,' but rather: 'There is one world and there is one God' in reason, as a practically-determining principle.

Like God (as the supersensible principle which combines the manifold of the world through reason) the world is thought a priori, as absolute unity.

Repetition upon repetition. The master was battering against the door, over and over, trying to break through to the larger truth governed in its first yearnings by the magisterial *principle of the poetic a priori.* He missed the mark, but he came so close!

The question: Is there a God? One cannot prove such an object of thought as substance outside the subject: it is, rather, thought.

Enough. The master was haunted by God his entire life, but he could never just leap into the Presence that was everywhere. He kept trying to fit God into a thought, like one more thing among things in the universe.

Lampe had to keep the manuscript. Kaufman would be furious, but Lampe was missing something important. He needed time to figure out what the old man was searching for amidst all the repetition and chicken scratch.

He might also be able to use the missing manuscript as leverage against Kaufman, or at least as a motivating force. "Johannes, my dear friend, what would Wasianski think if I sent a note telling him that a fascicle is missing from the great and crowning book?" He tingled at the idea of this possibility, but it was a risk. It had to be weighed carefully. He would bide his time and decide what to do in the moment. He knew too well the consequences of rashness.

When Kant was in his seventies and Lampe was in his fifties, some of the king's men became interested in the elderly philosopher. It was Lampe's considered and firm opinion that old men such as the master should not criticize the king's laws, especially since little, harmless, theorizing Kant ensconced in his self-contained world of everything-as-it-ought-to-be could easily undo Lampe's world with a few strokes of his pen. The king was a lustful Pietist with a taste for concubines, poetry, and flute playing. He would never have paid attention to a little scholar tucked away in the backwater swampland of Königsberg were it not for the Rosicrucians he hired as censors.

Kant seemed oblivious to the dangers of a loose pen in such volatile times. His book *On Radical Evil in Human Nature* passed the test of the censors. But they took notice when he wrote *Of the Struggle of the Good Principle with the Evil Principle for Sovereignty Over Man*. With the publication of *Religion within the Boundaries of Mere Reason* Kant succeeded in attracting their complete attention.

"Why are you writing these books?" Lampe complained one day.

Kant said, "A philosopher must say the truth and be done with nonsense."

"Not when the nonsense is the king's nonsense."

Kant dismissed Lampe's concern as nothing more than the fretting of an old woman. "Just do your work, Lampe. Don't worry your head over things you'll never understand."

But Lampe's fear was justified. A Rosicrucian named Wollner had gained power in the king's court. He was different from his predecessors. Lampe imagined him in magician's robes with a gaggle of pale and subservient wraiths following him around in court.

On October 1, 1794, when the cold had begun to chew its way into the marrow of old men, a letter appeared on Kant's desk. It had been sent from the king by way of his counselors, and it began, *Wollner, by order of the King*.

Before Lampe read the next sentence, Kant appeared in the doorway. "Does that scare you, Lampe?"

"I only glanced at the heading."

"Well, as long as you're prying into my private affairs you might as well read the entire letter."

Lampe read the letter outlining the reasons the King of Prussia—*THE KING OF PRUSSIA!*—was unhappy with little, wheezing, constipated Immanuel Kant, philosopher. He laid it on the desk and said, "It's an honor to get a letter from the king."

Kant looked hunched and tired. His eyes had none of their usual bright focus. He shook his head and sat down at the desk, looking at the letter.

Lampe said, "It's written on such high-quality paper!"

"I need to think, Lampe."

"Can I get you a glass of wine?"

"I need to think clearly."

"Wine always helps me," Lampe offered.

"Alone."

"Just a glass?" Lampe urged.

"I need to talk with Wasianski."

Kant kept the letter folded on his desk, so Lampe read and reread it. There was no ambiguity. According to Wollner, the king thought Kant was undermining royal paternity and using his philosophy to distort the truths of scripture. The first assertion might have concerned the king, but the second was absurd. Kant paid no attention whatsoever to the truths of scripture, and the king was probably not much different.

Dinner guests recognized how distracted Kant was. "We do hope your health is steady," they said, noting the sagging of the master's eyes and skin and bones and soul.

"My health hasn't changed. I'm as frail as ever!" Then with a somber expression, he reached into his pocket and said,

"Gentlemen, a letter from the king. I want your opinion. Speak freely."

What a fool.

The responses were unhelpful and dangerous. "This is merely Wollner's strange opinion about scripture," one of them said. "He's a Rosicrucian. The king is probably more bothered by that essay, *On the Old Saw: That Might Be Right in Theory, but It Won't Work in Practice*. You argue that revolution is never justified, and citizens may never disobey the law. But then you go on to insist that they can still question the law?"

"If Immanuel had stopped there, the king would never have noticed," another said. "But why press so hard on the question about whether the human race should be loved or disdained?"

"Sorry?" said a dullard. "I'm not familiar with the professor's answer to that question."

Yet another man equal to the dullard responded, "He says it depends on whether the human race can progress or is condemned to evil."

Lampe poured the wine slowly, lingering to eavesdrop on the gathered friends. They had nothing to risk, but Lampe's livelihood in old age depended on Kant's safety.

Another wedged in and said, "You took a bold turn in your attack on Frederick's hypocrisy."

Several nodded. One of them said, "Do you think he understands it?"

Another said, "He's not stupid."

A third complained, "The problem is that the Rosicrucians serve up bizarre ideas to him. They cast Immanuel's thought in their own language, with their own odd view of the world."

"Ever since the revolution in France," squeaked another, in a small, scholarly tone, "Wollner and his crew have been busy resisting this enlightenment. You, Immanuel, are the beacon shining in the darkness."

Kant wiped his thin lips and said, "They don't resist it. They just misunderstand it. They want a 'Rosicrucian enlightenment,' whatever that might be. In any case, I'm no fool. These counselors to the king are drunk with power, and I have enough interest in my own hide to take care of it."

"I doubt Frederick was happy with your suggestion that even he will ultimately have to submit to a cosmopolitan constitution."

Kant stiffened in his chair and glanced at Lampe who glared back with his eyebrows raised. He then looked at Wasianski who had nothing to say, but who looked toward Kant with the angelic confidence of a moron.

"I didn't name the king," Kant finally said. He took a sip of wine, holding it in his mouth for a moment before swallowing, and then allowing a transient grin to come to his lips. "The Rosicrucians eventually figure out the implications of my ideas, but I'm doing nothing more than reporting the way things are and the way they must be. I should be rewarded for warning the king to get his affairs in order."

"Here, here," Wasianski said, raising his glass with the others while Lampe snorted and looked to the ground, dejected. None of them understood. Where would this leave him and the master if the king responded in earnest?

One of them said, "Socrates told the Athenian court that they should reward him with a lifetime pension."

"And then he drank the hemlock," Kant said.

"Now, now," said Wasianski.

But Kant's comment led to a long and worried silence as Lampe poured wine, focusing on keeping his hand steady, invisible to the men who turned their concern toward the master.

"You all look so serious," Kant said. He surprised them with a grin, and the guests relaxed before his eyes. "I will not crawl before this threat." The strength of his voice grew as he continued. "Minister von Zedlitz protected me for years. Now that he's gone, I simply must amend my strategies."

"Who is von Zedlitz?" one of the guests asked.

Kant said, "My point exactly. Zedlitz was in the educational department of the ministry. He was quiet and quite sane, and he knew how to avoid ideological annoyances. Good work was good work. But now this cleric, this Wollner, is warning everyone, and apparently me in particular, against rationalistic errors, as he calls them. Well, gentlemen, I will not crawl. And how can I afford to be so bold?" He looked around the room, then he glanced at Lampe. "Because of my wisdom in personal economics. I'll be fine, don't you worry."

Kant's reassurance to his friends didn't ease Lampe's anxiety. He saw the folly, and he intended to punish Kant with a few days of testy silence.

On the second day of October, the air suddenly turned toward true winter cold. The birds were silent. Kant's friends had scattered to their own concerns, but Lampe remained, stoking the fire and tending the professor. The letter bothered the old man more than he admitted to his friends, but his anxiety was obvious to his loyal servant who observed Kant's incessant pacing and saw the sweat stains from his small hands on the tattered edges of the royal paper as he brooded and tended his doubts.

Deacon Wasianski had fully awakened to the scent of opportunity, and the letter from the king gave him an instrument to usurp Lampe. He made himself excessively available to Kant for counsel, intruding farther into each day. When Lampe would enter the room, Wasianski would say something like, "Do you mind doing your chores elsewhere? I must speak to Professor Kant about an issue of some sensitivity."

For decades—decades!—Lampe had stood to the side, mostly unnoticed. But he had never been excluded from conversations of any kind. Access made his tutorial possible, and that was his true pay for the many services he provided. Lampe expected Kant to defend his right to stay, but when the master just looked away, his eyelids at half-mast, Lampe said, "This is absurd!" He meant to think the words, but he yelled them instead.

The next day when Lampe arrived at the usual time, Kant was already awake. His study door was closed. Light from his lantern glowed under the door. Lampe leaned toward the door and listened. No sound came from the study. At least the master was alone.

Kant did not come out of his study until noon. When he did, Lampe saw his look of concentrated distraction. He had slept poorly. He didn't even greet Lampe before putting on his coat and leaving the house. A moment later he came back in and said, "Don't go into the study." Then he left again.

Lampe was a soldier to his core. He wanted to protect the master from harmful forces. He wanted to be armed to respond to dread or need. Because of this, he had to glimpse whatever was consuming Kant, despite being ordered to stay out of the study.

Crumpled pieces of paper were on the floor all around the desk. The draft of the letter that was still on the desk began, *Your Majesty.* Then nothing. He reached down and picked up several of the crumpled letters. Each began in the same way, *Your Majesty.* The pain of royal displeasure was clearly wearing away at Kant.

Lampe read each of the crumpled versions. Only one of them made even a start towards getting to the point. *I understand why you think I have misused my philosophy to disparage religion. And so, as your majesty's most loyal subject, I will refrain from lecturing, writing, or engaging in any sort of public discourse regarding religion . . .* Lampe added out loud, "Blah, blah, blah."

"What are you doing Lampe?" He had not heard the front door open and couldn't put down the crumpled draft before Kant saw him.

Lampe said nothing. He began dusting the picture of Rousseau that hung over Kant's desk.

Kant asked again, "What are you doing?"

"I'm dusting. What does it look like I'm doing? Someone has to clean up this mess. What a waste of paper."

"Dusting?" Kant walked towards him with his walking stick. Lampe thought he might hit him with it. But instead, the old man bent down and lifted one of the crumpled drafts. "You're reading my private letter."

"Why would I read your letter?"

"Do I have to lock up my own writing, in my own study,

in my own house, just to have some privacy of thought?" He leaned in and sniffed. "You've been drinking. It's the middle of the day, and you're drinking. And rummaging about."

Lampe said, "I wasn't rummaging."

"You were rummaging," Kant insisted.

"I wouldn't call it rummaging."

"And the house is a mess!"

Lampe held out his dusting rag to prove that he was trying to remedy the messiness.

"You're prying into my thoughts," Kant said. "Fine, then! I'll explain the letter to you."

"I don't want to know what the letter means."

"Ha!" Kant said, pointing his finger at Lampe. "So, you did read it!"

"I didn't want to throw away something important!"

"Now I know whom I can trust and whom I can't trust." Kant took the most recent draft of the letter and slipped it into the desk drawer. "You think I'm a coward, don't you?"

"Not because of this letter."

"Well, I'm not a coward, and I'll explain why."

"I don't want an explanation," Lampe said. "I just want to dust."

"And leave me standing here accused of cowardice in my own house? No! The letter must be answered, and I know the way. If the king's law dictates that I must not make certain public pronouncements, then I shall not … as long as he is alive." The old man grinned, as though he had accomplished something truly clever by adding that phrase.

"You took long enough to answer that poor woman, Maria von What's-her-name. I'm sure the king isn't nearly as distraught over your books as she was."

"Why bring up Miss von Herbert? I'm telling you something of great importance and you distract me by bringing up that woman. I can't have a servant who thinks I am a coward."

"You're not listening!"

"Look here." Kant pulled out the letter again as Lampe sighed. "Here, where I say, 'As your majesty's most loyal subject' … Do you see? When he dies, I will be free of this vow."

Lampe looked at the floor.

"What? Do you still think I'm a coward?"

"Not because of this," Lampe said again.

"So, you do think I'm a coward!"

"If I do, it's only because of the way you are treating that woman who put her trust in you."

Kant said, "We're not talking about her."

"You gave her letters to Elizabeth Motherby, didn't you? Admit it."

Kant looked genuinely surprised. "Where did you hear that?"

"To give her letters to another woman … And not even a woman. Elizabeth is still a girl!"

"Where did you hear that?" Kant asked again.

"Servants talk. We sit in kitchens and talk."

"What other parts of my private business have you pried into?"

Lampe rolled his eyes. "I pay no attention. None."

"Ever since Green died, Motherby has devoted himself to my financial security. I shared those letters as a gesture of gratitude. They are an example of what not to do. It was for Elizabeth's moral training."

"What about poor Miss von Herbert? She throws herself at your feet, begs for your help, and asks to visit you ..." Lampe stopped, regretting the way vodka loosened his tongue.

"You could only know that if you had read her second letter," Kant said. Then he added, "Without permission!"

"I can't help it if words on your desk force themselves into my eyes."

The master's cheeks were red with anger and exposure. "You're swimming in treacherous waters."

"I've been with you for most of my life."

"And the longer you're with me, the more your tongue wags. The more you argue. The more you rummage through my papers."

"I don't rummage!" Lampe said.

"Lampe, you understand nothing about Miss von Herbert, nor Elizabeth, nor my letter to the king."

"No?"

"No!" Kant turned and walked out of the room.

Lampe, who was losing the gift of silence that was so valuable to a servant, called after him, "I thought that freedom of the pen was important for a philosopher."

Kant stepped back into the doorway and glared. But not merely in anger. He also seemed surprised. "I'm a lawful man. My actions follow my maxims. That's all you need to know."

"How is being a slave to maxims any different from following orders the way a soldier does? But you despise soldiers."

"You're wrong."

"You despise me?"

"I do not."

"You do," Lampe said.

"I'm hungry. Get dinner ready."

"You despise me. Admit it!"

Kant breathed in deeply and said, "If you must know my reasons, Dr. Erhard was the one who convinced me that I should share the letters."

"That fawning little doctor from Berlin?" Erhard had begun corresponding with Kant once the professor became famous.

"Yes. And he didn't fawn. He merely said that my moral philosophy sent thrills through his soul as nothing else in life ever had."

"Fawning," Lampe said.

"He was friends with Miss von Herbert. Since you insist on pressing the point, he confirmed her lack of delicacy in giving herself to a man. She's past saving. It's done, and finally done."

"What's finally done? One mistake? A woman's passion? Why is it final?"

Kant held up his hand. "I extended the lesson to a young girl before she made the same mistakes. Motherby is my friend."

"Why are you telling me this?"

Kant glared at Lampe. "You accused me of cowardice and betrayal! I can't have someone in my own house who ..."

"I did no such thing," Lampe said.

"Tell me on your honor you didn't think it."

Lampe said, "If I let you pry into my thoughts once, you'll never stop." And he walked out of the room to set the dinner table.

Kant followed and said, "Lampe!"

Lampe looked back. "What?"

"My principles demand that I send this letter to the king.

They demand it!"

"Fine."

"So, you understand, then?"

"Yep."

"I'm merely being faithful to my principles."

"Sure thing."

Kant seemed to have nothing else to say, and he walked away under Lampe's flickering glare, which was bolstered by vodka, a magical substance.

The next morning, while Kant lectured on Meier's tired old *Logic*, Lampe went into the study to see the progress the professor had made on his letter to the king. But there was no letter on the desk. Lampe tried to open the desk drawer and found it locked for the first time. He looked on the bookshelf where the key was kept. The key was still there. Obviously, Lampe would know where the key was kept. Was the professor testing Lampe? Or did he have some other reason to lock the drawer but not hide the key?"

That afternoon Kant continued to explain his strategy to his friends, reading from a copy of the letter he had sent to the king that very day. And as he read, he periodically glanced at Lampe. Lampe refused to look at him.

Kant said, "Listen to this part." The guests stopped talking. "When I agreed to curb my speaking and writing about these topics, I wrote, *As your majesty's loyal subject.* Do you see? I didn't give myself over entirely to the king's pleasure. In this little phrase, *As your majesty's loyal subject,* I said to his very face that as soon as he is dead, the vow no longer applies. Ha!"

Wasianski responded with admiration, "Well done, Immanuel.

Well done indeed!"

Lampe left the room. Public controversy in religion was not the point. God was wandering in the garden of the great mind, and Kant was hiding his nakedness behind a bush. But death was approaching, and he should have been mining the true riches of an immortal philosophy rather than provoking political pawns. If only the old man could see things as Lampe saw them.

—⁂—

Once Kant decided that his exoneration depended on the death of the king, he deepened his attention to the tender extension of his own fragile life cord. News of colleagues growing ill and close friends dying became more common. Kant turned the powers of his intellect toward the goal of avoiding death, though he continued to become noticeably thinner, with fewer teeth, worsening eyesight, and an unsteady gate.

His efforts to preserve his longevity were guided by a book given to him by the famous Dr. Hufeland. He kept it at his bedside for nightly reading. The book was called *Macrobiotics, the Art of Prolonging Human Life.* Dr. Hufeland was physician to the royal court, and Kant was persuaded that he had discovered a deep secret about prolonging the body's life, a secret that became more important to the old man than obscure metaphysical mysteries.

One evening, while tucking Kant into bed, Lampe asked about Hufeland's book.

Kant lifted the book like a Pietist preacher lifting the bible. "It's the very thing I've been looking for. Medicine is wrong when it insists that all illness is an enemy. Macrobiotics proves that some illnesses can actually prolong life. It's a veritable revolution in thought!"

Lampe took the book and placed it on the side table. Then he smoothed out the wrinkles in the blanket that weighed down the small body of the professor. "Brilliant."

"You might nod respectfully and leave it at that," Kant said. He reached for the book again, wrinkling the bedsheets Lampe had just smoothed out, and he read a passage out loud.

The custom prevalent among our forefathers of exciting laughter at the table by jesters and buffoons was founded on true medical principles. Endeavor to have cheerful and merry companions at your meals. What nourishment one receives amid mirth and jollity will certainly produce good and light blood.

"That's it, Lampe! Good and light blood! Hufeland is a genius. I wager that this will also help my bowel movements. From now on, only the jolly can eat at my table. My life depends on it."

"Who could have known that the secret to long life was so simple?"

"You're becoming a cynic, Lampe. Laugh more! Drink less!"

Lampe said, "If you want to me to laugh, I have to drink."

"Well, at least don't bring your melancholy into the dining room."

"I can dress more festively, for a slight increase in my wages."

"I give you more bonuses than most servants get."

"Buffoons are in high demand," Lampe said. "Everyone wants to live a long time."

"Good night, Lampe."

———

Kant was outliving all of his friends. With each death, he more doggedly attended to every new brown spot on his pale skin and to the texture of his thinning hair. He was less and less able to combat the accumulation in his bowels, nor the bothersome variations in the beating of his heart, nor the decreased ability of his dry nose to adequately warm the air before it descended into his ever-struggling lungs.

Lampe tried to be patient, but sometimes he couldn't restrain a blurt of annoyance when the miserable old man complained about his bowels for the thousandth time. "Just sit there and shit until you're empty."

Kant was more like a worn-out spouse than an employer, and Lampe worried when Wasianski allowed him to play the frail, elderly man. That would kill the master. The only thing Lampe knew to do was to provoke him, hoping for an energetic and caustic snap in return. But the blunter he became with Kant, the more the master just nodded, or seemed confused, or expressed embarrassment.

Only in exile did Lampe see that he should have managed the master's worries better. He had been far too bold as he instructed the professor about bowel habits, worried over his clothes and table manners, criticized the excessively thick consistency of sauces on the sea bass, and pushed for bonuses. This last detail, he would readily admit, was mismanaged indeed.

Hippel's illness had turned Kant into a truly old man. The mayor was nearly the last friend from early days who was still alive. Lampe was, of course, selected by providence to deliver the news of Hippel's frailty to Kant. "Hippel's cook told me that he's partially blind because his eyes pussed up a week ago blind." It was an accidental misfortune that he reported on the illness just as he set out the cream sauce for Kant's solitary meal.

"Blind?" Kant's hand trembled as he dipped a piece of bread into the sauce.

"They say his eyes have started to cloud over, but I didn't see him."

Kant put down the wet piece of bread and pushed back from the table. "Was it important to tell me this catastrophic news just now, just at this moment, the one stretch of peace I have all day?"

"I thought you'd want to know."

"Hippel. Blind." Kant stood and walked out, leaving his fish and wine untouched.

Lampe never wasted food. So, he quickly ate the leftover fish and drank the remaining wine before clearing the table. Then he went to the study to reconcile himself to the moody old man through some ingratiating comment, or some small service such as covering him with a blanket or stoking the fire. Kant didn't look well after this new bout of cachectic dread.

Lampe said, "What do you need?"

The tremor of Kant's head and hands made him look older than ever. He said, "Life is becoming a burden to me."

"I know what you need. An extra bowl of tobacco and a good glass of port."

"Life is a burden," Kant repeated.

"Come now. Take your pipe."

Kant didn't take the pipe. He seemed scarcely to hear Lampe.

"Listen!" Lampe said. "I think it's that little titmouse you love. I think she's singing despite the cold."

Kant looked toward the window and then back to the floor. He had always been horrified by blindness, but his lack of interest in the titmouse was worrisome.

Lampe asked, "What else is wrong? People lose body parts all the time."

"I want to be alone."

"What you need is a dose of your own medicine."

"Please, Lampe." The old man was dejected, defenseless.

Lampe asked, "When dear old Hippel lost his sight, what did he really lose?" Then he took down Kant's copy of *The Critique of Pure Reason*, turned to the relevant passage, and began to read out loud. "All our intuition is nothing but the preservation of appearance. The things we intuit are not in themselves what we intuit them as being."

"Put that away Lampe." Kant stared down at his old hands folded in his lap.

Lampe continued. "If we annul ourselves as subjects, or even annul only the subjective character of the senses generally ..."

"Why are you doing this?"

"... then even this entire character of objects and all their relations in space and time—indeed, even space and time themselves—would vanish."

"Lampe!" Kant tried to appear threatening by standing up, but the effect was diminished by his need to push on the arms of the chair as he slowly achieved the position. "Give me the book."

Lampe stepped back and continued reading. "Being appearances, they cannot exist in themselves, but can only exist in us."

"Why are you reading that?"

"To comfort you," Lampe answered.

"It's not comforting."

"My point is that Hippel only lost appearances. But he's still Hippel!"

"Lampe, I want to be alone."

"No, you don't."

"What?"

"You don't want to be alone."

"Blindness leaves you alone!" Kant sat down.

Lampe asked, "What about God?"

The master closed his eyes and said nothing. Lampe put the book back on the shelf and walked toward the door.

Kant's eyes were still closed when he said, "Life is a burden to me. But I'm no poltron."

"No sir, you're definitely not a poltron" Lampe wasn't sure what a poltron was, but he would agree with any assertion that had a little of the old energy in it.

"Bring me a glass of wine."

Lampe smiled and, in his most respectful tone, he said, "Yes, professor."

As the old man's body became frailer, he steadied his mind by tethering it to the material world. He found that focusing on the steeple of the Löbenicht church provided the most effective material support for his speculative work, and when the poplar trees became thick with leaves and blocked his view, his frustration was bitter indeed.

Without material support, speculation hurled his mind into darkness. The blind were intolerable because of this philosophical reality. They were a threat to Kant's world, even though they usually sat calmly, expressing the usual gentle desires for friendship common to all humans. But the blind knew something that was dreadful to Kant. They knew how to be alone with themselves. They dwelt in absolute darkness where the thing-in-itself whispered and coaxed.

—⁓—

By the twelfth day of mourning, Lampe felt how forgotten he was.

Even the Dunce, who had threatened to retrieve the manuscript, failed to show up. He left Lampe staring out his window, waiting, watching, wanting.

And what was it that he craved after forty years of being cruelly tutored under the force of Kant's ambiguous longings? This question was interesting, and he knew the answer. He craved philosophical friendship. It wasn't good for a man's mind to be alone. Especially a mind like his, a mind shaped and contoured by persistent encounters with genius.

The master was not yet buried. That was simply a fact. In the flicker of candlelight, he stared at the sheet of paper on which the drop of ink had fallen, taking stock of the idea that was emerging from the fog of his mind's penumbra and establishing itself in the clearing. And then the idea made itself known.

The corpse of Kant is the secret to the thing-in-itself. As the appearance rots, fading into the nothingness beyond appearance, the mind grasps the thing-in-itself, readable only through that ultimate blindness inflicted upon the frail body: death.

He stood up in front of Ding and repeated those sentences. He picked up the fascicle and paced, saying the sentences over and over, trying to feel whether he was saying something that was true or something that was not true. Or perhaps he was saying something that was completely stupid. He didn't know.

How could he know whether he was thinking philosophy or becoming a charlatan? His mind needed to be pressed, ground, and polished. But the grinding stone was gone. The master was dead. It was too late. Everything was too late.

But he was alone, cold, and frightened in the dark, and he shouldn't trust his judgment in such circumstances. He had to imitate the master. As Kant had used the steeple of the Löbenicht church to give material support to his speculative thought, Lampe had to tether his mind to some material support. Otherwise, he too would be utterly lost.

Only one material support was adequate. As long as Kant's body was in the house, Lampe might still see him. The saving anchor for the loose tether of his mind was located in the master's final, fading, physical appearance.

Day Thirteen

Clausula Salvatoris

KANT'S RIDICULOUS FASCICLE, with its excruciating lists of mundane chores written in the margins, and his repetition of the same concept over and over, tempted some to view it as a chronicle of decline. But these details were nothing more than distractions from the treasures he had hidden beneath the dense foliage of absurdities. Kant was leaving clues about the ideas Lampe was ordained to take up and develop into *The Highest Point of View*, if only he had eyes to see and ears to hear.

Kant's ghost drew closer, as though the borrowed manuscript was a window on the dark world of spirit where Kant was finally gaining his bearings, using Lampe's mental activity as a lantern.

Nonsense! the master's voice grumbled from deep inside Lampe's mind.

Lampe soldiered on. Sheet two, page four.

There is a being in me which is different from me, and which stands in an efficient causal relation (nexus effectivus) toward myself (agit, facit, operatur); itself free (that is, not being dependent upon the laws of nature in space and time), it judges me inwardly (justifies or condemns); and I, man, am this being myself—it is not some substance outside me. What is most surprising is that this causality is a determination to action in freedom (not as a natural necessity).

Lampe suddenly saw the astonishing, overwhelming truth. Kant was trying to become God. If Kant was God, Kant was not Kant. No longer held in a dark and inaccessible dungeon with the thing-in-itself, the Divine Kant could stand in an efficient causal relationship to the Kant who called himself *Immanuel.*

Lampe opened his wine jug. After a few swigs, he felt much better. Perhaps he was misunderstanding, but if so, his misunderstanding felt like it was lighting up the innermost truth of the manuscript.

Sheet three. Page one.

God.

Lampe said, "God."

There was a note in the margin.

What compels from us the idea of God? No concept of experience, no metaphysics. What presents this concept a priori is transcendental philosophy.

"You were so close, old man," he said out loud. He pulled his blanket tight around his shoulders. The sun was just beginning to rise, lighting the snow that was falling outside his window.

Sheet three. Page two.

The totality of beings (the universum). The latter divides into God and the …

The sentence stopped.

This was enough for the moment. Lampe wrapped up the

fascicle and put it under his mattress, in case the Dunce visited and tried to force it from his weak clutch.

The totality of beings divides up into *God and the* ...

But what if it doesn't divide up into *God and the* ...?

Lampe wasn't thinking clearly. He lay on his mattress and went to sleep.

When he awoke toward noon the snow had stopped. The sun was hidden behind thick grey clouds. The light was subdued.

The time had come to take up the fascicle and read it to the end. He would sip wine, eat black bread, and stop indulging in nonsense and pathetic self-pity.

Unfortunately, his wine jug was empty. He could read without wine, of course. But wine elevated the mind. It released him from the prosaic realm of his boring life and allowed him to contemplate the very mind of the philosopher, which was, in turn, hunting down, or else becoming, the very mind of God.

The obvious thing to do was to go to the tavern near Kant's house, not for a drink, but for inspiration. He would hide the fascicle under his coat. With the little money he had left, he would buy a bottle of wine and some vodka. Then he would settle down in the corner with the mind of the master. Yes, good. He quickly dressed and followed through on the excellent plan, though the fresh snow slowed him down and the cold thickened his marrow into syrup.

Many years before, Kant enjoyed playing billiards in the tavern while Lampe looked on, holding his coat and umbrella. Since Lampe's exile, the old tavern owner had sold the pub to a middle-aged man who spoke little German, a man with a red face, tall, with a great belly and huge hands covered in red hair. The man glanced at Lampe when he shuffled in, joints stiff with cold.

The tables were filled with strangers who were either coming from Kant's house or on their way to it. Lampe sat at a long table, away from the men huddled at one end.

The young woman who was tending tables asked him what he wanted. "Vodka."

When she brought the bottle, he watched her freckled hands uncork it and pour a glass.

Lampe said, "You're busy for this hour."

"Visitors," she muttered. "A famous writer who lived up the road recently died."

Lampe gulped down his vodka and motioned for a second glass and then a third. The owner eyed him from behind the bar.

The woman asked, "What's your name?"

The vodka and the presence of a young female warmed him and lifted him from the pit made of dreams and dread. "My name is Martin Lampe."

"Really?" she said with a look of surprise, as though she had suddenly been given a revelation that all things are possible in strange times. "I've heard students from the university mention you."

He looked down at his glass. "As a joke?"

She shook her head. "As a question. Whatever happened to old Martin Lampe?"

"Whatever happened to old Martin Lampe?" He held up his glass and she filled it.

"That's right. I didn't hear much, but they said you were always with him."

Lampe swallowed hard before responding. "If you see them again, tell them that Martin Lampe endures. Alone."

She asked, "How long did you work for him?"

He looked at her eyes and smiled. "How old are you?"

"Almost twenty, sir."

"I had been with him over twenty years the day you were born. I stayed twenty more."

"That's a long time."

Lampe nodded and glanced at her breasts. "I'm an old man."

The beautiful young woman looked down at the floor, allowing the moment to pass in which the melancholy of impossibility covered its nakedness. Then she said, "You'd never know he was so famous if you looked at him now. I think of famous people as being bigger."

Lampe gulped down his vodka. "You've seen him?"

She poured a fifth glass without asking. "He's practically nothing, like a little doll, sort of grey and wrinkled. And his head is shaved."

Lampe looked away from her when she mentioned that his head was shaved. He asked, "Do you know anything about him?"

"I know we've had more customers in the past two weeks than the past two months. Everyone in the world seems to want to see that little man."

"What else do you know about him?" Lampe asked.

"He used to stomp past the window. I noticed him because of how he lifted his feet straight up and planted them hard on the ground. I didn't know who he was until I saw his little corpse lying there."

Lampe mustered his reserves of solemnity and, forcing words past his thickening tongue, he said, "Immanuel Kant was the greatest philosopher in the world." He held up his glass and she poured a sixth shot of vodka. "I was his assistant."

"What did you assist with?" she asked.

"The work."

"The work?"

"Philosophy," Lampe said.

She thought about this for a moment and said, "The students come here to argue about ideas while they eat and drink. They talk about him a lot. I listen, but the ideas are strange."

"Listening is education," Lampe said. "Do you want to know a secret?"

"Yes."

"When the professor died, he was working on his final and greatest book in the very house you visited."

She said, "After forty years, you probably know more than anyone about him and his books."

The vodka and the young woman made him feel so warm, and he felt his mind clearing. "Did you see his writing desk when you visited?"

"Only through the doorway. The man who works there …"

"Wasianski?"

"Not Herr Wasianski. Him I know well enough. He comes here for meals sometimes, but he's not much of a drinker. I mean the servant. Johannes?"

"Kaufman."

She nodded. "He seems nice."

"I suppose," Lampe said.

"Was he your replacement?" she asked.

"No." Lampe didn't explain. The explanation was as long as a life.

She said, "He tried to show me the professor's desk. That seemed to irritate Herr Wasianski, and he pushed me toward the freezing room where the professor's body is kept."

"He can be rude."

She nodded. "Herr Kaufman seems to know a lot about the history of the dead professor."

"What sort of history?"

"Mostly about his work habits. As we walked through the house, he told us how the professor used to get up early in the morning to write his great books, and he told the story of his death with a tear in his eye. It's enough to make you cry even if you never knew him. When I visited, students from the university gathered around Herr Kaufman and asked all sorts of questions. Imagine university students asking questions to a servant."

"Imagine that," Lampe said.

"I should get back to work. Be careful out there. I slipped and almost fell this morning."

"Thank you." He stood up and bowed. "You've helped me more than you can know."

Lampe held the fascicle tight against his chest and left the tavern, weighted down by the image of the Dunce surrounded by curious university students. His eyes locked onto the chimney of Kant's house. Smoke rose toward the white sky.

The snow had started to fall again, but there was still a long line of people at Kant's front door. The snow made the world feel closed in and small. Lampe considered covering his head with a scarf and trying to sneak in among strangers. If he was not discovered, at least he could briefly stand beside the dead master to make the absence more real.

But the thought of being a stranger in that house squeezed his heart with the teeth of a hunter's trap, the way his heart used to feel when he watched men turn his mother into someone besides his mother.

Instead of joining the line, he tucked his head, pulled up his coat collar, and quickly walked past them. Then he snuck up to the window of the house around the corner and looked in for the first time in two years. He stood on his tiptoes and felt his legs tremble. Because he was too weak to stay on his toes for long, his head bobbed up and down at the window.

There, a few feet from the window, was the master. Lampe trembled from the cold and the terror. Wasianski was there, looking down at the small corpse. Lampe let his feet relax for a moment and then pushed back up on his tiptoes just as Kaufman entered the room. The two of them spoke for a moment, and then both of them left. The old man was alone in the cold gray room, no fire, no warmth. His hands were crossed over that little belly that had given him a lifetime of trouble.

Through the open door, Lampe glimpsed the writing desk in the next room. Wasianski probably sat there and used Kant's pen to write his biography. He probably used the professor's pipe. Unthinkable sacrilege.

Lampe let his feet relax again. He was suddenly so sleepy, so full of grief. His feet were going numb. He stretched on his tiptoes once more to see the tiny body in the gray room. The frost on the window blurred his vision.

"Can you finally breathe wherever you are?" he whispered. "Can you eat without being tormented by bloat and your silly little inadequate shits?" He felt ridiculous, speaking through a closed window to a corpse. But he said a little louder, "How could you do this to me?"

Around the corner, someone knocked at the front door. Lampe peaked and saw the line of impatient gawkers dressed in drab browns and grays and blacks, infiltrating strangers who would pass by the very thing inaccessible to Lampe, the only thing he cared about. They had no idea what they were looking at, no idea who the man was.

The wind was rising. He hid his face with the collar of his coat like a man consumed with shame and fear, and he walked past the line of unknown souls who would freely gaze upon that which was forbidden to Lampe. Grief became the madness of desire for something beyond his grasp. Kant had warned about this danger.

He needed warmth and rest. Because of the snow, the Dunce would probably wait another day before retrieving the manuscript. His only consolation was the thought that he might use his last few thalers to buy a jug of wine, sit in his cold room with his candle, and continue to read the thoughts of God.

When he was back at his desk, he opened the fascicle and continued tormenting himself.

Experience is itself a species of knowledge which involves understanding; and understanding has rules which I must suppose as being in me prior to objects being given to me, and therefore as being a priori.

He read the line again. It led up to one of those sentences

that formed the prison bars through which Lampe peered into the professor's mind:

We can know a priori of things only what we ourselves put into them.

That was the problem! The master didn't see others. He only saw what he himself put into them. Lampe agonized over how close Kant's horrid formulation was to the golden phrase his mother had learned from one of her lovers, the student of some famous philologist in Naples. It was a philosophical nugget traded for a night in her bed and supplemented with wine and a promise of breakfast. But it was a hazelnut containing a whole universe: *The true is the made.*

The true is the made. The made! *Poesis!*

His mother mentioned the phrase when he was a boy. When he asked what it meant, she told him to figure it out himself. So he kept the phrase in his toolbox, and occasionally he pulled it out and looked at it. No one could have guessed that this singular sentence given to him by Providence would become *the principle of the poetic a priori*, the secret to completing the system of the world's greatest philosopher. It provided partial redemption for his mother, and this lightened Lampe.

From then on, he collected illuminating passages in his memory, and he carried them with him like a bag of precious, but curiously odd, stones he could take out and admire. He collected some of them because they were mysterious or wonderful. But he added others, including many from the master, only as terrifying examples of the horror that comes from excessive consistency.

One of the worst was a fable from the essay *On the Old Saw*, which was the piece that most infuriated the king's censor. In it, Kant told a story about a poor man who was holding money for a friend. When the friend died, his heirs, who were loveless, terrible, wealthy spendthrifts, knew nothing about the money. The money would make no difference to them. None! But it would pull the poor man and his family out of poverty.

What should the poor man do?

Kant had first posed the problem with his usual delight at the dinner table. The guests waited to hear Kant's great wisdom and judgment, but Wasianski outdid them all as he leaned in with exaggerated attention, though his puppet face registered no true comprehension.

Kant wiped his mouth with the napkin he had draped across his chest, then returned it to his chest in preparation for the next course. Finally, he said, "Any eight-year-old child would be able to see what duty demands. The poor man must hand over the money to the rich heirs."

"Nonsense!" Lampe blurted out from the corner where he was stacking dirty plates.

The traitorous wretches at the dinner table gasped, forcing Kant to respond rather than ignoring Lampe as he usually did in private.

Kant turned and said, "You've become quite a philosopher." He was never happy if the jovial atmosphere at the dinner table was disturbed, especially by Lampe. He had few remaining teeth to bare, but his gaunt face increasingly allowed a disturbing protrusion of his eyes. "Sit! Let's discuss philosophy!"

"I have work to do," Lampe mumbled.

"Surely philosophy is more important than any silly task I asked you to complete several hours ago."

Lampe said, "I don't want to sit." He was more disturbed by Kant's fixed grin than he would have been by any frown.

Kant said, "You may become a philosopher yet! Indeed, are you not already a philosopher, destined for fame? You should hang a placard over your door. *Martin Lampe: Reason at Reasonable Rates.*"

Lampe reached down and took away Kant's glass. "You've had enough wine for the day."

Wasianski said, "You've gone too far, Lampe. Give him his glass."

Kant closed his eyes as Lampe stood before the guests pondering whether to admit defeat and return the glass, or to defy Wasianski and endure Kant's unbearable mood that evening.

Wasianski sensed the opportunity for victory "Enough, Lampe. Put down the glass!"

After an awkward moment of silence, Lampe put down the glass.

"Thank you," Kant said to Wasianski, leaving Lampe in outer darkness, where there is weeping and gnashing of teeth. "Gentlemen, may I tell you about a manuscript I recently finished? I call it *Toward Perpetual Peace: a Philosophical Project.*"

"Yes, please do!" Wasianski said, aggressively grinning at Lampe and wearing the mantle of boldness bestowed upon him through his new proximity to Kant.

"You'll love this one," Lampe said.

"Stop interrupting," Wasianski demanded. Then, basking in

Kant's approval, he said, "Tell us, Immanuel, what is this eternal peace?"

"Perpetual peace," Kant gently corrected. "The argument is too complex to share at the dinner table. But the crux is that there should be no national debt, no standing armies, no forced interference with the government of another state, and no extreme measures in war."

"Ah, the richness," Lampe chirped from one dark corner of the world.

Kant tossed his napkin on the table and said, "Again, my friends, imagine how stunned I am after all these years to discover that I've been living with a great philosopher! To think what mistakes I might have avoided if only I had known to submit myself to the critique of this singular light in the world of philosophical fog—Lampe!"

"Scoff all you want," Lampe said. "But I've been a soldier, and I've fought in a war."

"Forty years ago," Wasianski said.

"Very well, Lampe," Kant said. "Enlighten us about war."

Lampe stood up straight with the military demeanor of a soldier. "When you fight a war, you fight to win. Frederick the Great pursued victory at all costs. He carried the banner of war with his own hands. I saw three horses shot out from under him in a single battle. He would run toward us, screaming, 'What! Do you want to live forever?' And we would follow his rage. If people could agree on the rules of war, they could probably agree on whatever divided them in the first place."

"Well said!" one unfortunate guest blurted out, only to be silenced by Kant's glare.

Kant clasped his hands together. "That's more than enough philosophy for one meal. Let's have dessert."

"Is that your only response to my objection?" Lampe asked.

Kant looked around at his guests, embarrassed by the insolence of his servant. "So now you object to getting dessert?"

"I'll get dessert if you tell me what you think about my objection."

Wasianski said, "Lampe, this is excessive, even for you."

Lampe knew he was approaching an abyss from which it would be difficult to escape, but he was incapable of silence. "The work of a mere servant cannot be threatening to a philosopher," he said, calculating a verbal thrust that only Kant would understand, "since the philosopher, who looks down on the servant, is under no obligation to listen."

With this sentence, Lampe's fate began to turn in a very bad direction. Lampe was accusing Kant of cowardice by paraphrasing the essay on perpetual peace in which he inserted an escape route he called the *Clausula salvatoris*, his little saving clause meant to deflect further anger from the king: *The work of a mere theoretician and academic can never be threatening to the state, since the world-wise statesman, who looks down on the theoretician, is under no obligation to obey.*

The comment went unnoticed by the guests, but Kant's grin disappeared, and he said, "Leave!"

"But don't you want dessert?"

Kant stood up slowly through the sludge of age and aches, and said again, "Leave!"

Before Lampe could reply, Kant pointed toward the door with a trembling hand, and he repeated his command a third time. "Leave!"

Lampe bowed and left the house. He knew he had probably gone too far.

—⁂—

Later that evening, fate delivered a reprieve into Lampe's hands. While he was medicating his spiritual wounds in a pub, he met one of Hippel's servants who told him that Hippel was now completely blind because of infection. Kant's horror at blindness was intensifying as he grew closer to death, and Lampe would have to handle the news carefully.

The next day Lampe knocked on Kant's study door and walked in without waiting for permission.

Kant put down his quill and turned to him. "I don't want you here."

Lampe put on his most humble expression and held his hat in his hands. "I heard something important and difficult about Herr Hippel."

Kant turned back to his desk and resumed writing.

Lampe waited for a moment and then began to retreat from the room, loudly shuffling his shoes on the floor so that Kant could hear his departure.

"Wait!" Kant finally growled. "Tell me about Hippel?"

Lampe stopped, stiffened dramatically, turned about-face like a soldier, and glared as though Kant was responsible for the events that had befallen poor dear old Hippel. "I've heard that he's now completely blind."

Kant's face drained of color. After a few moments of solemn reflection, Kant asked, "Will you check on him for me?"

Lampe's timing had been perfect. "Certainly, professor. I'll visit every day."

"You exasperate me beyond tolerance sometimes," Kant said. "But other times you seem like my only family."

Lampe bowed. "You honor me too much, sir."

And so, Lampe resumed his duties, sparing the professor the horror of looking upon the blind.

He arrived at Hippel's home, bolstered with a bit of vodka to steady his nerves. The servants led him to Hippel's room to deliver greetings. When Lampe entered, he was glad for the vodka.

Hippel was in bed, propped up with a pillow. He had become very thin. Both of his eyes were filled with pus, which he gently wiped away with a wet towel his servant handed him, wringing it out in a basin of water occasionally. Even when the pus was wiped away, both eyes were clouded over and gray.

"Lampe! Good to see you!" Hippel chuckled at his own joke.

Lampe stared, uncertain what to say.

"Have my gelatinous eyes finally silenced you? I bet even the professor hasn't found such a trick for deflecting your abuse."

Lampe said, "What do you mean, sir? I've never abused the professor."

"With great cheerfulness, I declare that to be nonsense. The two of you bicker like a little old married couple. It says a lot that he has kept you all these years."

"It says a lot that I've stayed," Lampe retorted.

"Ha! So it is you, Lampe. For a moment I thought a polite imposter had invaded my room. What have my two favorite philosophers been doing these days?"

"I'm no philosopher, sir."

"After all these years with Dr. Abstraction? Trust me, Lampe. You're a philosopher, alas."

"Not if Immanuel Kant sets the mark for a philosopher."

"You should tell him that. Old men need encouragement."

"I'm an old man myself," Lampe said.

"I'm younger than both of you, and yet I'm blind and probably dying," Hippel said. Then he added, "But don't say that to Immanuel. He doesn't like reminders of human frailty."

"He's prepared," Lampe said.

"For death? Really? And how do you prepare for death, Lampe? Give me some little consolation from your philosophy. I could use it."

"I'll ask the professor if consolation is possible."

Hippel grinned and wiped the pus off his cheeks. "Tell him the only consolation I want is for him to visit me. He can add me to his registry of fascinating blind people."

"I will," Lampe said.

"Thank you. But you know he won't come. He's terrified of blindness."

"That he is, sir."

"Forgive me, Lampe, my head is killing me. I'm going to drink a bottle of vodka and try to sleep away the pain. Sorry for the disgusting goo my body is producing. I'm glad you're not afraid to visit."

"I'm glad I came, sir. And if I might say, your goo goes well with your hair color."

"Don't make me laugh!" Hippel said. "My head hurts. Vodka!"

Lampe smiled at the eccentric, perverted mayor of Königsberg. "Goodbye, sir."

"And Lampe?" Hippel said.

"Yes sir."

"Thank you."

Lampe bowed, even though Hippel couldn't see him. "You're welcome, sir."

Hippel soon fell into a febrile state of unconsciousness. A week later, when Lampe knocked on the door, he was met by a hushed, clumped-together clod of servants who tip-toed, dazed and confused, as though suffering and death were rare events on the earth.

He followed them to Hippel's room and saw the dead mayor with his pus-filled eye sockets directed toward the ceiling. His mouth was frozen in an eerie grin. Lampe suspected that he purposefully willed the grin to stay until the end.

Lampe returned to Kant's study and slipped in quietly, waiting until the whisper of his own breathing finally made the master look up from his book.

Lampe said, "Your friend has …"

"Oh my," Kant said. He sank deeper into his chair. "Poor, dear Hippel."

Lampe looked down at the old man. "I'm sorry."

—⁓—

Now that he had seen the master's dead body, Lampe could barely get through a single paragraph of the final manuscript. He felt the shadows of dull gods everywhere, gods who did nothing but hover vaguely at the threshold of death, like ancient gossamer curtains blowing at an open window.

He needed something visceral and real. His mind burned with the fire of dread. Masturbation would have helped if his floppy organ hadn't long ago lost that function. But he needed something that would allow him to escape his mind by diving completely into his body.

Suddenly, his imagination filled with the memory of his mother. She had died before he knew enough to grasp the reasons for her profligate rip into the physical world. She had a gift for desire so expansive that no remedy on earth was sufficient. If Lampe were God, he would accept her ravenous hunger as an expression of gratitude for creation's wild goodness, a gratitude that was infinitely sweeter than the bland endurance of the fearful who could only say at the end of life that they had kept all the rules.

In that moment, he knew he had forgiven her. It was so simple and so complete. And though he almost never thought about the particulars of religion, he was flooded with certainty that Jesus would have joyfully welcomed her, even as the sanctified, the righteous, and the pure tossed her aside.

A calmness descended upon him, and he returned to his calling. Kant had buried his talent in the soil of the final manuscript, but Lampe would dig it up, invest it, and bring forth a ten-fold profit.

He poured a glass of wine, and in the strangely homey presence of an unnamed holiness, he resumed reading.

Transcendental Philosophy's Highest Standpoint—God, the World, and the Thinking Being in the World (Man).

The idea of a highest standpoint made him dizzy. The master had always preached caution. Let us not risk error. Let us not risk being wrong. Let us not, let us not, let us not. It was such a truncated liturgy of life. But in his final work, he was trying to soar to the highest point of view.

Even if God is to be regarded in philosophy merely as a thought-object …

Thought-object. Merely as a thought-object. Lampe saw that Kant's wings had probably long ago withered beyond repair.

As death crept up the cold stairs towards Lampe's door, he knew he needed a God who could forgive and redeem—not some thought-object.

God and the world are the two objects of transcendental philosophy; thinking man is the subject, predicate, and copula, the subject who combines them in one proposition.

In a proposition? No! In a life!

God, the world, and the free will of the rational being in the world. All are infinite.

Infinite! Yes, at last!

Can immortality be included a priori among the characteristics which belong to freedom? Yes, if there is a devil. Since the latter has reason, but not infinitely.

If there is a Devil? Oh, master. There is most assuredly a Devil.

Lampe wrapped the manuscript, placed it under his mattress, and laid down. Kant had devoted his life to gathering everything, including the mind, the world, war, and God into the thick walls of his philosophical citadel. But as he tried to save himself from the Devil, he ended up handing over everything that really matters. Between Kant's way of life and his mother's way of life, he would say his mother's was closer to wild righteousness.

As he drifted toward sleep, listening to Ding gnaw on a piece of stale bread, he thought of Kant's *Clausula salvatoris* and smiled. At least the professor, true to his word, had outlived the king.

The master was his true father. How he wished they had achieved perpetual peace, or any peace at all.

Day Fourteen

A Theory of Cats

LAMPE WOKE UP THE FOURTEENTH MORNING with unanswerable questions creeping towards him from the shadows of his dreams and smothering him. Then he felt Ding curled up under the blanket and nuzzled against his hip. The little dog's tumor had grown during their two weeks of waiting, but it didn't stop her from wagging her tail when he returned from errands or merely looked up from his desk and noticed her. Could there be a more important clue to the truth of the universe?

Before the minute hand on his cuckoo clock moved, the ghost of the dead professor yawned in his mind.

What would he have done without the master? The philosopher had been his highest good, but he had also muted the rest of life. The universe forced Lampe out of his bed with the only question he could act on: *What would he do now?*

He sat down at his desk, lit his candle, and looked at the pathetic black splotch on the otherwise blank page. The pot of ink contained too much possibility. This made it impossible to begin.

But he had work to do. He pulled out the manuscript.

Sheet four, page four.

God. What does reason think in the idea of God?

He sat up straight and said, "Ding! He didn't ask what reason thinks *of* the idea of God, or *about* the idea of God. He asked what reason thinks *in* the idea of God. Don't you see? He was almost there!"

He stood up with his candle and searched his walls. When he found what he was looking for, he raised his finger in the air in the way Kant used to do at the crucial point in a lecture, and he read out loud, "The shape of God's mind and intent is revealed through the veil of nature. It is also hidden by the veil of nature. We reach the mind of God residing in everything by seeing through the veil of nature with the imagination!"

He felt Ding staring at him in silence. Ding was right. If it was that easy, he would have already seen the mind of God shining through nature.

He turned to his window and stared at his reflection laced with frost. His image flickered when he breathed toward the candle.

He couldn't tell is he was getting close to something true, or just using the yarn of obscure sentences to spin tales about the universe. How could he know whether he was spinning tales as an imposter, or getting closer to the truth?

Lampe's mind felt like an airy thing that was easily untethered from reality. But even if his walls contained nothing more than a fable about the universe, he had lived a real life. He could keep it from dissipating a little while longer if he could touch the physical form of the old man and breathe in the familiar smells in the house. That was his tether, his only way to be reminded. He turned back to the first page of the fascicle.

Title-Sheet
The Highest Standpoint of Transcendental Philosophy
In the
System of Ideas: God, the World, and Man in the World,
Restricting himself through Laws of Duty Presented
By

By whom? And then he saw it. The master had not written *By Immanuel Kant* because, like Abraham standing next to Isaac with his knife raised above the heart of his dear son, Kant's hand had been stayed by divine providence, leaving the space blank so that one day this precious blankness might be replaced with the only just and right attribution:

By I. Kant and M. Lampe

Once he saw this miraculous absence, he too felt compelled to say with his master, "Now let your servant depart in peace, for I have seen the glory …"

Lampe was suddenly overwhelmed by a longing to return to his final months with the professor, and to intervene when Wasianski played his parlor tricks on Kant, so that the true gold of the master's finest thoughts might be extracted from the ore of distraction that tempted the old man with an easy surrender to senility.

What a coward Lampe had been when he allowed Wasianski to waste the remaining light in the professor's mind, prodding him to recite random passages from dead authors as a way of showing off for guests. Kant didn't have the strength to refuse, so he would reach into the treasures of his memory for a beautiful idea inscribed in that wonderful work of Erasmus Darwin, *Zoonomia,* and say, "*Principio coelum, ac terras, camposque liquentis, lucentemque globum lunae, titaniaque astra, spirito intus alit, totamque infusa per artus mens agitat molem, et magno se corpore miscet.*

To begin: the heavens, the earth, the watery wastes, the lucent globe of the moon, the sun, the stars exist through inward spirit. Their total mass by mind is permeated: hence their motion.

Lampe had allowed the master to be turned into a pretentious, performing monkey instead of helping him to distill the divine nectar of his as-yet unspoken thoughts. Kant had retained islands of clarity in the fog of decrepitude, but it took a subtle art to discern the places where the old professor was seeing new things in the sleepy realm of age, where the scaffolding of reason's constricted demands dropped away, so that the whole of reality might be grasped, including the dread thing-in-itself.

Discernment required a lifetime of honing the ear, becoming attuned to musical variation. Wasianski might elicit phrases from the old man that struck the nerves of gawking visitors, but the rhythm of the philosophical life Kant and Lampe had developed over forty years would always be inaccessible to the flittering, fawning mind of the deacon. Wasianski was deaf to the poetry of the master's final thoughts.

Unfortunately, as Kant declined physically, it was easier for Wasianski and the endless dinner guests to assume his mind was following the same course as his body. Kant didn't help matters when he would say to his guests, "I am old and weak. Consider me as a child." He would repeat this multiple times during meals and conversations, driving Lampe to distraction. Was the old man just giving up?

Lampe comforted himself with wine, along with his defense of fairness, as he pressed Kant for larger and more frequent bonuses to compensate for the burden of enduring the professor's ever-shorter temper. But he continued to serve with martial order, faithfully acting out the role demanded of him as the morality plays the old philosopher directed at the dinner table grew drearier and more predictable.

"Gentlemen!" Kant would say as he sucked the flesh off the skeleton of the white fish he was eating, holding everyone's attention with those blue eyes staring out from their bony sockets, his face looking more and more like that of the rodents in stories Lampe's mother used to tell him. "I am old weak …"

In the inevitable dramatic pause that followed, Lampe interjected, "Consider him as a child!"

Kant glanced at Lampe, but not with the look of a man ready for a battle of wits. Instead, it had become a look of weary resignation. Lampe mistook this for a sign that they were becoming partners with a shared understanding between them.

The moment of solidarity dissolved when Wasianski blurted, "Please excuse Lampe. He's finding it harder these days to hold his tongue. It's the drink."

Kant's body and face relaxed as Wasianski took on the burden of controlling Lampe-the-sideshow. Lampe had fatally underestimated the role Wasianski was creating for himself, as the old professor identified himself as a child and eased himself into the care of the deacon.

One evening Kant said to Wasianski, "Twenty years have passed since you were at the university."

"Your lectures were the high point of my studies," Wasianski replied with milky submission.

Lampe swept dust balls from the corner.

Kant said, "I need an assistant. So much work remains to be done."

"The man you choose will be fortunate indeed," Wasianski purred.

Lampe thought Wasianski would slobber on himself soon if he didn't contain his enthusiasm.

Kant said, "Come look at this."

Ignoring the presence of the faithful and ever-present Lampe, Kant led Wasianski to the sacred writing desk where he was collecting scraps for his final and greatest work, which Lampe had inwardly titled *The Tale of More than Everything*.

"Look!" Kant said as he opened his hand toward the crumpled slips of paper with ideas written on the front and back.

"Ah!" Wasianski spurted into the vacant air despite being innocent of any insight into Kant's ritual of scribbling thoughts and stuffing them into his pockets as he paced around the room, wringing his hands, rubbing his forehead, and clapping every now and then when some idea came clear.

Lampe had been created by Providence to help Kant write *The Tale of More than Everything*, a book miraculously flawed by the poetic power that extended philosophy to the textured realities of minerals, sheep in Cashmere, the ways in which women compare to haws and hawthorns, nitrogen azote, the shapes of stones, and the slippery etymologies of words.

The buds of the ideas would bloom on those slips of paper. But with the passing of seasons, whole pages would begin to appear all over the house. The master was onto something, and he needed Lampe to coax him toward connections that had to be apprehended by a method not accessible to mere reason. The scraps and pages placed speculation about the starry heavens next to the most local of observations about the blooming, walkable earth, and plans for the next day's meals. The master would quickly become lost without Lampe's guidance.

If poetry does not grab the heart in the heat of youth, it will grab the mind and tongue in the darkest and coldest parts of old age, and the poetry of love that inflames the young heart is cruel to an old man who has waited too long. Kant needed more than a lackey who sustains the physical conditions required by the genius as he painted long sentences onto paper with his quill. He needed a loyal protector who had served as a soldier for a poet-warrior-king.

"You see," Kant said, eyes brightening as he bent over the desk and pushed scraps into piles. "This will be the great work that unifies everything."

Instead of paying attention to the miracles Kant was revealing, Wasianski stared at Lampe over the top of the professor's head. "Herr Lampe!" he said, with a weak but malevolent grin. "Is it necessary that you sweep just now, right at this moment while we are reviewing the professor's most recent work?"

"Yes, Lampe," the master said, echoing the moron and

waving his hand around a bit. "Perhaps the sweeping can wait until later." He continued scratching his dried-up rodent fingers on the sacred papers without looking up to give Lampe a chance to display a grimace of annoyance.

Lampe stomped out, trying to make his boots sound angry. He continued to stomp around the house, but the two men didn't notice.

When they walked out of the room an hour later, Wasianski's arm was around the old man's frail and drooping shoulder. "Immanuel, you may rest easy. Your work will be brought to completion, and I will see to it that nothing is lost."

Lampe despised the deacon's undeserved intimacy with the master. As he watched Wasianski remove a stray thread from the sagging shoulder and straighten the master's coat collar, calling him *Immanuel*, he knew that everything was calculated to crush his spirit. But the greatest outrage was Kant's willingness to trust the imposter with the philosophy itself.

Lampe had never coddled the old man. Why was that? Because coddling would be death to the little weakling. Only a dim-witted man could fail to see what was at stake in the final book and how hard it would be to achieve. Wasianski was luring Kant into an unwarranted confidence about the writing that remained to be done.

Lampe was not afraid of Wasianski, and when they were away from Kant, he said, "Only a poet can mine the old man's remaining secrets. You're neither a poet nor a philosopher."

Wasianski's face screwed itself into an expression of revulsion. "Well, at least I'm not a drunk. A man could get tipsy just smelling your breath, Lampe."

"I could dictate an encyclopedia on the care and maintenance of an old philosopher—details that no one could guess. I know the sounds he makes at night when he is having a nightmare. I know what to say when the dream jerks him out of sleep. And most important of all, I know the reasons he has nightmares."

"If that's true, it's only because you take the liberty of rummaging through his private papers."

"Private papers? I'm not talking about paper. I'm talking about life! I've emptied his pathetic little output from the chamber pot for forty years. For forty years I've listened to him describe his bowels, his lungs, and his opinions about masturbation in excruciating detail. He hardly notices that I exist because I'm his right hand, and his left. But I've heard more of his lectures, in public and in private, than anyone in the world. I am his greatest student."

Wasianski grunted a chuckle. "His greatest student, indeed. You've embarrassed him many times in my presence. Who knows how often you embarrass him when I'm absent?"

"You think I embarrass him? I'm the one who's humiliated! One more public discourse about his plugged-up bowels and …"

"Enough!" Wasianski raised his plucked eyebrows over his momentarily sleepy eyes. "It's your duty to carry out the few tasks entrusted to you, but even these are increasingly neglected as you drink earlier and earlier in the day."

Lampe pulled out a flask of vodka from his coat pocket and took two swigs. "What do you know about my duty? My duty goes far beyond anything you can imagine."

"That's the vodka talking," Wasianski said.

"No, it's the master's disciple talking. The vodka just helps me get out of my own way."

"When you drink you speak too loudly, too often, and on subjects of which you know nothing. The house is not tidy, the guests are insulted, and the professor no longer feels safe around you."

"Nonsense," Lampe said. "I'm an old housecoat."

"On the contrary, he feels bullied. Think about that, Lampe. An old, frail man, bullied."

Lampe said, "Bah! I'm comfortable slippers."

"His delicate manners, and some measure of fear regarding your volatility, prevent him from directly confronting you. I'm standing in for his sake."

"You want to stand in? Well then, stand in for the rest of it." He pulled out his flask again and took a swig. "I'll stay out of your way, and you can see how much work it is to meet his endless needs. Maybe then old Lampe will get the respect he deserves."

Wasianski looked over Lampe's shoulder. "Immanuel, I wouldn't take that to heart. It's the drink speaking."

Lampe's eyes tried to poke out Wasianski's eyes for goading him into speaking while Kant was right behind him. But the clergyman was enveloped by the protective armor of his smugness, so Lampe collected the last fragments of his dignity and walked out of the house.

When Lampe arrived the next day, as he had done every morning for nearly forty years, he was shocked to see Kant sitting in front of the fire, smoking his pipe, reading his book on longevity, and generally looking like a dehydrated rodent in a stocking cap.

"Did you wake yourself?" Lampe asked, disturbed by the grin that was formed around Kant's gums as he clenched on his pipe.

"No, Lampe," Wasianski said. He had hidden himself in the corner, no doubt positioning himself to enjoy Lampe's reaction. "I woke him."

"Why?" Lampe demanded.

Wasianski strolled over and placed his hand comfortingly on Kant's shoulder. "Because it's his usual hour to rise, and I was at hand."

"You're conspiring to destroy me!" Lampe felt his eyes moisten against his will.

"Nonsense," Wasianski said. "You're becoming suspicious in your old age."

Kant stretched his grin, exposing his gums, an inflamed display of mortal fragility.

This was unfair. Lampe alone was the prime mover. Lampe alone was ordained to pull the professor from his river of dreams.

"Why the tears, Lampe?" Wasianski made a quick calculation to stave off any pity the professor might feel. "Are you already drunk at this early hour?"

As the elderly professor relaxed into the fluff of Wasianski's presence, Lampe began to know real hatred for the first time since war had owned his heart.

—⁂—

"I am old and frail. Think of me as a child."

Kant's refrain was so predictable that none of his table guests bothered to dissent. They all smiled at each other in response to his comments between bites of soup. Lampe hated Wasianski, but he could no longer protect the master from humiliation. He may have rolled his eyes when Kant came up with the idea of the schemata. He may have cringed when venereal fulfillment was disrupted by the professor's obsession with financial security. He may have howled when the master blathered endlessly about his bowels. But Kant was a philosopher like no other, and Lampe had never mocked him.

Wasianski handed out more and more invitations to guests who wanted to behold the great Immanuel Kant talking gibberish about nothing before drifting off to sleep during dinner. When he would wake up and go to the chamber pot, the conversation among the guests would immediately shift to observations about his decline and his strange language. Wasianski would tune his face to a look of grievous concern, but he had a sly way of averting his eyes and grinning when dinner guests made subtle jabs at Kant's expense. This allowed him to share in the joke while also appearing to offer a light rebuke.

"It's surprising to see how far his keenness has dulled," one guest would say.

Wasianski would respond, "It comes and goes." When the guests nodded politely, he would add, "But it mostly goes," and the guests would inevitably chuckle.

Lampe's heart slammed against the cage of his chest when Wasianski said such things. No one understood that the master's occasional fogginess of thought was part of his ascent toward the highest standpoint of all.

"But don't be fooled," Wasianski warned. "Immanuel is still

a veritable fountain of ideas. He has a theory for everything. Have you heard about the mysteriously dying cats?"

"The cats in Basel?" an infernal guest said.

Wasianski nodded. "Piles of dead cats everywhere, with no explanation for why they are dying."

"I smell a rat," the guest quipped, confirming Lampe's suspicion that the man was irredeemably stupid.

Wasianski looked around to confirm that Kant was still occupied with the chamber pot. Then he said, "Immanuel attributes the pressure in his head to electricity. So, when he heard about this massive death of cats, he decided the cause must be electricity."

"Electricity?" a couple of the guests asked simultaneously.

Another of the anonymous consumers of Kant's food and wine, who would no doubt disappear into the black hole of history along with whatever tiny talent or contribution they had made to the world, presumed to say, "Why on earth would he believe such a thing?"

Lampe agreed that Kant's silly theory fell into the same pineal category as his schemata. But to hear such degrading criticism come from these pedantic writers of footnotes, who would be forgotten within days of their solitary death, infuriated him, and he said, "It's a brilliant theory! You just don't understand cats. Cats are very electrical animals. When you rub your hand down the fur of a cat, you hear the crackle of electricity. That's a scientific fact!"

"But how does it lead to their death?" a ridiculous guest asked.

Kant walked into the dining room and said, "Enough Lampe! You're botching the theory."

Lampe felt his face go red with frustration, and he stabbed Kant in the forehead with his eyes. "How am I botching it? I explained it the same way you explained it to me."

"That's why I don't bother explaining things to you." He laughed as he sat down, waving his bony claws in the air and inviting the chuckles of the guests. "You failed to mention the clusters of clouds, Lampe. Without the clusters of clouds, the electrical theory of cat death makes no sense." Kant paused and looked around at his guests with a traitorous grin, making sure they all followed the subtlety of his theory. "It's a stupid theory if you don't factor in the clouds."

The guests and Wasianski offered disingenuous nods of approval, but their raised eyebrows and the darting of their eyes were obvious. After that, Kant stopped mentioning the theory in the presence of guests, but he continued to bring it up when he and Lampe were alone, especially during lightning storms. He would peek out the window, ever so carefully, and claim to see sparks along the castle walls when all was dark. Where else would they come from, if not from cats walking on the walls? And any time he saw cats near the castle gates while he was on a walk, he would say, "Mind your hands! Stuff them into your pockets! You touch a cat at your peril!"

Though Lampe seemed to be the only person whose opinions mattered nothing to the professor, the faithful servant nonetheless willed himself to consider the possibility of a world strung through by loops of cats, conduits of electrical fur lighting paths in forests as they hunted for food. He listened for any fine mysteries hovering beyond the walls, waiting to be discovered by Kant's boundless mind in the late poetic stages of his universe-building.

Cats tend to be less electrical when the sky is clear. Lampe didn't know how the master discovered such truths, but he was interested in this property of cats. Kant had no fondness for cats, nor for any other animals. But he admired the order of nature that compels birds to throw out a few babies for the sake of the rest. Lampe was occasionally disturbed by the brutality of nature's order, but he was appalled by the joy it provoked in the professor.

There were many cats in Königsberg foraging for food and finding shelter in the crawl spaces of houses and the unoccupied corners of the horse stables. One evening a cat wandered into the house from the street and trotted to the study where Lampe was poking at glowing embers.

The cat surprised both of them when it jumped onto the hearth. At first, Kant gasped his wheezing gasp. But he surprised Lampe when he patted his thin legs, leaned forward slightly, and whispered, "Kitty, kitty, kitty."

After a moment of purring the cat jumped into his lap.

"Kitty, kitty, kitty." He began to pet the cat, softly. "Do you hear that, Lampe? The crackle? It's a wonder more cats don't catch fire when they rub against each other in lightning storms."

"Or turn into cinders once their mother's water dries from their fur," Lampe added.

Kant petted a bit harder when no sparks ignited. The cat's purr deepened. Suddenly the cat let out a great meow and jumped from the old man, digging its claws into his thin legs. He cried out and stood up from his chair too quickly. He would have landed in the hot embers of the fireplace if Lampe hadn't caught him.

Instead of thanking Lampe, he said, "Throw this cat out the window!"

They were on the second floor of the house, and Lampe didn't want to sin against the cat, so he opened the window and made a show of tossing it. But it landed on the ledge and climbed down the fence to the low grounds of the proper cat world.

"I'm bleeding!" Kant said.

Lampe looked at his leg. "It's just a scratch."

"It takes me forever to heal."

"You petted it too hard."

Kant asked, "Why do you always torment me with your stubborn opposition?"

Lampe answered, "I have a good teacher."

"And look! There's a small hole in my trousers. This will need to be repaired."

"Tomorrow."

The next day Kant showed the scratch to Wasianski and told him the story. Wasianski screwed his face into shock and outrage at Lampe's neglect of such an urgent matter. "We must take care of this immediately. Lampe! Prepare water and soap."

"It's a scratch, not a gunshot wound," Lampe said, and he went to the kitchen to get water and soap.

Wasianski followed him. "Why didn't you wash and bandage his leg?"

"We were having a philosophical discussion. If he can tend to the ideas of the heavens, he can tend to such a tiny scratch."

"It was that silly theory about electricity and the cats of Basel, wasn't it?"

Lampe looked astonished. "Why does a discussion about

life-forces count as philosophy, but talking about the force of electricity in cats doesn't?"

"Because the theory of cats is ridiculous."

"That's very unscientific of you," Lampe said.

"You should have tended his leg."

"What do I know about wounds?"

Wasianski said, "Then you should have called on me."

"You're here enough as it is."

Wasianski locked eyes with him. "Apparently not."

———

In the late afternoon of the fourteenth day of misery, while Lampe was pondering the final fascicle of the final great book, he looked down from his window and saw Kaufman approaching the front door of the building.

The Dunce walked with the leisurely pace of a confident man, a man who didn't need to scurry around for survival. He was whistling.

Lampe locked the door to his room.

The Dunce called up from the street, "Lampe! Lampe! Are you there?"

Lampe ignored him and continued to read.

Transcendental philosophy is the act of consciousness whereby the subject becomes the originator of itself and, thereby, also of the whole object of technical-practical and moral-practical reason in one system—ordering all things in God, as in one system, (Zoroaster).

Zoroaster?

Kaufman knocked at the front door. Lampe peeked out his window and saw the Dunce come inside. Eco was far too trusting and hospitable.

But the Dunce couldn't have the manuscript. Not now. Not at the moment in which he arrived at the crucial word, *Zoroaster*.

Kant had mentioned Zoroaster a few times in his lectures on logic, and he and his friends frequently discussed the famous book *Zend-Avesta*. Lampe didn't need to read it to figure out that Zoroaster was the lawgiver, shrouded in vagueness, who showed up whenever Kant was trying to sew together the abstraction of a heavenly God and the muck of the daily world.

But here, at the heart of the final philosophy, Zoroaster appeared in a completely new way, charged with bringing God and the world together within Kant himself.

Kaufman knocked loudly on Lampe's door. "Lampe! Lampe! I must speak with you!"

Lampe read on as quickly as he could, feeling his mind grow confused as he skimmed words that should have received the most careful thought.

Of the argillaceous aroma, in breathing on alumina (through decomposition) …

Kaufman said, "Lampe! Don't be silly. Are you angry just because I didn't visit for a few days?"

"Go away! I'm busy!" He read on.

The melon must be eaten today—with Prof. Gensichen—and, at this opportunity, the income from the university.

Lampe's eyes grew damp at the precious little note the master had written in the margin.

"I need the manuscript, Lampe. Wasianski has asked one of the university professors to read it, and he'll notice the missing pages. I'll be in trouble!"

"Which professor did he ask?" Lampe yelled through the door.

"Schultz. Professor Johann Schultz."

"Schultz?" Lampe howled. "Oh, good God. He'll never understand it."

Kaufman said, "More than once, I heard the old man say that this person, Schultz, was his best interpreter."

"But he'll never recognize these great advances for what they are. He'll only see repetition, odd digressions, strange side-comments! Everyone will listen to his opinion, and then the book will die!"

The Dunce said, "The choice isn't yours."

Lampe didn't answer. As he read on, he had a pain like that of Tantalus, knowing the unpaid bill of an incomplete philosophy.

Religion is conscientiousness, the holiness of the acceptance and truthfulness of what many must confess to himself. Confess to yourself. To have religion, the concept of God is not required (still less the postulate: 'There is a God').

The concept of God is not required for religion?

"Lampe!" the Dunce said. "I will demand that Eco open the door. I will take the manuscript and never bring you any more news."

Air is a liquidum, but not a fluidum.

"Lampe! Lampe!"

Granite consists of quartz, feldspar, and mica. Mica includes muscovite, or Russian glass, of which there are large panes and the portholes of seagoing ships.

Lampe heard the sound of Eco's slow, heavy stomp as he climbed the stairs. Eco was gloomy-sounding when he said,

"Martin, your friend seems terribly upset. He insists that you have a book that belongs to him."

"It doesn't belong to him," Lampe yelled. "He doesn't even know what it is. No one knows except me."

Sheet six, page four.

Reason inevitably creates objects for itself. Hence everything that thinks has a God.

Silence. Maybe the Dunce gave up and left.

It is not even in the divine power to make a morally good man (to make him morally good): he must do it himself.

Yes!

Transcendental philosophy is the self-creation (autocracy) of ideas, into a complete system of the objects of pure reason. In the Bible it says: Let us make man, and behold, everything was very good.

Lampe stopped reading. What were they doing out there? Maybe Eco was choking the Dunce into silence. But that wasn't likely. Despite being the Königsberg executioner and as big as a lowland bison, Eco was the gentlest person Lampe had ever known.

Lampe read as quickly as he could, skimming past the irrelevant passages in search of the secret the master sensed as he wrote. He felt Kant's mind reaching toward the voluptuous darkness of the idea of God.

That this idea has objective reality—that is, that it has the force appropriate to the moral law in reason of every man who is not wholly bestially crippled—and that man must inevitably confess to himself ...

The handwriting whispered to Lampe that Kant was rushing toward something he desperately wanted to grasp.

There is one and only one God, requiring no proof of its existence, as if it were a natural being; its existence already lies, rather, in the developed concept of this idea, according to the principle of identity: the mere form here counts to the being of the thing. The enlightened man can do no other than himself to condemn or to pardon, and that which pronounces this judgment in him (moral-practical reason) can, indeed, be anesthetized through sensible impulses, so that ...

The sentence broke off. *To condemn or pardon?* Yes, this is where everything that matters begins to take shape.

To anesthetize judgment so that ... So that, what? So that Kant, along with everyone else including Lampe, might flourish, rather than enduring judgment without end?

Sheet ten, page one.

Yesterday Lampe forced a bonus from me for the first quarter of 1802, and he forced me to enter it on my writing-slate, with my own hand.

Lampe cried out, "Unfair!" He stood up and paced in front of Ding, trying to accommodate the shock of yet another unexpected and unjustified blow to his dignity. "Unfair, unfair, unfair!"

When Wasianski had taken over the professor's finances, he had canceled Lampe's bonuses. But Lampe needed them. He had earned them!

Lampe forced a bonus from me ...

Forced? Did he not merely cite his need, his long service, and his endurance of abuse at everyone's hands? Did he not merely point out that Kant had built an empire, while Lampe had nothing to show for his life except his service to the professor? Was that not sufficient to justify an extra two thalers for his wine, the only thing that enabled him to endure?

Lampe heard Eco stick the key in the lock. For once he was glad the lock stuck.

Eco said, "Patience, Herr Kaufman, patience."

Sheet twelve, page one.

The love of wisdom is the least that one can possess; wisdom for man is the highest—and hence, transcendent.

Yes.

Zoroaster: or philosophy as a whole, comprehended under a principle.

Yes! The master was nearly there.

The lock turned, and the door opened. The Dunce unsuccessfully tried to loom darkly in the doorway.

Lampe quickly read the last sentence of the manuscript.

Poltron (pollex truncatus).

How lost tired and the old man must have been.

The Dunce said, "Lampe!"

As Lampe tried to wrap the fascicle, he noticed that Kant had scribbled something on the wrapper:

God, as a holy being, can have no comparative or superlative. There can be only one. Transcendental philosophy precedes the assertion of things that are thought, their archetype, in which they must be set.

That was it, a message from Kant to Lampe, written on the wrapper covering the final fascicle of the last and greatest book. The philosophy of transcendence precedes thought. Obviously, only the imagination can reach so high. The master had finally seen it, and in the last words he wrote before he died, he had scribbled his affirmation of the great *principle of the poetic a priori,* and of Martin Lampe.

Lampe looked up at Kaufman and folded the wrapper around the manuscript. Then he held it out and asked, "Is this what you wanted?"

"I'll leave the two of you alone," Eco said, and he retreated to his room.

Kaufman stepped toward Lampe with a confidence he had lacked the day of Kant's death. He sat down without asking permission and said, "When Wasianski sees the wrapping all crooked and crumpled, he'll know someone's been at it."

Lampe scratched his chest and said, "You'll have time to wrap it to your satisfaction. He won't give it to Schultz before the funeral."

"Maybe not, but I can't take a chance." The Dunce looked around the room, gawking at the half-chewed bone beside Ding, the scribbles on the walls, the disheveled bed, the disheveled Lampe. He sniffed and made an exaggerated and unnecessary grimace at the smell of dog and unwashed old man.

Lampe sat in silence, glaring. Then he said, "You never looked at those jobs, did you?"

Kaufman's face wrinkled into a quizzical expression, before ironing itself back into placid smugness. "No need. Wasianski promised to get me a good position when everything is settled."

"What a relief that your many gifts won't be wasted."

"I'll just be glad when it's all over. I've never seen so many people care so much about a dead man. The whole world seems sad. And the questions! They want to know everything. I didn't mind for a day or two, or even a week, but this has been exhausting."

Lampe pulled out his precious jug of wine and asked, "Do you ever mention me to the visitors?"

The sphincter of Kaufman's face contracted into the look of a man reaching for a memory that was scarcely important enough to keep, but that might be lying around somewhere in his mind. Then he said, "Yes, actually. A visitor asked about the soot that had built up on the walls. I said, 'That's a question for Martin Lampe. He used to keep house for the professor.'"

There was no reason to resist. Lampe would be forgotten. He would be lucky to show up as an unread footnote, a curiosity mentioned for completeness in a biography of the great professor. The sum of his life was reduced to nothing more than, *Martin Lampe: He Kept House for the Philosopher.*

Lampe mumbled, "So people are interested in the private life of the professor?"

The question animated the Dunce like a pull on a puppet string. "Their questions take up half my day. Wasianski's almost finished with his book about the professor, and I wouldn't be surprised if everyone in Königsberg will want a copy."

Lampe's thoughts were cold molasses as a sense of doom settled on him. "I can hardly wait to read his great insights into philosophy's greatest mind."

"He has a good way with words. He calls the professor a mighty shade, a phantom from a forgotten century. That's sort of mysterious and spooky, don't you think? He says the greatest honor of his life was being chosen to care for the mighty shade until the end."

Lampe wanted to drown the Dunce's enthusiasm in a pool of gloom. "I lived with this mighty shade at the height of his powers."

"That may be, but Wasianski says the soul is only truly known on the death bed." The Dunce was almost perky as he tutored Lampe. "He's earned the right to brag about it."

"To brag about what?" A ghost inhabited Lampe's voice.

"About the last hours and how he created a singular bond with the master."

"A singular bond?"

"Toward the end, the old man could barely speak. But a few hours before he died, he signaled that Wasianski should kiss him. So he kissed the old man. I couldn't have done it, but he said it was a solemn act of tenderness."

Lampe's face went pale. "He kissed him?"

"Right on the lips," the Dunce said beamily, rousing himself and filling the room with his delight.

"He was asking for water!" Lampe howled. "He hated when his lips and mouth were dry! He would never ask for a kiss, least of all from Wasianski!"

"I think Wasianski could tell the difference between being asked for water and being asked for a kiss."

"All is lost!" Lampe cried.

"You seem awfully upset."

"All is lost," Lampe said again. He poured another glass of wine and quickly drank it down.

"If it bothers you so much, maybe you should write your own book."

Lampe ignored the comment. He breathed in and breathed out. Then he asked, "What were the master's last words?"

"He said, 'It is good.'" The Dunce shrugged. "Sort of a disappointing way to end a life of wise pronouncements."

Lampe had never seen a glimmer of curiosity or a flicker of insight in the Dunce, but when the answer came forth from his mouth, it was as though he were delivering a message in a divine language, causing the mind of Lampe to become radiant like the face of Moses on the mountaintop. He leaned forward and asked, "Are you sure he said, 'It is good'?"

"Completely sure. Wasianski had given him a little wine mixed with water, so we figured he was saying how good it tasted, and that he had had enough."

Lampe ignored the hermeneutic of the two imbeciles as he basked without fear in the presence of an unnamed mystery, even though he knew it was the master filling the room with light like a lantern in a cave, with the wind of the great spirit stirring, rising up from a place too deep to be explored. After a few moments, he opened his eyes and asked, "Where will he be buried?"

"The Professor's Vault. Wasianski says they've got music, poetry—the works. He's really putting his heart into the funeral. Königsberg will always remember Wasianski for his devotion to the old professor. That's what he tells me, anyway."

"We can only hope." Lampe wiped his eyes with his sleeve. "Do you know the day of the burial?"

"Not yet. But the lines are short now, and things have slowed down. It won't be long."

Lampe needed to be alone. He opened the door and said, "You should be getting back."

"I suppose you're right," The Dunce blushed as he picked up the manuscript that meant so much to Lampe, and he left the room.

Lampe was a soldier who had killed many men in his youth.

He knew that the point of a large sword and the point of a small sword are equally as sharp, and equally capable of penetrating a man's heart.

Day Fifteen

The Highest Point of View

LIGHT FROM THE MORNING STAR outside Lampe's window dusted the back of his eyes, and he hurled his imagination towards it. He allowed his mind to float by the homes of Königsberg toward the swampy lands that lay outside, past the cold sea that reached to the top of the earth, and then off to the farthest darkness of the universe.

He needed to urinate, but he hesitated to get out of bed in the bitter cold of winter. The confluence of mind, bladder, and bowel wearied him after spending a life as the one who had been ordained to support the world's greatest mind, which sat atop the world's most incompetent coil of intestine, ending in an utterly inadequate arse. The thought stabbed Lampe's memory with regret.

If Lampe ever knocked on the bedroom door while Kant was using the chamber pot, he would bark, "I'm occupied."

Lampe would respond, "Tell me when you're finished."

"I'm never finished!"

Lampe was aware of this, but if he always waited for the

master to be done with his little shit, he would never get anything done. "You could have produced a magnum opus in the time it's taking you to produce a …"

"Lampe! Leave me in peace!"

One afternoon, when Kant was taking an especially long time, Lampe was more insistent. "The guests will be here soon. The food is getting cold, the sauces are congealing, and the cook is upset."

"Leave me to my misery," Kant whimpered. "I'll come when I can."

As guests arrived, Lampe led them to the parlor. "He'll be here soon. It takes him longer to dress these days." How many lies had Lampe told to keep the appearance of the Great Philosopher intact?

"The professor will come when he can," Wasianski added, taking over the conversation, the introductions, and everything else that was rightly Lampe's. "We all know about his increasing challenges."

"Yes!" Kant said. He walked into the room with the odd stomping gate he had recently adopted to keep his body stable, lifting his feet high and then driving them firmly into the ground. He sat at the table, clapped his hands, and looked around at the several guests gathered for dinner. "I simply cannot empty my bowels, however much I try. I don't know how long I can carry these bloated intestines inside me."

Wasianski said, "At least we're all alive for one more meal together."

"If I have any room remaining for food," Kant said. "What a misery it all is. Even wiping my bottom with newspapers irritates my skin. Deacon Wasianski got me some hemp, which was certainly an improvement. But it costs more, and we need to watch the finances. Old gummed up philosophers are unpredictable, and you never know how long they might last."

A visitor named Karl Ludwig Porschke jotted down the professor's statement in a notebook. Then he said, "Here's something that might interest you, Immanuel. I recently used a flushable toilet on a visit to London."

"I've heard about that!" Kant's eyes were suddenly enlivened by a focus and light that was becoming rarer.

"It's marvelous," Porschke said. "You turn a crank valve and suddenly your waste is gone."

In a droll tone, Wasianski said, "No more emptying famous men's chamber pots? Lampe, you'd be out of a job."

Lampe was picking his nose in the corner of the room. He stopped when everyone looked towards him.

Before Lampe could think up a response, Wasianski turned the conversation to the one topic that no longer had competitors—securing Kant's immortal reputation.

Porschke saw the opportunity first, and he leaped. "Yes, Immanuel, I'm working on a wonderful poem about you."

After Porschke's pushy claim on the poem to celebrate Kant, everyone at the table expounded on the legacy Kant would leave, planning for his death right in front of him until his eyelids began to droop.

They spoke with such unearned confidence about Kant's life and work that Lampe, the singular witness, had to fortify his patience with a nip or two of vodka. But despite, or perhaps aided by, the wonders of this beverage, in the end, he could not stop himself from proclaiming the truth. "Do any of you know his true glory? I've devoted my entire life, and sacrificed everything, including my wife, to sustain his work. I've been ..." Lampe choked, felt his stomach rise, and then swallowed hard. "I've tried to be the light in which he wrote his philosophy."

Kant had slumped into full sleep. There was an embarrassed silence among the guests until Wasianski waved his hand toward Lampe and said, "Gentlemen, behold Martin Lampe, without whom none of the famous books would have been written. We can all be grateful that he lent the world his skills as a craftsman of precise philosophical language."

Kant suddenly blurted out, "That's right!"

Was he making a joke? Surely he didn't agree with Lampe's presumptuous self-assessment.

Then Kant straightened up and said, "A flushable toilet would put you out of a job!"

"Immanuel!" Wasianski laughed, jabbing a glance at Lampe.

Kant opened his eyes fully. "I must have slipped away into sleep, but I feel much better. Have we had dessert?"

Wasianski said, "No, no. We would never have dessert without you."

"Lampe!" Kant called out. "Where is Lampe?"

Lampe was standing just behind him, blushing with anger. "I'm right here."

"May we have some pie?" Kant asked.

"You may have some pie," Lampe answered, stating a mere fact in a voice suited to the stating of such a fact.

"Thank you," Kant said.

"Certainly," Lampe replied without moving from his place.

Wasianski asked, "May we have some pie as well?"

"You also may have some pie," Lampe politely answered. But he still didn't move.

Wasianski looked around the table at the baffled guests. "Lampe, why aren't you getting the pie?"

"You didn't ask me to get the pie. You asked if you can have pie."

"Lampe!" Wasianski said.

Lampe bowed. "Would you like a large piece or a small piece?"

"A moderate piece," Wasianski answered.

Kant's eyes were slowly closing again. He was tired. The wine had been a bit stronger than usual.

Lampe pursued clarity. "By moderate do you mean slightly larger than small, or slightly smaller than large?"

Wasianski again grinned at the guests, embarrassed that he didn't have better control over this servant. He reached out and propped up Kant who was leaning in his chair. "Somewhere in between."

"Somewhere, or exactly?" Lampe asked.

"Exactly!" Wasianski said.

"Excellent. Exactly. Very good."

Lampe stood still, staring across the room at the picture of Rousseau.

Wasianski said, "Lampe! What's the problem today? Why are you still standing there?"

Lampe answered, "We must establish what we mean by large and small in order to know exactly where the middle lies."

"Lampe!"

"Isn't this what philosophers do?" Lampe inquired.

"Bring in the whole pie and I will serve it myself."

"I can't bring in the whole pie," Lampe said, committed to speaking only the truth.

"And why not?" Wasianski stood up in frustration.

"Because the cook ate a piece earlier."

One of the guests chuckled as Wasianski glared.

Lampe said, "Words have meanings. They matter."

The poet Porschke said, "Lampe has a point about words. I'm sure Immanuel would agree."

"Words have meanings," Kant said, eyes still closed. "My name is …" He stopped. The guests leaned in to hear the rest of his thought, some of them ready to jot it down.

"Yes, Immanuel?" Wasianski's grin was fixed on his face like an actor's mask. "Words? Names?"

When Kant didn't finish his sentence, Lampe stepped in as only he could do. "The professor was about to tell you the story of how he changed his name from E-mmanuel to I-mmanuel many years ago."

Porschke asked, "Why on earth did he do that?"

"To make it more faithful to the Hebrew," Lampe answered. "You'll have to ask the professor if you want to know why faithfulness to the Hebrew is more important to him than faithfulness to his mother who gave him his name."

"Eh?" Kant said, sitting up a bit more, eyes still mostly closed.

"Sleep, Immanuel," Wasianski purred. "I'll take you to bed soon."

"While we're on the subject," Lampe added, "he changed his last name too."

"Really?" Porschke asked, frantically scribbling in his notebook.

"Yes," Lampe continued, feeling Wasianski stare daggers into him. "His birth name was spelled C, A, N, T, but he changed it to K, A, N, T because he was embarrassed when anyone called him 'Tsant.' Abandoning history is one of his gifts."

Wasianski grumbled, "You're certainly full of informative stories today."

"He's been my whole life," Lampe said.

"He doesn't feel well, Lampe." Wasianski stomped on any further questions the guests might ask the impertinent servant. "Take him to bed while I get the pie."

Lampe was weary of the gawking guests and Wasianski's fawning, so he complied. Kant followed him to the bedroom in the dim lantern light. His hand fluttered a brief wave goodbye to his guests.

In the bedroom Kant sat down on the side of the bed, holding his tiny belly. His small body nearly disappeared in the folds of the nightgown he had put on. "Lampe, get me a piece of sugar with some rum on it for my intestines."

"You know those remedies are absurd. The mind of a philosopher ..."

"Lampe," he said quietly. He reached out and touched his servant's hand, then let it drift back to his uncomfortable belly. "Just get the sugar with rum. I feel like I'm going to pop, and it scares me."

Lampe dipped a lump of sugar in rum and brought it to him from the kitchen. He avoided the guests who were busy eating pie, drinking port, and talking about the declining professor and his fool of a servant. When he entered the bedroom Kant had covered up with a blanket.

"Here," Lampe said.

"Ah, thank you," Kant said. "My faithful Lampe. I am … I am …"

"Shhhhh," Lampe said.

Kant closed his eyes and quickly drifted away into sleep.

———

Months before Lampe was exiled, he began to see something glowing in the piles of scraps Kant was scribbling as he came closer to the highest viewpoint that would transform the mind of humanity finally and for all time. Sometimes he would see the direction an idea was trying to go, and using his best imitation of the professor's handwriting, he would scribble a note in the margin to prompt the old man. When Kant would discover the note that looked like his own, he would write with a frightening focus for several more pages, occasionally turning over the ink well as he jabbed the quill into it. When the work stagnated and the master seemed to drift, Lampe would follow the dictum Kant gave to his students, and he would start a new paragraph by restating the question.

The master was searching for a priori principles so rich and so full that physics would no longer require instruments of measure. He craved a singular principle that would make even the physical reality of the stars unnecessary for the deep truth he felt. The great mind turned to a kind of a priori ether that filled the universe and penetrated all bodies.

Wasianski never asked questions about the ideas when Kant tried to explain them. He just nodded and smiled like he was humoring a dullard. "How interesting. How very interesting."

Then he repeated the ideas to friends in private with egregious mistakes, missing the subtle points that made the ideas interpretable. There was always a good laugh.

Lampe would have no part of this, and he pushed the old man to go farther. Kant had pages and pages of outlines about the apparent contradiction that obsessed and possessed him—a priori matter. It was lunacy and genius at the same time. So, when Kant mumbled to himself about an idea, Lampe goaded him, saying, "I don't understand!"

"Of course you don't understand," Kant said. "How could you understand?"

"Show me the proof" Lampe replied. "All you have are silly outlines."

Kant held his belly as though it was aching, "You wouldn't understand the proof."

"Do you even have a proof?" Lampe asked.

"I would have a proof if I had any peace. But you clatter and clink dishes, and you shuffle your shoes on the floor instead of lifting your feet ..." He paused and grimaced. His grimace was connected to real pain, but he exaggerated it when Lampe was near. He pointed to his belly. "And how can anyone think when he has to live with this? Get me some naphtha, Lampe. I will try anything."

"Anything?" Lampe asked.

"Anything."

Lampe paused before saying, "Let go."

"What do you mean?"

"Let go," Lampe repeated.

"Let go of what?" Kant said irritably.

"Let go of everything."

"You're making no sense. Go to the apothecary! I'll never finish this work, never. But it must be done!"

"I can help you." The words came as though they had a will of their own, as though God had formed the words from nothing in his mouth. Calm relief swept over Lampe as he came closer to asking for what he most wanted, and what the professor most needed.

"You want to help me? Go get the naphtha!"

"I understand more than you think," Lampe persisted with equanimity.

Belly pain forced Kant's face into a frown. "If you understood you would be off to get the naphtha."

The demon of irritability again possessed Lampe, and he pulled out his flask and took a couple of swigs to numb it. "Ask Wasianski. He's good for nothing except errands any boy could do."

"At least he does that much!"

"He's an idiot," Lampe said.

"Lampe!" Kant shifted his body into one position, and then another, trying to find comfort.

"Fine," Lampe said. "I'll go get your naphtha."

"Hurry!"

Lampe went out into the cold, wearing his old inadequate coat. When he returned Kant took the bottle of naphtha with no word of thanks, and he swallowed a dose. He waited a few minutes, staring at the floor. When nothing happened, he swallowed another dose, sitting, looking around the room, hoping his insides would soon churn.

Lampe was still in his coat, his organs and marrow chilled. "Try sitting on the pot as an act of faith." He took a couple of swigs from the flask to warm himself.

Kant scowled at his drinking.

Lampe moved close to Kant's face and said, "What? I'm cold! We each have our medicine. Go sit on the pot."

Kant raised his eyebrows. "I think I feel something."

"Did I finally scare the shit out of you?"

The chamber pot was behind an ornamental divider. Kant hid, awaiting his miracle.

Lampe followed Kant with some of the notes from the desk. He took a few more swallows of vodka from the flask. His mind floated upwards towards the heavens, and he began to read aloud.

"Put down my notes!" Kant demanded in a voice strained with pushing.

"But they're marvelous, your greatest work," Lampe said with a flicker of sincere intent from a heart warmed by spirits.

"Put them back in the study!"

"Listen, old man!" he said, shocking himself with his boldness. "I've figured out something that can turn all this scribbling into the greatest thing you've ever written."

"Leave me in peace and hand me my naphtha. I need another dose. Maybe that will help."

Lampe said, "First listen to the secret I've discovered. Then you'll know who can truly assist you in finishing your work."

Kant was silent behind the screen, probably rosy-faced from straining to evacuate his unfortunate bowels.

In the silence, Lampe felt the truth unveil and name itself.

"The secret has never been spoken outside my own mind. It's a principle. A great and guiding principle. We must work together to draw it out of the darkness, but I'm certain it will unlock the secret of your final great work. I call it ..."

As Lampe finished his sentence, "... *the principle of the poetic a priori*," Wasianski walked in and filled the room with his preaching voice.

"What is this, Lampe? Have you lost all respect for the man? Will you invade even this most private of exercises?" Then he looked down at the papers in Lampe's hand. "What are those?"

Lampe looked down at his flask in one hand and Kant's notes in the other.

Kant called out from behind the curtain. "What was that you said?"

Wasianski answered, "Nothing, Immanuel. I'm taking care of it." Then he asked again in a strained whisper, "What are you doing? What are those pages in your hand?"

"No!" Kant said. "I mean Lampe! He said something. What was that? What did you say?"

Lampe glared at Wasianski's eyes and answered his question. "This, sir, is my work." And he took a long drink from his flask.

Wasianski leaned toward Lampe with an expression on his face like that of a man who just bit into rotten cheese, and he said, "Your work here is nearly done."

Lampe grinned at the thought of the rotten cheese as Kant strained his voice to repeat, "What was that? What did you say? Lampe!"

"It's only me, Immanuel," Wasianski said. He reached out to squeeze Lampe's elbow, and he nodded for him to leave the room. "Take your time, Manny. Don't strain too much. You'll pop a vessel."

Lampe left, but as he closed the door he heard Kant say again, "What was that? What did you say?"

What indeed? Wasianski had ruined the moment by colluding with Kant's uncooperative sphincter muscle. Lampe would have to be patient. If he presented the principle at the wrong time, he would be summarily dismissed, the way he was always summarily dismissed, as a fool, a dullard, a drunk.

When Kant finally emerged from his room, he walked up to Lampe and looked at him with an increasingly rare lucidity and clearness of eye. "Lampe, you make no sense, and you smell like spirits."

No sense? The master needed help. Death was fast approaching, and Kant was moving without a rudder in the fog-strewn seas he had run from his entire life. Poetry prevailed over critique as he tried to navigate the connections of meals to flowers to heavens to rocks to ether to morality to God, and to stay upright among the towering waves of metaphor that overwhelmed him in his desperate attempt to gather it all into the great book of everything. He also began to have bad dreams of the sort that accompany the twilight of genius when it glimpses a harbor it will never reach.

As visitors came to watch the phantom's decline, Lampe stayed by his side. Even though the master refused to see that Lampe offered a way through, the faithful servant stayed with the old philosopher in faith, hope, and, yes, love.

In the winter of Lampe's impending exile, a lump began to

313

appear on the upper part of the master's belly after every meal. It frightened him, and he didn't want to be alone with it.

"Lampe," Kant said with a whimper of doom. "There it is. Touch it."

Lampe poked it with one finger.

"Not so hard, Lampe. You'll punch a hole in my skin."

"Does it hurt?"

"Only when you poke it," Kant answered.

"You told me to poke it."

"I told you to touch it."

Lampe touched it more gently. "I think it's nothing."

"It's not nothing, Lampe. Look at it! It's right there! It has returned!"

"Returned? You've never had this lump before. What's so scary about it?"

Kant didn't answer. He tried to unfasten his clothes to relieve the pressure it caused. He rubbed his hand over the hard place, gently, as though his belly would pop open if he rubbed any harder. "I wonder what it is?"

"The thing-in-itself?" Lampe said, immediately regretting his rebellious tongue.

"You're the one who gives me nightmares," Kant said as he continued to fuss with the top of his trousers.

Lampe reached over to help him unfasten the top button, and Kant's hands dropped to his sides. Lampe said, "I can't be the one who gives you nightmares. I have no power over you."

"And don't forget it!" Kant didn't thank Lampe for getting the button loose, but he did sigh with relief, which was reward enough.

Kant tried to pull off his shoes, but the lump kept him from bending. Lampe knelt down and carefully pulled at the shoes filled with the old man's swollen feet.

"I'm only trying to help you," Lampe said.

"Help me do what?"

"Finish the work!" Now that he had said the absurdly enormous thing once, it was easier to repeat.

"Don't be ridiculous. Just get my shoes off."

"Why is it ridiculous?" Lampe asked.

"I won't even talk about this. It's inconceivable. You're always chattering on about this thing or that thing. You argue with guests. And you show no respect to Wasianski, even though he's the one who actually helps me with my work."

Lampe's throat clotted with blood and feeling as he said, "Wasianski doesn't understand the first thing about your work."

Kant answered, "Drink less. Argue less. Talk less. Work more." Then he paused and reviewed his own words. Once he felt sure about his advice, he compressed it. "*Less talk, more action.* This should be your maxim, Lampe."

"You're not listening!" Lampe's voice thinned into an unfortunate whine just as he needed to say things clearly and calmly.

Kant said, "I'll pop if I don't find a way to achieve a more sufficient exoneration of feces!"

"Exoneration of feces? That's what you're thinking about? I'm baring my soul, and you're fantasizing about a big shit?"

Kant mumbled, "That's vulgar, Lampe. Vulgar and unnecessary."

Maybe it was the late hour. Maybe it was Lampe's weariness after a day of service. Maybe it was the vodka Lampe allowed himself as a reward at the end of another meal, well-served and unappreciated. But Kant's lack of gratitude was suddenly, over-whelmingly intolerable.

Less talk, more action.

Lampe knew that lifeless maxims could ruin common sense. He knew they could blind a person to the consequences of actions in the world. But as A causes B, and as B causes C, with no apparent room for undetermined freedom, Lampe could not stop the series of events that made his exile inevitable.

In that moment, Lampe and Kant were no longer servant and master, but rather two old men who had known each other for forty years. Lampe looked down at the brown spots on his own hands, and he said, "Less talk, professor? More action, professor?"

Kant eyed him with alert caution.

Lampe reached out and poked at the lump on his belly, not with any real force, but just to make a point. "Forty years! Forty years I've listened to you talk about your bowels." He drank from his flask and watched his own hands shake as though they belonged to someone else.

Kant's look of alarm increased.

Lampe said, "You talk endlessly about the sphincter in your ass, but you won't talk to me about ideas. I'm a man, professor, even if I'm only a servant. I've spent forty years with you and your ideas, and yet you treat me as though I'm the only person in the world who will never understand. Am I alone not worth the trouble of an education? Well, here's a piece of news from the foreign land of my soul. You educated me against my will, and now you have to live with your creation."

Lampe's eyes went wet, and his nose began to run. He forced

a smile onto his face, a great and magnanimous smile laced with slobber, and he continued to choke out his words. "How many times do you think I read my copy of *The Critique of Pure Reason*?"

Kant leaned back in his chair and performed a little shrug in the face of this astonishing question.

"Twenty!" Lampe said. "More than twenty! It's my book. My only book!"

Kant raised his eyebrows with genuine surprise. This made Lampe bold, and he wiped his mouth with one sleeve and his eyes with the other. "I'm the only man in the world who has been present with these ideas from the beginning. Long, faithful presence. Ah, but I'm a drunk. Yes! Irritable. Yes! Lazy. Well, what if I do choose leisure over work sometimes? What if I polish the spoons too often, while resting my swollen feet? I'm an old man just like you. I'm closing out my time on earth and asking what I've done with my life. Do you have any idea what my great work is?"

Kant shrugged again, glancing left and right, looking for help or escape.

"You!" Lampe cried. "You are my great work!"

Kant rolled his eyes, just a flick of the pupils upward, scarcely perceptible. But with that slight rolling of the eyes, Lampe felt his dignity deflate. He relinquished, surrendered, stopped. "You seem to think there is only one topic fitting for me. Your bowels." He took a drink from his flask. The urge to weep left him. "Fine. From now on, we talk of nothing else."

"Nonsense, Lampe. This is all nonsense, unnecessary, and a result of too much drinking."

"Yes, it's all nonsense. What else am I capable of besides nonsense?" He drank again. His flask was nearly empty. "I shall write a short history of your bowels for posterity, so to speak. I may be ignorant of any crumb of wisdom contained in your philosophy, but alas, no one comes close to having my understanding of your intestines."

"Stop, Lampe. Just stop."

"Or!" Lampe said, raising his finger in the air and leaning toward the old professor so that he could look directly into his eyes. "We can do away with chatter and finish our discourse on the philosopher's bowels using a bit of Aristotle." Lampe finished the vodka in his flask and capped it. "You look surprised that I mention Aristotle. Why? I've heard you lecture on his principles at least a hundred times. We'll conclude this lesson with a practical syllogism, in keeping with the only guiding maxim you have bequeathed to me. *Less talk! More action!*"

Lampe stepped over to the chamber pot where Kant had deposited his little pellet. He dropped his pants. Staring at Kant's eyes, he shit greatly into the pot of the famous philosopher.

He stood and pulled up his pants.

"And that, my master, is how it's done. A great and satisfying shit in the old pot. Less talk, more action. Nothing could be simpler."

Kant stared with an intensity of astonishment that Lampe had never witnessed. With weak arms and legs, he pushed himself up from his chair. He walked past Lampe and looked down into the chamber pot. He stared in silence.

Shame began to creep up on Lampe, but he held his expression firmly in place. As his shame deepened, he took a step back. The silence was unbearable. He whispered, "Professor."

They were on the threshold of a new honesty. Is anything impossible between two old men who know the deepest parts of each other's lives?

Lampe said, "I've listened to forty years of your lectures and your conversations. You think I'm ignorant, and indeed I was when you hired me. But I'm not anymore. I've listened, and bit by bit I've collected and stored away your entire philosophy in my mind. I know you."

Kant continued to stare into the chamber pot with an almost childlike fascination.

Lampe was encouraged, so he continued to speak. "I know you, but you don't know me. How have forty years passed without you knowing who I am?"

Kant looked up at Lampe with a blank expression on his face, as though he was seeing Lampe for the first time.

Lampe's throat filled with the words that were all trying to get out at once, but he overcame the choking sensation and, with an unstuttering eloquence building toward a crescendo, he said, "I suffer from my horrid vulgarity. But I want to help you. I want to serve you. I alone can help you finish this final work. Let me fill my flask and we can drink deeply, remembering everything we've lived through together."

Lampe suddenly felt wonderful and ashamed at the same time. He knew he was drunk, but there was a sober core that was on the verge of declaring his unconditional devotion to the professor that was, indeed, a kind of love.

Kant turned away from Lampe and the chamber pot. He took a couple of steps toward the window with his head hanging down, his hands clasped behind his back. His voice was firm but quiet when he said the word, "Leave."

At first, Lampe didn't understand. It was impossible. This was not the response he expected.

Kant turned back towards him and said again, "Leave!"

Lampe's confusion deepened. "But … I … I … Let me clean the chamber pot."

"Leave!" Kant said with whatever small fury he could pull into his aging voice, spitting the word past his nearly toothless gums. His hands were trembling, his eyes were dull.

A servant knows when to leave, when to give space to an angry employer. He had not meant to be cruel. He had not meant to cause pain. How many times in forty years had he made the professor angry? They always managed to repair things. He just needed to give the professor some time. Sleep would calm the master. He would also forswear alcohol, at least for a day or two. That always helped.

Kant followed Lampe silently, breathing heavily and glaring as the servant gathered his rag of a coat and his whittled walking stick. Lampe opened the door and looked back toward Kant. He wanted to fall on the ground at the master's feet and beg forgiveness. But he knew there had been sufficient folly for one day.

Kant would not look at Lampe's eyes. He merely stood there, wheezing, waiting.

When Lampe stepped into the snow, Kant immediately slammed the door shut with all his might. Lampe heard a clamor on the other side of the door and knew that the force of slamming the door had caused Kant to fall into the umbrella stand next to it.

Lampe put his ear close to the door, listening for the old man, just in case he cried out for help. He heard the sounds of Kant using the umbrella stand to lift himself off the floor. He heard the sounds of footsteps fading down the hall. Then there was silence. It was finished.

That evening Lampe lay on his bed contemplating his folly. *Just wait*, he thought. The old man would sleep, and in the morning Lampe would be precisely on time, ready to wake him at five before the sky grew bright. He resolved to accept his place in life. He was no longer a soldier. He was not a student. He was not a philosopher. He was Martin Lampe, servant. Once and for all, he would take pride only in his excellence as a servant. And he would be satisfied with his wages, never again asking for a bonus.

His resolve was clean and complete. But his sleep was fitful and full of anxious thoughts and dreams. Though he was exhausted in the morning, he rose and dressed urgently. Both dread and joy nipped at his heels as he clomped through the snow, leaning on his walking stick like it was half of a bishop's staff.

The darkness of Königsberg winter had an ancient being of its own. It wrapped around Lampe, slowing him and resisting every step he took. But he walked on. He was devoted to the master with a will that was as real as his very breath. He turned the final corner at last and walked toward Kant's front door.

Then he saw the heaped-up glow of Wasianski's pipe, overstuffed with tobacco. Something wasn't right.

Lampe crept closer and said, "I'm here to wake the professor."

"No, Lampe," Wasianski said. "You will not wake him."

Lampe stepped forward. "You're going too far this time, Deacon."

Wasianski said, "You're done, sir. Your service is no longer needed."

"Well, sir," Lampe retorted, clicking his heels together and preparing for something that was only vaguely forming in his will. "I'm here to say that it's your presence that is no longer needed! It never was needed! We were fine until you arrived." Then Lampe formally asserted, "You, sir, are dismissed!"

Just then he noticed another man in the shadows tapping his palm with a police bludgeon. Lampe wilted. "I'm an old man, Wasianski. Do you need the police to protect you from me?"

"You may leave," Wasianski said.

A third man appeared in the shadows, but Lampe couldn't see his face.

"Why?" Lampe cried.

Wasianski answered, "Because the professor said so. He refused to say why. You are fortunate indeed to have served a man who is so discrete."

"I demand a reason!" Lampe bellowed.

"You're in no position to demand anything. You should have thought of consequences earlier."

"Consequences for what? Serving him with my life? No, this is absurd. I must talk to the professor. This is all a misunderstanding. I have served him for forty years. He would never fire me."

Wasianski stomped with one foot and said, "Immanuel will not tell me why you have been dismissed. But dismissed you most assuredly are. Assuredly. Finally. Absolutely."

Lampe leaned on his walking stick. He didn't want to give

himself over to further shame with whimpering and tears, but there was no strength in his voice. "What will become of me? I'm an old man. I've devoted myself to him and to his work. I'll be destitute."

"Your good fortune has an undeserved robustness. Whatever passed between the two of you has clearly agitated him. But Immanuel will provide a pension for you. You'll be cared for."

"I'd rather work for him. I want to be with him. If only he could hear my voice and see my devotion. I'll change. I *have* changed!"

"That's quite enough." Wasianski tapped his pipe against his hand, emptying burnt tobacco onto the fresh snow. "Listen closely. Your security depends entirely on what I'm about to say. He is frail and he cannot endure further agitation. Not the slightest. If you so much as knock on the door or call out to him in the street, I will see to it that your pension comes to an irrevocable end that very day. Then, God help you. Do you understand?"

Lampe knew with the tenor of a maxim from Kant. His exile had formed in the night as a maxim and therefore had become a new and unchangeable fact about the world. Even Wasianski, who had been chosen to deliver the news, could not grasp the finality of such a thing.

Lampe said, "I understand as no other man ever will."

He turned to leave. In the window of Kant's study, the dim light of a lantern glowed. Lampe saw the dark outline of the professor's head appear and then disappear.

For two years, Lampe had relived that memory in his imagination. He had tried to grasp how a whole life can change in a moment. Sometimes, consumed by sorrow, he would forget to take Ding outside. Then he would look over to the corner and see her hunched up, shitting her little shit, eyeing him with guilt. He never reprimanded her. Never. He was no better than that beast.

A lifetime of work had made him what he was. Language, ink, paper—that was all he was left with. And Ding at his feet.

His own old body with all its scars was pale and small in the moonlight. His genitals were limp and shriveled. His navel reminded him that he was once curled up in his mother's belly. His nipples were useless. His hair was gray. His skin was wrinkled. Everything reminded him that he was nothing more than a thinking tube that excretes and contracts. But at least he had that.

And he had the night sky. And half a bottle of wine.

His inventory was nearly complete. He would fully and finally accept things as they were. He would lie down uncovered and feel the cold. He would stare at the great corpse of the moon, his twin brother, for he too was nothing in the world apart from the reflection he gave of Kant's light.

He would think of clean stars and of the clarity of nightmares offering no justification beyond what they are.

He would become what he was at last, with philosophy nowhere in sight, except for the three words that repeated in his mind, over and over: *It is good.*

Day Sixteen

Toast and Cheese

LAMPE WAS SULLEN and didn't have the energy to feign gratitude toward the traitorous Dunce.

After a few moments of apparently thoughtful silence, Kaufman said, "I'm glad it's all coming to a close."

"Why do you say it's coming to a close?" Lampe asked flatly. "Have people stopped visiting?"

"Most of them. And the funeral arrangements are finished. A funeral's more complicated than you'd think."

"When will it be?"

"Has no one told you?"

Lampe was too weary to exaggerate his exasperation for theatrical effect. "Who would have told me?"

The Dunce shrugged his shoulders and said, "It's tomorrow. Then we'll clean up and close the house. Wasianski plans to execute Kant's will from his own home."

"The only truly good thing is a good will," Lampe said.

"What's that?"

Lampe ignored Kaufman's dull oblivion to wit. "What about the manuscript?"

"Wasianski will take care of that too. I rewrapped the fascicle and put it on top of the others. He never knew it was gone."

Lampe didn't bother to point out that it was the final fascicle and should have been placed at the bottom of the stack. Not that it mattered. A wise reader could start in the middle, read outward in both directions, and still get to the underlying sense of what is real. That might even be the best way to read it. Lampe asked, "What will you do now?"

The Dunce said, "I'll take some time for myself. The old man left me two hundred and fifty thalers in his will."

Lampe's chest tightened.

Kaufman leaned toward Lampe. "Are you okay old man? You don't look well."

Lampe said, "That's more than six times my annual pension." He wiped his eyes with his sleeve. "So the funeral is tomorrow?"

"Yes, tomorrow," the Dunce said with a worried look on his face. "You might want to drink less wine for a stretch, and maybe see a doctor."

"Wine kept me from dying these past two weeks." He poured himself a glass of wine.

Kaufman refused a glass.

"Please drink with me," Lampe said.

"One glass," Kaufman said. "There's no time for a nap today."

They sat sipping in silence. Then Lampe's eyes filled with tears, and he said, "I would have traded anything to be in your place for the past two years, or even the past two weeks."

Kaufman tried to console him as far as his staggering ignorance would allow. "You missed nothing, Lampe. Nothing, I tell you."

Lampe knew exactly what he had missed. The Dunce and

Wasianski had neither eyes to see nor ears to hear, but two of the most important years in Kant's life had been wasted on them.

Kaufman patted Lampe's knee and tried again. "You were better off being away. Yes, better off! The frailer the professor became, the more he complained. He complained about everything from some silly electrical headache ..."

Lampe held up his hand to silence the Dunce. "I knew his every complaint before he said a word. And I always knew what to do."

"No one would have tolerated him if he weren't so famous. I shouldn't criticize a dead man, but he could be mean."

"I tolerated him when he wasn't famous. For half his life he was barely known in the city and wasn't even paid by the university."

"Well that sure changed, judging by the thousands of footprints I've had to mop up these past two weeks."

"He was the greatest philosopher in the world!" Lampe cried. "Don't you understand how meaningful it was to care for him in his last days? Don't you see what a gift that was?"

Kaufman looked down at his feet. "I was only doing my job. I didn't think of it as a gift to him."

"No! I mean that it was a gift to you!"

Kaufman blushed at the misunderstanding. "You're an old widow woman, Lampe."

"I am," Lampe said, his voice emptied of lifeforce. "I've been sad for a long time."

"How long?"

The question surprised Lampe, and he wasn't sure how to

answer. After a moment, he said, "Longer than you can imagine. But my sadness grew after the cheese."

"Ah, the cheese that was the beginning of the end."

"I've dreamt about that cheese. I've dreamt of the professor floating over the seven bridges of Königsberg with that cheese floating along at his heels like a dog."

Kaufman snorted when he tried to suppress a laugh, then he wiped his nose with his sleeve.

Lampe said, "Don't laugh. If I had been there, he would never have eaten so much cheese. It stopped him up, and his brain couldn't take the pressure from below. I know it."

"You couldn't have stopped him," Kaufman said with authority.

"I would have hidden the cheese!"

Kaufman shook his head. "He loved nothing more than dry English cheese on toast. Wasianski begged him to stop eating so much cheese. It didn't matter. He stuffed himself until one morning he just fell to the ground and couldn't say a word."

"Silenced by an English cheese," Lampe lamented.

The Dunce persisted in his awkward attempt at consolation. "He was a husk, Lampe. He could scarcely do anything for himself. He was always afraid, and he was always having dreams about murderers and thieves."

"He would have felt safe with me," Lampe mumbled, glancing at Ding who was curled up on the bed, asleep.

Kaufman looked at the pale old man in his musty sleeping gown. "Tell me why he made you leave?"

Lampe stared toward the meaningless shapes of the clouds kneaded by the slow wind, and he felt the familiar warmth of wonder as his intractable mind imposed the patterns of things and faces on them. Then he said, "I was forced to leave because Immanuel and I disagreed about the nature of philosophy."

"Immanuel?" The Dunce snorted again.

Lampe blushed, but he kept his eyes fixed on the clouds. "I wish I could have become a philosopher."

Kaufman said, "It's just a bunch of words, if you ask me. I suppose the professor made a lot of money by saying a bunch of words. But it still seems useless."

"That's why it's so beautiful." The movement of the clouds and the sharpness of their bloom against the deep blue of the sky was such a lovely simplicity, focusing Lampe's thoughts. "What do you want Kaufman?"

The Dunce thought for a bit. "A wife, I suppose. A couple of children. A roof to sleep under. Plenty of food. And I do enjoy billiards."

Lampe nodded without looking away from the clouds.

Kaufman asked, "What about you? What do you want?"

Lampe said, "I want to be happy."

"Oh, well, we all want that. But life isn't over yet, eh Lampe? Life isn't entirely over just yet." The Dunce looked out from the rippleless puddle of his dull expression, devoid of anything resembling a spark of curiosity about truth.

Lampe said, "You're right, Kaufman. You can't call a man's life happy or sad until it is over. Let's drink to this and get back to our work."

They tapped glasses and drank. Then Kaufman left the old man behind.

The Dunce understood nothing of the vast reservoirs of

Lampe's memory, but he seemed to be satisfied tending the idea of a wife, children, a house, and food. Perhaps that was something in the world about which Lampe could say, "It is good."

Lampe sat at his desk with his jug of wine, his paper with the single splotch of ink, and the quill. Nothing had changed, and everything had changed. He was a dog. A dog snaps once at the wrong time, and he finds himself no longer sitting by the master in front of the fire. Suddenly he is shivering in the streets, trying to avoid the rocks of cruel children. He had always been a dog in the alley waiting for scraps. But the thing-in-itself had found Lampe-the-alley-dog, and it was begging for help from within its meditative terror of eternal silent solitude.

Strange thought, he thought. Maybe misunderstanding ideas was one way of doing true philosophy. Maybe God was the one who blessed fools and madmen with the gift of misconstrual.

However it happened, Lampe had a philosophy, but it was made up of leftovers. His *principle of the poetic a priori* was just a rearrangement of crumbs dropped from the philosopher's table. And yet, though all of Königsberg might see him as the town idiot, he cherished this little philosophical worm making its way through the hard earth of his mind, this seed reaching for the sun. *The principle of the poetic a priori* was, in truth, *the principle of the rummaging dog*, allowing him to delight in everything that was discarded from the master's table, and doing so without a hint of cynicism. So be it. Let it be so.

———

Immanuel Kant, dead sixteen days. *Sixteen days.* The soul of the master had crossed over into oblivion, or into the presence of God, or into cosmic goo. Who knows? Sixteen days of solitary vigil, tormented by the vagueness of mystery, staring at a black splotch that was all potential and no act, mocking Lampe by containing every idea that could haunt the imagination, but saying exactly nothing.

Everything was concealed in the blackness of the accidental shame-splotch, but only the alchemy of a mind could transform it into truth, the one real mind that was now concealed in the blackness of death.

Sixteen nights of desire had brought Lampe into the house of fear. What a mind-wandering waste of time and feeling his life had become, always numbed with vodka or wine.

Ding's tumor had grown in the weeks of fitful waiting. She was in pain. That was part of the fear. Her flesh was threatening to become mere rotting matter. Kant was gone, Ding would soon be gone, Lampe was going.

He started to weep over the small bundle of water, muscle, bone, and fur that was his dog, and that tributary of feeling quickly found a river as he turned and faced the thought that he should have loved the old philosopher, with his frail, dust-bound body, better than he did.

There was only one day remaining before the corpse of Immanuel Kant would be buried, forever out of reach, separated from Lampe by a few feet of dirt and stone, and by the dread of annihilation.

He looked at the feather he had borrowed from the professor.

Or, perhaps, just maybe, one could say he stole it.

He didn't mean to steal it. He had intended not to steal it. And yet, with no apparent change inside his mind, he had stolen it. The master had used the quill to write the first hundred pages of his ticket to intellectual immortality, *The Critique of Pure Reason*. The quill had called to Lampe, promising the possibility that one day he too could write a great work he would bequeath to humanity in return for being fondly remembered in centuries to come. What a fool he had been. He had kept it like a sacred object, awaiting the arrival of his own philosophy, and now he couldn't return it. Now the borrowed quill was truly stolen, and his soul was permanently stained by his black deed.

The professor had looked all over the house for the missing feather, complaining that important ideas would fade before he could get them onto paper. He finally gave up the search and said, "Lampe! Go buy a quill!"

Lampe felt red shame splash onto his face. "But it won't be the same feather you started with."

"It doesn't matter!" Kant said, pacing back and forth, gnawing on his empty pipe.

Lampe was shocked. "How can you write with a different feather? That makes no sense at all."

Kant stopped and glared at Lampe. "Find me a twig in the yard if it will hold ink!"

The rotten old philosopher didn't have a single spark of magic in him. He practically gave Lampe permission to keep the first feather.

"Go!" Kant commanded.

So, Lampe ran out and bought another feather. He used his own money, hoping this might absolve him.

Then he discovered something horrible as he handed the new quill to Kant. The professor's never-ending talk about maxims and morals had wrought a devastating change in Lampe, and he was overwhelmed with the unwanted conviction that the only way to truly absolve himself would be to return the feather, to confess, and to beg forgiveness. And yet, the history of an object mattered. Ink had flowed off the end of that bone, sanctified by a great mind, and words had appeared on paper, transforming the way the mind viewed the mind and the world viewed itself. Lampe couldn't relinquish the quill.

But the quill stopped functioning in his hand when he tried to write. His small crime had emptied it of its magic, and his vigil with the silent ghost of Kant, evoked by the feather, was absurd.

Ding raised her head when Lampe said out loud, "Stop!" But he couldn't will his mind to be free of the thought that *Immanuel Kant used the same quill to write the book that changed the world.* The feather was his only real connection to the master's great mind from which the entities of Lampe's own shadowy and ghostly ideas grew. A sudden, painful urgency overcame him. He craved not to think but to touch. To touch anything and everything that belonged to the master—the desk, the spoons, the books, the dead old man.

The setting sun was almost gone. Kant would be buried the next day. If Lampe didn't lay his hand on the old man's body now, he would be out of reach forever. He had squandered sixteen days staring at clouds, drinking wine, twirling a stolen quill, and pondering morbid intangibles such as the dread thing-in-itself. What a fool he had been to choose financial security over the risk of demanding to be by Kant's side at the vigil, in the place of honor he deserved, or at least desired. He had missed everything.

"I'm a coward!" he cried into the cold air, empty of ears that might hear him, affirming or denying his charge against himself. "I'm a coward to the core!"

He lit his candle. The light reflected on the windows, bringing forth the face of his twin hovering on the other side of the window against the darkness of falling night, staring at him.

Lampe stared back.

What a ragged end to a life. Face gaunt, hair long and disheveled, nightgown hanging off the bony body. Drunk. Alone. Poor. With nothing to show for his life work besides a worn copy of *The Critique of Pure Reason*, a stolen feather, and a single ink splotch that was the sum of his philosophy. The scribbles on the walls were a distraction. He was a monkish husk in a cell learning penance from the moldy and earthly elements of rot and decay moving within him, taking him over. He felt himself disappearing, dying.

When he leaned toward the window, the face on the other side of the window did the same, ghostly in the candlelight. He stared at himself sitting and staring at himself. His mind asked his mind, "Why are you still sitting here? Why don't you choose the only right path? This is your problem, Lampe!"

He couldn't say what changed as he looked at himself on the other side of the window, summoned from cold darkness by the light of one small candle. But something moved him.

He put on his worn shoes and threadbare coat, took up his whittled walking stick, and set out on a journey to Kant's house, ready to confront Wasianski and take the consequences in exchange for the only thing that could bring him rest.

He ignored stares from passers-by as he walked through the streets, shaking from cold and nervousness. He didn't care what he looked like to strangers. With every step, he felt the presence within him grow, the presence of the master and the presence of his singular, unified self. Everything was merging into one. He was being pulled by the presence emanating from Kant's little body as it strained to be fully untethered and to be released to the stars and planets, the sight of which had been the preamble to his philosophy and the postlude for his mistress metaphysics who had shown him that there was still a remainder untouched by all his books. There was so much left to do.

When he came to Kant's street, he reached within himself for the resolve he needed to confront Wasianski. But as he walked toward the house, he saw that all the windows were dark, and he felt a great relief. Maybe no one was home.

Maybe he could do the work he needed to do in peace, with no begging, and without losing the security of his pension in old age. But whatever happened, nothing on earth mattered to Lampe except this final task. He found the hidden key he had used so many times before the exile, and he unlocked the door, scarcely able to control the shaking of his hand.

In the darkness of the house, the familiar smells suddenly crowded his mind with memories of countless meals, bowls of pipe tobacco, wood fires, and the subtleness of fresh ink drying on new paper. These endless, mundane events populated every corner of the thing Lampe called his life. They were constituents of his soul. The confluence of memory and feeling, and the conflagration ignited by the scents that pervaded the house, confirmed how desperately he needed to be present in this place to find the evidence for his mind and its work.

There was enough light from the moon to make out the

shapes of furniture. Lampe didn't go straight away to the freezing room where Kant had been all these days. The presence of the old master was too dense, and Lampe was struggling to breathe.

He moved into the study with friendly and familiar wonder. Maybe Kaufman was right. Maybe he was just a grieving old woman. He had endured the brilliant, ridiculous man for forty years, but the daily activity he once took for granted was transformed by a mysterious process of mind close to mysticism, or magic. The strange presence suffused the walls, the floor, the furniture.

He stepped toward the desk where the final work was wrapped in bundles. The master's thermometer was in its usual place. Why did he monitor the heat of his small body? Lampe suddenly loved this absurd habit the little man indulged.

Two feather quill pens were neatly arranged next to the manuscript. In a lightning strike of illuminated regret, he realized that he could have brought the stolen quill with him. He could have left it on the desk as a private gesture of confession and reconciliation. But he had not thought about it. Why was he so unable to live his life well?

He could bring it in the morning. Of course he could. He felt a cooling breeze of relief as he rehearsed a scene of repentance in his mind. Wasianski would open the front door. No doubt he would say, "Lampe, you insolent …"

But with a raised hand, Lampe would silence him. His hand would flutter out from his coat pocket in the bird-like fashion the professor so often used, grabbing control of a conversation as words whipped about in the air, holding them like reins, and pulling them taut as his hand settled back into his pocket. "I came to return this. Nothing more." Lampe's tone would be humble, but resolute and firm. "It's a quill I borrowed."

No. This required complete honesty.

He would say, "It's a quill I stole from the master. It's the very quill he used to write the first part of his world-changing *Critique of Pure Reason.*"

Perhaps Wasianski would look at it reverently. Then he might return to his effeminate snarl and say, "What gall you have, Lampe. Why return it now, on the very day of the funeral?"

But this could still be a moment of hope rather than despair. "I'm returning it today because I've changed. You're a deacon of the church. You know a man's heart can change. This is the one wrong I can try to undo in some small way. This will be enough. This will satisfy an old, sad man."

And then, at last, Wasianski would feel his heart touched, moved by old Lampe's humble act, and the momentum of forgiveness would build.

Lampe breathed in the ten thousand memories that made his tired soul soar, and he closed his eyes in the delicious relief of finally feeling that he was home.

His thoughts were halted by the rattling of the door handle. The front door opened, and the foyer filled with lantern light. He had barely a moment to hide behind the couch before Wasianski walked in.

Lampe couldn't control the trembling of his legs and hands, his pounding heart, his dark terror as Wasianski rummaged in a drawer. His body was utterly other than himself and out of his will's reach. Then the light faded as Wasianski walked out of the study and across the hall. Lampe peeked over the top of the couch. There he saw Kant's little body. Wasianski stood beside it with his back to Lampe as he looked down at the philosopher, continuing his private vigil.

Walk to him, Lampe thought. *Just walk over to him and kneel and beg forgiveness. This is the moment.*

How hard the heart is. How hard it is to have a heart.

Just go, Lampe. Seize this final chance to be with your master, to touch him, to make your memory real one last time so that the meager remainder of your life will not be lived in the throes of longing, with no way to close the door against the winter of regret.

He stood up in the darkness and walked around from behind the couch, moving slowly, but with confident steps from his long habit of navigating the house in early morning without light. He crept toward the light in the room of vigil, the horizon of salvation, when suddenly his foot kicked the umbrella stand, sending umbrellas and walking sticks in a clatter to the floor. Surely it was Kaufman the idiot, the instigator of iterative interruptions in Lampe's diligent search for redemption, who had moved the umbrella stand to the wrong location.

Wasianski dropped his lantern as he jumped back. The glass shattered, plunging the two men back into near-total darkness with only a faint glow from the moonlight.

"Who's there?" he cried out in a voice tense with fear, this believer in spirits and ghosts.

Lampe watched in horror as Wasianski's shadowy shape bent down to lift the broken lantern, as though that would help him see.

"Speak up, I say!" Wasianski's voice trembled, and he took

a step toward the hall separating the rooms in which the men stood, glass crunching beneath his shoes.

The floor creaked as Lampe shifted his weight. All was lost. He couldn't bear it. He covered his face with his coat and ran into the foyer and out the front door. Behind him, Wasianski yelled in a thin voice, "Whoever you are, stay away! This is an outrage! It's a crime against holiness!"

Lampe ran as well as he could until he reached one of the seven bridges of Königsberg. Halfway across, his chest was burning, and he stopped. He looked down at the black river. It would be so easy. One jump and he would be gone.

He listened to the wind. It was only wind, saying neither yes nor no. And then he heard something else. Three words repeating in his mind again and again. The master's voice was speaking to him. *It is good.*

Day Seventeen

The Kingdom of Ends

LAMPE AWOKE, exhausted and clouded with weariness. He gently scratched Ding behind her ears. The scribbles on his walls looked like the markings of a lunatic. How strange that he had tried to use them like constellations in the universe, a self-made astrology, peering through his walls to find the truth.

What is truth?

This is truth. Ships were unloading at the docks, as on every other day. Men and women were waking up and staring at each other before going about their daily tasks. Horses were clomping here and clomping there. The market was opening. The morning was growing brighter as the plain blue sky blotted out the vast expanse of the universe, the simple, single light of the sun making the thousand thousand lights of the starry sky disappear.

This too is truth. The body of Immanuel Kant would soon be buried. And the next day ships would unload at the docks, men and women would awaken, horses would clomp, markets would open, and the sun would rise.

Martin Lampe lay in bed thinking about the many funerals

for faculty members he and the master had attended together. His imagination traced the path to the Professors' Vault next to the University Church. He pictured the old man sealed in a box, placed in the ground, and covered with a great stone.

What was left to do but to follow the professor into death? He was dying, disappearing. He would die alone in his vault, made up of dreams and poetic nonsense, hidden until Eco or some neighbor smelled his remains. Then he would be tossed in a pauper's grave, and the walls with his ideas would be painted over with whitewash.

Seventeen days the sun had shown on a world with no master. Seventeen times the sun had hidden the starry universe from the eyes of Königsberg, the monotonous sun allowing the oblivious, happy citizens, unburdened by the curse of philosophical longing, to meander about the town toying with trinkets and trading their days for shiny baubles, even as the tidal wave of death rose up.

The master's death had left Lampe's world thin and empty. *The principle of the poetic a priori*, his only discovery in the philosophical spying out of high and mysterious truth, had evaporated. He felt the cold of the air, the weight of his blanket, the warmth of his ailing beast. He felt his own fragile unnameable ghost. He felt the cobwebs that strung his mind to the verities transcending the world of forms, but also to grasshoppers, to the saffron-dyed hides of animals, and to young women who made the world fit for a homely beatitude that tastes like the first bite of a pear in spring.

But he was lost. His dear old half-gestated philosophical idea seemed to have miscarried.

And yet, even if the idea turned out to be stillborn, with the mystery of its potential never to emerge from the coffin of its ridiculous name, *the principle of the poetic a priori* continued to stoke the fire of his mind. His entire philosophy resided somewhere in that black splotch on the white page, just as goodness resided somewhere in the memory of his mother who, with her many imaginative dives into darkness, was the soil from which Lampe had grown.

As the sun rises and the sun also sets, doubt greeted his reverie with the words, "Stupid, stupid, stupid."

What practical problem could ever be solved by something called *the principle of the poetic a priori*? What bridge could be built? What government organized? What peace, justice, or scientific insight could follow a blunt statement of such a principle? What if his one idea was nothing more than a few words that found each other accidentally, exploding into the fragments of nonsense that were slowly being covered by soot on the four walls of his room, in one building, in one city, in one country, on one planet, in one unimaginably enormous universe?

Something had become clear, slowly and grievously, over seventeen days of fits and starts. As servants make their lives out of discarded remains, as his clothes were patched with pieces of cloth salvaged from the tailor's floor, and as the body rotting on his mattress was built of leftovers from the master's table, he knew that his *principle of the poetic a priori* was made of abandoned philosophical scraps.

"Very well!" he said to the air and to Ding. "I am what I am. The written works of Martin Lampe might never amount to more than one ink-splotch on a single piece of paper. But the remainder of his works will consist of fully lived days!"

He looked at Ding. "You are my new teacher. You are the only fully unabstracted thing in my universe."

Her tumor was more inflamed. Lampe wanted her suffering to end, but he also dreaded the day of her death. He could not bear to lose the only other soul in his room.

Alone on his mattress with Ding, pondering the eruption of a tumor that would end such a good life, Lampe held before his mind his one perfect, whole, unsayable idea. He thought about the possibility of simply, suddenly, and completely being content in the moment he called *now*.

He was startled from his thoughts when bells began tolling. Were they marking the start of the funeral? He listened. No. It was only the mark of noon. Soon everything was silent again, though his heart still raced.

There was a little pile of dog shit in the corner of the room. The tin bowl on the floor still held his dribbles from the night. His quilt stank, his nightgown stank, his beard was tangled, and he had gray stuff under his long fingernails from scratching.

He suddenly felt deep compassion for the master who had spent his life stuck in an uncomfortable, small, wheezing, constipated body, reaching up and out in thought even in the middle of his daily struggle.

He returned to his principle and held in his mind the idea of the idea, unopened. The idea of the idea. Maybe it could only be thought, or perhaps felt. Maybe he could relinquish the burden of writing once and for all. He could *feel* the idea of the idea in the middle of the absurdity known as being a body.

An unexpected thought drifted into the space of his mind. If he was going to surrender himself fully to the formation of this perfect jewel, never written down, never spoken to anyone, but simply held in the mind as the pure idea of the idea, he should give back the magical feather.

But it was not enough to say that he should return it, as though the act was somehow hypothetical. The act was necessary. It was the only necessary act. He had to return the feather and walk away cleansed of theft and misguided ambition. All his sins and errors would attach themselves to the stolen quill, and he would be free. This would be repentance of the highest magnitude, an act that would honor his master. Then he would be free to take up the only credible work remaining in his life, which was to think the idea of the idea for the rest of his days, until blood no longer reached his brain, and he obeyed the divine command to let go.

Light and lightness suddenly erupted in his soul, coming from he-knew-not-where. The idea of the idea. This was the sole and proper object of *the poetic a priori*. The moment the feather was returned, he would be free to do nothing other than to contemplate the idea of the idea of *the poetic a priori,* and then to die.

A sense of urgency flooded him. The burial of an inaccessible corpse was soon to be accomplished in the vault for dead scholars. But Lampe was not dead. One day he would die, yes. But he was not dead at the moment. Far from it. Lampe was alive!

The feeling of life may have been present all along, but he had failed to notice. What buoyancy! What energy! He was not yet a dweller among the dead, so there was still time to accomplish his act of repentance, to right a wrong, and to be absolved!

He had suffered greatly in the days since the professor's

death, but he saw that most of it came from his own selfishness. As the old man had dwindled, Lampe had never gone to him and risked saying what he most needed to say. An apology? Perhaps, but more than that. He should have sacrificed his security and gone to the master just to say, "Thank you for such a wonderful life. Thank you. Thank you. Thank you."

How could he have missed this lesson of simple gratitude? *Thank you* was the one thing that Lampe had never said.

He felt Kant's last words suffuse his mind. *It is good.*

The master wasn't saying that he had quenched his thirst for water. He was saying thank you. He had been given the gift of a good life, and he was saying thank you to the God who was the placeholder, or to the placeholder who was God, or to whatever mystery allowed the greatness of the master to show up in the world.

It is good. That was the secret for overcoming the darkness of isolation, the dread of the lonely thing-in-itself.

It is good. Was there any better statement of *the principle of the poetic a priori*? The master had uttered the secret as he died.

Lampe suddenly saw the truth, and his heart pounded as he felt himself having an idea. *The principle of the poetic a priori* was not merely a light that shined upon the surface of things. No. The principle revealed the inner light of things. It made him see that everything is illuminated from the inside, showing forth goodness.

It is good. It, It, It!

How long It had haunted Lampe, even from the days when his feet were frozen in the swamplands of war. For forty years he struggled with It, in the bowels of the professor and in the palpitations of the heart. It was in the executed official thrown outside the city wall. It was in the strange and toothy grins of Hippel, and in the thoughts of their lustful but Pietist king. It was in the French Revolution aiming for perpetual harmony. He hardly knew what he was thinking as his thoughts tumbled forward, but he knew It was in the river, in the stars, in the moss covering the damp stones at the base of the castle. What was It? It was in the very coldness of the castle library and in the prisoners' wailing songs of praise. It was in Lampe's dreams and in his fear of death. It was in the eyes of Ding, the old dying beagle he loved.

And, *It was good.*

Lampe was not a failed project in a world obsessed with underlying mechanisms. No! Lampe was a man of the surfaces, of truth as it appears, of the goodness of all that shows up, all that cannot remain hidden. Lampe was a man of inward illumination. With his principle, he would set his own small world on a new path, not toward enlightenment, but toward illumination! He would henceforth see the world as it appears and say, "*It is good!*"

This was madness. Everything suddenly seemed to be whispering to him—the sky, the river, the swamp, the dog. Was this what the professor experienced when he sat at his writing desk and universal truths appeared in his mind? Was his own mind touching reality or departing from reality? How would he know?

Madness! He lay on his bed, tired and cold, but alive, thinking only of the professor's final gift to him, the words, It is good.

This was the time for action. This was the last opportunity for action.

But nothing happened.

This was the time to move. But where was his will?

He just lay there, unmoving, fantasizing. He imagined going to young members of the philosophy department and telling them that he was ready to speak, ready to give something that later philosophers would only be able to hope for—the chance to interrogate the witness to forty years of life with the master, the man who acted as moon to Kant's sunlight, reflecting his wishes, thoughts, and desires.

"Young sir," he might say, "I can tell you tales. Oh, listen, my young scholar. If you think this old man was the lighted orb forcing darkness to recede, then let us sit together over a glass of wine, or maybe two, while you take notes."

"What's your name?" the hypothetical stunned student might ask.

"My name? Ah, my name."

And what should he say in answer? If he said Martin, then he would surely be forgotten as one among many Martins, named so by the whims of their mothers, but rooted neither in history nor in the humor of Providence.

No. There was only one acceptable answer.

"My name? Good sir, my name is Lampe."

Who would believe the confluence of circumstances that took the history of Lampe and allowed it to land in the arena of enlightenment's greatest thinker?

Lampe!

The malleable young philosopher, if truly formed in the golden light of *the principle of the poetic a priori*, could at last accept the eternal fittingness of that apparent little accident.

Lampe sat up. The bells were ringing again. The time was finally upon him. Two bells rang out, then four, then ten. Soon all the bells of Königsberg were crying up from earth to mark the loss of the Colossus.

He was overcome, drowning in a wave of sorrow sounding out beneath the sky. The part of the master that could still appear to the world was soon to be pulled into the streets as bells threw death tolls into the clear winter air.

He got out of bed and went to his window. When he opened it, the chill wind hit his chest through the thin nightgown and made him gasp. He looked down to the river of people dressed in black.

He yelled down, "Where are you going?" as though the question needed to be asked.

Several people looked up. One shouted back, "Are you the only man in Königsberg who hasn't heard? The famous philosopher Immanuel Kant died and today is his funeral. Are you coming?"

Are you coming?

He didn't answer. He couldn't answer. The man moved on.

Suddenly, urgently, Lampe yelled out, "Yes! Yes, I am going to the funeral!"

Finally, he knew what to do. He closed the window and patted Ding gently on the head. He put on his boots and coat. Then he took the magical feather in his old fist and went downstairs. In the kitchen, Eco sat eating black bread, plucking straw from the loaf. He was dressed in his black coat.

Eco said, "You're going?"

Lampe said, "They're carrying the old man to the vault now. I must hurry."

Eco, the pale reservoir of ghostly spirit who carried the weight of Königsberg's executions so that fellow citizens could live their lives unencumbered, said, "I'll join you."

The street was dense with people moving towards Kant's house. Thousands filled the small streets of the city in rivulets flowing toward the professor in his coffin. Eco's head was high above the crowd as he walked behind Lampe.

The streets were packed with onlookers, jostling Lampe. Crowds flowed into the streets, lining up behind the formal procession that would go from Kant's house to the Professors' Vault at the University Church.

Lampe looked around at the masses chattering to each other. There was no mention of the great works. Probably none of them had read any of his books. They knew nothing of the master's life beyond the bare fact of his fame. They had no access to the ethereal glory of the thought that rose up in the midst of the muck of Königsberg. And yet they were out in the cold to honor the man, the great philosopher. This filled Lampe with gratefulness for the privilege of being his servant. But he was also overwhelmed with the sense of not belonging, a sense of sadness at being nothing more than a single, unknown person bobbing in the sea of the uninvited masses who knew nothing about the great man.

Eco, who was exquisitely sensitive to the emotions of those around him, said, "It must be bitterness and gall to move anonymously among the hoards."

A woman next to him glanced disapprovingly, and Eco blushed the faint pink that was the only color his body could manage to produce.

Lampe said nothing. He just walked and looked around at the faces of all the people who were honoring his master.

Eco spoke again. "You should be in front, Martin, in a place of honor."

They walked along in silence. Soon they turned onto Kant's narrow street, pressing against the backs of strangers. Eco saw that the procession had indeed begun. The coffin was at the far end of the street, held up by a great flock of young students who came to bear the hero to his grave. Soon, the distant, tiny coffin disappeared around the corner in its winding moves towards the church.

Lampe tumbled along in the river of flesh. Suddenly he felt a firm grip on his arm. He nearly fell as he was pulled to one side.

Eco bent down to Lampe's ear and said, "You'll never catch him this way." As always, the doughy face of Eco-the-Executioner seemed tuned to some far away and inscrutable thought as his eye roamed over the river of people. Then he opened the front door of the house nearest them and said, "Come. Everyone is in the street. We'll take our chances."

They met no one inside the house, and soon they were out the back door. They galloped across a small courtyard and went into another house through the back door. They rushed through and then stepped into a larger stream of people. Eco held Lampe's arm as they crossed the street and went through another house. Again no one was home. When they opened the back door of the next house, an old man was smoking his pipe in the kitchen with his feet by the coal stove. The deafening bells occupied every space, and the old man didn't even take his pipe out of his mouth as he glared. Eco and Lampe ran to the front door before the surprise wore off.

When Eco opened the door, Lampe stepped forward into a slower, more formally arranged group of people. Eco remained in the doorway, waving with the placid neutrality that softened his face.

Lampe moved into step beside the rear pallbearer. He walked in the shadow cast by the small, nearly empty coffin of his master carried on the shoulders of young students. It was inches above his head. As he felt the presence of death thrust through him, he saw Wasianski just ahead, dressed in black coat and tights, wearing a perfectly whited wig, and carrying the very walking cane the master had carried on his ten thousand walks with Lampe.

Wasianski turned, as though he felt Lampe's arrival. There was no escape.

"Lampe!" he said in a forced whisper.

Lampe felt the urge to run away, but where?

Wasianski stepped back toward Lampe, grabbing his elbow. Lampe looked around for the policeman who would take him away the moment Wasianski signaled. That which he feared had come upon him. He had become a disturbance on this singular day, an intolerable presence that had risen out of the swamp, defying the rule, the irrevocable maxim of exile.

"Lampe!" Wasianski spoke so close to his ear that he could feel the warmth of his breath on his cold skin. "I'm so glad you've come. I wondered why you didn't pay a visit. But I knew that after forty years you might have difficult feelings of your own. So I let you be."

Lampe tried to pull away, but the crowd forced them close together beneath the shadow of Immanuel's small coffin.

"Let me be?" Lampe's whisper was husky and thick. "I was in exile!"

"Exile? But surely, Lampe, you wouldn't suppose that this exile, as you call it, would preclude a simple visit to the vigil."

"Of course it would!" He caught his breath, felt blood in his throat. "It was the rule! I was not to come again upon pain of losing my pension, my only support. Nothing but an invitation could have overcome the rule, the maxim!"

"An invitation?"

"Yes!"

"To a funeral?"

"Yes!"

"I've never heard of such a thing." They walked along in the presence of the dead. Wasianski ran his thin fingers along his pale and beardless face while he stared at the ground. "Then how is it that you're here now?"

The crowds pressed in, and Lampe could hardly breathe. "I ..." He choked on his own grief. "I came to return this feather." He clutched the accursed feather in his hand.

"Feather?" Wasianski said.

Lampe overcame the choking sensation in his throat and said, "I took it from him some years ago. I never gave it back. I'm so ashamed."

"I see," Wasianski said.

"The professor wrote the first parts of the great *Critique of Pure Reason* with it." Lampe searched Wasianski's face for the judgment that he craved.

Wasianski walked silently. Finally, he said, "Keep it. He certainly doesn't need it now."

"What about ..."

"Enough," he said, putting his finger to his lips. "Keep it. You served this great man for forty years, and now we are going to the Vault to bury him."

Lampe stepped back as Wasianski turned to another person in the procession. Several students noticed the attention given to him by Wasianski. Lampe even exchanged little bows with them.

The students whispered among themselves. Who is this man? An old friend of the professor? A philosopher from some other university?

Lampe stood by himself at the service, and the students continued to whisper about him among themselves.

As he watched the coffin lowered to its final resting place, covered with a stone slab, forever out of his reach, he held the feather in his hand, the final gift.

When the slab was in place, nothing remained for him there. The master's work was done. It was finished.

He pushed his way through the crowd and began to run as well as he could through the streets of Königsberg. He had to get back to his room and to Ding. He had to distill everything into a perfection he could carry contentedly in his mind. He wished he could fly, because at last he knew how to conclude the works of Martin Lampe, asker of questions. He knew exactly what to do. The master had given him the secret to everything, a secret so simple that it made him laugh out loud.

It is good.

Acknowledgments

Endless thanks to Sam Wells, in whose home we were living when I finished the first draft of this novel, and to Marc Estrin and Donna Bister, who supported me with such generosity as I brought it to completion. And thank you to my family—Karen, Micah, Alexandra, Crew, Ali, Julia, Ray, Pearl, Carole, Flannery, Sadie, Sophia, and the Worms who sing the song from Whoville all year long—for lovingly allowing me to scribble before work, settling inward things as a preamble to evenings of play, chitchat, movies, and food.

About the Author

Raymond Barfield is a writer and physician in Asheville, North Carolina. *Dreams of a Spirit Seer* is his third novel.

Fomite

Writing a review on social media sites for readers will help the progress of independent publishing. To submit a review, go to the book page on any of the sites and follow the links for reviews. Books from independent presses rely on reader-to-reader communications.

For more information or to order any of our books, visit:
fomitepress.com/our-books.html

More novels from Fomite...

Joshua Amses—*During This, Our Nadir*
Joshua Amses—*Ghats*
Joshua Amses—*Raven or Crow*
Joshua Amses—*The Moment Before an Injury*
Raymond Barfield—*Dreams of a Spirit Seer*
Charles Bell—*The Married Land*
Charles Bell—*The Half Gods*
Jaysinh Birjepatel—*Nothing Beside Remains*
Jaysinh Birjepatel—*The Good Muslim of Jackson Heights*
David Borofka—*The End of Good Intnetions*
David Brizer—*Cacademonomania*
David Brizer—*The Secret Doctrine of V. H. Rand*
David Brizer—*Victor Rand*
L. M Brown—*Hinterland*
Paula Closson Buck—*Summer on the Cold War Planet*
L.enny Cavallaro—*Paganini Agitato*
Dan Chodorkoff—*Loisaida*
Dan Chodorkoff—*Sugaring Down*
David Adams Cleveland—*Time's Betrayal*
Paul Cody—*Sphyxia*
Jaimee Wriston Colbert—*Vanishing Acts*
Roger Coleman—*Skywreck Afternoons*
Stephen Downes—*The Hands of Pianists*
Marc Estrin—*Et Resurrexit*
Marc Estrin—*Hyde*
Marc Estrin—*Kafka's Roach*
Marc Estrin—*Proceedings of the Hebrew Free Burial Society*
Marc Estrin—*Speckled Vanities*
Marc Estrin—*The Annotated Nose*
Marc Estrin—*The Penseés of Alan Krieger*

Fomite

Zdravka Evtimova—*Asylum for Men and Dogs*
Zdravka Evtimova—*In the Town of Joy and Peace*
Zdravka Evtimova—*Sinfonia Bulgarica*
Zdravka Evtimova—*You Can Smile on Wednesdays*
Daniel Forbes—*Derail This Train Wreck*
Peter Fortunato—*Carnevale*
Greg Guma—*Dons of Time*
Ramsey Hanhan—*Fugitive Dreams*
Richard Hawley—*The Three Lives of Jonathan Force*
Lamar Herrin—*Father Figure*
Michael Horner—*Damage Control*
Ron Jacobs—*All the Sinners Saints*
Ron Jacobs—*Short Order Frame Up*
Ron Jacobs—*The Co-conspirator's Tale*
Scott Archer Jones—*A Rising Tide of People Swept Away*
Scott Archer Jones—*And Throw Away the Skins*
Julie Justicz—*Conch Pearl*
Julie Justicz—*Degrees of Difficulty*
Maggie Kast—*A Free Unsullied Land*
Darrell Kastin—*Shadowboxing with Bukowski*
Coleen Kearon—*#triggerwarning*
Coleen Kearon—*Feminist on Fire*
Jan English Leary—*Thicker Than Blood*
Jan English Leary—*Town and Gown*
Diane Lefer—*Confessions of a Carnivore*
Diane Lefer—*Out of Place*
Rob Lenihan—*Born Speaking Lies*
Cynthia Newberry Martin—*The Art of Her Life*
Colin McGinnis—*Roadman*
Douglas W. Milliken—*Our Shadows' Voice*
Ilan Mochari—*Zinsky the Obscure*
Peter Nash—*In the Place Where We Thought We Stood*
Peter Nash—*Parsimony*
Peter Nash—*The Least of It*
Peter Nash—*The Perfection of Things*
Michael Okulitch—*Toward Him Still*
George Ovitt—*Stillpoint*
George Ovitt—*Tribunal*
Gregory Papadoyiannis—*The Baby Jazz*
Pelham—*The Walking Poor*
Christopher Peterson—*Madman*
Andy Potok—*My Father's Keeper*
Frederick Ramey—*Comes A Time*

Fomite

Howard Rappaport—*Arnold and Igor*
Joseph Rathgeber—*Mixedbloods*
Kathryn Roberts—*Companion Plants*
Robert Rosenberg—*Isles of the Blind*
Fred Russell—*Rafi's World*
Ron Savage—*Voyeur in Tangier*
David Schein—*The Adoption*
Charles Simpson—*Uncertain Harvest*
Lynn Sloan—*Midstream*
Rana Shubair—*And No Net Ensnares Me*
Lynn Sloan—*Principles of Navigation*
L.E. Smith—*The Consequence of Gesture*
L.E. Smith—*Travers' Inferno*
L.E. Smith—*Untimely RIPped*
Robert Sommer—*A Great Fullness*
Caitlin Hamilton Summie—*Geographies of the Heart*
Tom Walker—*A Day in the Life*
Susan V. Weiss —*My God, What Have We Done?*
Peter M. Wheelwright—*As It Is on Earth*
Peter M. Wheelwright—*The Door-Man*
Suzie Wizowaty—*The Return of Jason Green*